The Dead Wake!

Something was disturbing the snow just by the hoofs of Aldric's horse. Then the thing broke surface. It was a hand, long dead, rotten leather stretched taut over a claw of old brown bones. But it was moving. Horrified, Aldric looked away, only to meet the empty eyesockets of a skull heaving itself from the earth. As he stared, mesmerized, other shriveled relics rose out of the past into the nightmare present.

Then suddenly, the hand he had first seen, now fleshy and filling out with muscle even as he watched, twisted and clutched his horse's foreleg. The horse reared with a neigh that was almost a shriek of outrage, and Aldric, thrown back in his saddle, his own wounds reopening, was overwhelmed by unbearable red agony. . . .

Gilbert

The
Horse Lord

Peter Morwood

DAW BOOKS, INC.
DONALD A. WOLLHEIM, PUBLISHER

1633 Broadway, New York, NY 10019

For my father,
who had to leave early

With acknowledgment and thanks to:

Alastair Minnis and Diana Wynne Jones;
Charles Redpath and David Lavery;
Rosie Freel and Trish Burns;
and my mother and sister, who put up with it all.

PREFACE

". . . bye virtue of his lady wyfe.

In this yeare also, being but ye eighth of ERHAL-OVERLORDE his holding of his Seate in ye fortress of Cerdor, was there war and stryfe in ye north kingdomes through ye Malice and foul Usurpationes of that Sorcerer since ynamen Kalarr cu Ruruc.

ERHAL-OVERLORDE having setten him forth with an hoste being of soche numberes as fyve thousandes of Horse and of Foote ten thousandes, he did bring defeate to his enemy and ruination utterly by force of armes at Baelen Fyghte.

But in that field did fall and perish ERHAL, most Noble and Gentle of LORDES (this of an Arrow betwixt ye Harness joyntes) and with him dyveres soche Honourable men as ykepen oath even unto Deathe, to ye numberes of seven thousandes both hygh and humble. And of hygh-clan yfallen are . . .

. . . And this is all their names that be yknowen slaine. Now to their sonnes hath ycomen fell Ambition wherebye each hath ycraven landes held of another for his own, and hath ytaken seizen of full many an halle and citadel each from another. Now indeed doth red War make of ALBA his dwelling-place to the dolour and exceeding Heaviness of all honest folke, and noble LORDES do slay those that were their hearth-friendes not four monthes agone.

May-be by HEAVENES grace this lande may be delivered from sore Travail, and by ITS Endless Mercy the people may be ysafen from blood and pestilence to live again in Peace . . .''

Ylver Vlethanek an-Caerdur
The Book of Years, Cerdor

PROLOGUE

Boots thudded in rotting vegetation, slapped in patches of slushy snow. As the sound grew, a solitary figure came stumbling through the forest gloom, slumped against a tree and then slid face-downwards into the dirt and wet dead leaves.

The runner was twenty years old and sick with fear. His tunic was open despite the chilly air, and the neck of a once-fine shirt hung loose. Sweat glistened on his face and body, sticking sodden clothing and tails of wet hair to his skin. The boy's chest heaved, veins beat in throat and temples and his whole frame quivered with exertion.

He listened, holding his breath and lying quite still in the clammy ooze of slime where he had fallen. At first there was nothing but the hesitant patter of raindrops and the slamming of his heart. Then he heard it—a soft, ponderous sound not quite drowned by the whisper of wind through autumn-bared branches. As it drew closer he clawed at the tree-trunk, struggled upright and then fell back. Though his left shoulder barely touched the unyielding wood, he convulsed and an agonised moan escaped his clenched teeth. Around the arrow jutting obscenely from torn flesh, crusted stains grew slick and oily beneath a film of fresh blood.

The arrow had ceased to pain him hours ago when all feeling had left his arm, and he had almost forgotten its presence. Until now. He had forgotten, too, how long he had been running. There was only the dull realisation that his flight was almost over. Fatigue was spreading a seductive

warmth through him like a drug—or a poison. It invited
sleep, stiffening his muscles even as he gulped the air which
kept them working.

Lightning flickered, etching the world starkly black and
white. Its thunder growled like some vast beast among the
trees and nameless things scuttled slavering through his brain,
sniffing the air for their quarry's scent. His scent. He fled
again through a flurry of rain.

Something struck at his leg and he flinched wildly, almost
tumbling headlong before realising it was his long sword. The
weapon's straps had slackened, letting it swing free; another
minute and it would have been lost. The boy fumbled to run
his hand into the complex hilt. He dared not stop, yet his left
arm was useless to halt the scabbard's crazy wavering. The
blade was only half-drawn when he fell.

The storm was to blame. Great banks of cloud had drifted
up in silence, then vented their fury directly overhead. Blinded
and deafened, the fugitive did not even see the tree-root
which jerked both feet from under him. Raising his head
painfully, he stared at the thing in his fist. Only a jagged
splinter remained in the hilt—the rest of his finely tempered
blade was gone. With a sound that was half sob and half
curse he flung the remnant away and reeled on.

After another crash of thunder it began to rain in earnest,
slashing sheets of water which drummed a knee-high haze
from the ground. A tree loomed suddenly from the murk and
raked crooked branches across his shoulder. The impact tore
a ragged scream from his throat.

Whimpering with pain, he knew that the running had ended.
Death hung at his hip; a short sword for them . . . and a black
tsepan dirk for himself. Its triple edges would be preferable to
being taken back alive.

The boy straightened with an effort, choosing with pathetic
pride to be found standing rather than grovelling in the mud.
He fell twice, for the ground had been hammered into greasy
mud by the downpour, but at last remained steady enough to
draw blade. He glanced down at the dirk, waiting loose in its
sheath; there would be no dignity for its use, no ceremony or
ancient ritual phrases. Just a hasty inward stab before they

could lay hands upon him. But they would be cheated. He almost smiled bitterly at that. And then he waited, while the rain fell steadily. And while nothing else happened.

Even the curses he began to howl were swallowed up by a long rumble of receding thunder. As the courage of desperation ebbed away his shoulders drooped and at last he began to cry, softly, like a child.

Suddenly the boy stopped abruptly and wiped his face with one muddy sleeve. There was a feeling—a tingling deep within his brain—that he knew from previous experience. He was no longer alone. Panic welled up again, and he would have run if only he knew which way was safe.

Then a hand came out of the dark and gripped his injured arm. With a croaking gasp the boy lashed out and staggered away, but made only two swaying strides before his knees gave way and a deeper black than the night closed in around his eyes.

He did not hear the footsteps padding closer until they stopped beside his head . . .

ONE

Hunter's Moon

Autumn sunshine warmed Gemmel's whitewashed cottage and gilded its thatched roof, making him smile. In the fifty years since he had first come here, he had often compared the modest dwelling unfavourably with his other home under Glaselyu Menethen, the Blue Mountains dimly shading the western horizon. But on days like this such criticism was out of the question.

The locals called him *an-pestrior*, the wizard, and he was content to let them do so. There were no words in the Alban language—or in any other, for that matter—to adequately describe what he really was. Which, when he gave the matter thought, was just as well. Even so, over the past few years he had done little to warrant his title. Gemmel Errekren had retired from active sorcery . . . and he was bored.

One of a long-lived race, during his years of exile he had performed spells, travelled the known lands and some un-known as well, learned the martial arts of half-a-dozen king-doms. He *had* . . . and there lay the problem. Everything had been done, was completed, past tense, and now ennui gripped him in soft and cloying paws.

The sun dipped behind a cloud and brought the old man out of his reverie with a yawn. He eyed the changing sky and decided it was time he prepared something to eat . . .

Outside was dark and blurred with rain, a curtain of drops briefly sparkling as they passed through the wash of lamplight from the cottage windows. Inside was snug and smelling of hot food as the master of the house, who could have stopped the storm had he chosen, sat down to his meal.

Gemmel stopped with a mug of ale half-way to his lips. The sound which had reached his ears was nothing to do with any storm. It seemed more like the howling of a wolf, he reflected as he finished his drink. Then he set the cup down with a sharp little click and turned to stare out into the night. There were words in this wolf's howl.

The sorcerer's eyes flashed green in the lamp-glow and a smile tugged at the corners of his thin mouth as he stood up. Hung over the fireplace was his *athame*, an iron knife inlaid with silver runes and whetted to a razor edge. It was a weapon potent against any foe, human or . . . otherwise. There were other weapons too, but Gemmel ignored them with an effort. He had made a vow not to use such things without good reason, and even a possible werewolf was not sufficient justification for him to unclip them from their racks. Instead, as he stepped out into the rain-swept night he drew the *athame*, holding it point-up like a practised knife fighter. Which he was.

The howling continued barely long enough for him to guess its source. Then it faded away and the hiss of falling water filled his ears once more. Despite the deluge he moved slowly, ready with the *athame* or matter-ripping spells should anything spring from the darkness. Neither was required. Before long a new sound reached him and Gemmel stopped, eyes narrowing as he listened to the wretched, heartbroken sobbing that had no place here. He hesitated, then sheathed the knife and walked on, peering warily through the gloom.

Then he came upon a vague, ragged figure crying bitterly as the sky opened above him. Moved to pity, Gemmel put out one hand to lead the stranger back to his cottage—and almost lost fingers as a blade hacked feebly at them. The muddy-faced youngster choked and wrenched away, wide-eyed with such terror as the enchanter had seldom seen. Then he tried to run, but after two wobbly paces went down in a heap.

Gemmel blinked, then rubbed his hands together. They felt sticky, and when he glanced down there were dark smears across both palms. With a surge of strength ill-matching his venerable appearance he lifted the slack-limbed body and bore it carefully back to his house. At every stride he felt warm blood soaking through his sleeve.

*

The wizard's guest lay on a hastily cleared table while Gemmel boiled water and rummaged for long-forgotten jars and bottles. Cutting away the boy's clothing, he swore softly when he saw what attempts to free the arrow had done to an originally clean puncture. The old man cursed again, damning the oversight that had left his proper healing materials back under the mountains. Then he shrugged and resigned himself to making the best of what means were at hand.

As he washed after dropping some instruments into the boiling water, a groan made him turn round. The youngster's eyes were open, wide and white in a mask of bloodied mud. "Get out!" he gasped. Weak though it was, his voice had a commanding edge that made Gemmel stare. "I'm being followed! I can't lose them. Get . . . *out,* you fool! Kill me clean . . . then . . . run . . ." The effort cost him dear, for his staring eyes unfocused and rolled shut as his lifted head dropped with an ugly thud to the table. With no reason to disbelieve him, Gemmel moved fast. Seizing a few items, he ran from the house. But not to hide—he was, after all, a wizard.

The rain had stopped as suddenly as it had begun and wind was shredding the remaining clouds. Instinct, mingled perhaps with a forlorn hope, raised the old man's gaze toward the remote glint of stars, searching . . . Then he snorted and marched around the cottage, muttering under his breath. At each compass-point he stopped, bowed, drew a sign in the air and flicked pinches of dust from the leather bags he carried. Both sign and dust glowed blue for an instant afterwards. At the front door he raised one hand and pronounced one of the lesser Charms of Concealment. As the spell took effect a bluish haze shimmered briefly, and though when it faded nothing had apparently changed, Gemmel breathed more easily. Now at least he would have enough time to patch up his visitor so that they could both get well out of the way. But charm or no charm, once inside he bolted the door. Twice.

Before long he had the arrow out, the wound bandaged after a fashion and his blanket-wrapped patient set in a chair by the fire. The wizard poured himself another drink with the feeling that he deserved it. Apart from where Gemmel had been working, the boy's skin and clothes were caked with muck until they were hard to tell apart. Knowing Albans perhaps better than they knew themselves, the sorcerer stoked his bath-house fire and turned the pine tub right-side-up.

When he re-entered the front room, his guest's eyelids fluttered up, only to squeeze shut again as pain seared his torn back. Gemmel hastily offered him a wooden beaker. "Drink this," he instructed. "It should ease the effects of my surgery somewhat."

Obediently the young man put back its bitter contents in a single face-twisting gulp, and after a time felt the throbbing dwindle. He nodded gratefully. "Thanks . . . for the surgery as well." His wry little smile went crooked when a determined twinge worked through the drug. "If you will excuse my ill manners, I will not bow just yet."

"I will excuse you until you've rested," said Gemmel considerately.

"And bathed," the Alban put in. "I stink."

Gemmel grinned slightly. "Well, since you mention it . . ." he conceded. "But tell me something, if you would. Who are you?"

Suspicion welled up in the boy's grey-green eyes, turning them cold and flinty. "Who wants to know?" Something in the demand—it was no less—made Gemmel very glad he had thought to set any weapons out of reach.

"I do. The man who took a broken arrow from your back."

"Oh . . . I beg pardon—my rudeness was—"

"Understandable in the circumstances."

Despite the way it obviously hurt him, the boy insisted on making an awkward bow. Gemmel took note, wondering what he was going to hear. It wasn't anything he might have expected.

"Talvalin," the youngster said *"kailin-eir* Aldric." Even though he didn't look the part, Gemmel was convinced. Little things indicated a high rank: the excellent quality of shortsword and dirk; a tunic where heavy embroidery glinted gold wherever mud had dried sufficiently to flake away; something which might be a crest-collar showing now and then as its wearer moved. Only the hair was wrong, hacked crudely short instead of tied in a queue.

"So . . . Aldric-*eir*, you are safe in this house, and my guest. Though I cannot offer food after that drug, there's hot water in the bath-house and a spare bed. Feel free with both."

Aldric's face was puzzled under its mud. "Why are you doing this?" he asked finally.

"I have a kind heart." The wizard grinned toothily. "Go to bed, boy. You'll have more questions in the morning, and by then I shall feel more like answering them." Opening a jar, he mixed its contents with hot water and held up the potion. "This should help you sleep—and ensure some pleasant dreams."

It occurred to Aldric as he clumsily undressed that he had not asked his benefactor's name. Then he dismissed the matter and had as relaxing a bath as possible under the circumstances. Despite the drugs it hurt to move his arm, but actually to be clean again, to wash away the dirt and the sweat and the smell, was worth a few aches. When at last he crept under a thick down quilt, he fell asleep almost at once. Not so the wizard.

Glancing once towards the silent guest-room, Gemmel put more logs on the fire and settled back into his cushioned chair. Mixed with the sleeping-draught was a generous pinch of *ymeth*, freezing Aldric's mind for probing by any wizard with the necessary skill. It was simple, fast, proof against lies—and gave both parties a splitting headache.

That was something Gemmel felt he could tolerate. He began to breathe evenly, and after a time his eyes went cold and dead, green crystals reflecting not even the dance of flames. Though the logs burned slowly, they had died under a film of ash before life returned to the old man's face.

By then he had learned all that he wanted to know.

*

There was an art to the use of *ymeth,* requiring great delicacy not to probe deeply and too slowly, yet not so shallowly and fast that facts were lost in the blurred recollections of another's brain. Gemmel was a master of that art.

At first there was only the beat of two hearts in a dark warmth. Then came light and cold and a kaleidoscopic whirl of colours. Faces focused and faded, voices swam together in a confusing babble, there were names meaning nothing and yet significant. Now and then the images of important memories grew clear, like an awareness of reality . . .

Swords glittered in sunlight. A voice issued crisp instructions. Steel grated, its shrillness deadened by the hot, heavy air. Blades met with harsh percussive music, again and again. These were fencing lessons.

Watched with sleepy amusement by his eldest brother Joren, Aldric went through the exercises of *taiken-ulleth,* the art of longsword fighting. It had once been an art in which blade and body, hand and heart and mind and eye all worked as one; but the last true master was more than two centuries in his funeral urn and *taikenin* were now just ordinary swords. Insofar as *taikenin* were ever merely "ordinary".

The boy was fourteen now, and in Joren's opinion very good—though he had not bothered to tell Aldric so, even after ten years' tuition. Praise was something hard-earned and not freely given. Nonetheless . . .

"That's enough for now." Joren waved away the soldier who had partnered Aldric's exercises, acknowledging the man's salute and his brother's bow with the same nod. Then he frowned as Aldric stuck his practice foil into the ground, and kept his stern expression until the blade had been withdrawn and sheathed with proper respect. Custom demanded the honourable treatment of honourable weapons, especially in practice where no true harm was meant.

"Joren," the word came out in a gasp as Aldric sank crosslegged on to the grass, "I would much rather swim. It's too hot for this."

"Later. You've another half-hour to go yet." Joren's toe nudged lazily at his little brother. "And sit up straighter. Look neat."

In response Aldric flopped back and grinned, untidily comfortable, raking his fingers through the hair which, though short and boy's length as it would remain for six years, still fell into his eyes whenever possible. "When I'm a *kailin-eir* like you I'll be proper and correct, I promise. But while I can relax, I will."

Staring at him doubtfully, Joren touched his own warrior's queue and high-clan earbraids, then shrugged slightly. He had come of age and been made *kailin* only that spring, and in all fairness to the boy there were times when his insistence on propriety bordered on the obsessive. But he had his position to think of, as eldest son and heir to ranks and titles, while Aldric was merely third son and heir to very little.

"All right. No arguments then. But if you cannot look like a gentleman, let's at least see if you can fight like one."

"Difficult, I'd say," cut in a suave voice and Aldric's smile died. There had never been much affection between him and his other brother Baiart, Joren's twin. There was little love between the twins either. Twin, and yet second son—by all of five minutes. That twist of fate had twisted Baiart somewhat, ever since he became old enough to understand it.

"Manners!" reproved Joren in a soft voice which bore the merest hint of menace. Baiart stepped out of shadow into the full wash of sunlight. He was tall, blond and blue-eyed like his twin and four sisters, and though the light flattered his hair it did nothing for his expression. Aldric was the only one of seven children to carry his Elthanek mother's dark hair and grey-green eyes, as if she had given up those as well as her life when he was born. Baiart had always suspected there might be another reason, though he dared not say so. And he hated the child who had usurped Lady Linnoth's place in the family after killing her. His love for his mother had always been more intense than that of the others. Almost too intense for comfort, his or hers. But that also was never spoken of.

"Dear elder brother," he said with a mocking bow, "I'm sure our little brother can speak for himself." If he had hoped to needle anyone into an unseemly outburst Baiart was disappointed. Then Aldric rose to his feet with feline grace.

"If you want to prove something, dear brother, I suggest you try it now. Here. With these." He extended the foils.

Baiart had spent most of his time at court in Cerdor, returning only at feast-days and when his allowance ran out, as now. Though aware that Aldric had learned *taiken*-play, he still had no idea how skilled the boy had become. Aldric knew of his ignorance; it was one of the reasons he had "allowed" the duel to apparently arrange itself in the first place. Baiart needed a lesson.

A formal Alban duel was totally unlike combat. Since the Clan Wars five hundred years before, when three-quarters of the ancient aristocracy had destroyed one another, it was illegal for *kailinin* to fight to the death except in war and raid—or with permission from their lord. Duelling foils were light, thrusting weapons, tipped with sharp spurs which did nothing worse than draw blood, and the movements were more of dance than duel.

What was fought that day under the shadow of Dunrath—hold's great citadel was no such cautious ritual. Saving only that the blades were blunt, it was the same whirl of cut-and-thrust which had characterised the fierce warrior clans for almost two millennia. Agile and swift, Aldric was able to score two quick points before Baiart grew wise and used his longer arm to keep the boy at a distance. Then he saw an opening for a thrust.

But instead Baiart cut with such force that, blunt sword or not, it would have ripped his brother's face apart had it been successful. Aldric felt the sting of skin peeling off his cheek even as he jerked his head aside. He retreated, shaken not by the insignificant wound but by Baiart's clear intention. And by something he had never met before—the feeling which had made him dodge. He hadn't ducked so fast because of training but because of the unsummoned warning inside his head, without which he would surely have been blinded. Knowledge of that made his temper foul, and Baiart's grin made it fouler yet.

The bigger man saw something in his brother's dark eyes that he did not like, and broke ground hastily. With blood bright across his face and shirt, Aldric shifted *taiken* to both

hands and came after him. Joren saw the change of position
and realised his pupil was no longer playing. He opened his
mouth to shout, then realised that an interruption now could
prove deadly—for someone.

When Baiart jabbed, a warning move to keep Aldric away,
the other blade beat against his own so viciously that the
weapon was almost knocked from his grasp. Aldric grinned
the grin of a cat whose mouse is secure under one paw, just
before the claws come out. Then he stamped and shouted
both at once. This surprised Baiart enough for the boy to
advance in a precise, gliding pass, reach out his left hand and
wrench his brother's sword away.

His own blade thrust home with unnecessary force on
Baiart's chest an instant later. With a painful grunt he held up
both empty hands, signalling surrender. Aldric stared at him
through slitted, feral eyes. "That, dear brother," he said very
softly, "was to win." Touching fingertips to his face, he
scowled at the blood on them, then suddenly swung his
sword.

The horizontal cut was invisibly fast, savage and perfect. It
hit Baiart across the waist, doubling him up; the same blow
with a live blade would have sliced him to the spine and
everyone present knew it. Except for the ugly sound of
retching it was very quiet in the fortress gardens. Joren
remembered that Aldric's name was seven centuries old in his
mother's line, Elthanek rather than Alban. Every man who
had borne it had been a warrior of the old style: a renowned
and ruthless slayer.

Aldric slowly regained his breath and eyed Baiart with
more sardonic mirth than any fourteen-year-old should have
possessed. "But that," he smiled coldly, "was purely personal."

*

Haranil Talvalin was Clan-Lord, master of Dunrath and responsible for the King's peace in the north. Unlike many of
his ancestors, who had often to cope with full-scale war,
Haranil's foremost worry was cattle-reaving along the Elthanek
border, and even that was more an over-rowdy sport than a

conflict. There was occasionally much more trouble under his own roof.

Against all the odds, Aldric was growing up. His father's first step was to forbid the boy, on his honour, to fight needlessly. With such a charge laid on him, Aldric obeyed, keeping out of most duels—but not, of course, all. He fought often enough with hot-headed comrades for his skill to become notorious; at last it became difficult for him to find anyone willing to chance even the friendliest contest. Though he never lost his temper or his control, there hung about him an air of restrained violence that was disturbing.

There was one memorable episode in a seedy tavern of Radmur's old town, when somebody had suggested that, since young Aldric had not yet found himself a woman, he probably bedded with his broadsword. Aldric had not drunk enough to find the comment funny, and the escalating argument had broken two heads, several limbs, an uncounted number of ale barrels and had ended with the whole unsavoury den catching fire and toppling sideways into the canal.

He had been seventeen then, at five feet eight inches not very tall for a Talvalin though average for most Albans. Approaching his twentieth birthday, he was broader in chest and narrower in waist—but only an inch taller. That was not good, for the five remaining clans of the old nobility each had their hereditary distinguishing feature, strong enough at least in the male line to survive inter-clan marriages. Talvalins were invariably tall, blond and blue-eyed—except for Aldric. By the time he neared legal maturity any remarks on this had ceased, though not through fear of Talvalin displeasure even though the clan was notorious for its implacable avenging of insulted honour. Aldric's skill with a blade was reason enough.

He spent the early part of that year with one arm in a sling after falling from a galloping horse in full armour. Even before the arm had knitted he was back in the saddle. *Kailinin* relied on mobility, not brute force, and the subtleties of horsemanship were of paramount importance. Learning to control a mount with knees alone was difficult enough with hands clasped on head. Over jumps it became painful as well.

With work so intense, it was only reasonable that recreation should also take extreme forms. One such was the hunting of wild boar, using a spear from horseback. It was lively, often dangerous and therefore popular with the highborn youngsters; also with those old enough to know better . . .

*

Two riders picked their way carefully down an overgrown bridle-path, arguing as they went. The silence of autumnal woodland was disturbed only by their voices and by the distant belling tones of boar-hounds.

"I tell you he's escaped," drawled Aldric lazily. Joren slapped his saddlebow irritably with one hand and waved the other in a huge sweep which took in most of the forest and came very close to taking off the end of his brother's nose.

"Listen to the hounds! They've got him at bay somewhere!"

"Those yapping puppies would bark at their own shadows; you know that."

"At my age I should know when hounds are giving tongue and when they are not!"

Aldric remained calm with an effort. "And at your age you should know when you're in the wrong," he pointed out. Their wrangle was over a boar which had somehow evaded Joren's favourite thrust, and it was injured pride rather than the loss of his roast pork which made the big man so peevish. Aldric did not much care for pork, which explained his lack of interest. Also he enjoyed gently teasing his brother; it always proved rewarding. All at once the yelping died away and Aldric shot an "I-told-you-so" glance from the corner of one eye before lifting a horn from his belt.

"It's too late to start again," he said. "I'm calling the others in and then we'll go home, eh?" Joren expressed his opinion in several crude syllables and began easing his horse round in the confined space of the path. Suddenly a cry went up away to the left and with it the renewed baying of hounds. Joren saw Aldric's face and laughed aloud, then jabbed heels to his steed's flanks and crashed off through the undergrowth, whooping as he went. Aldric rolled despairing eyes heavenward, then shrugged, put the horn away and followed—rather more cautiously.

The scene was familiar enough; dogs raved in a semicircle

round the base of a tree, while horsemen fussed and fidgeted behind them. Their quarry hunched almost invisible in the shadows between a fork of roots, huge and black with a drool of froth hanging from his champing tusks. The boar regarded them with mad red eyes, secure in his defensive redoubt and quite content to wait for his antagonists to make the first move. His wait proved to be short.

When cries of encouragement failed to move the hounds, one hunter used his spear-butt. The beasts snarled and one twisted to snap at the iron-shod ashwood. Through this opening the boar came charging like a bristled thunderbolt, chopping one of the hounds as he passed before sidestepping a clumsy jab and shooting away with the hunt hot after him. As the bracken gave way to open woodland the speed of the chase increased, heedless of the low branches which scraped an occasional rider from his saddle.

The forest ended abruptly in a smooth valley, dotted with clumps of gorse and carpeted with poppies. The setting sun glared across it, making everyone blink and slow down. All except the boar. Instead of crossing the valley he fled along its rim in an attempt to double back, only to find stragglers emerging from the woods all along his escape route. And still he tried to avoid running in the obvious direction. A thrown spear changed his mind; faced with immediate death or the strange fear welling from the valley, he galloped over the ridge and began to descend the slope.

The hounds' baying stopped in mid-cry, while that of their masters redoubled as horses reared, wild-eyed and whinnying. Neither soft words nor hard blows would induce them to enter the valley. Normally fierce hounds backed off with tails curled to their bellies and hackles bristling. Adding to the hunters' rage was the boar; no longer pursued, he slowed to an insolent amble and then stopped with a piggy sneer seeming to curve his chops.

"What in hell's the matter?" snarled Aldric, his coolness slipping. He thumped his stamping, sidling horse. "Why won't this brute follow that one?"

"Sorcery," said Joren flatly. "And I don't know why it's

here,'' he put in quickly as Aldric's mouth opened for the inevitable question. "This is an ancient part of the forest."

As Joren spoke, his brother looked around with dark un-Talvalin eyes wide with curiosity. That same curiosity had driven him to read many of the writings which lay forgotten in Dunrath's great library, and had given him knowledge beyond that offered by his most liberal-minded tutors. "It was here before the fortress was built," Joren continued, "though mother's people were here even before that. You'd better read the Archive when we get back."

"And leave the boar?" Aldric's imagination landed, returning him to reality. "Not I!" He favoured the beast with a thoughtful glance.

"The horses won't . . . " began Joren, then stopped as Aldric dismounted. "Idiot! We haven't cross-head spears— he'll come right up the shaft to get at you."

"Let him try," grinned Aldric, but the grin was a little thin and stretched. Drawing a heavy falchion from its sheath under one saddleflap, he thumbed the edge, nodded and strapped the weapon to his belt. Joren made a disbelieving noise and then exploded.

"What the hell d'you think you're doing?" he blazed. "You're not impressing anyone . . . ! Light of Heaven, if you get killed what am I to tell father?"

"You'll think of something," mocked Aldric gently.

"I . . . just be careful." Joren playfully ruffled his youngest brother's hair and Aldric flinched away. It was *kailin*-length now, and he was close enough to the *Eskorrethen* ceremony to resent its being touched by another warrior. No *kailin* put hand to another's queue except to lift his severed head. That was a tradition old enough to be almost law.

Then he regretted the hasty move and smiled crookedly up at Joren. "Me, careful? But surely, aren't I always?" He hefted his spear, loosened the falchion in its sheath and walked down towards the boar. The animal watched him, snapping its tusks nastily as he continued to advance.

Then it charged.

Aldric dropped to one knee, spear braced, and let the boar run straight on to its levelled point. As Joren had said, the creature came on up the shaft as if nothing had happened, but by that time the boy had let go his spear, sidestepped quickly and drawn the falchion. Its wide blade lifted, hovered and whipped down across the boar's thick neck even as Aldric skidded and fell flat. Even so, he was in no danger. With its head half off the boar was down and dead before its slayer could pick himself up. Aldric shook his head, feeling foolish. There was a lot of blood and its coppery stink clogged his nostrils, making him sick and giddy. His head buzzed inside and the walls of his mouth went dry and sour.

Then he shuddered violently and stared about him. For a few ugly seconds the valley had become a battlefield, the ground scarlet not with poppies but with gore, strewn with corpses in ancient, ornate armour all hacked and torn with fearful wounds. He rubbed his eyes and the fit was past. A skylark chirruped faintly high up in the blue dusk, and things were all so ordinary now that Aldric thought he had been dreaming. But looking at the carcass he felt more than willing to leave without it.

He lost his chance when the others came running and sliding down the slope, bubbling with congratulations and good-humoured banter. When they started the butchery Aldric retreated hastily. Then a hound whined and licked his hand. Dogs and horses alike had followed their masters into the valley as if they had never feared it. Odd . . . Aldric shook his head again, to clear it of confusion this time, and looked across to the far slope. A few hazy mist-patches trailed like forgotten scarves along the ground, ghostly pale against the shadows. Remnants of sunset glowed amber behind the trees silhouetted blackly on the skyline. Aldric sighed and sat down.

With a yelp he sprang up again, rubbing an injured rump. There were no trees nearby, so the offending object could hardly be a root. He kicked at it irritably, but when something shifted under the turf he looked more closely. Then his eyebrows went up and he dug the object free with falchion and fingers. It was a sword-hilt, in the blocky, massive style not made since the Clan Wars so long ago. He had seen one before in Dunrath; horseman's weapons both, as the chained pommels and wrist-bands bore witness. They were constructed so that, if the weapon was knocked from its owner's hand in battle, with the band around his wrist at least his sword was not lost underfoot. There was something strange about this rusty remnant of someone's forgotten battle, something Aldric could not at first pin down. Although the weapon had been lying out under the sky for years uncounted, and was deeply corroded, it was still in passable condition for something which one would have expected to have been entirely eaten away.

Aldric recalled his hallucination, wondering now if it was anything so simple. Before *an Mergh-Arlethen,* the Horse Lords, came out of the sea mist to claim Alba for their own, Cernuek and Elthanek scholars had already been writing history, legend and plain gossip for an age and an age. But some things they had not written. These survived only as tales told in winter by the great log fires, stories for children and the credulous. Or truths no one dared to believe.

A wolf howled balefully among the distant trees and Aldric's fingers clenched the ancient hilt. He scowled, both at the display of nerves and at the beast which should have been miles further north at this time of year. Making a mental note to organise another hunt, he moved the hilt towards one of his hunting-jerkin's deep pockets. Then an odd thing happened: between one heartbeat and the next, he lost all interest in the relic. If it had not been easier to complete the pocketing movement, he would have dropped it back on to the ground, and even so he had forgotten the hilt's existence before it had completely slithered out of sight.

As he mounted up, Aldric's mind wandered down macabre lanes, the back alleys of imagination. He recalled stories read, overheard or gloatingly told by Baiart when they were both much younger. Stories of men who, willing or not, became beasts at the full of the moon.

He sat back in the lofty Alban saddle—then shivered involuntarily. Just visible through the eastern trees was a disc which shone like a newly minted mark: the full moon. Wiping chilly moisture from hands and face, Aldric laughed hollowly at having worked himself into such a state.

Joren, laden with joints of boar, overheard the laugh and gave him a strange look, but witheld other comment. Stars had appeared before they were ready to leave, and as the moon rose further it washed woods and valley with a frosty sheen. Aldric felt cold, and as the others rode off he gladly turned his horse to follow. Then he jerked on the reins and stood up in his stirrups.

A fragment of shadow had detached itself from the forest and was flitting from one gorse-clump to the next. Without reason the fine hair on Aldric's arms and neck stood on end. There was a crossbow hanging in a loop by his knee, and he reached for the weapon's cool walnut stock as if seeking comfort from its weight. He had had enough irrationalities for one night; at least the bow was heavy, solid and real. Spanning and loading it, he strained his eyes to see what the lean shadow might be. He thought he knew already.

He was right: a monstrous wolf, its grey coat tipped silver by the moonlight, came padding up the slope. It ignored the dark patch where the boar had been cut up—most unwolflike and suspicious, had Aldric been noticing such things—and made for the small patch of disturbed earth where something had recently been exhumed. Aldric frowned slightly as a faint memory nagged him for a moment, but could recall nothing of importance. Whimpering eagerly the wolf began to dig, carefully at first and then with increasing frenzy until soil flew in all directions. Then abruptly it stopped and raised its long muzzle in a wary sniff.

Downwind, and invisible under the trees, Aldric levelled his bow, hoping the uncertain light would not spoil his shot. Taking a deep breath he set finger to trigger, noting absently how the beast's eyes reflected the moon, glowing like tiny bluish candles. They seemed almost to be watching him; ridiculous of course, or the creature would have run long ago.

Just before he tripped the sear a low, rumbling snarl reached his ears and the wolf crouched, not to flee but to pounce. A beast of that size could have him out of the saddle in two bounds and a snap . . .

"Aldric!" Both boy and wolf started and the crossbow went off, its bolt flinging the animal backwards in a squirming heap. Wood snapped as it bit the missile from a hind leg and rose unsteadily, blazing eyes fixed on Aldric as if etching his shocked face into its memory. Then Joren came trotting up, the younger man glanced towards him and when they both looked back the wolf was gone.

"What's the matter with you?" After hurrying back in case his little brother had fallen foul of roots or hanging branches, Joren was none too pleased to find him shooting at shadows. "Well?"

"Nothing," Aldric replied, far too quickly. "Nothing at all."

Joren eyed him narrowly. "Does 'nothing' usually make you sweat like a wash-house window?" he asked rather more gently. Aldric realised with clammy distaste that his whole body was damp and cold, and he tugged a shirtsleeve away from sticky skin.

"I saw a wolf down there," he explained lamely. Joren blinked.

"Oh, did you? I think I heard one earlier, but . . . Pity you missed it—if it was there at all."

Aldric coloured. "It was! And I didn't miss!"

"Then where's the body?"

"I . . . it ran off when you appeared . . ."

"As I said—pity you missed." There was something in Joren's tone of voice which stopped any further protests. "Now come on home, or you'll catch a chill."

Aldric stared doubtfully across the valley one last time, then shrugged and did as he was told.

TWO

Rites of Passage, Rites of Blood

On an evening some five weeks later, the great feast-hall at Dunrath was filled with music and ablaze with light made brilliant by the shifting hues of *elyu-dlasen*, the formal Colour-Robes of the Alban clans. It was Aldric's twentieth birthday, his coming of age, and Haranil-*arluth* was making an occasion of it, inviting relatives and friends to the least degree. He was even willing to welcome total strangers.

"My lord?" The *arluth* looked up to where his steward had appeared silently by his chair. The man bowed low. "There is a man at the gatehouse, my lord. He craves shelter."

"So?" Although travellers were unusual at this season, it was equally unusual to be told of their arrival. Normally they were simply admitted with courtesy, since such hospitality was expected by the fortress-lord. Looking uncomfortable, the steward bowed again, twitchily.

"My lord, he will not come in." Haranil raised his brows at that. "You must invite him across the threshold yourself, it seems. He says it is a custom of his country, and only polite that a host should see what guest enters his home."

The lord groaned softly; he was very comfortable where he was, but in such circumstances a refusal was out of the question. Signalling those at his immediate table to remain seated, he rose, shrugged into an overmantle and strode out. Returning alone some minutes later, he met a quizzical glance from Joren.

"He's changing into more suitable clothing," the *arluth* explained. "A very courteous gentleman—unlike some." His gaze touched an empty chair; Baiart had refused to attend the feast.

When the guest eventually appeared, he proved arresting enough to mute conversation for several seconds. Not that he was impressive in himself, being stocky, round-headed and balding. What little hair he retained over his ears, and the small beard framing his thin lips, was brindled silvery grey like a wolfhound or a wolf. But his clothing was in stark contrast. Over unassuming grey trimmed with silver fur he wore an over-robe of royal quality, ankle-length and pure white lined with azure. Its stiffly embroidered surface rustled when he knelt to give Haranil Talvalin the respect proper to his rank.

"Gracious good my lord," he said, somehow projecting a murmur clearly from the door, "may the warmth of hospitality be always in the hearth of this house." Haranil acknowledged the compliment with a nod and indicated Baiart's empty seat. As the stranger moved to take it he limped, wincing and favouring his left leg before sitting down with an air of relief. Seeing the lord's concern he patted the limb and smiled.

"My horse and I argued with a tree, lord—I lost." Then his smile was replaced by a concerned expression. "But your pardon! Here I sit at your table, nameless." Putting one hand over his heart, he spread the other wide. "Duergar Vathach, an indifferent scholar and historian, very much at your service." His eyes glittered as he smiled again; they were the palest blue Haranil had ever seen, and seldom blinked.

The scholar's slight accent and occasional difficulty with Alban didn't prevent him from talking virtually all the time he was not eating. It would have been most unmannerly had his conversation been boring, but he spoke entertainingly about every subject raised at the lord's high table. Except for one put forward by Aldric.

"Duergar-*an*, did you come south from Datherga?" The pale eyes stared at him, and Aldric noticed how the man's face went cold and sinister when he forgot to smile. Actually, Duergar was trying to decide whether this young man merited a title.

"Sir, you are . . . ?" he ventured cautiously. Aldric inclined his head politely.

"*Kailin-eir* Aldric *un-cseir* Haranil-*arluth* Talvalin. Third son." He rather enjoyed saying that—it was the first time he had chanced giving anyone his full rank and title and it sounded good. Duergar concealed slight surprise, then realised that he was after all seated at the lord's high table.

"No, my lord—I came by Elmisford and Baelen Forest." Aldric leaned forward eagerly.

"Did you see or hear any wolves—wounded, irritable wolves?"

"I confess I did not, my lord. Is it important?"

"I shot one over a month ago; it was never caught. Certain people"—he stared hard at Joren—"would say, and have said, that I missed. At that sort of range I don't miss, so the brute's wounded and dangerous. I want it found before someone gets hurt." He caught an odd expression on the scholar's face and stopped. "You disapprove?"

"Well, yes," Duergar admitted. "You don't know who the wolf might have been." His grin was stillborn as an awkward silence fell on those who had overheard.

"That," said old Lord Dacurre, "is not amusing." Further down the hall, rowdy normality continued with such gusto that the silence became painful. When Duergar stood up and bowed, very low, someone cleared his throat and began to talk again, the uneasy moment forgotten.

Two retainers set a carved stool on the gallery of the great stairway and the murmur of voices died to an expectant whispering. An old, white-bearded man was helped to his seat and a harp of black wood was put into his hands. He made obeisance towards the high table and spoke in a resonant voice, thick with a Hertan burr.

"Gracious good my lords and ladies fair," he said, "I would have your leave to sing." With equal formality Haranil-*arluth* and Lord Santon's wife granted him that leave, and he sat down with a smile. The old man did not begin at once; he ran one finger across his harp, stroking a rippling chord from the strings. The hall fell silent as he played a liquid melody, long fingers flickering delicately across the instrument. As the old bard plucked the harp's strings, he also began to touch the hearts of his listeners.

He played of sunrise and spring, courage and love and laughter, the sheen of swords and maidens' golden hair; he played of the wind in the trees, the waves on the sea, of luck and the joy of living. Then he began to sing at last, and though older than any in the hall, his voice still filled its every corner with cunning music and subtle words.

He sang the old stories of magic and adventure, when lean firedrakes flicked flaming across the sunlit sky and sorcerers worked their spells by starlight. He sang of battles lost and won and the love of kings' daughters for brave strangers. Archaic names sprinkled his songs like rare jewels, and earlier ages flowed from his music in a golden haze of memories. Long-forgotten voices spoke again through the harper's mouth, captains and kings and beautiful ladies who returned from the dust to live for a space, warmed by the suns of past summers.

The old Hertan struck three crystal notes which shimmered to silence in the vast hall, and bowed his head. There was a pause and then his audience erupted, most un-Alban, into waves of applause. Haranil had the old man brought before his chair, where he filled a guardsman's high-crowned helm with golden deniers and placed it in the harper's hands. Then he unclasped a ring of massy Pryteinek gold from his wrist and snapped it shut about the minstrel's arm. This was something more personal than mere wages and the old man knew it. He traced the deeply-incised crests on the wrist-band and bent his head deeply in gratitude. They were the Talvalin spread eagle, set within the double border of a Clan-Lord; such tokens would greatly increase his fame, for they were never presented lightly.

"*Arr' eth-an,* a question for you," Aldric said quietly, giving the old man his proper title. "Have you heard any tale about Baelen Forest—and a valley filled with dead men's bones?" He was conscious of curious stares, for until now he had made no mention of what he had—or thought he had—seen after the hunt. There had been sparse mention of a battle in earlier Archive volumes, but no details either there or anywhere else in an exhaustively searched library. Although Aldric did not admit it even to himself, the experience had worried him. Thus his willingness to try any other source, and thus his mixed emotions when the harper replied.

"I know that legend, lord. It is called *'The Fall of Kalarr cu Ruruc.'* " He paused and studied Aldric with eyes blue as faded cornflowers. "It is not a tale for this occasion. Your pardon, lord, but I will not sing that song tonight." His departure was marked by Haranil-*arluth*'s bow to honour him, an action which by custom the entire hall must copy. It served at least to mask the expression of slight horror which rested briefly on Aldric's face.

Only Duergar noticed it. "An interesting story, lord, even though untrue," he pointed out. Aldric's mouth shaped a silent "Oh?" at him and the historian started to explain. By accident or design his lecture was complex, boring and obscure, so that before long Aldric had stopped paying any attention whatsoever and was regretting he had ever raised the subject.

Kalarr had been a sorcerer in the days before the Clan Wars, when Alba had been divided into petty kingdoms whose rulers paid only lip-service to the dominion of their Overlord. It was a situation bubbling with intrigue, as the lesser lords plotted their own advancement. None could say from whence Kalarr cu Ruruc had come; he simply *was*. At first the sorcerer made pretence of aiding the conspirators until such time as he could get them all in one place under his eye. That day came at a feast in his citadel of Ut Ergan, where he slew his allies with fire from the air and seized their lands for his own.

The Overlord, undeceived by soft words, gathered his warriors and rode north to destroy the usurper. Cu Ruruc's army was broken utterly in Baelen Forest and the sorcerer himself was cut down. But the Overlord and many of his nobles were also slain, which by the succession of their ambitious sons led directly to the Clan Wars and all that followed.

Aldric had read these bare bones before, but worse than learning nothing new was the way Duergar talked down to

him as if he was a child. At length the rather haughty
youngster yawned—a slow, exaggerated and supremely insolent yawn like a cat's. Duergar stopped in mid-sentence. "Do
I bore you, dear my lord?" he enquired silkily.

"In a word, yes. I'm twenty years old, man, yet you treat
me like an infant. I do not like that." Duergar's smile was
beginning to set his teeth on edge, and when the scholar
made several benevolent noises as if to a squalling baby,
Aldric's temper flared.

"Duergar-*an*, I dislike your manner, your condescension
and your smile," he said, and though his voice remained soft
and pleasant, thinned lips and narrowed eyes gave ample
indication of his feelings. "In short, historian, I dislike you!
Good evening." Rising without a bow of courtesy, he stalked
away.

Without even blinking Duergar watched him go, then smiled
a slow smile to himself and drank more wine with satisfaction.

Aldric was seething inwardly, at himself this time. He had
broken one of the many customs surrounding high-clan *kailinin*
by showing both boredom and irritation to a guest. It made
him look foolish. It made him lose face. It made him damned
angry!

He was saved from further brooding by the retainer, who
appeared before him with the information that everything was
ready for his coming-of-age ceremony. Regaining control of
himself, he followed the servant out of the hall to be prepared
for the rituals.

*

Kneeling before his father, Aldric bowed until his forehead
touched the ground between his hands. It was the only time in
his life he would be expected to give First Obeisance to
anyone other than royalty, and he took care to do it correctly.
Then he sat back on his heels, took the Book of Ancestors
from *yscop* Gyreth, bowed to the priest and pressed the
ancient holy relic to his brow. From Lord Dacurre's hands he
received his father's *taiken*, unsheathed a handspan of blade
and touched that cold, keen metal lightly to his lips, careful
not so much of the weapon's age as of its edge.

Haranil Talvalin rose from his seat, laid both hands on his

son's head and swept up the hair at the back. Uncut for six months except to keep it neat, it fell at once into the queue which Haranil secured with a crested clip. Though some clans required that the full head of hair be put in queue, this single tail had sufficed for more than twenty generations of Talvalin warriors.

After that the lord pulled free the long locks Aldric had kept anchored over and behind his ears, letting them fall one along each cheek to the jaw-hinge. Then he stepped back and bowed as one warrior to another. Aldric acknowledged with forehead against hands crossed on the floor, Second Obeisance, from a *kailin-eir* to his lord. Then he stood up, bowed as an equal and spoke the oath which would bind him from this moment onward.

"I am *kailin-eir* Aldric Talvalin," he said in a clear voice. "Know me, and know I have a Word of Binding. On it I swear now to keep the laws of Heaven and the King, that my name and ancestors be not dishonoured.

"I do also swear to keep true the honour of my House and Clan, even to the ending of my life.

"I lastly swear to be the King's liege man, to live and die as may best serve him. Under Heaven and upon my Word, I do truly swear."

Everyone present bowed respectfully when he had finished speaking. When they straightened, Joren looped the shoulder-belt of a sword about his brother's neck, taking care not to touch his hair, then fastened a silver crest-collar around his throat and made way for Lord Santon.

Aldric's mouth went a little dry—not because of the warlord's sinister appearance, his *elyu-dlas* of purple and dark blue contrasting with the pale skin of all the Santon clan, but because of the slender rod he bore so carefully in both hands. Lacquered a hard, intense black, it was capped at either end with silver. Santon moved his hands and the rod broke in two, revealing a five-inch triple-edged stiletto blade, toylike and glittering, sharp as a needle. An icicle of steel. A *tsepan*.

Now it was a badge of rank and a piece of masculine jewellery, its materials of the very finest for the sake of the wearer's honour. But it remained an echo of the older, harsher codes which once laid down both the living and the dying of a warrior. The *tsepan* was for suicide; it had no other purpose.

There had been a time when the reasons for its use were petty: shame that a word could have erased; dishonour; the ultimate emphasis to a protest. And there were reasons still justified now: avoiding capture by an implacable, dishonourable enemy; self-execution as repentance and admission of guilt—an act which also kept forfeit lands from seizure by the crown.

But in war, where commonsense prevailed over pride and bloody obsession with honour, the dirk took on another aspect: that of mercy. When a man lay in the dirt split asunder by a *taiken*'s sweeping stroke, it could never be anything but kindness to end his irreparable pain. Though it was never admitted, there was tacit acceptance that each *kailin*'s dirk was carried, at the last, for himself. A man was luckless indeed if in the hour of his hopeless agony there was neither blade nor compassionate hand to make his passage to the darkness quick and clean.

Santon spoke the old phrases in High Alban, the Horse-Lords' priestly tongue, forgotten save in rituals such as this. It was a language rich, rhythmic and musical, but hard and stern as those who had first pronounced it.

"Behold this blade, black and belt-borne," the lord intoned slowly. "Honourable it is, pride-protecting, death without dishonour's darkness. Mark its meaning in your mind with Word of Binding and with blood." From the corner of one eye Aldric saw servants unroll a length of bandage and shivered slightly.

"Word and blood will bind me. I will bear the blade." The young *kailin* held out his open left hand, muscles taut to stop the fingers trembling. Lord Santon laid the *tsepan* on the offered skin and cut once with each edge, marking duty to Heaven, to Crown and to Clan.

White-faced and barely breathing, Aldric watched dark blood welling from the parallel wounds until they were covered with white gauze and a fine linen bandage. He felt very slightly sick. The cuts themselves had hurt little, so keen was the fragile dirk, but now a throbbing crawled hotly up his arm. Clenching his fists he bowed, then retired for a while as was his right.

The ceremony was over and his life for the next few years was laid out in orderly fashion. A youth spent in weapon-training had been to prepare him for this: service in some high lord's garrison before officer rank if he earned it and promotion perhaps to the Guards' cavalry barrack in Cerdor. Not an appealing prospect, but better at least than the other choice of a lord's third son—Aldric had never seen himself as a priest. Grinning at the thought, he gathered himself up and went to find something to drink.

*

Sitting astride his roan gelding at the crest of a small rise, Aldric twisted in the saddle to look back at Dunrath's distant bulk. The donjon of the citadel and the loftier fortress turrets gleamed straw-gold in the sunrise, but the rest was still lost in mist and pre-dawn gloom, with only a few firefly specks to show where people were up and about. Aldric hunched deeper into the fur of his travelling cloak, for autumn was drawing to a close and the days were both short and chilly. The horse stamped and shook its mane; it at least was eager to be off, and with a final glance Aldric settled back and let the beast make its own way down the slope, towards the broad army road that led to Radmur.

*

"Radmur? At this time of year?" Joren had been startled when he first heard Aldric's plan. He had been inclined to treat it as a joke until he realised his young brother was quite serious. Then he began to grow suspicious. "Why, may I ask, are you so set on going?"

"I've told you once—I want to see my friends before winter closes in, because there won't be time come spring before I go to Leyruz." Joren cleared his throat. "To *Lord* Leyruz. Sorry."

"Eight leagues is a fair distance even in summer," muttered Joren dubiously. "You'd not find me doing it."

"But then I'm not you, am I?"

"No, praise Heaven!" The big man's vehemence made Aldric laugh. Joren was right, of course; nobody he knew about was worth a twenty-five-mile social call in the present weather—but it made a good enough excuse . . . Unlocking a chest, Aldric hauled out clothing, then swore softly and began to dump three month's accumulated debris from the pockets of his favourite leather jerkin. Something clanked loudly on the bottom of the trunk and he fished out a decrepit, rusty sword-hilt with a broken chain through its pommel. Flakes of corrosion sprinkled his clean clothes, and he muttered something under his breath. Joren stared out of a window, wondering how his little brother had grown up to be such a wise fool. Collecting rubbish, going visiting in such weather . . . "It wouldn't be a woman, hmm?" he speculated idly.

If he had not been watching the clouds Joren might have wondered about the glance Aldric shot at him. Then the expression vanished as he realised Joren was only joking. He dropped the sword-hilt and resumed his packing with a careful laugh.

"Wrong again. When I find a lady, she'll live a damn sight nearer home!"

*

Now Aldric cantered on, whistling between his teeth. Apart from a peasant or two who gave him "Good day" and respectful bows, the road was deserted and winter unquestionably drawing near. Everything seemed draped in grey— the sky, the hills, the clumps of woodland—and Aldric wondered why he had not stayed at home. Haranil-*arluth* had given him three days—pleasing enough until the old man elaborated. A day to go, a day to stay and a day to return. Aldric had made the mistake of protesting, forgetting he was no longer a child whose whims were humoured. Haranil had simply said, "I am your lord, warrior," and Aldric had wisely argued no further.

The smooth sad wail of a wolf floated down from the woods beyond the ridge, and Aldric resisted the temptation to jam in his heels. He had not forgotten the strange events after the boar-hunt, nor Duergar Vathach's enigmatic remark at the feast. Strange man, he thought idly. Spends all day wandering about the woods, never minds the weather, seldom gets back till after dark. Weird . . . his musing was interrupted by the raindrop which hit him in the eye. With a shower coming on, he shook the gelding to a gallop and reached a way-house just in time to watch the downpour from beside a roaring log fire.

He and the horse were both tired when at last he reined in and looked at the walled city of Radmur. Stiff and saddle-sore, he stood in his stirrups as the beast trotted towards the gates where already lights were glowing yellow, newly lit and smelling of oil and resin. Exchanging a brief greeting with the guards, more polite than usual when they saw his hair, he handed his steed over to one of the city ostlers. As in other Alban cities, horses were forbidden beyond the perimeter roads, and as his aching thighs complained he toyed with the idea of a palanquin or chair. Then he reminded himself that he was still only twenty and not fat, and walked.

Tewal's inn was much as he had last seen it, dim and snug under adzed oak beams. At this time of night it smelt mouthwatering, with various things cooking in the kitchen, and in the common-room a fire like a forge and bowls of salted dainties—both deliberate, to encourage thirst and deep drinking. Aldric didn't care about that. Hitching his sword's crossbelt so that the scabbard hung comfortably across his back, he took a handful of beef slivers and began munching. Unmannerly, but then he was hungry.

Tewal himself was not long in appearing, summoned by one of the serving wenches. Short, fat and cheerful, he emerged red-faced from the kitchen where by his smudged nose he had been blowing life into a brazier. "Well now, my lord. I thought I'd seen the last of you till spring," he said, and slapped Aldric on the shoulder, warrior-rank or no. Aldric winced—the little man had big, broad hands—and grinned at him.

"There's no need to sound so disappointed," he said. Tewal tugged his ginger beard and shook his head.

"Oh, no, dear me no, not like that at all, my lord. I was only saying to Egyth, Egyth my dear, I said, that young lord Talvalin—" Aldric held up one hand for silence. Tewal always made him feel out of breath.

"Tewal," he said firmly, "I'm tired and hungry. Feed me and then you can tell me everything you've said to everybody this week. But please, not just now, eh?"

*

The tavern slowly filled with other customers as the evening drew on and Aldric, never fond of crowds, retreated to a quiet corner with his wine and carried on a sporadic conversation with the innkeeper's wife. They had been swapping scraps of gossip for perhaps half an hour when Aldric's flow of speech faltered and an odd expression crossed his face. Not because of the drink—his head was harder than that—but he had the feeling that someone was watching him.

Setting down his tankard, the *kailin* swept a quick glance across the smoky taproom. Merchants with long-stemmed pipes—a curious habit Tewal also affected now—mingled with off-duty guards and their ladies of the moment. Otherwise there was nothing out of the ordinary—until his gaze reached the doorway.

Her name was Ilen; that was all she had admitted and he had not pressed her for more. Their relationship was a complicated one, since she was the lady of a good friend of one of Aldric's good friends and he was reluctant to do anything which would break these long-standing ties. The young man had absolutely no previous experience of women to guide him; Joren had guarded his morals with the same energy as he had taught him to fight, and at the age of twenty Aldric was shy, frustrated, obsessively honourable and nervously virginal. His visit to Radmur was intended to rectify this uncomfortable situation, since at their last meeting—at somebody else's birthday feast—Ilen's friendship had shown signs of becoming something more intimate.

As Ilen crossed the room Aldric half-rose and bowed with as much grace as his apprehension allowed. He was downright scared of doing something which might appear foolish or awkward in the girl's eyes, and was consequently becoming reluctant even to move. Then he did move, very smoothly and with a speed even Joren would have applauded.

Ilen had come too close to the table where three soldiers just off punishment drill were drowning their sorrows, and one had made a grab at her. His fingers had closed around the girl's slender wrist and he was hauling her closer with as much finesse as a fisherman landing herrings. The man's drunkenness was some excuse—but in Aldric's opinion, not much. "Let her alone, friend," he said harshly, tugging the guardsman's shoulder and relying on his rank to gain obedience.

As he sorted out his legs from those of an upturned table and wiped blood from his lip, Aldric realised such reliance had been a little optimistic. Scrambling upright, he intercepted a tray of tankards and helped himself to one, then moved in on the little group of soldiers—rather more carefully this time. They were trying to kiss Ilen and laughing heartily as she tried to flinch away. Aldric's teeth showed briefly and he tapped the nearest man on the back. The soldier swung round, blearily looking for trouble, and found it in the shape of a tankard smacking him very hard under the chin. Not surprisingly he fell down with a crash that took his comrades' table and their drinks down with him.

In the ensuing silence Aldric extended one hand to Ilen. "Let us leave, now," he suggested calmly, and there was a clattering as several of the more timid customers took his advice, just before somebody grabbed his queue from behind with an excessively vicious jerk.

Nobody did that to a *kailin-eir*! Without looking, Aldric slammed elbow backwards at mouth level and felt the crunch of a good square impact shoot down his arm. The "somebody" let go of his hair and tried to yell, a sound muffled by several displaced teeth. It gave Aldric the chance to roll sideways under the shelter of a friendly table, where he could watch the developing fight in relative peace and quiet.

Something heavy hit the ground behind him and he found himself no longer alone. Not that his visitor was anyone he could talk to—the spice seller had been on the wrong end of a bottle, brandy by the smell, and was in no fit state for conversation. Judging by the rising uproar, things were getting out of hand and Aldric guessed that *kailin-eir* or not he had best not be around when the Watch came calling. Radmur's Prefect of Police doubtless remembered the last time well enough.

One of the chairs by his table shot straight up out of sight, followed by loud noises and a rain of splintered wood. Drawing his sword was out of the question, of course; this was only a friendly fight and while brawling was one thing, bladeplay was quite another. As two squealing wenches ran for the door Aldric stood up and followed them, oozing innocence.

This fooled nobody, as three swinging fists made quite clear. By the time he had sorted out that problem—easily enough, since he was sober and his attackers were not—someone else had departed noisily through the window and Aldric hastened his own exit. The sound of breaking glass drew Radmur's city Watch like wasps to syrup, and Tewal's big front window had held enough panes to attract the deafest constable.

Then, despite the risk of being jumped on, he stopped. Ilen had been backed into a corner by her drunken acquaintance of earlier on, and by the look on the man's ugly face he was after more than a kiss this time. There was a small knife in Ilen's hand, but the guard was in no mood to sweet-talk her out of using it. Instead he drew a dagger from his boot and advanced with a nasty grin.

When Aldric shouted he looked round—having learnt nothing from the fate of his colleague—and then lunged. The young *kailin* dodged, grabbed the knife-hand's wrist and used it to hurl the soldier over his shoulder and headlong into a handy pile of chairs. "All a matter of balance," he said dryly, then led Ilen out into the dark, cool peace and quiet of the street.

Opening his mouth to make some comment, Aldric shut it again as his mental alarm sounded for the first time that evening. He spun, one hand flying to his sword-hilt—then lowered it as a halberd prodded his stomach.

"So, my lord Aldric," said the Prefect of Police with a gentle smile. "At least there is nothing in the canal this time. Yet."

*

Heavy flakes of snow wavered to the ground as Aldric galloped fast for Dunrath. The fall had begun just after he left

Radmur and was making the paved road treacherous, but he was in no mood for caution. The magistrates had taken two days to decide who was responsible for the riot in Tewal's inn, and though they had finally given Aldric an honourable discharge they had taken too long over it. The damage was already beyond repair; it would now seem to Haranil-*arluth* that he had been deliberately misunderstood. And deliberate disobedience was one thing the old man had never tolerated. He would be in just the right frame of mind to hear the real reason for the delay; Aldric's stomach went cold at the thought.

He stopped perforce at the way-station, not to feed himself but to rest his lathered horse before the beast dropped under him. Not all the stamping up and down nor the rapping of quirt on boot could hurry the weary animal's recovery and at last Aldric gave up trying. He went inside and stared in grim silence at the fire.

Nearer home the sky began to clear and he approached the fortress in cold, brilliant sunshine. The frosty air was still and silent, the only sound his steed's hoofs muffled by the snow. He could see no guards, no sentries . . . not a soul. The roan passed over the outer drawbridge, and still no one challenged his presence.

Aldric frowned and scanned the courtyard, then dismounted. Though the stables were empty of grooms there were horses in the stalls and even his new battle armour still boxed in one corner, not yet unpacked. Intrigued and by now wary, he moved quietly up into the citadel itself.

Inside was cold, its gloominess accentuated by the dust-flecked shafts of light streaming from the western windows. There was neither movement nor sound save that made by Aldric himself. He had never seen the long corridors so still and dark; even late at night there were usually lamps and servants, but now there was nothing except the slow eddy of golden specks washed by the evening light. Aldric shivered and his sword appeared in one hand almost of its own volition. Very carefully he eased back one of the great hall's doors and slipped inside.

The vast chamber was completely deserted; the ashes of dead fires slumped grey in the hearths and of lamps and

candles only charred wicks remained. Crossing the hall at a
run, Aldric took the stairs four at a time, up the right fork
leading past the galleries, into the donjon and towards the
lord's private apartments. Twice he almost went headlong,
for apart from a little light filtering in the passages were in
total darkness.

At the foot of the spiral stair leading to his father's tower
rooms, he paused to regain his breath and to listen. All the
corridors with access to that door had *en-canath,* singing
floors, uncarpeted loose-laid boards designed to creak at the
slightest pressure. Now they were silent; almost as silent as
the young warrior who slid upstairs like a stalking cat.

The planks groaned thinly when Aldric set foot to them and
he hesitated briefly before continuing to his father's door.
Beginning to ease it open, he grimaced—with the floors
announcing his every step, further caution seemed superflu-
ous. He threw open the door and went inside.

The sword slid from his slack fingers. A thousand thoughts
became one vast silent scream ringing endlessly through the
echoing caverns of his mind.

Haranil-*arluth* Talvalin sat in his high-backed chair by the
fireplace, with his great *taiken* resting on his knees. His head
drooped forward on to his breast and it seemed that the old
lord slept. Only the spear which nailed him to his chair
destroyed the illusion.

A few feet away Joren and his four sisters lay heaped
against the wall, their rich garments glimmering like so many
cut flowers in the wan light. The women had each been stabbed
once, in the neck from behind, but someone had fought.
Blood puddled thickly on the floor, spattered the walls and
smeared across ripped fabrics and hacked furniture. Aldric
stared for a long time at Joren's face, at the loosely gaping
mouth and the obscene emptiness of wide, dead eyes.

Then he began to cry.

When he had recovered from the convulsive sobbing, Aldric
pressed his face to the cool wood of the door and tried to
comprehend the enormity forced upon him. He had been late.
He had promised his father, his lord, that he would return at a
certain time and he had broken that promise. Broken his

Word. Logic nagged that this was not of his choosing, that he would anyway have done no more than die with the rest. But logic had no place in a *kailin*'s honour-code. Without a Word he would be better dead.

As his arm hung limply by his side something touched it. Aldric glanced down and his scarred left palm seemed to burn with a fresh and freezing pain. The hilt of his *tsepan* glittered coldly at him, and his stomach lurched.

Slowly he drew the thin blade. Its lacquered hilt was chill against his hand, and the hand itself trembled. Staring at the bitter point and cruel edges, he quailed at what was expected of him. To die . . . And for what purpose? It would neither avenge the killings nor mourn them; nor even carry out the funeral rites. But not to do so would dishonour his name throughout eternity.

"No!" The word spat from bloodless lips, chasing the *tsepan* as it flickered across the room to thud into a panel. Thrumming with the impact, its pommel swayed so that the blue-enamelled crest—his crest—winked at him like a sardonic eye, mocking his cowardice. Aldric rubbed his throbbing hand, but the pain would not go away. His haunted eyes looked far into the distance, towards the sun hanging low over the Blue Mountains, edging a lapis lazuli sky with gold. A gentle breeze passed through the shattered window, caressing his face and the sweat beading it.

I have lived as well as I may, Aldric thought. I have eaten good food and drunk fine wine, I have had worthy friends. I might have loved . . . I have never slain a man. Why then fear to die? All must go out into the darkness, and only *kailinin* may choose their time of passing. It is an honourable right, that one may leave this melancholy world to return reborn in the great circle.

Quietly he crossed the room and twisted the *tsepan* free, then returned to kneel at his father's feet, laying the dirk before him. Caring nothing for the still-wet blood upon it, he bowed and pressed his brow against the floor. Cold stickiness spread across his skin. The formal phrases for the rite of *tsepanak'ulleth* refused to form in his head and he was ashamed. Quickly he opened tunic and shirt, then reversed the dirk and nuzzled its point into place under his breastbone. The weapon stung.

"My lord father," he whispered at last, "I am dishonoured and full of sorrow. I ask forgiveness and offer my life as recompense."

"Do . . . not!"

The barely audible words shocked Aldric like the stroke of a mace. Blood trickled from where the *tsepan*'s point had broken skin and jabbed deep, but the boy felt nothing. He stared into eyes lit from within by the effort of holding off death by force of will alone.

"You live . . . good. Good . . ." Aldric kept quiet, knowing that Haranil-*arluth* must have had good cause to cling to this half-life so long. "Duergar has done this . . ." the old man gasped hoarsely. "Destroyed us . . ." As Aldric listened, his father choked out the story. It made grim listening. Duergar Vathach had been a familiar figure at all hours of the day or night, and when he appeared just before dawn the doors were opened. But hiding in the shadows had been a gang of hired bravoes who had rushed the sleeping citadel, slaying all who refused to serve their master. Duergar was no scholar, but a necromancer of the Drusalan Empire, aflame with some mad scheme. Clan Talvalin had been convenient hosts, now no longer needed.

"Forget *tsepan*—laws—honour if you must. But live—let the clan survive. It must . . . not die . . . as I die . . . Please . . . my son . . ." Aldric clutched the old man's hand desperately as his father stiffened, dragging in a shuddering breath. That breath came out again in a faint little moan as Haranil, the Clan-Lord Talvalin, in his sixty-sixth year, relaxed in his chair for the last time. Aldric felt the life take its leave, released at last by the stubborn will to brush past like a movement in the air. And then it was over.

Although his face was taut with grief and tears ran down his cheeks, Aldric had no time for mourning; he had much to do. Reaching down, he lifted the *tsepan* and pressed it to his lips.

Then he sliced it deeply across the scars on his left palm, cancelling all other oaths in a scarlet spurt of blood. The pain purged him of confused emotions, and he was able to stare dispassionately at the pulsing cut before putting it to his mouth and swallowing some of the sweet-salt flow. It was warm in his cold throat.

"En mollath venjens warnan," he said harshly. "The curse of vengeance be upon thee, Duergar Vathach my enemy. Thy life will pay the weregild for my father. On my blood I swear it." Gripping his queue in smeared fingers he slashed it off with the dirk, then did the same to each ear-lock and flung all three to the ground. The cropped hair gave him a strange, youthful look belied by his eyes and by the blood oozing down his face. "I renounce my duty," he intoned as each tag of hair came free. "To Heaven if it guard thee; to any King whose laws protect thee; and to my honour lest it make me fear to slay thee—by any means I may." It was a sentence of death for Duergar and maybe for himself as well. He completed the old ritual of the *venjens-eijo*, the avenging exile, by sheathing his dirk and saluting with his sword before returning it to the scabbard across his back.

Then from the corridor outside a singing floor began to squeal.

Only a muscle moved in Aldric's cheek for perhaps three seconds. Then he snatched the heavy *taiken* off his father's lap and shrank into the shadows just before the door opened to admit torchlight and men. Their faces were familiar: men who had called themselves traders, on their way from Datherga to Radmur with a wagonload of swords. So they had claimed. They and others like them had trickled through Dunrath like a rivulet of dirty water—Duergar's raiders. With hindsight it was all so very clear.

Both wore *taipanin*—shortswords—through their belts, and armour of a kind, but the first also had a visored helmet and Aldric coldly marked him down. Such headgear would be useful when he had to walk unnoticed from the citadel. Cocking the *taiken* double-handed behind his head, the boy took a soft step forward.

Even now he was not ready to strike without warning from behind like an assassin—but giving this murderer fair warning was downright stupid. Then his problems vanished as, for some reason, the helmeted man looked round. His head tumbled to the floor wearing the slightly confused expression of a man who literally never knew what had hit him.

Aldric stepped across the corpse, *taiken* already in attack position and concentration focused on the second man who gaped, foolishly forgot his torch was a useful makeshift weapon and dropped it in favour of his sword. The delay was nothing less than fatal.

Something flickered across his body from shoulder to hip and the hand which steadied his scabbard. It was a stroke so old that it came from a time when *taikenin* were curved—but neither time nor straight blades reduced its efficiency. The mercenary stood for a moment, eyes and mouth wide with shock. His left hand dropped from its wrist just an instant before his body split along the huge diagonal cut.

Aldric stared at the exploded corpse for several minutes. After his near suicide and the shock of everything that had followed, he was close to fainting. Only adrenalin had kept him on his feet, and now it ebbed swiftly to leave him nauseous and unsteady. This revelation of his own appalling skill was too much. He had never killed before, and to start like this . . . And why that cut—something out of the distant past? The sour taste of vomit rose in his throat and his head spun. Then, as he had been taught, the *kailin* breathed deeply, pushing the shattered dead from his plane of awareness. They ceased to be sickening, just as they had ceased to be threatening. Regrets, qualms and conscience would remain, but they would no longer interfere with his survival.

He did three things in rapid succession: broke his father's sword against the fireplace and left its shards respectfully at the old man's feet; picked up the soldier's helmet, shook out its ex-owner's head and set it on his own; and set a torch to the place. Noting with grim satisfaction that not even fresh-spilt blood stopped the flame from taking hold, Aldric bowed once to the funeral pyre and walked away.

There were still only one or two people to be seen, and he wondered where they had been earlier on. It was only when Aldric rode out of the stable that he realised with horror that he had seen no other horsemen. The roan gelding seemed to

be shouting for attention as he trotted quickly for the drawbridge, but since an alarm gong began to sound as dark
smoke billowed from the donjon, nobody showed much interest. It gave him the chance to pause near the winding-gear for
the drawbridge and delicately saw through the ropes holding
its counterweight portcullis. There were no guards anywhere,
although the icy wind slicing in from outside should have told
him why.

As the cords began to unravel and snap of their own accord
under their burden, he set heels to the horse and went over
the bridge as fast as he was able. Even then he felt a sudden
upward lurch as a rattling rumble broke out behind him. His
mount jumped the last few feet as the drawbridge made a
violent, uncontrolled ascent and slammed behind him with a
huge hollow bang.

Aldric rode straight for Baelen Forest, though had he known
of the guards sheltering from the wind within the gatehouse
his course might have been more crooked. Instead it remained
as unerring as the arrow which slammed into his left shoulder. The boy might have gasped, even screamed—he could
not remember. His only recollection was of the world spinning away down a long polished tube that had utter blackness
at the bottom.

*

When he came to his senses there were trees all around him
and the horse had slowed to a walk. The high saddle had held
him in place, as it was meant to do, despite the way he
swayed drunkenly with every step the gelding took. Aldric
straightened up as best he could. The wind was still sighing
about his ears, and when he looked up past dark branches to
the sky he could see stars. There was a vague threat of rain in
the air; it was marginally warmer and the snow was turning
slushy. At least that would make his tracks harder to follow . . .

Then the trees came to a sudden end and a valley yawned
before him. Aldric tensed, knowing this place all too well,
but with nowhere else to go he rode out from the tumbled
light and shadow on to the upper slope. He glanced back
painfully, listening for sounds of pursuit and hearing none.
What might have been a fragile laugh formed in his throat,

only to die in a gurgle when he saw what hung above the forest behind him.

Away to the north-east, above Dunrath, a bloated spiral cloud was swallowing the sky. Long tendrils stretched towards the forest until it resembled some vast hand extending taloned fingers southward to clutch and rend. A flicker passed through the cloud, throwing its coiling bulk into sharp relief—but no lightning Aldric had ever seen was that vivid, venomous green.

Raw fear welled within the youngster's brain and was not dispelled when he tore his eyes from the convoluted sky. Something was disturbing the snow just by his gelding's hoofs. Then the thing broke surface.

Starting backwards in horror, Aldric yelped and clenched his teeth against the stab of pain his sudden movement brought. Then he stared in disbelief. On the ground was what had once been a hand. It was long dead, rotten leather stretched taut over a claw of old brown bones. But it was moving. The Alban looked away, only to meet the empty eyesockets of a skull heaving itself from the earth. Its jaws worked, dribbling ancient mould across the clean snow, and pulpy white things squirmed in its hollow nostrils.

There was a sonorous droning in the air and a humming more felt than heard. Other shrivelled relics rose out of the past into the nightmare present until the whole valley was bubbling like putrescent broth. A vile stench clogged Aldric's mouth and nose until, despite the scarf around his face, he hung retching over his saddlebow.

The hand he had first seen was thrashing more violently now. It had become fleshy, filling out with muscle even as he watched, and the reek of decay lessened somewhat. Then the hand twisted and clutched his horse's foreleg, sending the animal rearing back with a neigh that was almost a shriek of outrage. Aldric was almost thrown and kept his seat more through adhesive willpower than any real skill. Trying impotently to quiet the shuddering roan, he looked down to see an almost exhumed body drag itself from the crumbling soil, then clung frantically to his saddle as the champing horse finally got the bit between its teeth and took off at full gallop.

Aldric reeled back and hammered the shaft in his back against a saddlebag. Red agony overwhelmed him and his mouth gaped wide, but long before any cry emerged he had slipped into the dark again.

THREE

Parting the Veil

In the grey light of dawn Aldric regained consciousness to find his left arm cold and stiff, hard to move and painful when he tried. But pain meant life. When he was dead he would no longer feel pain; nor love, nor joy, nor laughter. Though in his present mood he might as well be dead, for he was sure that he would never laugh again in this life. The dead felt nothing—even when they moved, he recalled with a shiver. But he was not dead yet, nor helpless either.

He slid clumsily to the ground, supporting himself with a stirrup when his knees threatened to give way. With only one hand, opening a saddlebag posed problems surmounted only by effort, ingenuity and much use of the teeth. Within was dried meat and wheaten bread for himself, grain and a feeding-bag for the horse, and a bottle of wine. Water he had in plenty from the melting slush around him.

Memory made the boy's appetite slighter than it might have been, and he queasily set the meat aside after a few mouthfuls. Instead he turned his mind to the arrow; it had struck into the muscles by his shoulder-blade and only the heavy leather jerkin had saved him from a fatal skewering. Panting for breath, he worked up his good hand far enough to hook two fingers over the shaft, whimpering as the head shifted in living flesh. Blood seeped stickily through his clothes, leaving a smell in the cold air that made the roan gelding stamp nervously. Aldric clenched his teeth and jerked the arrow hard.

It snapped and he fell forward into slush and dead leaves,

sobbing. He only regained his feet again because the horse leaned over him, so that he could grip the reins and let the gelding lift him upright. Patting the beast's nose, he buzzed affectionate nonsense into its ears.

In the clear autumn-to-winter sky a black crow drifted endlessly. The bird was still circling overhead more than an hour later, descending in lazy spirals wherever the trees grew thick. Now that pain no longer fogged his mind completely, suspicion found some room again in Aldric's brain. He stopped, listening for any sound of pursuit, but Baelen Forest answered only with the noises of small living things. Then a wolf howled thinly in the distance and the crow cawed. Twice, then twice again. The *kailin* looked up with a strange expression on his face and carefully dismounted.

There was a *telek* holstered on his saddle, and beside it the crossbow which stayed there all the time. Aldric led the gelding under a tree, forcing deep into the shelter of its needled branches, and saw how the crow swung lower. It was then that he took down the crossbow and painfully cranked it back. Above him he could see the crow straining to sight him, and glared at it. "Stay there, bird," he muttered, "and you'll soon find out what I'm doing."

A bolt ripped up through the screening pine-needles and feathers burst from between the crow's wings. Aldric swore softly, but not at his good shot; rather because the bird did not caw as it died—it screamed.

The wolf howled again, an anguished sound like hunger made audible. Aldric mounted again and let the horse move off at an easy jog. Panic tempted him to lash his steed to a gallop—but panic was no longer a luxury he could afford.

*

There were dead leaves and mud plastered on his clothes where he had skidded face-down across the ground. Raising himself painfully on one elbow, Aldric tried to shake the whirling stars from his head. How . . . ? The booming in his skull made it so hard to think . . .

Then he rolled over and swore hopelessly. The horse, the poor faithful horse, the blasted brute that was his only hope of escape lay on its side, flanks heaving. Its eyes were rolling with pain and fear, and the cause was all too plain.

Some small animal had dug itself a burrow, and the horse's leg had gone into it almost to the knee. They had only been trotting, but the gelding's leg had snapped like a stick of celery.

Aldric could do nothing for such a break and only one thing for the horse. Kneeling by its head, he gentled it with soft words and drew the short sword from his belt. When the horse relaxed, trusting him, he drew the blade across its neck and felt like a murderer. He regretting killing the horse more than the two men yesterday. They had been unknown killers; the roan gelding had grown up with him since it was a wobbly-legged foal and he a skinny boy in his teens. What he had just done was like severing a limb; *kailin* and mount were a single unit, and the loss of one diminished the other.

There was nothing on the carcass he needed, not even the crossbow, since his need was now to travel fast and light. Taking only a little food and the water bottle, he began to walk.

*

The wolf's howl was much closer now and what Aldric had thought—hoped—was an echo was without doubt an answer. He started to run. It was late afternoon now and the sky would soon be growing dark. Though the full moon was almost a week past, Aldric was afraid of nightfall. His breath hung in smoky clouds on still air that grew more harshly cold every time he sucked it into his lungs.

Then the snarl came; a harsh ripple of ferocity right at his heels. In a desperate attempt to run faster and look behind him, his legs went from under him and he finished up in an untidy limb-flailing bundle with his throat well placed for ripping. It remained undamaged and cautiously he raised his head. The undergrowth rustled, then emitted a throaty, malicious chuckle. When nothing else happened Aldric hauled himself up and sidled towards the bracken. Then he whirled and sprinted away.

After that the flight became a nightmare. Things snarled and giggled out of thin air; bushes and gnarled roots took on distorted shapes in the shifting evening light; and still he ran, though now his muscles were dull and his legs as slow to move as if he was wading in honey. Sweat soaked him, running down his face and blinding him to the hooked branches which tore at his back. Times without number he collided with trees or fell headlong, dragging himself on by force of will and little else. His grey-green eyes took on a glazed, dead look ghastly in a living face.

Night rose from the ground like a fog, made darker by the clouds shrouding the sky in grey. A small breeze began to hiss among the branches, carrying a few drops of rain from the iron sky. Thunder rumbled distantly, chasing the flash of its lightning across the heavens. Reeling from tree to tree, Aldric knew his mind and body were failing fast. Then the thunder bellowed in earnest and he took another tumble, snapping his sword as the rain came down in a solid mass. Finally he gave up and stood cursing and crying in a storm that slashed rain against him like a hail of arrows. When a hand clutched the raw agony that had been his shoulder there was a brief, blinding moment of abject fear.

Then the ground came up to meet him and all the lights went out.

*

Aldric struggled awake with a pounding headache, hauled up eyelids made leaden by weariness and drugs and looked around him. He saw low wooden beams, simple sturdy furniture and daylight oozing past painted shutters. None of it meant a thing until he tried sitting up. Then a flare of pain tore through the narcotic haze and his memory returned.

After a few minutes spent gathering his wits, he got out of bed and began to dress. There was no trace of his own clothes, except for the leather jerkin and his weapon-belt, but the strange garments were a reasonable fit and clean besides. He finally squirmed into them, even though the operation was punctuated by oaths and gasps of pain, then slung his belt so that both blades were close at hand. Only then did he open the door.

Gemmel saw him from the corner of one eye, blinking owlishly in the watery sunshine, and glanced up from his book. He started to say something, but the words died on his lips at his first clear view of Aldric's face. Last night it had been concealed by a flaking crust of dirt and gore. Today it was the face of his own dead son.

Closer inspection revealed differences: the Alban was not as tall and his hair was lighter. Where Ernol's eyes had been a clear and honest green like Gemmel's own, this young man's gaze was like a cat's: hooded, cold and unreadable. The eyes were discs of flint sheathed in green glacier ice. But the likeness was still close enough to tighten the old man's throat.

Aldric knew the expression "to see a ghost". That was why he felt uncomfortable about Gemmel's intense stare, and he laid one hand on the reassuring metal of his shortsword's hilt. The old man at once looked disapproving. "You won't need that," he said. Aldric's hand stayed where it was and Gemmel felt a twinge of annoyance; suspicion was one thing but ingratitude was quite another. When he spoke again his voice was crisp and commanding. "Let go of that *taipan* at once!" The finger which stabbed out seemed only an emphatic gesture, but Aldric jerked his hand from the weapon as if it had stung him. Which indeed it had. He eyed the old man and forced himself to relax a little.

"Who are you, anyway?" he asked.

"Gemmel Errekren fits most comfortably on short Alban tongues," was the rather condescending reply. "You can call me that."

"Errekren—Snowbeard—that's no clan-name."

"Since I haven't a clan it should not surprise you," Gemmel returned tartly. "Now hurry up. The spell wears off at sunset."

"Spell . . . ?" Aldric repeated the word as if making sure of it. "Perhaps I should have asked *what* are you? Well?"

"I have already—no, I haven't, have I? Forgetful . . ." He rubbed his cropped beard and smiled faintly. "The villagers call me *pestrior* and *purcanyath;* dialect I know, but you understand the words." Aldric did, and to Gemmel's surprise a thin, humourless smile appeared on his face.

"Wizard and enchanter," the boy muttered half to himself. "Ironic really, to be hunted by one and rescued by another.

For which I thank you." He bowed as well as possible. "But this isn't your affair. I'll leave at once."

"You'll stay until I have tended that arm properly," snapped Gemmel in a tone brooking no refusal, and met Aldric stare for stare until the Alban flinched and looked away. He nodded, half in defeat and half in gratitude.

"As you wish. But only until then. I owe too great a debt already."

"Debts are for merchants," observed Gemmel. "Put this on." In the old man's hand was a thing like a long-dead mouse and Aldric eyed it distastefully.

"Where?" he wanted to know. A shake of finger and thumb revealed the object to be a false beard. Aldric fitted the whiskers round an expression of faint disgust and found, as he had feared, that they itched. Even so, though he looked unlike anyone with a shred of self-respect, he also looked nothing like a high-clan *kailin*—which, he reflected with a gloomy scratch, was the whole point.

Gemmel had acquired mounts for both of them and Aldric studied his own steed with some dismay. It was a stocky, barrel-bellied, shaggy little pony, and not the sort of horse he had ridden for almost thirteen years. It also tried to bite him, twice. Gemmel watched the young man mount the skittish beast without difficulty, even one-handed, and wondered about the Alban's other and more sinister skills. Then he shifted in his own saddle—on a horse much finer than Aldric's, something already noted with some envy. "Best come on, son." If that "son" was noticed it passed without comment. "Twenty riders passed at first light, and it won't take many questions in yonder village to bring them right back here."

"How did they miss this place anyway?" Aldric thought aloud. The wizard waved one hand in the air.

"A simple spell that stops you seeing in a straight line." His explanation explained nothing. But as Aldric rode away he saw—or more correctly, did not see—what the enchanter meant. Stone and thatch faded from sight as if round a corner and left an empty space where grass waved in the wind. He said nothing, being consumed with curiosity while doing his best to seem unconcerned. Gemmel found his facial gymnastics most amusing, but very wisely kept the fact to himself.

Riding as fast as the wizard deemed sensible was still not fast enough for Aldric's liking. He kept thinking of those twenty horsemen. After half an hour of cantering across the moorland, always due west and mostly uphill, the *kailin* reined in and turned his horse around. There had been a tingling across his back for several minutes now and he felt sure he knew the cause. Gemmel watched him and wondered.

On the horizon a thread of black crawled into the sky. "I thought there was somebody behind us," the Alban said quietly. Drawing a long-glass from its case at his belt, Gemmel opened it and peered towards the smoke. Aldric did not understand what he said then, but it sounded nasty. "If they were told about the cottage," he pointed out, "they will know about you as well."

Gemmel ignored him.

*

It took almost a week for the Blue Mountains to change from a saw-edged shadow to the tumbled mass of crags which now reared vast and vaguely menacing almost overhead. Snowflakes whirled from a dirty yellow sky and settled thickly on anything they touched, including the two men carefully walking their horses along the treacherously iced mountain path.

"Almost there, lad," called the taller of the pair, shaking a small avalanche from his hood as he moved. The other looked up without much enthusiasm.

"You said that yesterday, and the day before." Aldric found the weather, his itchy beard—mixed now with real stubble—and Gemmel's unfailing optimism depressing, so that he no longer even tried to produce the right responses to his cheerful conversation. Bored, wet, sore and miserable, he neither expected nor was able to see anything other than rocks, even though Gemmel seemed to think otherwise.

"Up there, by the standing stone," he insisted, and Aldric dutifully strained his eyes through the blurring snow before giving up. Handing over his horse's reins, Gemmel scrambled up to the monolith and laid both hands against its side. Following to give what help he could, Aldric realised that the old man's pressure was barely enough to mark the crust of snow under his fingers. He stopped, threw back his hood for a better view and watched. As if finding the right spot Gemmel pushed once, very hard, and the stone shifted with a grinding clearly audible in the snow-silence.

There was an instant's pause—then twenty feet of the rock-face slid open without a sound. Aldric's eyes dilated, for he had never read or heard of anything like this. The cavern thus revealed was no dank cave, but a smooth, polished tunnel whose walls and ceiling were lined with globes of some crystalline stuff. Dropping lightly to the ground, Gemmel touched his hand to a metal plate set into the stone. Immediately the first few crystals glowed, and as Aldric watched the illumination spread from globe to globe down the tunnel until it was filled with a warm golden light.

When he looked back the horses had vanished and Gemmel was shouldering the few items he carried on his saddle. The *kailin* blinked, but realised that if one lived with an enchanter one must learn to live with enchantments. Well then, now was a good time to start.

At the end of the tunnel of lights there was a spiral stair, made of metal but otherwise identical to those in donjon towers. Its upper end was sealed by a smooth metal slab which hissed aside as Gemmel approached, releasing a harsh glare which made Aldric flinch and shield his eyes. He followed the old man when he judged himself used to the brilliance, and discovered it was virtually the only thing he was used to.

The cave—now that was ordinary: sensible. He could grasp the principles of it, even though it was triangular in section and flooded with light of unreal whiteness which struck sparkling reflections from the burnished machinery recessed into both walls. There was a humming in the air and a slight vibration underfoot as of incalculable power hidden somewhere in the rock below. But it was the yawning vault at one end of the cave which totally defied all comprehension.

The vault was vast: more than big enough to swallow an entire fortress and sufficiently high for the loftiest citadel turret to fit in comfort. More of the glowing crystals shone from its walls, but they cast just enough light for the colossal size of the place to be marked out in tiny rows of jewels, being nowhere near bright enough to actually be of use. All around the entrance, pipes and conduits emerged from the floor and went snaking off into the shadows; some were bunches of metallic filament finer than a cobweb, but one slashed with black and yellow stripes was as thick as Aldric's waist. A slight, cold drift of air moved out of the cavern, swirling slightly as breezes will in such monstrous empty spaces. Except that this space was far from empty.

There was . . . something . . . crouched squarely in the middle of the cavern floor, an ill-defined mountainous bulk of dark smooth shapes and glinting edges. It dwarfed all else both in mass and in the eerie suggestion of dormant power. On trembling legs Aldric stepped towards it, all his senses tingling—and then Gemmel laid one hand on his uninjured shoulder and steered him away without a word of explanation.

Warrior stared at wizard for several minutes before Aldric spoke. "Meneth Taran," he said very softly. "So this is the Mother of Storms." Gemmel met the boy's unwinking agate eyes and nodded. Meneth Taran, Thunderpeak, was the heaven-scoring crag where the great tempest was born in the story. People gave the name half in fun to Sil'ive, tallest of all the Blue Mountains and one perpetually wreathed in cloud. Half in fun, but never completely so, and with the very air thrumming in his ears Aldric could guess why. Even if he gained no other knowledge from the old enchanter, he had at least learned the meaning of awe.

*

By contrast, the living apartments were reassuring in their air of comfort. Most of the rooms were panelled in wood like a fortress and for the same reason—to conceal the fact that the walls behind were stone: in this case half a mile of living mountain rock. Live flames danced in elegant fireplaces and even Aldric wasted no time wondering where the smoke went to. With warmth around him for the first time in six days, his shoulder was taking precedence over frozen feet and hands. It throbbed wickedly.

Gemmel noticed the slight wince with which Aldric took a

seat by the fire in his study and nodded to himself. "Enough of this," he said with a touch of impatience. "Your arm will heal in time, but it will be time wasted. Shirt off, please." He set down a box of instruments on a handy table and opened the lid. Aldric blinked apprehensively at a row of tiny knives and probes, but made no move to obey.

"I'd much rather have a bath and a shave first," he ventured nervously. Gemmel tutted disapprovingly and shook something from its clear case.

"And I would much rather have that wound dealt with. Now!" He set out two metal bottles, three small pads and a pair of gloves which he removed from their sealed pouch and worked onto his hands. With an uneasy swallow born of memories of having his arm set last spring, Aldric did as he was told. Gemmel peeled away the bandages and selected a knife. "This won't hurt . . ." he said. The *kailin* jumped and yelped, then twisted round to fix him with a baleful glare. "Much," the wizard amended.

He told the truth and within five minutes was packing away his medical kit while Aldric felt with increasing delight for a scar that was no longer there. Gemmel grinned broadly; he had forgotten the great satisfaction that surgeon's work always gave him and was pleased to discover that it had not diminished with the years. Then he returned to more basic matters. "Aldric, do you want something to eat now—or would you rather take that bath you mentioned?"

Aldric was definitely in favour of eating first and said so. Emphatically.

*

Even so, being high-clan Alban and as fastidious as a cat, he went to wash directly after the meal, leaving Gemmel to stare at the fire, drink Hertan grain-spirit and try to shape what he wanted to say to this young man with the unsettlingly familiar face. So alike, and yet so totally different. Though Aldric had begun to smile a little in the past week, there was a freezing menace about him that Ernol had never possessed. The *kailin* was—Gemmel at first rejected the word but found it returning to his mind—frightening. "Frightening," he said aloud, as if hearing the word would change its meaning.

"Who is?" asked Aldric from the door.

He had found a clean white shirt and breeches somewhere and there was a towel in one hand. With his short, wet hair and a face freshly shaven smooth, he looked so young that Gemmel's chosen word seemed more out of place than ever.

"I was thinking," the wizard said. Aldric relaxed in a chair by the fire and picked at a loose thread in the towel.

"So was I." He hesitated, watching unobtrusively through the lashes of half-closed, seemingly sleepy eyes. The fireglow carved deep trenches in Gemmel's face, giving him an eldritch appearance. That strange expression had returned; echoes of recognition and regret, all mingled with a bitter memory of loss. It was enough to make Aldric sure his half-formed guess approached the truth. "You knew someone—a long time ago—who looked like me. Or I like him. And he died. A friend? Maybe a relative . . ." What flickered on the old enchanter's features then had nothing to do with firelight, and with an inward wince of sick embarrassment Aldric bit his tongue before it did more hurt. "I—I'm sorry," he finished lamely.

The sorcerer stared at him, wishing he was more stupid or at least less forthright. More like Ernol. At least the Alban was in his own country; he could never—and Gemmel hoped would never—know what it was like to live down the long years, to walk through a crowded city, to exchange friendly words and yet be alone—always, eternally alone. And now this boy with his dead son's face; surely it was some cruel joke perpetrated by an ironic fate. Gemmel regained his composure with an effort and twisted thin lips into a thin smile. "No matter," he said. "I was miles—years—away." Aldric inclined his head in polite acknowledgment that the subject was now closed.

"You started to say something when we were at table, then decided it was best left till later," he said. "this is 'later'."

"Very well." Gemmel leaned back and steepled his fingers, staring intently at their nails for a few seconds. "Recall your last boar-hunt—in as much detail as you can, but without speaking." Aldric gazed into the shifting embers of the fire and let his memory work. He sat like that for some minutes, hardly seeming to breathe, then straightened and blinked several times.

"Now what?"

"There was a spell on that valley to keep animals out, as you know. It wasn't to preserve the honoured dead from scavengers but to prevent anything being killed there. Blood is the catalyst for many powerful forms of magic. The wizard who cast that spell must have suspected that the spilling of blood would have some terrible consequence. As you must guess now, he was right. You can blame Duergar for that."

"Duergar . . . ? But what had he—"

"You have shown yourself to have intelligence, boy. Use it!" That flash of irritation was a warning which Aldric judged it wise to heed. He sat up straighter and prepared to make sensible remarks. Remarks for which he wasn't asked. "You shot a wolf. Did you really fail to notice which leg you hit—or which leg Duergar Vathach was limping on . . . ? He's wily, that one; he should really have taken the shape of a fox, it would have suited him better."

"You *know* that bastard?" The young *kailin*'s voice was incredulous.

"We . . . met once. In a professional capacity. I didn't like him then either. Agents of the Empire always make my skin crawl."

"What is an Imperial agent doing in Alba, or is that obvious too?" Aldric bit off the words, hoping Gemmel would snap at him again and give him a really good excuse to lose his temper. The boy was seething inside, as much with a feeling of helplessness as anything else. At mention of the Drusalan Empire his own hopes and aspirations began to look very small. Seek to be revenged on that mighty realm—as well make war on the sea for drowning your friend. Gemmel saw his face change.

"It is obvious, Aldric," the old man said quietly. "Your family may be only the first to die. When Grand Warlord Etzel turns his mind to conquest, he is as inexorable as the incoming tide." Aldric wondered at the wizard's choice of words, and wondered too whether his own mind was still being read. "But even a spring tide can be stopped, if a hole in the sea-wall is plugged before any water passes through."

"Sifting through your metaphors, then," said Aldric with an acid little smile, "if I succeed in my intention to kill Duergar, and do it soon enough, I'll save Alba from an Imperial invasion?"

"Basically, yes."

"I see." From Aldric's face and tone of voice Gemmel could tell he was not very impressed. "And why would the Imperial Grand Warlord want to invade in the first place? Alba has nothing to do with Imperial policies." Gemmel smiled sardonically at that.

"How little you know of power politics, *kailin-eir* Aldric," he said.

"That was Baiart's field, not . . ." The young man's voice trailed off and his eyes went very distant. "Baiart . . ."

"Forget him for now," Gemmel said impatiently. "What do *you* know of the Empire?"

Aldric shrugged. "It's big . . . The Emperor holds most of the countries across Bian-mor in the palm of his hand. Their borders have expanded almost constantly for almost a century—" Seeing Gemmel shaking his head, he stopped. "What did I get wrong?"

"One thing only. The *Empire* rules across the Narrow Sea—the Emperor is lucky if he can command the running of his Palace. Etzel, like all his predecessors as Grand Warlord, is true master of the Empire. But that may change. Emperor Droek is an old man—old before his time, and that time is running out. I predict—no, not by sorcery—that he'll die in a year or so; even though, for a change, the Warlord does not want this to happen. You see, Droek's eldest son had been trained by Etzel's people to be a good Emperor; weak, fond of pleasure, a puppet whose strings would be pulled by the Warlord. But he fell off his horse six months ago and broke his neck."

"Joren said that somebody helped him on his way. I thought the Warlord might—but from what you say, I doubt it."

"He probably helped himself, with a bellyful of wine and a headful of smoke. Or his brother could have done it."

"His brother?" Aldric sounded disgusted and Gemmel remembered the closeness of Alban family ties. "Baiart didn't like me, but he wouldn't have—Or I don't think he . . . might well, given the chance," he finished lamely.

"How much better reason with an Empire as your prize, eh? But Ioen is a better man than his brother. Much better—or will be. He's only sixteen. Though since he wasn't brought up in the sort of decadence Etzel provides for his puppets, he's probably more adult now than his dear, late brother ever was." Aldric had been paying attention once his interest was aroused and he could see how things fitted together now.

"So like it or not, the next Emperor won't be just a figurehead. And the Warlord is going to do what he can, while he can, because if the Empire stops expanding by war, there will be no need for a Warlord. And he picked on Alba because—because if the worst happens, he'll have a bolt-hole out of the Emperor's reach. And the fact that he's using a filthy, treacherous, back-stabbing . . ." The boy took a deep breath and calmed down a little. "The very fact that he's using a necromancer as his agent, when all sorcery is forbidden in the Empire, shows how desperate he must be to succeed."

Gemmel applauded, with only the faintest trace of an ironic smile creasing his lean face. "And the fact," he mimicked Aldric's slightly pedantic tones with good-humoured mockery, "that Alba's king has condoned acts of piracy against Imperial shipping, has drawn up letters of marque for the commissioning of privateers, already signed and only awaiting issue, and that his High Council have been instrumental in the smuggling of arms and gold to insurrections in the Imperial provinces . . . all these have nothing whatsoever to do with it."

"Ah . . ." breathed Aldric. Then with sudden violence: "How in the name of the Highest Hell did you learn all that?" There was no anger in the outburst—just an extreme curiosity.

"I am a wizard, you know," Gemmel pointed out. "Though

friends in high places are also useful. But . . .'' He paused, deliberately.

"But *what*?"

"But I think you may have it all wrong.'' Aldric eyed the enchanter and gave up. Trying to keep track of Gemmel's mental processes was worse than trying to read a book at night, without lights, in a thick fog.

"So what is the solution?" Gemmel stood up and wandered across his study to the big oak desk, returning with a long slender pipe which he proceeded to carefully fill and light. Since it was obvious that he was not going to get an answer until the ritual had been concluded, Aldric also rose and helped himself to the sorcerer's wine.

"Now why would Vathach have been sneaking about the old Baelen battlefield?" Gemmel muttered to himself. Aldric glanced towards the enchanter, drained his goblet and then filled it again in anticipation of more convoluted discussion. Then he spilled about half the contents as Gemmel thumped his chair and barked, "Yes, of course!"

"Of course what?" Aldric shook wine from his fingertips into the fire and finished what was left before it too was spilt. "I grow tired of asking simple-minded questions which you never seem to answer." Raising his eyebrows, Gemmel looked at the young man with new respect. There had been an edge to his last words that was more than mere petulance; he had sounded like someone accustomed to obedience—like a *kailineir*.

"The sword-hilt which you found,'' Gemmel explained, only to be met with a quizzical blankness. Then he recalled how the images in Aldric's mind had faded during the *ymeth*-trance. There had been a charm of forgetfulness cast across the valley—but one cast hastily and without due care, or there would have been no trace of the hilt in Aldric's memory at all. So Duergar had been watching the valley either in the form of a wolf, or with witch-sight from a distance. He had been searching for one particular artifact, had been interrupted by the boar-hunt and had seen his trophy unearthed quite by accident. After failing to make Aldric drop the old hilt, he had followed it to Dunrath and laid his plans accordingly. The Talvalins had simply been in the way, and as was the manner of such wizards he had snuffed them out without a thought. That thought might have made him more careful to do a thorough job—and the lack of it, Gemmel realised grimly, could prove the end of his scheme. The old enchanter told Aldric his theory, for once without rhetoric, and waited for a reaction.

"It must be Kalarr cu Ruruc's sword!" the boy said firmly. "I can't think of anything else—especially after Vathach took such pains to bore me out of any curiosity on the subject." Gemmel smiled around his pipe-stem.

"He must have considerable talent to do that," the wizard observed dryly. Getting to his feet, he faced one of the bookcases which ran from floor to ceiling around the walls of his study. "There should be something here to enlighten us on why . . . ah, and indeed there is."

He pulled down a thick leather-bound book and leafed rapidly through its pages, then marked one with his finger. "This is not unlike your clan Archives, Aldric," the old man said. Then his teeth showed in a crooked grin. "Except that no hall-scribe would dare write some of the things this book contains, for fear of his very soul." It was an explanation which did nothing for Aldric's peace of mind. "Now let me see . . ." Gemmel read the page quickly, muttering some of the words under his breath; what Aldric caught of them sounded like an archaic form of Alban, not quite the ancient High Speech of religion and ceremony but certainly closer to it than to the language Aldric spoke. He felt suddenly reluctant to hear whatever it was the sorcerer was reading, and was about to say as much when Gemmel set down the book on his desk and stared hard at him.

"Aldric, would you go now and fetch me your old jerkin?" he said, and his voice was strange. Aldric went at once. When he returned, the sorcerer was toying with the pen he had been using to construct a complex table of words and symbols. He tapped his chin with one finger, then drew a large question mark right in the centre of the page. "Turn out your pockets, please," he told the boy without looking up. This revealed the usual mixture of fluff, small coins, notes on scraps of parchment and threads from a hole in the pocket lining.

Gemmel looked at the unprepossessing rubbish, then lifted one of the broken threads and frowned. The frown deepened when scrutiny revealed the jacket's lining to be still intact. A moment later it was anything but, as he took a knife from the desk and sliced the seams apart. Opening his mouth to protest, Aldric quickly closed it again. Something had fallen from the rent and rolled clattering across Gemmel's desk; as it stopped and fell over sideways, the boy could see quite clearly what it was. The wrist-band of a horseman's sword, with three links of rusty chain remaining of the length which had once threaded through a pommel.

"So then," said Gemmel quietly, "Duergar has the hilt and we the band to it. Which is more important, I wonder?" He made no move to touch the age-corroded bronze, but Aldric did. Save only where the chain had left russet flecks, the band was green with verdigris, covering even the studs decorating its surface. The more Aldric studied it, the less he felt it had anything to do with Kalarr. Plain bronze was too . . . too cheap for the trappings of a master sorcerer. With a disgusted noise he dropped it on the table.

"Deceptive, is it not?" Aldric cocked an eyebrow, not quite understanding Gemmel's comment. "But then, such things were meant to fool more than your uninformed scrutiny." He began scratching the band with his small knife, talking the while. "The outward appearance of any object is seldom an indication of its true worth; an older man may be stronger than a young one; a ring plain and unadorned may have greater value than any set with gems; and a band of rusty bronze with simple ornaments may prove of—ah!" Metal squeaked under stress as Gemmel prised back his blade.

"*Has* proven of greater interest than one made of jewelled gold. Aldric . . . look!" He twisted the knife away and a flickering nimbus of pale blue light sprang up around his hands. The radiance poured from one of the studs on the wrist-band, from which Gemmel had scraped a concealing layer of metal, and which now glowed like a sapphire lit from

within by cold, fierce white light. It was altogether beautiful—
and at the same time as awesome as the vast dark shape
Aldric had half-glimpsed in the cavern.

"This," said Gemmel, holding it up carefully, "is one of
the seven spellstones of Echainon. They have been lost for a
long time—and now I have one in my hand. But I can guess
from this what Duergar has in mind." Gemmel laid down the
spellstone and gazed for a while into its throbbing core.
"And Aldric, had I the choice, an Imperial invasion would be
preferable by far."

                                    *

There was a slab of crystal resting on top of the stone plinth,
making it look like a catafalque for the lying-in-state of some
great man. A slow dance of green flames surrounded it,
burning without heat, without smoke and without fuel.

Duergar dozed before it in a cushioned chair, undisturbed
by the shifting light. He was so weary that little could disturb
him now; the rituals had lasted four days and their completion
had left him with an exhaustion such as he had seldom
experienced. Held firmly in one hand was an old sword-hilt,
scratched and shiny from a recent, over-vigorous cleaning but
the letters on its guard and pommel carefully outlined in fresh
black ink. Duergar had read them and others like them from
the many grimoires scattered about the room. Intricate symbols covered the floor, some drawn with chalk and others
outlined in coloured sand. The square, heavy letters were
everywhere. A casual observer would have called them ugly,
but even the least of closer glances would have changed the
adjective to brutal—sinister—menacing. They were all of this
and more besides.

Settling in his chair, Duergar drifted into a deeper sleep. As
he slept, he dreamed that the sluggishly fluttering flames
swirled upwards into a tapering needle like translucent virid-
ian ice. A globe of amber radiance grew at the heart of the
fire until its golden light swallowed every trace of green, and
then the honey colour darkened through incandescent scarlet
to a smoky crimson. The globe began to spin, attenuating to a
spindle of dark red poised atop the catafalque. Then even its
sullen glare faded and everything grew dark.

Waking with a nervous jerk from something close to night-mare, Duergar found that his dream had become reality. A solitary candle was the only illumination, barely enough to discern outlines, but even so he could see . . . something . . . standing on the granite plinth. Fear rose within him, for like all sorcerers who meddle in such things he lived in dread of the day when the thing he had summoned up was not that which appeared. Today was that day, for whatever he had expected this tall, rustling object was not in any of the possible shapes his grimoires had described. The candleflame sparkled back at him in a hundred ruby-red reflections, from polished metal, from cut gemstones—from gleaming eyes . . .

The eyes blinked lazily, savouring his terror, and then with a susurrant motion glided closer. Sweat coursed down the necromancer's face and his tongue stuck within a dry mouth as he fought to utter the words of a defensive spell. Then the being stopped abruptly and the glowing eyes glanced down. A vivid white line crossed the floor, blocking its path, before joining another part of the pentacle Duergar had drawn so carefully around the catafalque. There was a soft, venomous hiss of indrawn breath, and the dark outline moved unhurriedly sideways, but always the lines of the pentacle flared before it as if tracking the movements. At last the thing retired to the plinth, and Duergar found he could breathe again without the constriction of fear clenched in iron hoops round his chest.

"Who . . . who are you?" he quavered. There was no reply, and made confident by the power of his restraining-spell Duergar began to grow angry. "I summoned you, I command you!" he snapped in a voice very different from his first thin tones. "Give me your name!"

There was a noise almost like a sigh of boredom, and suddenly all the candles sprang to life revealing a man leaning nonchalantly against the catafalque, smiling, but with a glint in his dark eyes that suggested he was anything but amused. "If you could remove this obstruction . . ." he said in a deep, urbane voice, gesturing towards the pentacle with a crystal-topped staff. The unwary could drown in that voice, thought Duergar apprehensively, and made no attempt to do as he was asked.

"What is your name?" he repeated. The man regarded Duergar with a trace of contempt from eyes resembling bottomless pits bored into his sombrely handsome face. His stare burned into the necromancer as if determined to read his innermost thoughts, then withdrew, leaving Duergar with the uneasy feeling of a hand unwrapping from his throat.

"You summoned me, you command me," the man echoed Duergar's words with undisguised sarcasm. "Are you so unsure of yourself that you dare not also name me? Then I will spare you the trouble." He left the stone plinth and sauntered with a predator's grace to the edge of the pentacle which flared with intolerable brilliance to hold him back.

"I am Kalarr cu Ruruc." He made a complex sign in the air with his hand; it was one of the sigils which identified him as a true summoning and not some shape-shifting demon. Almost shaking with relief, Duergar bowed low, almost but not quite abasing himself.

"Your pardon, my lord, but I was not sure . . . welcome, welcome! Let me open a way through the pentacle for you."

Kalarr studied him with icy humour. "You bade me welcome, so there is no need. The ancient binding-spell still holds good, does it not? Somebody invited *you* in, eh? Foolish of them." He jabbed the staff at the glowing line before his feet and it split asunder, leaving his path clear. "You see . . ." He stepped through, smiling.

Duergar cringed like a dog before a beating, but failed to sidestep the long-fingered hand which wrapped around his head. "Don't be concerned," Kalarr reassured him. "I merely want to learn. Although I feel *ymeth* takes too long." The sorcerer drew in a deep breath and tightened his grip.

It was not the grip but a feeling of having his mind wrenched asunder which sent Duergar reeling backwards with a harsh scream of agony. Kalarr did not follow him; he flexed his fingers and nodded slowly, then smiled again, like a shark. "And that method doesn't give *me* a headache."

His face was lean and high-cheekboned, with distinguished features framed by dark, grey-flecked hair swept back in a widow's peak from his lofty brow. The nose was thin, high-bridged, bounded above by the notch of a slight frown and below by a mobile, ruthless mouth and a heavy moustache. It was a face of saturnine humour; of suppressed power; the face of a man who seldom hears refusal of his wishes.

"So you want my aid in wrecking this kingdom of Alba, because you think I would enjoy taking revenge for my defeat . . . ? How very true. But instead of turning it over to your Imperial masters, you would hold it for yourself. Laudable ambition—if you succeed. And since you hold the last thing I touched in life"—Duergar nervously raised the sword-hilt as if it was a protective amulet—"I have no choice but to obey your wishes." Cu Ruruc's smile faded as if the implications of what he had said were sinking in, although if Duergar had seen the sardonic glitter in his eyes when they observed the broken chain, he would not have felt so comfortable. "So be it, then," Kalarr's voice was resigned. "I shall obey."

He turned away and as if for the first time, though he had known it all along, Duergar realised that his . . . guest was dressed entirely in red. He had intended to ask how a summoning came into existence fully clothed in the height of half-millennium-old fashion, but thought better of it. No Alban would ever wear red without some other colour; red, and particularly vermeil, that shade of deep scarlet or rich crimson which Kalarr wore with such arrogance, was the single most unlucky colour in the spectrum. It was associated with blood, with misfortune and violent death.

Cu Ruruc and his chosen colour were well matched.

FOUR

Isileth—and Kyrin

Aldric lay back, half-dozing, and let his mind wander over the past three years. It still surprised him that they had passed so quickly and that he was already into the spring of his twenty-fourth year. He felt no different, even though he was: not merely older, but with a thin white scar under his right eye and a mind better versed in certain subjects than an honourable *kailin-eir* would care to own. Gemmel called it "survival".

Gemmel . . . When he first told Aldric how long he was to stay, there had been an undignified scene when the youngster lost his temper. To defer his vengeance for so long was the act of a coward, he had snarled, and whatever else he might be he, Aldric, was no coward. Gemmel had weathered the storm of abuse with a little half-smile on his face, thinking to himself how very fitting was the *kourgath* wildcat on Aldric's crest-collar. His smile was that of a man who knows he will always have the last word in any argument, and this one was no exception.

An *eijo*, an honourless wanderer, had nothing to lose by accepting some tuition in the Art Magic. So Aldric thought when the old enchanter offered, since he had already picked up a few *pesok'n*, as the little spells were called, from old books filched from his father's library. Filched, because *Haranil-arluth* considered sorcery sly, devious and no concern of a warrior. Not that ability with dogs, cats and horses, or finding lost trinkets, was anything more than toy magic for women and children. Aldric came face to face with the real

73

thing that day and saw how much chance his intended revenge would have had against Duergar.

None at all.

A few days later he was calling the old man *altrou*, meaning foster-father. It seemed fitting somehow, and Gemmel's unfeigned pleasure at a title meaning more to him than a lordship had broken down the sometimes formal host-guest attitudes once and for all.

Even so, Aldric should not have laughed aloud when the wizard announced he was a *taiken*-master—for one thing, if it was true his mirth was most unwise. The young man knew, as did every warrior, that there had not been a true master since Baiel Sinun died two hundred years ago, and said so. Gemmel was unruffled and his response took Aldric unawares.

"Sinun was passable," he said blandly. "Not as good as some, but he taught me some moves and I him." Before Aldric could recover sufficiently to start asking questions, Gemmel had found a pair of foils and shown him the truth of his words. The lean old man had taken him off-guard three times within the first four passes, and that was something not even Joren had ever done.

Despite his apparent age—and Aldric had not the nerve to ask what it might be in years—Gemmel's gaunt frame concealed a wiry strength and his hands the kind of skill harpers exaggerated about. Gemmel was not a master—he was a genius, a virtuoso, perhaps the finest swordsman Aldric had ever met, seen or heard of. Without false modesty, the *eijo* knew himself to be good—in latter years he had beaten Joren several times and that needed more than luck—but against Gemmel Errekren he was like a child with a stick trying to harm a battle-harnessed *kailin*.

Whenever Aldric thought about fencing now, he could see the wizard, eyes glittering like emeralds, whirling and stamping like some dementedly graceful dancer. Gemmel, when his wizardly dignity was set aside, was opinionated, excitable, quick to argue and impatient to a fault. *Taiken*-master or not, he had no time for any of the rituals Aldric associated with swordplay. He knew, from the *ymeth*-trance, that the boy could fight and not merely duel—he had done so against

Baiart so long ago, after all. So when Aldric took up a
stylised guard-position with both hands on his hilt, Gemmel
copied him and then shot out a free hand and slapped him
across the face.

"Two-handed rubbish!" the old man barked. "Had I a
dagger, your throat was cut. Only one hand on the hilt,
except when you need both. Secure your index finger—thus—
over the quillon. The hilt-loops will guard it."

"What hilt-loops?"

"I know what I'm talking about! These are only foils,
remember. Again!" His moustache bristled with the intensity
of his passion.

Aldric was slapped frequently during the fencing lessons;
his teeth were rattled and more than once his nose was caused
to bleed. He bore it as calmly as he could, because he had
seen early on what Gemmel-*altrou* was doing—having lost
one son already, he was trying to teach another how to stay
alive.

There came a day when the boy's cheek was opened by an
accidental stroke. It was not a dangerous cut, not even un-
sightly although he would bear its mark to the day he died.
But it meant he was too fast for the wizard to slap any more.
As the realisation dawned, a grin twisted the stream of blood
on his face into grotesque tributaries. Gemmel grounded his
blade and leaned on the pommel, watching as Aldric saluted
politely. He had no objection to saluting; as he said, in a real
fight only the winner *can* salute.

"You'll have a scar when that heals," he observed. Aldric
looked at his right cheek in the polished sword-blade and was
forced to agree. "Make sure it's the only one you ever
receive in single combat." The old man's voice grew severe.
"Being wounded in a mellay is excusable; if you heed my
teaching at all, being wounded in single combat will be
damned careless! Remember that."

This fierce tuition was to continue for three hours a day on
six days out of every seven. Aldric did not enjoy it, but he
had not expected to do so, even though without a doubt he
was improving. When Gemmel lectured him on other subjects
while they fought and he could remember the discourse; when

he was able to think out the often abstruse questions and answer them—sometimes even correctly; when a sudden flurry of Jouvaine or of Low Drusalan words no longer left him floundering in a morass of bad translation and worse parrying: then he knew within himself that he was growing more skilled.

As Gemmel had so waspishly pointed out, Aldric had intelligence. He had guessed long ago that whatever the sorcerer was planning, it was more than simply helping an *eijo* who happened to look like his son to achieve a difficult task. All the lessons in languages, politics and geography added up to something on a scale Aldric preferred not to think about. Even so, one day soon he was going to ask for a full explanation, and not hints and guesses. One day . . . probably after a meal when he had bolstered his courage with a cup of wine—or perhaps two. Interrogating Gemmel when he did not feel like answering questions was definitely a two-cup enterprise and more probably three. As a smile began to form around his mouth, Aldric fell asleep. For once, he did not dream.

*

"Where can he be?" Kalarr cu Ruruc's voice was a soft, introspective murmur, but it stung Duergar like the shrillest accusation of guilt. He shrugged and made helpless gestures, but on looking up from the books on which he had been working he found that the other sorcerer was ignoring him. The tall, lean figure was outlined against a window of coloured glass, his red *elyu-dlas* blending eerily into the carmine-tinted sunlight. "Where . . . ?" he breathed again.

Duergar did not know, despite hunting Baelen Forest and beyond for almost two years before abandoning his search. In all that time there had been no trace of Aldric Talvalin after his trail went cold at a strange cottage. It had been magically concealed, an insignificant lesser charm which might well have been cast by the Alban himself—Duergar had seen the little cache of dubious books hidden in the youngster's room— but he privately opined that the boy was long since dead from the arrow he had taken as he fled from Dunrath. Kalarr, however, was not so easily convinced, even though had

Aldric been alive no power on earth would have stopped him from coming back in a quest for revenge. There were times when Duergar felt that his . . . colleague . . . was trying to find something other than just the *eijo*, irritation though he might prove. What that something might be, the necromancer did not yet know, although he was trying to find out—without cu Ruruc's knowledge.

Aldric was not his only problem. Locked in his desk were five letters, four of them enciphered but one, the latest, written in dangerously unequivocal plain language—and the language was plain indeed. Warlord Etzel was losing patience with his agent's carefully worded excuses; he wanted action and an end to subtlety. The Alban Royal Council, stated the letter, was blatantly financing an insurrection by two prominent Jouvaine city-states and arms of Pryteinek manufacture had been seized in the province of Tergoves, right at the heart of the Empire. Where was the political instability he had been sent to foster? it demanded. Why had his much-vaunted seizure of a fortress not borne fruit before now? What, snarled the spiky letters, did Duergar Vathach think he was doing?

The Drusalan necromancer was perfectly aware of what he was doing—but by the letter's interrogative tone, nobody else was. Not yet, anyway. Except of course for Kalarr, who seemed to derive cynical amusement from Duergar's intended treachery. As always whenever he thought of things which cu Ruruc found humorous, the necromancer put one hand to the sword-hilt which he wore now like a tau cross, around his neck on a chain. Its cold metal afforded him little comfort, and less when he realised Kalarr had caught the gesture. For some reason his mouth curved slowly into a smile that was thin and yet so heavy with malign significance that it made Duergar's stomach clench like a fist inside him.

Although the necromancer had requested that his companion start something—anything—to justify his rebirth and aid Duergar's mission, Kalarr had . . . not actually refused, but been so evasive that the Drusalan's wishes were never carried out. The ancient charm which imbued cu Ruruc's sword-hilt with power over its previous owner should have allowed Duergar to command, not merely request—but the necromancer was strangely reluctant to test his strength even though at present he was unable to define his reasons. He had not recalled all the spies sent out after Aldric and was certain Kalarr remained unaware of the fact.

Duergar was equally unaware that Kalarr had posted spies of his own, under the same orders: find Aldric Talvalin and bring him, with everything in his possession no matter how insignificant, straight back to Dunrath.

It was the wrist-band from the sword, of course. What Duergar had read from an old grimoire given to him by Etzel was a spell of summoning, where any artifact of a sorcerer's previous existence may be used near the place of his death to restore him whole and entire. There had been a rider to the incantation, stating that if such an artifact were the last thing touched before death, it would grant control to whoever held it. While a skilled sorcerer, Duergar knew nothing of Alban military history—otherwise he would have known that a dying man may drop a sword from his fingers but not the metal band clasped about his wrist. It was the sort of niggling oversight which slew many otherwise careful wizards, and when Kalarr no longer had need to pretend subservience he would make sure it slew another. All he needed was to destroy the wrist-band, render it inaccessible by sealing it within a sphere of magic or sinking it in deep water—or best of all, lay his hands on the Echainon spellstone.

If he did that, it would negate the charm of the wrist-band and bring into his grasp a means of focusing his own considerable power, as he had been able to do so many years before, until that stupid day when fear of loss had made him conceal the spellstone under a sheath of bronze on the band of his war sword. The stone's power had been muted by its metal shroud, but he had never foreseen a time when he would not be granted the few seconds needed to free it—until that last suicidal charge by Clan Talvalin's cavalry which had burst his battle-line heedless of their losses and had swept him dying to the ground. He could not remember the then-*arluth*'s name, but if he closed his eyes he could still recall the man's wide blue eyes, the bloodied teeth bared in a fixed snarl under his sweeping blond moustache, the helm buckled and scored—and the shining *taiken* which had lopped his hand in two through the palm. Kalarr could remember the sword's name: Isileth, it was called, so long, long ago. It had ruined his hand and even as he killed the Talvalin *arluth* with a lethal blast of sorcery the long blade had come whirring back towards his face. There had been a flare of red and black, pain, heat, cold dark silence and the deep fall which never reached bottom . . .

Kalarr drew a shuddering breath and massaged his right hand with his left; the palms of both were damp with sweat. It was fitting that he should now hold the Talvalin citadel, but at the same time terrifying that a Talvalin should hold his spellstone. A Talvalin who in defiance of the *kailin* honour-codes read books of sorcery, who failed to kill himself when it was expected of him—what might such a man not do to achieve the vengeance he had brooded on for three years? If he regained the spellstone Kalarr would be invincible; he would show Duergar, and Rynert of Alba, Emperor Droek and his Warlord, show the Earth and the Sun and the Moon the dark majesty of a true Overlord, for after half a thousand years there would be no wizard with enough schooling in the Old Magics that he knew to defy him, once his spells were amplified through the stone of Echainon.

If he regained the stone . . . Even without it he was a power to be feared, but the spellstone was held by one whom he could not judge by any of the rules with which he was familiar. What if this boy, this Aldric, somehow bent the stone to fulfil his own desires? He could pay an enchanter to use it on his behalf if he had not the skill himself. Any enchanter . . . Kalarr shot a sidelong glance of horrid suspicion at Duergar's bowed head and considered several possibilities—but killing him now would be too soon, for his own deep-laid plans would benefit most from the confusion of an imminent invasion and the Drusalan had not yet sent the proper secret codes. But when he did . . .

A bead of perspiration trickled slowly past Kalarr's eye, tickling the skin and making him blink. His teeth showed and in a sudden excess of frustration he flung the window wide and roared: "Where are you, Talvalin?" into the afternoon air. Duergar started, but only the hollow echoes of cu Ruruc's voice came distortedly back from the citadel walls. Kalarr bowed his head as the door of the chamber opened, then shifted his sombre gaze as the man in the shadows bowed low.

"Is anything wrong, my lord?" he said humbly. Kalarr's face twisted.

"No!" he barked. "Get out!" The man bowed again as he backed through the door.

"As my lord pleases," said Baiart Talvalin.

*

For the first time in longer than he could remember, Aldric snapped out of sleep with an alarm tocsin's clangour in his mind. Without taking time to think about it, he rolled sideways off the bed with one hand already reaching for the holstered *telek* behind the headboard. It cleared leather as he hit the floor and emitted a small, sinister double click as he wrenched its cocking lever back. The spring-gun had a magazine of eight stubby steel darts, and inside twelve paces would put each one through an unarmoured target just as fast as he could crank them out. It was the favoured weapon for places where a sword had insufficient range but a crossbow or longbow was too powerful—such as bedrooms. Such as now.

"Very impressive," said Gemmel from the doorway. "All I had to do was think hard about attacking you and your sense of danger did the rest."

"That wasn't very clever," Aldric replied severely, disarming the *telek* cautiously—it was all too easy to put a dart through one's own foot. "You've trained me not to ask questions in a situation like that one. If I hadn't remembered where I was . . ." Gemmel was not very concerned and said as much.

"The day you take me off guard when *I* set up the ambush, I'll give up sorcery for keeping chickens," he grinned. Aldric snorted and returned the *telek* to its hiding-place.

"Don't be too impressed with this sixth sense of mine, by the way," he pointed out. "I've noticed it doesn't always work."

"Such things seldom do. Don't rely on it, that's all."

"I don't, *altrou*."

"Wise of you. But enough of this dazzling conversation. It's time you found out what has been going on in the world these past few years, because within the next few days you're going to rejoin it."

"You mean I'm leaving? But . . . why?"

"Strange; I would have thought you much more eager to be away."

"I *am* eager, but . . . well, this is one of the situations where you don't like me not to ask questions. Isn't it . . . ?"

*

". . . and that, I guess, is why Kalarr hasn't given Duergar any assistance so far—and why I think that Duergar himself doesn't want to risk forcing the issue yet. But he isn't a fool; if he hasn't already worked out what the true controlling talisman is, a look at any contemporary sword will show him what it must be. Whether he has any notion about the spellstone I cannot say—but if he does enough research a process of elimination should tell him. I doubt if Kalarr will."

"But *altrou*, you're a wizard." Aldric's finger tapped the table to emphasise his words, making the cabochon stone wobble slightly in its velvet-lined case. Cold azure fire spilled out and made a dancing shadow-show on the young *eijo*'s intense features. "Why not use the stone yourself—let it focus your power instead of his?"

Gemmel smiled wanly and shook his head. "Sorcery isn't as easy as picking up another man's sword," he said. "You could probably use a Jouvaine *estoc*, but a man skilled with it would defeat you easily. With any of the seven spellstones I would be the same; I could control them, but they're not one of my fields of study. An expert could turn them against me without even touching the stones himself. And Kalarr cu Ruruc is an expert."

"So then, what do I do?"

"You find out why I gave you such an elaborate education."

They talked over dinner, or rather Gemmel talked and Aldric listened while he ate. The youngster never bothered to ask where food came from; he simply enjoyed it. This meal was a rich stew of three meats, served peasant-style with fresh vegetables on separate dishes and a little bowl of hot red spicy sauce which by the matching colour of Aldric's face he was using liberally. Without the elaborate high-clan table manners Aldric took care to observe at all times, Gemmel finished in half the time and lit his pipe. Not that he was a gluttonous eater, merely that he saw no reason to use salt only left-handed, in three shakes only and setting down the cellar before another three, knife in right hand only and never lift drink with the left. Aldric did—it was a link with what had once been and he was unwilling to break that link, because there was so little else left to him.

"Since I can't use the spellstone, you must get me something I can make use of. I spent this morning trimming down a list made last week, and you'll be glad to hear you won't have to go as far as I had feared at first. Look . . ." The old man cleared dishes to one side and spread a map on the table. "I marked the locations of various talismans on this, and although the closest is here"—his finger touched a red dot in the central Jouvaine provinces—"that's much too close to the Imperial frontier. The provinces are usually lax in the matter of magic, but right now two city-states are in rebellion and Imperial law is stringently enforced. The fact that you come from the country funding the rebels wouldn't be in your favour, and looking for a sorcerous talisman would virtually guarantee your summary execution. However," and a pleased smirk appeared on Gemmel's face, "this ban on enchantments has rebounded on Warlord Etzel. Duergar Vathach isn't his only agent and a Vreijek overlord caught one inside his city walls. The man was . . . induced to say who sent him, and since he was a wizard of some small cult his confession of Etzel's name has that worthy embroiled in a scandal it will take him some time to live down. I was afraid that if old Droek should die Etzel would have tried to usurp Ioen's authority, but now he won't have enough support to risk the attempt. Indeed, the wonder of it is that he is still in office."

"*Altrou*, why are the Imperial lords so much against magic?" Aldric was genuinely interested, because Alba had no such ban and yet the clan-lords had never bothered to use sorcery. Perhaps the two facts were related.

"Not just the lords, Aldric. The common people have been taught that magic is irreligious and disrespectful to Heaven."

The young Alban instantly noticed what Gemmel had hinted. "So that's the teaching. What's the fact?"

With a little shrug the old enchanter poured himself wine and took a careful sip. "I travelled, before I came to Alba. We travelled—my son and I. For no other reason than to see other countries, other cultures. Curiosity, if you like. We came to a village in Tergoves province which for some reason was being . . . 'disciplined' is the Empire's word. I would have left, for we could do nothing, but Ernol tried to rescue a girl and killed two troopers in the process. We fled. Later that afternoon the soldiers came.

"There was a young man with them, unarmoured but in rich robes. He called Ernol over and looked him up and down, smiling pleasantly. 'Did you kill my soldiers?' he asked. 'Yes,' said Ernol. 'Why did you do that?' Ernol told him 'They are expensive to train—can you repay me?' 'I cannot,' replied Ernol. 'Oh, but you can,' said the young man. And then—then . . .

"He slew my only son.

"I went a little mad. I think I screamed—I know I wept. I saw the young man, smiling, wiping his sword, and he was red: his horse was red; the grass and the sky and the sun were all red with the blood of my son and the hate in my brain. Then I raised my empty hand and spoke the Invocation of Fire.

"He burned. He sat on his tall horse with a smile on his lips and a naked sword in his hand and he flared and died like dry straw in a furnace. It mattered little to me that he was the Grand Warlord's second son, Etzel's uncle, or that my action would make the Empire ban all magic thereafter on pain of death. All that mattered was that I had killed him too quickly. I had not repaid him in full for the death of my own, my only son."

Aldric stared unblinking at Gemmel for a time, then poured wine and drank it, not in a careful sip but in a single long gulp though he hardly felt the liquor's warmth through the icy knot in his stomach. He had only ever seen the gentle, studious side of the man he called *altrou*, and had sometimes wondered whether he knew the true meaning of Aldric's own desire for revenge. It seemed that he did. ''Not repaid him in full . . .'' echoed again through the *eijo*'s mind—it might have been his own voice.

''What am I—'' now that was his own voice, raspy and shrill from a mouth the wine had barely moistened. Aldric cleared his throat and tried again. ''What am I to look for, then—and where?''

''There is a talisman which I think will answer my needs best. It's called Ykraith—the Dragonwand.''

''Dragon . . . ?'' Aldric wondered aloud. The word had a Drusalan sound.

''Firedrake,'' Gemmel translated. ''There's a cavern on the island of Techaur. That's where you'll find it.''

''Where's Techaur?'' asked the Alban, squinting at the map. It was a strange thing, drawn on stiff glass-clear parchment with letters much too small to read unaided. The wizard touched a smudge of islands in the Narrow Sea south of Cerenau. Aldric realised what they were and groaned softly. ''Not the Ethailin Myl! They're not called the Thousand Islands for a joke!''

''Even so, they're only five days' sailing from Erdhaven.''

''And how many days finding one particular unnamed lump of rock, eh?''

''Less than you might think—there are only so many 'lumps of rock' big enough to contain the size of cavern this is supposed to be. If in doubt, ask one of the local fishermen.'' Aldric grunted, then found something else to quibble about.

''Look here, isn't Kerys much closer? Two, three days sailing at most. Why don't I—''

''Why don't you look at the rest of the map? There's a lot more riding from here to Kerys than there is to Erdhaven— and that much more time for you to be spotted by a spy and dealt with before you have the Dragonwand.''

''Oh . . .''

''Yes, 'oh'. Now, I think it's high time you had a sword of

your own. Follow me—unless of course you have a few more objections for me to dispose of.'' The old man's voice wasn't unkind, more dryly amused, and though Aldric could have mentioned pirates, Imperial Fleet patrol-ships and even water-monsters, he decided to save his breath and follow.

*

"This is my armoury," said Gemmel, indicating a door with one hand and fishing in his pocket for keys with the other. As the door hissed open on well-oiled hinges, Aldric caught his breath at the multiple glitter from within. After so long with a wizard, he was prepared for and accustomed to wonders where he least expected them, but the armoury was some-where he had long wanted to see. He saw it now, lit by a cool, pale light pouring from slots in the ceiling, and realised that he was not completely inured to the marvellous after all—which he considered privately was just as it should be.

He spent a long time simply wandering up and down, looking at things. Though he could not put the sensation into words, he felt that there was one particular weapon he should be looking for. The feeling was vague, amorphous, but still strong enough to bring him back to Gemmel empty-handed. The enchanter nodded as if he had expected something of the sort and took a sheathed blade from a locked cupboard on the wall. He locked the door again carefully afterwards, then extended the weapon to Aldric. "Try this," he said. "I think it will suit you.''

The young *eijo* bowed politely, as was the custom when receiving the gift of a sword—though in truth it was just a blade, cased in a black battle scabbard chaped, clasped and throated with silver. Its tang was shrouded in a binding of soft leather, with the parts of the proper hilt in a box which Gemmel set out on the armoury work-bench—a metal box enamelled in deep blue shot with silver stars, its edges ornamented with designs of significance. How significant, Aldric was soon to learn. Within, each piece was cradled in its own nest of quilted satin; the metal was black and shiny, not because of lacquer or enamel but because the steel itself was jet black. Even the strips of tooled leather braided crisscross on the long grip were black, relieved only by an under-lay of silver wire.

The weapon was a *taiken* of exquisite quality, and with sensuous care Aldric revealed part of the straight blade. By tradition no *taiken* was ever drawn by a new owner for the first time except under the light of Heaven, and he contented himself with a mere handspan of the mirror-burnished metal. It flashed under the harsh artificial lights. Smoky blue-grey lines of incredibly hard steel outlined the cutting edges, shift-ing in a constant play of reflected shadow as he turned the longsword this way and that. Slightly embarrassed to find his hands trembling, Aldric ran the shining blade home with the gentlest of pressures and unwrapped the leather binding from its tang.

This was the only part of the blade where writing was permitted; any other decoration was limited to stylised or abstract engraving. As they scanned the precise, beautiful uncials, flowing as elegantly as if they were penned and not gouged from the unpolished grey metal, Aldric's eyes nar-rowed and he glanced at Gemmel for a nod of confirmation before staring more intently at the graceful letters. Both they and the language they constituted were in an old form of the Alban High Speech, so that he had to work at the translation— and even when the meaning was clear, his mind found it hard to accept.

"This can't be true!" he breathed.

"The words are true," intoned Gemmel quietly. "It is fitting that this ancient evil should be matched by this ancient blade."

"Forged was I of iron Heaven-born," Aldric read, half to himself. "Uelan made me. I am Isileth."

The weapon Aldric held was almost two thousand years old, older than the coming of the Horse Lords, and though the hilt had been changed many times as fashion and need dictated, the blade itself had a lineage few clans could match. Clan Talvalin did, on the Elthanek side. Aldric did.

The ribbon of steel was too hard to bend, too flexible to break, and the legends said its edges had only once been honed, and then still wet from the quenching bath. A named-blade, its formal title was Isileth; but down the years and in the stories it had become known by a simpler, sinister, more accurate epithet: Widowmaker.

Aldric secured the complex hilt, noting absently the quillons deeply forked for parrying or snapping an opponent's blade, and seeing that there were indeed loops to guard his fingers. He locked the pommel in place, lifted the *taiken*, then knelt and pressed the cool smoothness of its lacquered scabbard to his brow. Gemmel bowed slightly, acknowledging his foster-son's courtesy. There were words to say when accepting such a gift, but Aldric could not remember them—and anyway they were probably insufficient to describe his state of mind. Instead he pulled the scabbard on its shoulder-belt over his head in silence and settled it on his left hip, withdrew the longsword's safety-collar a bare half-inch and then sheathed it with a solid click.

"I'll have your horses and armour ready by tomorrow," said Gemmel, interrupting the *eijo*'s reverie as gently as he could. Aldric came out of his waking dream with a start.

"I'll pack my travelling gear," he said quickly. "There are things I don't want to forget." The enchanter looked at him curiously.

"I don't think there's anything I've overlooked."

Aldric smiled a small, enigmatic smile which told Gemmel nothing. "Probably not . . . ." was all the young man said.

*

Aldric limited his selection of clothing to essentials, functional rather than fashionable. Apart from the white of shirts and linen, everything was unrelieved black—and some garments were even more functional than their tailor had originally intended. Upending a boot, the Alban shook three sheathed knives from their place of concealment. Neither his family nor, he guessed, his foster-father would have approved of them, since even *venjens-eijin* were expected to have a modicum of honesty and carry their weapons in plain view. He intended to do no such thing. One, a balanced throwing-knife, buckled round his calf where it was hidden by the long moccasin boots he favoured. Another was a thin stiletto

strapped to his left forearm, hilt foremost under the shirtsleeve.
While the third . . .

That was the most dubious of all. It was a T-shaped punch
dagger whose scabbard hooked to the loops he had secretly
sewn inside all his collars. It was dishonourable, an assassin's
weapon—and a possibly-fatal surprise for anyone who thought
him unarmed. That, Aldric reflected as he settled the tiny
knife against his spine, was justification enough for him.
Fitting Isileth carefully to one side of a new double weapon-
belt, he bowed very slightly, very privately, before slotting
his *tsepan* into place. Then quite quickly he gathered up his
clothes and left the room, pausing only once to look back at
what had been home for three years. Then he closed the door
with a sudden, final movement.

In the armoury he packed his saddlebags and waited for
Gemmel. When the old enchanter appeared, he strode without
pausing straight for the wall which shot up smoothly into the
ceiling at his approach, revealing a dusty flight of stairs lit
with the yellow dance of live flames. In the dust were traces
of feet coming and going, with the latest so recent that
nothing had yet dimmed the shiny stair. Aldric smelt the
odours of hay and horses. Beyond a green door was his
pack-horse, already partially loaded with cased armour—but
the youngster made at once for the stall beside it.

Within was a courser, midnight black and gleaming. It was
harnessed in black leather bossed and inlaid with silver,
saddled in black leather with tassles of silver-shot blue—the
Talvalin colours, but too subtle for the idle glance—and
geared with bow and quiver, holstered *telekin* and a cased
shield. The beast was Andarran, a pure-bred stallion of a
breed extinct this hundred years or more, and its value was
beyond price. "The horse's name is Lyard," he heard Gemmel
say as he made his saddlebags fast. Aldric's mind was whirling,
despite his efforts to control it. There was an overpowering
sensation of having slipped unnoticed into a harper's tale, and
reality was something harder to grasp than the horse at his
shoulder or the sword at his hip.

He led the war-horse forward and secured the pack-pony's
reins to a stirrup leather, then glanced around for the way out.

Gemmel noticed his enquiring look and gestured with one hand, at which the back wall of the stable ground ponderously open. A breeze whirled in, bringing with it birdsong and the smell of the open air. Walking beside his charger, Aldric stepped back into a world which should have seemed real—except that he was no longer sure just what was real.

Gemmel watched as the warrior with his son's face reached the saddle in a single easy swing, then stepped out behind him into the watery sunshine. "I'm sorry the weather isn't more pleasant," he said apologetically. Aldric didn't care. He had never really appreciated landscapes before, but this was the first scenery he had laid eyes on in far too long and he drank it in.

"This is gold, this silver," the enchanter said, and held out two leather bags. "Six hundred marks should be enough, I hope. If not, and you hurry, you can earn something at the Erdhaven Spring-Feast. Now remember, don't touch anything but the Dragonwand, no matter how tempting. Watch out for spies—and they won't all be human. Trust nobody, especially after dark."

A tiny smile tugged at the corners of Aldric's mouth; it was typical of the old man to give a lecture when all had been already said. "And Aldric . . ." the words hesitated.

"Yes?"

Gemmel shyly rubbed the toe of his boot into the grass. "I was only going to say, come back safe." Aldric smiled and bowed. With a rush of warmth the wizard realised it was the small, informal nod of son to father.

"I'll do my best. *Tau k'noeth-ei, altrou-ain.*" He twitched the stallion's reins and cantered off into the sunrise. Gemmel watched him go.

"And with you also, Aldric . . . my son." Then he turned away.

When Aldric looked back he saw only the grass—but he waved anyway.

*

Behind a securely locked door, Duergar Vathach read the words on a ragged scrap of parchment for the third time, as if hoping they might have changed their meaning. They had not. There was nobody in the room to see how pale his face had become, nor how his fingers trembled before they clenched into white-knuckled fists that clawed the pendant sword-hilt from around his neck. Links of broken chain scattered across the floor with a multiple laughing tinkle, and then the hilt itself went crashing against a wall.

Cradling his sweat-slick head in both hands, Duergar mumbled incoherently to himself. He had long been troubled by the way cu Ruruc showed neither fear nor respect, but ill-concealed amusement, whenever he saw the talisman that supposedly controlled him. And there was the way he had sent out spies to find and bring him . . . something.

Duergar had not known what cu Ruruc sought until a year ago, when some errand had brought him from Dunrath's great library into the Hall of Archives next to it, a place which housed both writings and objects from past history. There he had seen old *taikenin*, relics of the Clan Wars—and seen too, for the first time, the chains and bands which held each sword securely on its owner's wrist. Bands which would remain in contact with the wearer's cooling flesh long after death-slack fingers had released the finest sword-hilt . . .

It had taken Duergar ten months to confirm his nightmare. Ten months of frantic, furtive searching through every document in a fortress all too well supplied with scribbled scraps of information. He had not known what he was looking for, only that he would know it if he found it. As indeed he did.

The evidence was not dramatic; rather, its insignificance was more redolent of some black joke. A bill. A coppersmith's bill, stuffed out of sight and out of mind in a heap of ledgers, destined to be discarded but instead forgotten until Duergar found it; after an interval of some five hundred years.

" . . . *from a* kailin *of Ut Ergan citadel, retainer to* Kalarr-*arluth, two markes of silver for ye ensetting of a jewel (this blue and most fair) under bronze on his swordes clasp against losing of ye same, it being a luck-token ygiven of his Lorde . . .*" Any sorcerer of intelligence knew that one of the seven Echainon spellstones had vanished from all wizards' knowledge during or before the Alban Clan Wars—

and to Duergar's frantically working mind the words he read
had only one possible meaning. He was aware, too, that if
Kalarr learned that his secret was discovered he, Duergar,
would die. But if he, Duergar, was able to retrieve the
wrist-band, then when cu Ruruc made his move the other
sorcerer would get the shock of both his lives. And if the
Echainon spellstone was still "ensetten under bronze" on the
sword clasp, then he would be no longer needed.

But if Kalarr should regain the wrist-band and the stone
. . . Duergar's mind quailed at the consequences. It explained many of his suspicions about cu Ruruc, and he had no
doubt that his so-called ally was also searching for Aldric
Talvalin. Except that if Kalarr felt unable to bring the *kailin*
back, then rather than risk the stone falling into someone
else's hands he would obliterate everything. Duergar had to
reach both it and Aldric first . . .

With the strength of extreme fear he dragged his laden desk
aside and began to draw a symbol of great power across the
wooden floor . . .

*

In the four days' riding since he had left Gemmel, Aldric
had encountered no more than a dozen people—but he had
already discovered that his status of *eijo* was accorded more
respect than a *kailin* of the same age. Reaction was the same
in every case: first a curious glance towards the sound of
hoofs, then a narrow-eyed survey of the covered shield, the
apparently uncoloured trappings, the *tsepan* from which Aldric
had prised his clan crest, the cropped hair and the faintly
sinister air lent by his scarred cheek. And then the bow,
invariably low, formal—and performed with a timidity the
young man at first found rather shocking.

An *eijo*, whether with hair unbound to indicate his lordless
state or like Aldric's, cropped to mark an oath-taken purpose,
was outside the law and without protection from House or
Clan. He had only himself to rely on—which made the *eijo* a
menacing individual and one for lonely travellers to be wary
of. While Aldric was comfortable in the presence of yeomen
and peasants—regardless of whether they were comfortable
with him about or not—he avoided large towns and the

occasional *kailin* he met on the road. When encounters were unavoidable he matched their bows precisely, neither offering nor expecting much respect. When they were low-clan and inferior, as most were, even that rankled.

It was another fortnight before the huge forest of Guelerd began to darken the horizon ahead of him. The place had a well-deserved reputation as a stronghold for ruffians and bandits despite the efforts of King Rynert's father, and what few steadings Aldric passed were large and well-fortified. Rumour had it that only fools and foreigners rode through Guelerd unescorted; a rumour the young man smiled at, since he had seen no trace of hostility all day. It did not occur to him that a full-armed *eijo* on a warhorse was not the most inviting of prospective victims.

By the time he passed under the eaves of the forest, afternoon was already tilting towards evening. He was grateful for the cool of the slanting shadows and almost wished it would rain a little, enough to settle the dust of the paved military road and wash the dry heat from the air. A pair of rooks hopped out of his path, then returned to whatever they had been squabbling over. A solitary fox eyed him from behind a tree before ambling off about its own affairs. There was a crow cawing lazily somewhere. Aldric yawned and tried to remember what the last yeoman had told him of the forest inns. They locked their doors at nightfall and did not admit guests after dark, that much he did know. A glance at the sky relaxed him; it would be a couple of hours yet before the light failed.

Watching darkness fall from a tavern common-room, Aldric sipped ale and sniffed the savoury aroma of his dinner being prepared. He knew now why he had not encountered any highway robbers on the road; after seeing the tavern's prices, it was clear they had all turned innkeeper. Such places catered for the wealthy merchants who travelled towards Erdhaven port, and charged accordingly. Even the third son of one of Alba's foremost clan-lords could not have stayed in such a house. It was wryly amusing therefore that a landless *eijo*, an enchanter's fosterling, could afford the best room and pay for it in hard coin.

As he ate Aldric became aware of unease among the other patrons; though to the innkeeper one man's silver was as good as another, he, Aldric, was probably not the sort of guest this place liked to attract. The plump merchants and their ladies—by the look of them, "wives" was not the word to use—did not like sharing their dinnertime with an *eijo*, no matter how young or well-mannered. Aldric was not concerned—although the fat woman who was probably the only merchant's wife in the building annoyed him throughout the meal. Languishing glances and rogueish winks did not go too well with a fine venison pasty. With a thin, sardonic smile he fixed an unwinking stare on the would-be-romantic, toying significantly with his knife all the while.

By the time he had to blink, she and her husband had hurriedly bustled out. Aldric's smile widened fractionally; there were advantages to being *eijo* after all.

With the heat and the ale and the feeling of being pleasantly full that gave the whole world a rosy glow, the young man decided it was time for bed. He rose, stretched mightily and ambled upstairs to where the room had been shuttered for the night and two lamps set out. The bed looked soft and inviting, so much so that he kicked off his boots and lay down fully dressed, intending to relax for a while before sleeping properly.

That, at least, was his intention. However, once his eyelids had closed, it soon became too much effort to open them again . . .

Merchants who lodged in an inn such as this paid too highly for their rooms to tolerate nocturnal noises. Floors were thickly carpeted, locks and hinges oiled and silent. Thus it was that Aldric slept on peacefully while his window-shutters were teased open and the window itself slid back. A thin glow of moonlight flowed in, and with it a dark outline which drifted like fog across the floor. The Alban whimpered softly in his sleep and rolled over, making the stealthy intruder freeze where he stood. Only when the youngster was breathing deeply once more did he continue about his furtive business. The same sharp knife which had forced the shutter-catch now sliced saddlebag straps and the lacings on well-filled moneybags too imprudently displayed earlier in the evening. The thief's gloved fingers checked their contents without chinking a single coin, then transferred them to his own belt-pouch before the man retraced his steps and vanished into the night. Lacking in all manners, he did not even close the shutters behind him.

Aldric's eyes flicked open half an hour later to a room streaked skimmed-milk blue by the moonlight pouring through his open window—a window that had been dark and secured when he fell asleep. And a window through which somebody was quietly entering.

He would have grabbed for *taiken* or *telek*, except that one was on the rack built into one wall for the purpose, and both of the other were still holstered in the stable . . . Instead he made the small noises of restless sleep and gathered his legs under him, sliding the stiletto from his sleeve. The shadowy figure paused warily, watchfully and then bent over his saddlebags.

One hundred and sixty pounds of irritated *eijo* in the small of the back would inconvenience most people and this burglar was no exception. The pair went down in a tangle of flailing limbs and began an impromptu wrestling match which did nothing for the room's furnishings. What with the uncertain light and the black clothes of both combatants, it was a confused and confusing fight, complicated by the fact that the thief refused to do much except try to escape. Though they were much of a size, Aldric quickly discovered himself to be the stronger of the two. Besides which, there was the stiletto to consider.

A dainty sting under the fellow's masked chin stopped the burglar's wriggling long enough for Aldric to drive one knee down hard, winding his opponent for the second time in a matter of minutes. Taking advantage of the man's helpless gasps for breath to open one of the lamps, Aldric raised it high and wrenched off his victim's mask with the other hand.

Only to discover that *he* was actually *she*. "Good gods!" the Alban exclaimed unoriginally, and then let rip with several more interesting swear-words when the girl jerked both knees up into his side and almost threw him over her head.

Had those knees struck their intended target, Aldric would have been in no state to prevent her escape and he knew it. That was why he straddled her and sat down hurriedly with his full weight in the pit of her stomach. Her breath came out in a gasp for the third time, and Aldric used the opportunity to make himself more comfortable—then delicately rested his stiletto point in the hollow of her throat as insurance against further attempts on his . . . person. This gave him the chance to look at his catch more closely:

Fine skin tanned to the colour of honey, electrum-pale blonde hair tied back under a black hood, slightly oblique eyes of a brilliant blue that reminded him of the Echainon spellstone, a full mouth half-open over white teeth. She was beautiful—and at the moment very, very angry. "Get off!" she snapped, and even in only two words Aldric noticed a slight, unplaceable accent. "Alban, take that knife away and get *off*!"

"You're scarcely in a position to make demands," Aldric observed with a smugness he did not really mean. "Now— what did you steal?" The girl spat inaccurately at him. "Listen, you," he rasped, waving the stiletto in front of her eyes, "I'm asking you nicely. The Prefect in Erdhaven won't be so pleasant. *What did you steal*?"

"Nothing," she retorted eventually. "There was no gold in your saddlebag."

"No?" Aldric's voice was sharp with disbelief. "I'm at liberty to search you unless you . . ." He cast a thoughtful gaze over the girl's clothing and realised the threat was useless. Her black garments fitted so closely—apart from where they had burst open in the fight—that anything as big as his moneybags would show quite plainly. There was nothing showing at all. The girl saw his face fall, and rather than trying to escape she smiled amiably.

"Your shutters were open, Alban. I doubt if I'm your first visitor tonight." Aldric cursed foully in three languages. "You shouldn't have taken the best room," she pointed out helpfully. "Nor paid for it in gold coins." Aldric stared at her and almost reluctantly grinned at the irony of it all.

"But I did," he returned flatly. "And much good it did

me.'' He studied the girl more closely, as if realising again how very pretty she was. ''Who are you anyway?''

''Alban, if you're going to talk, I'd rather you sat elsewhere—and removed your hand.'' With sudden embarrassment Aldric jerked his knife hand from between her breasts, having rested it there quite absently the better to keep his stiletto under her chin. The girl closed her shirt and stared up at him levelly. ''The second part, Alban. Find a chair.''

''Don't try escaping,'' he warned. ''I wouldn't want to—'' he thought of various things he would and would not do, then chose the least offensive. ''To miss hearing what you're going to tell me,'' he finished and stood up. Backing away, he turned quickly and slammed the shutters, but when he looked round the girl had merely risen to a cross-legged seat on the floor. She put her head on one side and fluttered her lashes at him mockingly.

''Convinced of my good intentions, Alban?'' Aldric nodded, but slung Widowmaker round his shoulder nonetheless.

''*You* aren't Alban, of course.'' It wasn't a question—her accent made one unnecessary. The girl untied her hood and let her hair fall free before answering him.

''I am Kyrin,'' she said at length. ''Tehal Kyrin, Harek's daughter, of Tervasdal in Valhol.'' Aldric was startled; he had expected almost anyone but a Valhollan.

''What in the name of Heaven are you doing here?''

''Trying to collect enough money for passage home again. My uncle's ship was wrecked on your so-well-mapped coastal rocks and no merchant will sail to Valhol without being well paid.''

''I'm not surprised,'' admitted Aldric. Then he grinned maliciously. ''But if you'd got to my saddlebags first you could have bought your own vessel. With near enough five hundred marks.'' Kyrin winced, and said something in her native tongue. It sounded vicious.

''So we're both in the same situation,'' she muttered despairingly.

''Apparently. And what do *we* do now?'' It was ''we'' already, he noted sourly; need breeds strange bedfellows. His eyes slid sideways at the thought of bed, then blinked and shifted away. Not so hasty—not with a Valhollan, anyway.

"We could rob," suggested Kyrin bluntly.

"No. There are limits even for *eijin*. It would be dishonourable."

"Albans and honour!" the girl flared. "You all think it's your exclusive privilege. Mine was the most honourable of honourless choices—rather a thief than a beggar and a robber than a whore . ." She stared grimly at the big bed. "I am—was—to marry at Spring-Return. It was to bind an alliance of families, so Seorth will have married my sister instead." She shrugged carelessly. "So, and so, and so . . . but if I had earned my money in bed, who would marry me for any decent reason? Eh?"

Aldric said nothing; indeed, Kyrin wondered if he had even been listening, because there was a thoughtful, faraway look about him. Then he grinned at her and clapped his hands briskly so that she jumped.

"Thanks for reminding me," he said cheerfully. "I can earn something at the Erdhaven Spring-Feast—not much, but enough."

"Earn? At a religious celebration?"

"Not religious—holiday. It's a market festival of some sort; I've never been to it, but I know they hold weapon contests, archery, *telek*-shooting, horsemanship—and all with prizes of minted silver."

"What about swordplay?" The girl's sharp eyes had noticed a fine *taiken* racked on the bedroom wall and Aldric's reluctance was plain when he shook his head.

"I daren't try single combat. With people looking for me it's too obvious to risk."

"The people who originally owned that money you lost, honourable *eijo*?"

Aldric didn't react to the jibe except with a mirthless leer. "Actually, no. But if they catch me and you're nearby, you'll wish yourself far, far away."

"I . . . see," muttered Kyrin, glad that she did not. Her father had been right all the time—Albans were crazy and this one was crazier than most. She would be well advised to have nothing to do with him; yet travel with this black-clad loon could prove entertaining and maybe profitable as well. "Why do you need the money anyway?"

"I'm taking a sea voyage for the good of my health. Want to come?"

"Why not? It might be interesting." Kyrin wondered then why the young Alban roared with laughter—honest amusement, without sneer or sarcasm. Then he looked at her, still chuckling.

"Oh, I think you'll find it that. Definitely interesting . . ."

FIVE

Resurrection

Aldric was too polite to ask where Kyrin's handsome grey gelding had come from, and she was not yet so sure of him that she would have answered anyway. Not that her daytime wear invited questions: thigh-boots of soft doeskin over tight, faded blue breeches, a loose white shirt indifferently fastened, a leather jerkin armoured after a fashion with a layer of chain mail and a lady's *cymar*—overmantle—flung over all as if to mark her sex. With the complex hilt of a Jouvaine *estoc* riding at her shoulder and the arm-plates from somebody's battle armour strapped over her sleeves, Tehal Kyrin made a brave show alongside the equally picturesque but rather more sombre Aldric. Neither was the sort of person idly approached by passers-by.

There were many such; peasants riding ox-carts or walking in noisy groups, well-heeled merchants in their carriages and those less wealthy jolting in horse-palanquins. Certain elderly *kailinin* cast disapproving looks at the younger set, fantastically tricked out in the latest fashion of the Imperial court, the Jouvaine city-states or wherever else took their current fancy. Aldric was relieved to notice that in this holiday atmosphere his and Kyrin's attire was dismissed as whimsical fancy dress.

As they came closer to Erdhaven, the crowds increased; judicious eavesdropping revealed that this Feast was rumoured to be the best and biggest for some years. For a man intending to lose himself among the press of people, that was good news. Aldric glanced up at the birds circling above the road;

they were attracted by scraps of food, occasional spillages of grain—and one of them maybe by himself.

The scream of a gull cut through the other noises and his eyes went narrow and thoughtful. Was he not being a bit unimaginative watching out only for crows—when a seagull would look less out of place near the coast? Reining in, he stared at one big yellow-eyed brute which seemed suspiciously disinterested in the scraps lying under its beak.

"What's the matter, Aldric?" Kyrin had seen the worried look on his face before she saw the gull, and when her eye fell on it she snorted dismissively. "Those pirates! Vicious—but no concern of ours."

"Of yours, maybe," he said softly, easing a *telek* from its holster. "For myself, I'm not so sure." He cocked the spring-gun and levelled it, taking care to adopt the proper arm's-length posture for contests of skill; with luck he would appear merely to be putting in a little practice. The *telek* thumped and the gull went down in silence. There was no human shriek of agony, only the reflex spastic flutter of one wing which soon ceased. Ignoring the ironic applause from other travellers, Aldric racked another dart into the weapon and nudged Lyard slowly forward, eyes and *telek* fixed on the dead bird. Kyrin followed, muttering under her breath in her own language and wondering again why she had bothered to come along with this madman. The *eijo* dismounted, nudged the corpse with a toe, rolled it over, then finally picked it up and tugged his missile free. Throughout all, it remained a seagull.

"If you don't tell me at once what this exhibition is about, Alban, I'll leave you to play-act on your own."

Aldric eyed her for a moment, then dropped the carcass and wiped his fingers on the grass. "If I don't, could you really bear to leave without finding out something?" he asked goodhumouredly.

"Don't twist words!"

"All right then, I won't. I'll tell you everything—that you need to know, at least—but not here. When we've found a room and a bed——"

"Beds, Alban. I've warned you already."

"Beds, then. Or privacy at least. But Kyrin-*ain*,"—the endearment was not accidental, nor was it just to tease her— "Kyrin-*ain*, I doubt that you'll like what you hear. Playacting has no part in it."

"Whether I like it or not is immaterial. What I do not like is all this secrecy. Why don't you trust me?"

"I do trust you. If I didn't, I . . . I wouldn't have told you my name. That's the truth."

The girl stared at him for a long time without saying anything, then bowed very slightly. "I believe what you say, Aldric-*eijo*. And I'll accept anything else you tell me about this business, however little that may be." Then she glanced towards the road and smiled. "Best be on our way if you want to find somewhere to stay for tonight—your small change won't last until tomorrow otherwise."

As they mounted up and cantered towards Erdhaven, neither saw a black crow fluttering heavily from the lower branches of a tree where it had been perched. Nor did they notice how it wheeled high into the blue spring sky before flapping with uncrowlike speed towards the north-west.

And the citadel of Dunrath.

                              *

Kyrin's guess was close to the truth; they found it almost impossible to obtain rooms and ended up sharing one in a tavern near the harbour. It was better than Aldric had anticipated, but consequently more expensive than he was prepared for. Even after an hour's haggling his meagre funds had been sorely depleted when at last they went upstairs.

"One bed," said the Valhollan in a toneless voice. "Well, at least there's a chair and blankets . . ." Aldric disliked the implication.

"I paid for this and I'm sleeping in it," he snapped. Kyrin shrugged, dumping her saddlebags before the fireplace as a footstool.

Aldric's irritation evaporated at once. "Kyrin . . . *Kyrin*." He met her stare, then gestured at the mattress. "It's easily big enough for half each. To *sleep*. We'll need rest, both of us. I know that you . . . that is . . ." He was getting embarrassed now and angry at himself for being so. Finally he drew a deep breath and released it hissing between clenched teeth, unslung Isileth Widowmaker from her travelling-place at his back and laid the sheathed *taiken* precisely down the centre of the bed. "Half—I promise."

The girl looked at him, head tilted quizzically. "You promise . . . like *that*?" Aldric nodded once, fiercely willing her to accept and not make him look foolish. "Very well. I agree . . . to the arrangement." She almost smiled and kept it to a twitching of her lips; the boy—she was older than he was, almost certainly—could be horribly intense sometimes. "But why that way?"

"It—it seemed right, somehow," Aldric tried to explain awkwardly.

"Sometimes, Alban, I wonder if you're real." There was no mockery in her voice and when Aldric remembered his own feelings about the sword and the horse, he matched the twinkle in her ice-blue eyes with a shy smile of his own. But when Kyrin lifted Widowmaker from the bed only her sex restrained him from harsh words; no warrior ever made so free with another's sword and though physically a woman, the Valhollan's sword made her as much a warrior as any *kailin-eir*.

Perhaps she sensed something or heard his gasp of outrage; whatever the reason, she turned almost hastily and bowed from the waist as she had seen her companion do along the road. Holding out the longsword, one hand already incautiously on the hilt, she asked: "May I draw?" Aldric nodded curtly, realising he could not expect customs and protocol from a foreigner, but acknowledging her untutored courtesy all the same.

Isileth hissed from her scabbard with a whisper as of stroked silk. Without raising her eyes from the cruel beauty of the steel, Kyrin murmured, "Have you used this?" and at once regretted the question, suddenly aware of an aura of cold menace settling over the blade as it slid clear. With a shiver she realised this same intangible grey veil sometimes hung around her companion and wondered, not wanting an answer, which of the two was its true source.

"She has been drawn in the dawn-light, under the eye of

Heaven, that she may know me," intoned the *eijo* quietly. "But used—not yet . . ." Kyrin sheathed the *taiken* and laid it down, affecting not to notice the slight, caressing touch of Aldric's hand on hers as he retrieved the weapon and secured it on his hip. "Someone tried to insult me once—said I slept with my sword. I can't imagine what he would say now." His small, crooked smile widened fractionally. "By the way, I'm not utterly penniless. Shall we eat now or later?"

*

"I guessed aright, then," Duergar muttered, his pale eyes fixed on a thin man in black who knelt before him. The man's hood was thrown back, revealing yellowish eyes and dark hair which hung in lank tails from perspiration. Had he been a horse he would have been lathered. Until a few minutes previously he had been a crow; he was still lathered. "You are certain of this?"

"Quite certain, lord," gasped the man. He was having difficulty in getting his breath back and Duergar's impatient questions were not helping. "From what I saw, indeed, had the boy spotted me I would have been"—he essayed a gaptoothed smile—"dead certain, as they say here."

"Spare me your feeble humour, man," returned the necromancer wearily. "I have much to do." He stood up and the changeling lowered his head respectfully. "You may rest; there will be rewards for this day's work. Would that all my servants did so well . . ." He crossed to the door and then glanced back. "Mark you, no word of this to lord Kalarr."

"No word?" Kalarr stood in the doorway as it opened, his teeth bared in a hard, mirthless grin. "Whyever not? I'm most curious." There was a *taiken* in his hand, its point resting on the door-ward's lips. "I learned that one of your changeling-crows had returned. Yet this"—his sword prodded delicately—"denies it." Kalarr's gaze swept the room and settled on the black-clad man, who stared back with fear in his eyes. "It seems he lied."

Dispassionately, without even watching what he was doing, the sorcerer crunched his longsword past lips, teeth and neck deep into the panelled wall, pinning the sentry like some grotesque specimen. As Kalarr released the weapon and sauntered past his victim, the unfortunate man slid forward down its blade until the hilt against his face held him in an eternal half-obeisance above the puddle of his own blood. He took a fearful time to die.

Kalarr paid him no further heed; his concentration was now focused on Duergar to the exclusion of all else. "Enough of this charade!" he hissed as the necromancer groped for the talisman at his neck even though he knew it was useless. "I grow weary of it." He emitted a chuckle like tearing metal and raised one finger of his right hand.

A whirl of yellow fire dissipated barely a handspan from Duergar's face, filling the air with heat and the reek of burning. Kalarr gaped; sooner or later every wizard laid a protective charm on himself and he had failed to consider that his erstwhile ally might have done the same. Such things required additional spells to breach them.

By the time he had repeated a fuller invocation Duergar was ready, made bold by his survival after being taken unawares. The changeling scuttled for shelter as power crackled through the room and then his world dissolved into harsh colours and raw, atonal noise. Under the lash of such ravening energies, even wood and stone flared away in coruscations of disrupted matter.

The magics died abruptly amid sparks and vapour. Nothing moved. Echoes of thunder rolled sonorously towards the mountains, while in the shadow of the citadel donjon, ordinary folk raised their heads from the dirt and looked around in terror. Only the sun shone placidly and unconcerned from a clean blue sky.

Kalarr passed one hand across his face and laughed shakily. "It seems we are well matched," he muttered, then coughed on a wisp of acrid smoke. Shaking with exertion and fright, Duergar sat down on the rippled, spell-warped floor but said nothing. Sweat glistened on his bald pate.

After a glance around, Kalarr chuckled again, and even though it still was not a pleasant sound, this time he seemed genuinely amused. What he had found humorous was the state of the room. It had somewhat . . . changed. Walls sloped giddily out of the vertical, floor and ceiling were corrugated into waves like a petrified ocean. The changeling was a greyish silhouette scorched into the window-frame where a blast of force had snuffed him out of existence. The whole place had a dizzy, nauseating look.

"If neither can defeat the other," he mused, turning back to Duergar, "then the obvious solution is to form a true alliance. There is, however, one problem."

The necromancer looked up at that. "Only one?" he repeated in contemptuous disbelief.

Kalarr smiled blandly at him. "Only one; the source of all others. A lack of mutual trust."

"You try to kill me and then you say I lack trust in your intentions?" Duergar choked on a bitter laugh.

"Certainly you lack manners, Drusalan. Hear me out."

"Then talk." Manners were far from Duergar's mind right now.

"What oath of mine would you accept as a token of good faith?"

The necromancer looked blank; such a question was so improbable that he had never considered his possible answer. Finally he shrugged. "Suggest one yourself."

"I was once *kailin-eir*, as much so as the Talvalin boy, before I learned . . . other skills. That clan—and my other name—is five centuries extinct, but I still have rank, and lord-right over lesser men, and honour when I choose to remember it. Those were never stripped from me." As he spoke Kalarr went to the door, twisted his *taiken* free of the wall and wrenched it from the sentry's face, then cleaned the blade with a silken kerchief.

There was a footfall in the corridor and Kalarr swivelled to see who was there. He smiled thinly, then drove his longsword into the wooden floor where it stuck, quivering. "So you alone have the courage to brave this sorcerer's den, eh? Then come in."

Baiart bowed low as he entered, ignoring the corpse in the doorway. "You are both unharmed . . ." he said without any inflection. Kalarr's smile widened into a cruel grin.

"Such deep concern touches my heart," he purred. "All went as usual in Cerdor?"

"Of course. How else would it go?"

"How indeed . . . Tell me, Baiart-*arluth,* Clan-Lord Talvalin, what great oath would a man take if he desired an enemy to trust him? An enemy, mark you." Baiart stared coldly at the wizard. "I don't mock you now, man—not with my question, at least."

"Do you not? Then surely the sun rose from the north today."

"It may well do so tomorrow," hissed Kalarr, setting his pleasant aspect aside like an actor changing character-masks. A flicker of something distorted the outline of his hand so that it seemed wrapped in flame. A dangerous glint awoke in his dark eyes as they bored into Baiart's face. The man flinched, but refused to look away. "Take care, or you might die before you see such marvels."

"Death no longer frightens me, warlock. Since you wove your spells about me I can wear a *tsepan* without you fretting I might use it. So I must take my ending as a gift; given in hatred, given in rage or given in mercy, my passage to the dark is now the only journey I would welcome."

"Quite so." Kalarr looked him up and down and banished the poised spell from his hand. "Then I may give it you in repayment—sometime. But remember Duergar's special skill, and bear in mind that death here is not an ending, but more often a new beginning to more . . . docile service. What you desire, Talvalin, is not your passage to the dark but your passage through the pyre. And I seldom like to see a funeral."

"It smacks too much of waste," said Duergar pleasantly. Baiart's face had long since drained of colour. "Now answer my lord's question." The necromancer's courage had returned now that Kalarr's attention was directed elsewhere. He could defer to whatever scheme was in cu Ruruc's convoluted brain, at least for the present. What happened later would depend very much on how things developed both here and in the Empire. And on whether Kalarr cu Ruruc proved worthy of trust.

Perhaps the sun would rise in the north after all.

"The oath is made in blood, for reasons you sorcerers well

understand," said Baiart. "Like all the High oaths, this one is made with a *tsepan*."

"Give me yours." Kalarr held out one hand, arrogantly refusing to watch Baiart when the *kailin* drew blade right behind his back. The weapon's blue and silver hilt was placed gently in the middle of his open palm, despite the savage expression which twisted Baiart's face. He had tried, anguished, to stab either himself or his undefended target, and his right hand had refused to obey him. Tears of rage and shame trickled down his cheeks, but Kalarr merely nodded absent thanks. "What now?" he demanded.

"You must cut, once only, from thumb to index finger, joining the Honour-scars. But cut shallowly; a man may need to swear many such oaths in his life—especially a man with many enemies." Kalarr ignored the remark. "Then you must make the mark of your crest in the blood, and the first rune of your name, swear the oath, and wipe all clean with a cloth which must be burnt at once."

"I see," said Kalarr. "And if there are no Honour-scars . . . ?" Baiart gasped in outrage and the wizard laughed at his scandalised expression. "Merely a question, Clan-Lord." He opened his hand to reveal the three parallel white scars, then sliced the *tsepan* across the top of each.

Both Baiart and Duergar were privately surprised to see that the blood running out was red, as red as the sorcerer's robes. Using one fingertip, Kalarr drew the crescent and double curve of his crest, the winged viper, and under it the character "Sre".

"The first rune of *your* name," said Baiart urgently, "or any oath is void." Kalarr gazed at him coldly.

"I know," he said. "Duergar Vathach, give me your hand." The necromancer started to protest, then thought better of it and did as he was asked. "You are no Alban, wrapped around with honourable codes," Kalarr said, "but the Empire has a custom of bloodbonding which you should respect. Bloodbond friendship with me, for peace of mind if nothing else."

Duergar shrugged, then jerked slightly as the *tsepan* nicked his thumb. As the two wounds pressed together he received

another surprise—Kalarr's blood was as warm as any other
man's, neither too hot nor too cold as the necromancer had
speculated it might be.

Normally never at a loss for something to say, whether
sharp and cruel or once in a rare while almost poetic, Kalarr
stared at the flowing blood and spoke not a word. Then with
a touch of his hand he closed both wounds, wiped away
marks and errant trickles with a kerchief and exploded the
wisp of silk into a flash of fire with a single gesture.

"Now that we are allies, my friend, what were you about
when I first came in?" he said to Duergar. The necromancer
jerked his head in warning at Baiart and a slow smile creased
the skin of Kalarr's face. "Ah . . . I understand perfectly."
He turned to the Alban and returned his *tsepan* with a sardonic bow. "Would you care to leave us now, *arluth*
Talvalin?"

Baiart nodded as curtly as he dared and made for the door.
Duergar called him back. "Cause some servants to come up
for yonder carrion," he ordered, indicating the dead sentry.
"He was a strong man and should make a useful addition to
the ranks of my *traugarin.*" Baiart's mouth twitched but he
nodded obediently and went to go out again. Once more he
was called back, this time by Kalarr.

"You can go—but if you should care to stay"—the tall
sorcerer paid no heed to Duergar's frantic hushing noises—"I
can promise that what we have planned should be more than
entertaining for you. And your brother Aldric."

Baiart's face stayed immobile, robbing Kalarr of much
satisfaction and pleasure. The *kailin* merely shook his head
and fled from the room, but the sound of sobbing drifted back
from the corridor. Duergar cringed inside himself, and cringed
even more when he could no longer hear Baiart's weeping—
for the noise of cu Ruruc's laughter.

*

There were tents all around the enormous competition field
beyond Erdhaven, and Kyrin sat in one of them with a pile of
silver marks in front of her and a sheet of sums on her knee.
The money came to almost a hundred marks, but no matter
how she added up the columns, her sums totalled nearer five.

The girl added them up again, then subtracted two entries and nodded to herself. If she could persuade Aldric to leave the horses here, they would be able to afford one of the ships to whose masters she had spoken. Except that parting the *eijo* from his Andarran charger was not going to be quite as simple as arithmetic suggested.

Hoofs sounded outside the tent and then the flap lifted to admit a figure wearing Great Harness, the full battle armour which Albans called *an-moyya-tsalaer*. Aldric unbuckled the straps of his flaring peaked helm and laid aside the war-mask covering cheeks and chin, then unlaced his mail and leather coif with a sigh of relief. Under the armour his hair was dark and wet.

"You should wear one of those new over-robes," observed Kyrin. "All that black metal must absorb a frightful heat from the sun on a day like this."

"Oddly enough, it doesn't," Aldric said, settling into a chair which creaked protestingly. The armour, from Gemmel's armoury, was remarkably light for Great Harness at fifty pounds, but not to a folding camp-chair. From the helm, mask and coif, through the four-panelled lamellar corslet to the peculiar idea of separate mail sleeves and strapped-on arm-plates—like those Kyrin wore—from neck to knuckles, and the equally strange jazerant scales arranged honeycomb-pattern on leather leggings, Alban armour was unique. Despite its cats'-cradle of laces, straps, buckles, belts and hooks it was eminently practical, for each part could be worn individually as the need arose.

Aldric wore it all, not because he needed protection but because it served to conceal who he was. Besides, wearing *an-tsalaer* for a mounted archery contest was entirely in keeping with the spirit of the Spring-Feast.

"Oh, by the way,"—he pulled out a wallet which had been stuffed for safety behind his weapon-belt—"second prize. One-fifty." Kyrin caught the wallet as it sailed through the air and added its contents to the money on the table and to her calculations.

"Better!" she said. "But be careful—too many second prizes and people will start talking just as much as if you

were taking firsts.'' Aldric laughed and poured himself some
wine.

"You needn't worry on that account. If young Escuar from
Prytenon hadn't been nursing a hangover, I would have been
lucky to manage fifth place. How are we doing for money?''

"Well enough, but slowly. Aldric, if we left the horses—''

"We'd never see them again, as I've told you before. I'll
try horse-riding or shooting the *telek*—but I will *not* leave
Lyard in the hands of some would-be thief.''

"You don't trust anybody, do you?''

"Not really. I have been given little reason to do so. But at
least we can afford to eat better than we have done during
these past few days.'' He punctuated his change of subject by
standing up with that creak of leather and metallic slither to
which Kyrin was still unaccustomed. "I, for one, am
famished.''

During festival time, almost all the prices in Erdhaven
tripled; however, there were some taverns too proud of their
reputations to indulge in such piracy. They were usually
small eating-houses, into the fourth and fifth generation of the
host's family—and very few people knew about them. Those
who did kept quiet about it and used their chosen eating-
places purely for epicurean gluttony or a little well-mannered
seduction. For reasons Aldric did not question, Kyrin knew
the owner of one such carvery—he was later to find it was all
quite innocent and a matter of family friendship—and was
able to persuade the man to find them a table. Comforted
perhaps by Aldric's meticulous courtesy, he did not object to
the young man being armoured from the neck down.

The food was even better than Kyrin had promised—and
her claims had been so extravagant that Aldric had thought
them exaggeration. All the wines were imported—red from
the Jouvaine Provinces, white from the Empire—and Aldric
was interested in how they had got through the various block-
ades and embargoes which made life so difficult for merchants. Then his steak arrived and he forgot the question. The
meat was just as he liked it: seared, but otherwise not so
much cooked as well heated, and he sliced into the fragrant,

almost-raw beef with a delicacy that totally belied the speed with which it was devoured.

"One thing I do intend to try, even if it has some risks involved," the young *eijo* said once the edge was off his hunger, "and that's *yril t'sathorn*—the Messenger's Ride. It's a kind of mock battle; obstacles to jump, targets for sword, spear or bow and a moat you have to swim your horse through. It's from an old story about a courier in the Clan Wars."

Kyrin drank white wine and smiled at him. "It all sounds faintly childish," she said.

"Perhaps; but you're allowed to bet on it all the same."

"Indeed?" Kyrin's eyes lit up; like most Valhollans she was fond of gambling, but being prudent disliked long odds if they could be avoided. "Tell me, Aldric," she crooned at him, filling his wine-cup to the brim, "who do you think will win?"

The Alban sipped his drink with relish and smirked like a cat with cream on its whiskers. "Who else but me?" he answered brightly.

Kyrin rather pointedly drank the rest of the wine herself.

*

Clocks in the town of Erdhaven were chiming for the sixth hour of evening when a man sat down at a bench and put fire to a bowlful of crystals. The stuff, sparkling like crushed diamonds, burst into brief flame and then settled to a slow crawl of sparks. Grey smoke coiled up, not dissipating but hanging at eye level, growing thicker and more opaque with every wisp that joined it. The man lowered his head and began to mutter in a soft monotone.

The cloud began to glow from within and an image formed, moving and distorting as the vapour shifted. Its half-seen mouth formed words. "You are late," said Duergar's voice, thickly warped by sorcery and distance.

"Pardon!" The man abased himself hastily. "I beg pardon!"

"It is of little matter. You have the holiday as your excuse, of course?"

"Yes, lord. I couldn't close my shop at the usual time and—"

"Enough. The article I sent you remains unharmed?" Glancing behind him, the man swallowed and nodded affirmation. "Excellent."

Filling most of the shop which fronted his small bronze-foundry was an equestrian statue, life-size, of a warrior scale-armoured after the style of an Imperial *katafrakt*. A masterpiece of casting, it was exclaimed over by everyone who entered the foundry, but the bronze-smith himself preferred not to go near it. There was an eerie quality about the image; its armour was not a hauberk, what the Alban stories called lizard-mail, but fitted more like a lizard's skin and gave the figure a scaly, reptilian look. The rider leaned back in his saddle, war-mask in hand, and stared into an unknown distance from under the peak of his helm. Goat-horns curved from that headgear and the essential inhumanity of the piece was completed when the face was made visible by the lifted mask. There was no face!

In profile the features were of classic, perfect beauty; from any other angle they became merely geometrical shapes, cold and precise. Shadows suggested a soft roundness to mouth and brows and chin, but clearer light revealed only stark hollows and harsh, flat planes. There was no mouth other than a flaw in the verdigrised metal, no eyes at all. Only a bleak power, like the desire for conquest given palpable form.

Duergar's eyes were closed as if in concentration, but the bronze-founder still felt as if he was being watched—and that by someone without his best interests at heart. Despite the threat of his master's anger, the man rose and backed quietly towards the door.

Then a vast shadow fell across him and he spun, mouth gaping in a shriek which never left his throat.

That throat was clamped shut by the inexorable pressure of a bronze hand as the statue leaned down from its pedestal and clutched him by the neck. "I can give it movement for a little while," came Duergar's voice from behind him. "But it must have a life of its own. Yours will suffice." If there was more, the founder did not hear it.

As the metal *katafrakt* straightened up, the workman's

wildly dancing legs left the ground in a hanged-man's jig as he was lifted with no effort at all and held dangling at the end of the creature's arm. The last thing he saw was the flawed mouth cracking into a smile, and then the hand on his neck closed to a clenched fist. Though flesh and sinew gave way like wet paper, there was hardly any blood from the frightful wound and what little spurted from the dead man's nostrils to fall upon the bronze armour was absorbed as if by a sponge. The corpse shrivelled in that icy grip, shrinking and contracting as life was sucked from the deepest marrow of its bones. When at last it was released, it fell not with the sodden thud of a body but with a clattering of dry sticks wrapped in a bag of skin.

The ponderous bulk of horse and rider left their pedestal without a squeal of stressed metal, or indeed any sound other than that of an ordinary *kailin*. Only a certain massive deliberation to every movement betrayed that this *kailin* was far removed from the ordinary. The horse stopped and knelt before the smoke-cloud as the warrior astride its bronze back raised one arm in a salute. His voice was deep, resonant as a flawed bell in an empty place of prayer.

"Command me, Lifegiver, my master."

"First you must be named," said Duergar. It was necessary; even such a creature of sorcery was incomplete without a name—but this was not "man" for its flesh was cold bronze, yet nor was it "statue" for it moved. It was Duergar's servant and more than servant—like an extra limb. "You are as one of my hands," the necromancer pronounced at last. "Your name shall be Esel, which is to say 'sword-hand' in the old tongue."

"It is a good name, my master. What is thy will?"

"My will is in your mind, Esel my servant. Seek Aldric Talvalin on the weapon-field tomorrow. You will know him. Yet do not slay him—in this the weapon that you bear will aid you—unless there is no choice. And if he must be slain, then destroy him and everything he carries. Utterly."

"Thy desire shall be fulfilled in all ways, Lifegiver, my master. Thy enemy is my enemy. My victim is thine."

*

Glancing down at himself, Aldric smiled wryly; *yril t'sathorn* really did seem like an elaborate children's game after all, for though armour and harness remained, most of his weapons had been replaced by wooden ones edged and tipped with dye-soaked wadding. He, Lyard and his opponents all wore white overmantles so that any impacts would show up like ink on paper.

The competitors had received instruction earlier that morning from one of the Prefect's officials, a small man over-full of his own importance. "Each rider will be given a scroll," he had announced fussily, "representing important despatches. This must be carried to the judge who sits on this moated island, representing Torhan-*arluth* in his fortified camp of Gorlahr. In various places there will be targets for spear and bow—the Great-bow only, sirs, since the lesser bow is not historically speaking correct—and five mounted *kailinin* of the Prefect's guard representing—"

"—five men on horseback . . . ?" speculated somebody, provoking laughter. The official reddened, coughed, rustled his notes and then continued in a less patronising manner. "Representing enemy forces," he said emphatically. "There is only one bridge to the island. It is guarded. A rider may, if he wishes, swim the moat. He will not then be attacked by any defender, but may I point out that swimming takes longer than galloping and each rider will have his Riding timed by turn of sandglass. That, sirs, is all."

That, thought Aldric, was enough. Personally he considered the best way to stop a courier was to shoot the horse from under him, but that was much too practical for a sport like this. He watched through narrowed eyes as Escuar the Pryteinek galloped out to ride the Courier's Ride.

A hidden target came up on its counterbalanced arm and Escuar, twisting in his saddle, drove an arrow neatly into it. Aldric pursed his lips thoughtfully; the young man's mounted archery was very good, but his swordplay was as wooden as the mock *taiken* he used. The fifth and last of the hidden warriors burst from ambush in a clump of trees where a leaf-strewn net had hidden him, and charged with levelled spear. Escuar half-turned, flinging up his shield—and his attacker threw the lance aside, whipped wooden sword from scabbard-tube to white-clad thigh in a single move and left a blue blotch visible all over the field. Somebody not far from Aldric groaned and swore, making the Alban grin as he recognised the sound of lost money. He wondered whether Kyrin would be loyally backing him or sensibly doing no such thing.

"Kourgath-*eijo*," said a voice at his elbow, "you ride now." One of the Prefect's retainers presented him with a small scroll. Aldric was tempted to pretend to read the thing and then destroy it, but fancied that such humour would not be well received and tucked it into the cuff of his shooting-glove instead. For a moment he wondered what his odds might be, then as the trumpets blared he dismissed all other concerns and kicked Lyard into a gallop.

Two warriors pounced before the big Andarran courser had got into his stride, and Aldric reacted instinctively as he had been taught to do—charging the nearer man, sidestepping Lyard at the last minute with tug of rein and touch of knee, then lunging past the displaced shield with his spear. The second warrior, sword-armed, was "dead" before he closed enough to be dangerous.

Children's game or not, Aldric found his heart was pounding with the excitement of something that was far more real than anything done in Dunrath's exercise yard so long ago. A target reared up and he lowered spearpoint, struck squarely home—and felt his spear disintegrate as some small unseen flaw gave way under the impact.

Cursing under his breath, he threw down the pieces and swept his longbow from its case, drawing an arrow from the ornate fan of shafts quivered at his back. He preferred the handier shortbow to this seven-foot assymetrical archaism, finding it clumsy by comparison. Like its modern counterpart the Great-bow of old Alba was thumb-drawn—but to well behind the archer's ear—and its arrows were correspondingly long, heavy and destructive. Aldric loosed one at close range and even over the noise of galloping in full battle armour heard the wooden target split from top to bottom . . .

Another target appeared, this time craftily set on his right.

The *eijo* bared his teeth in a hard, appreciative grin; whoever had built the course knew that no horse-archer could shoot to his nearside. Heeling Lyard briefly away to the left, he launched a shaft backwards over the animal's rump—almost missing altogether in his haste—and then turned back towards the judge's island.

The three remaining *kailinin* were waiting for him at the bridge. Lyard reared as Aldric reined back, eyeing the other riders apprehensively. Without a spear, attacking all three would be a risky undertaking, yet he did not want to waste time swimming his horse across the moat. Deciding at last that boldness would be best, he pulled the peak of his helmet down a little, settled more firmly in the saddle and touched heels to his stallion's flanks, aware that the judge had risen from his canopied seat to get a better view.

But the official was not watching him. Aldric's head jerked round, all plans and strategies forgotten as something surfaced in the moat with a hiss of displaced water.

As an armoured horseman surged towards him through the shallows, he thought for just one instant that it was all part of some trick staged by the Prefect. Then weeds fell from the rider's spearhead to reveal not a dye-pad but a long, sharp blade. This trick, if trick it was, had no part in *yril t'sathorn* . . .

There was time enough for his stomach to turn right over as the lance slashed towards his head, then reflex took over and his shield came up. The impact punched it back against him, rocked him in the saddle—and chilled him with the knowledge that such a blow striking home would drive clear through him, armour or no armour. Throwing aside his useless wooden weapons, Aldric rode with desperate haste towards the judge's escort, the only men in range who wore real swords.

The soldiers broke and scattered as he approached, terrified not of the *eijo* but of that which followed him. Aldric snarled and rode one of them down; before Lyard had skidded to a halt he was on the ground and wrenching the dazed man's broadsword from its scabbard. The weapon was no *taiken*—but it was steel, and that was enough.

Before he could regain his saddle the bronze rider was upon him. Aldric twisted away from the jabbing spear and hacked at its shaft, but almost dropped his sword from stinging fingers as it bounced off solid metal. With obvious intent the *katafrakt* continued his charge at Lyard and Aldric screamed a warning. The battle-trained Andarran knew well enough what was meant by that and galloped out of reach.

In the deathly stillness which had fallen over the crowd, Kyrin's whistle rang out clearly. The black stallion hesitated, ears pricked, recognising the signal but knowing that his master had not given it. Kyrin had to repeat the summons twice before she was obeyed.

Rather than press home his advantage, the scaled horseman descended with a harsh metallic slither from his own steed. The sound had an eerie echo, almost a hollowness, as if there was emptiness within both the reptilian armour and the horse's hide. Aldric swallowed sourness and tried not to think what that might imply.

"I am Esel, o enemy of my master," pronounced the *katafrakt*, his voice so deep that Aldric felt it vibrating in the marrow of his bones. That, too, had an ominous metallic quality which confirmed the Alban's fears. His enemy, no matter what he looked like, was not a man. "Return to me the thing ye stole aforetime, ere I take it from thee." Esel paused, the empty glare of his war mask not wavering from Aldric's face. "Speak thy choice."

The *eijo* cleared his throat, trying to still the tremor lurking there. Gripping his broadsword and settling his shield, he smiled a mirthless smile that did little to conceal his fright. "I r-really think—" he tried again: "I really think you have to take it." His voice sounded insignificant.

"As ye will." The monstrous figure turned towards his horse, standing immobile like something cast from metal, and when he swung back there was a sheathed sword in his hand. "My master desires that ye be brought before him, that he may visit condign punishment upon thee at his pleasure. This shall be. It is my master's bidding."

Kyrin shouldered her way furiously through an audience who stood as if spellbound, trying to reach the spot where

Lyard waited patiently. She approached the stallion as warily as her need for haste allowed, knowing how dangerous a war-schooled horse could be. When she vaulted into the charger's saddle Lyard reared, pawing the air and shrilling his anger and excitement; but he did nothing worse, knowing the woman on his back as a companion of his master, as someone who had treated him kindly, and was at least familiar with the strangeness which had frightened him. Kyrin sighed with relief, then dug in her heels and rode full-tilt for Aldric's tent and Widowmaker.

Backing away from Esel's stealthy advance, the *eijo* glanced around. Nobody moved, whether through fear or horror . . . or some more sinister reason. Then the bronze *katafrakt* shook the scabbard from his sword, flicking it at Aldric's head. The Alban almost forgot to duck, such was his shock at seeing what Esel cradled easily in one scaly fist.

It was not steel, nor even bronze, but a shimmering translucent stuff like glass which drew the eyes and held them. Aldric gulped as bile rose in his throat and wrenched his gaze away with an effort, feeling sweat begin to film his skin. For perhaps a second the world had tried to slither out of focus, and he knew another second would have left him helpless. It was more rage and fear than courage which sent a whirring cut at Esel's helm, and it was more luck than judgement that permitted it to strike.

With a snap one of the bronze goat-horns spun away, but Esel ignored what should have stunned him and kept on advancing. He had not parried, nor even tried to, and his shield sat uselessly on his arm as he gripped his great sword like a blacksmith's hammer. Or a bronze-founder's maul.

Then heavy feet approached from Aldric's left as one of his erstwhile opponents came charging in with an axe raised in both hands. Why this man had moved when no one else did, the *eijo* did not know. Not that it was of use. The bronze warrior blocked clumsily, his blade emitting a piercingly-sweet chiming note, and Aldric saw the nacreous shimmer drain from the weapon to leave it clear as ice, almost invisible in the sunlight.

Then it chopped home.

The stricken *kailin* dropped his axe and tottered back a pace. There was no wound, no blood on the white robe covering his *tsalaer*—but those robes had gone strangely rigid and crackled at each sluggish movement. It was a sound Aldric had heard before. As the warrior fell over stiffly, his face frozen into a pallid mask of shock, Aldric knew what Esel's sword had done even before the wave of icy air billowed over him. The man was frozen in very truth, his body, clothing, armour all frosted over—within half a heart-beat on a hot spring day.

Another great sweep of the sword left a trail of chilly white vapour hanging in the air as Aldric ducked, then straightened and smashed his iron-bound shield rim into the bridge of Esel's nose. It should have blinded the bigger man with pain; but the only blindness was that of a war-mask buckled beyond recovery. Esel made a grinding, impatient noise and tore the mask aside to reveal his non-face.

In the next exchange Aldric lost his sword. Not through clumsiness but because, made brittle by appalling cold, its blade abruptly flew into a score of tinkling shards. With blood streaming down his face from where a splinter had ripped skin, Aldric flung the useless hilt—a hilt which frozen perspiration had almost stuck to his hand—at his enemy before backing out of reach. Esel followed, making no attempt to lengthen his stride. He came on with the calm assurance of an executioner.

Aldric knew now that he could not outlast Duergar's sending, because though he was sodden with sweat, exhausted by the dragging weight of *an-moyya-tsalaer* and growing rapidly unsteady on his feet, Esel's movements were still the same: no slower, no faster, patient and inevitable. Resignation joined fatigue in Aldric's brain, combining into the despair of vast weariness so that he almost knelt and waited for the inevitable. Almost . . . but not quite. He was Alban, *kailin-eir* Talvalin. If this thing was to finish it would be on his own terms. Aldric's hand began to close around his *tsepan*'s hilt.

Hoofbeats and shouting cut through his daze and his unfocused eyes finally settled on the blonde figure riding swiftly closer on a black horse. Perhaps, he thought, perhaps there is another way. He forced himself into a shaky run.

Kyrin slid Isileth Widowmaker from her lacquered scabbard and breathed a soft apology to the *taiken*, then flung it as hard and straight as she was able. The weapon came cartwheeling down and quivered in the turf for barely a second before Aldric's fingers closed around its hilt and he turned to face his tormentor.

He turned almost into a cut across the eyes and though he jerked his head a handsbreadth back, the frigid wind which whipped into his war-mask's trefoil opening left frost rimed thickly on eyebrows and lashes. He had no illusions about crossing swords, even with Widowmaker, and made no attempt to press home an attack. Instead he concentrated on the opening that he wanted . . . needed . . . had to have sooner or later.

Bronze was brittle. That helmet-horn had not been cut but broken off like a dry stick. Given the chance—Aldric threw his shield invitingly away—he would test his theory on the bronze man's armour.

Or his arm. Esel's blow was huge but clumsy and Aldric evaded it with ease even in his weakened state. There was nothing weak about the double-handed cut which came down on Esel's sword-arm. The limb shattered half-way to the elbow.

With a shrill noise barely recognisable as a scream, Esel clutched his stump with the remaining hand. There was no blood and instead of flesh an oily pulp bulged from the ruptured metal. It dripped clear ooze that had a sharply chemical stench, and it pulsed with a slow rhythm which in the severed portion fluttered briefly and then stopped.

Aldric fought the churning in his stomach as he lifted the amputated half-arm and twisted the sword-hilt from its slack grip. He moved forward, stiff-legged both with anger and exhaustion.

"Esel . . ." There was no longer any quaver in his voice, only hatred fired and tempered by the memory of how this— this *thing* had frightened him. "If you ever truly lived, you are truly dead now." Aldric poised the huge sword momentarily, then stabbed it home. The iceblade slid into the bronze *katafrakt*'s chest as easily as into a scabbard and there stuck fast. A convulsion wrenched the hilt from Aldric's grip—not that he was reluctant to let it go—and Esel staggered drunkenly towards his horse.

Somehow the bronze warrior crawled into his saddle and sat there, plucking feebly at the sword protruding from a torso already thickly caked with ice. Then his horse jerkily raised one foreleg and stopped in that position. Esel leaned back, stump raised as if to hold his missing war-mask in a hand no longer there, and gazed fixedly into the distance.

Both man and mount slowly overbalanced and fell with a vast splash into the moat. As the mass of metal rolled over and sank, the sword reared into view—and in that instant the whole surface of the moat froze over. Then the hilt slid out of sight, dragged through the crust by the weight of the metal in which it was embedded.

Aldric watched it vanish. There was a full minute of shocked silence before the cheers began, and he turned a face curdled with disgust to watch how armed and armoured men came running up. Now that it was safe! The *eijo*'s stomach heaved and tearing off his helmet he started to vomit.

Kyrin bent over him and gently, with a kerchief wetted through a crack in the ice, she began to clean the flaking blood-streaks from his hair and chalk-white face. Reaction struck and, making a tiny whimpering noise, Aldric wrapped his steel-sheathed arms around her waist and clung on tight. Even through the armour she could feel the waves of shudders racking his body. The girl knelt and cradled his head, murmuring soft comforting sounds until the shaking died away.

She glared as soldiers came clattering towards him—then blinked in shock as they levelled curving halberd blades. Their officer, a slight man whose face was sallow inside his rank-flashed helmet, surveyed her with a cold eye, then studied Aldric's face. The *eijo* licked dry lips and whatever flicker of expression crossed his face made the officer take a long step backwards. "Somebody get his sword," the soldier snapped, angry at being startled by a frightened boy in armour.

But the fright had almost gone by now and Aldric was not so immature as he appeared. There was a glitter in his grey-green eyes suggesting that after a sorcery-created monstrosity like Esel, a mere officer of guards would give him little trouble.

After several deep breaths he felt capable of speech and straightened his back unconsciously. "What is going on here?" His voice was soft, controlled once more and deliberately laced with menace.

The officer tried to ignore his tacit threat and levelled one gloved finger at Kyrin. "You," he said, "help him to walk. Guards, watch them. Especially the *eijo*. I wouldn't think of escaping, *an-kourgath*," he finished, bolder once his soldiers had closed in.

"I asked you a question," Aldric said. There were no more threats; he was too weary for play-acting an unconvincing role and no longer cared whether or not he was given an answer. But he got one just the same.

"My lord wants you," the officer returned. "Both of you. Now. At once."

SIX

Contact

Neither Aldric nor Kyrin had any idea of where they might be—there had been curtains tightly fastened over every window of the carriage which had brought them here. At least, the *eijo* reflected grimly as he glanced around their place of confinement, the cage was a gilded one.

Gilded was an understatement, for the place was magnificent. Its walls were panelled in maplewood and carved burr walnut, the inlaid floor was thickly strewn with rugs. Scented oil in lamps of gold and crystal filled the air with fragrance and struck a myriad reflections from gems and precious metals. The place should have been coarse and garish; instead it was tasteful, restrained and of such elegance that Kyrin found herself considering every move she made, lest it destroy the room's sense of graceful order.

Aldric felt no such compunction; he was long past being overawed by mere fine furnishings and had been irritated both by apparent arrest and by his own brief, shaming loss of face. Slithering comfortably into a chair—and pointedly ignoring what his *tsalaer* was doing to the polished wood—he tried without success to work out who had captured him. If "captured" was the right word, and he was inclined to doubt it. Despite their brusque early treatment, it seemed now that they were less prisoners than guests—reluctant ones of course, but there had been a lack of threats, of locked doors or anything else suggestive of captivity. Wondering just how far his guesses would be borne out, he rose and walked quietly to the door.

It was indeed unlocked and he eased it back a whisker—
then bit on an oath and all but slammed it shut. There was a
file of soldiers in the corridor outside, at ease, talking quietly,
but all with weapons at their sides. So much, thought Aldric,
for another fine idea. Closing the door, he leaned back against
it until the latch clicked home.

Both he and the girl had been disarmed—except for his
tsepan, which was either criminal oversight or a deliberate act
in keeping with the strangeness of this strange place. That his
own armoured body was a useful weapon he knew already,
but bareheaded against a dozen men it was nowhere near
enough.

There was a small table near one wall; on it stood flagons,
goblets of worked metal and tiny, fragile glasses. The *eijo*
filled two of these with a wine which was the brilliant,
sinister colour of fresh blood and offered one to Kyrin. No
word had passed between them since they had been taken and
even now she thanked him only with a nod. Looking at the
trembling hand she extended for her wine, and at lips com-
pressed so tightly that they had no colour left, he could guess
the reason why: Kyrin was terrified.

Forcing his own lips into a smile, yet knowing it must look
more like a grin of rage, Aldric slipped one mailed arm
around her. "Drink up," he murmured. "If they'd meant us
any harm we'd have found it out by now." That was not
necessarily true, he thought sombrely, but kept it from dark-
ening the false and brittle brightness of his voice. Kyrin
blinked nervously at him and he heard the crystal clink
against her teeth as she gulped down its contents. "Another?"
he offered, holding up his own glass. "If it does no other
good, it will help you to relax. You're shaking." He tightened his embrace a fraction and leaned towards her face.

"I bid you welcome to my house," purred a voice from
just behind them. Aldric controlled himself in time, but Kyrin
jumped and failed to stifle her gasp of shock. When they
turned around, it was with the slowness of exaggerated calm.
The speaker stood in a sweep of darkness just beyond the
lamplight; his outline was vague, and only the points of light

from jewels and embroidered garments gave them any indication of possible shapes.

"I would offer you refreshment—but it seems no longer necessary," the voice observed rather tartly. There might have been some disapproval in its soft tone; there was certainly a thread of accent which put Aldric on his guard at once. Despite the precision of his Alban words, this man was still more accustomed to the guttural consonants of Drusalan: the Imperial tongue.

"I beg pardon," the young *eijo* responded insincerely. He gestured towards the cups and flagon. "May I pour you some . . ."

"My thanks, but no. I do not drink wine. The sun has not yet set." That last irrelevant statement struck Aldric as odd and he stared at the intruder when at last he deigned to leave his cloak of shadows and walk forward so that they could see him. The man was several inches taller than Aldric, but his height was offset by a burly, powerful frame which reminded the Alban of a bear; a weatherbeaten bear whose dark hair was greying, but a cold-eyed, scar-faced carnivore for all that.

Flicking a glance at the worn hilt of a low-slung sword and the blunt, capable hand resting on its pommel, Aldric inclined his head respectfully. He bowed not merely to the physical strength so apparent here, but to the power of authority which the big man wore like a garment; Aldric had possessed a little of such power himself and knew politeness to be just good sense.

"Might we be offered some explanation for what has been happening today?" Aldric speculated warily. The man stroked his moustache, perhaps to hide a smile, perhaps not.

"Curious," he muttered. "Almost the words *I* was going to use." Then he did smile, if anything so small and fleeting deserved the name. "Explanations will be given and received presently. For now, sit down; be still; make free with the wine—I am assured it is excellent."

Aldric opened his mouth to continue this diplomatic exchange, but was interrupted by four soldiers who stamped in and snapped to attention on either side of the door. The

moustached man drew himself more upright, while his two
unwilling guests forgot about making themselves comfortable
and instead waited apprehensively for the next development.

This took the form of a man in a gold-worked purple
over-robe who swept an interested gaze around the room. In
his forties, he was slightly built and wore his thinning fair
hair in the three braids of a high-clan *arluth*. He limped as he
entered and the padding of his under-tunic almost—but not
quite—concealed the crooked tilt of his left shoulder. A
golden crest-collar at his throat bore a pendant rayed-sun
centred with a single ruby the size of a thrush's egg. The eyes
in his clean-shaven face were a clear hazel, like sunlight
through water, and tiny crows-feet wrinkled the skin around
them as he stared long and hard at the two strangers in this
tranquil room.

Aldric did not return the stare as he normally would;
instead he knelt with studied feline grace and touched brow to
floor in First Obeisance. Kyrin copied him, wanting to ask
questions but knowing enough to realise that this was neither
the time nor the place. She had gleaned one important answer
from the *eijo*'s bow alone.

This slender man was Rynert, the King.

"Up, you two," he said, taking a seat and accepting an
offered glass of wine. "Now, Dewan . . . what is all this?
Your report was a trifle . . . garbled, shall we say? Give me
the translation, please."

Dewan . . . The name rang a long-forgotten bell in Aldric's
memory; the name of King Rynert's captain-of-guards, personal champion, adviser, confidant and friend. Dewan ar
Korentin, late of the province of Vreijaur on the edge of the
Empire's influence in Jouvann, and equally late a much-
decorated *Eldheisart*—lord-commander—of the Bodyguard
cavalry in Imperial Drakkesborg.

Ar Korentin spoke briefly, his accent and mode of speech
clipping the words shorter still. As Aldric listened, he wondered that the King even bothered to hear such an improbable
episode, much less give it any credence. Yet Rynert set down
his wine-glass and listened closely, twisting at a signet ring
on his little finger, turning it round and round again . . .

Then he looked up and Aldric almost fancied he could see the thoughts swimming like fish in his lord's translucent eyes.

"*Eijo-an*, you call yourself Kourgath—that's only the beast on your crest-collar. Tell me your true name."

"I . . . *mathern-an arluth*, lord king, I was once *kailin-eir* Aldric Talvalin."

There was a hiss of indrawn breath from ar Korentin, and the faint slither of steel as he half-drew his sword all but drowned a gasp uttered by one of the soldiers near the door. "You lying—" started the Vreijek angrily, then fell silent at a gesture from Rynert.

"Put up your sword, Dewan. There will be time for it later, if need be. You, *eijo*, why do you claim to be one of the Talvalins, when everyone knows of the plague in Dunrath three years ago? And choose your explanation carefully."

"Because the name is mine, *mathern-an*. If 'everyone' knows of this plague, why would I be so stupid as to use a dead man's name?"

Rynert's eyebrows lifted; he had expected some intricate excuse, not a blunt admission of guilt. Or was it guilt . . . ? The warrior's reasoning was sound enough. "Can you give me any proof?" he demanded. Aldric shook his head; Gemmel had warned him not to carry anything which might identify him as other than the *eijo* he was supposed to be. His foster-father had not foreseen *this*.

"Unfortunate." Rynert's voice was cold and sceptical. "You almost convinced me for a moment. I fear that Dewan's inquisitors will have to prise the truth from—" he broke off as one of his guards stepped forward and slammed a salute.

"Why do you interrupt the king?" snapped ar Korentin dangerously.

"Proof, captain," muttered the soldier, frightened now by his own boldness. He pulled off his helmet and dropped to one knee, revealing a homely, well-battered face and a spreading broken nose.

"Well?" asked Rynert, curious to know what light a mere sentry could throw on this situation. Aldric doubted it would do much good; the man's face meant nothing to him and he doubted if he would have forgotten such misshapen features if he had ever set eyes on them before.

"I've seen that one before, sire," the soldier said. "Him in the black armour. Wore his hair properly then and didn't have that cut on his cheek, but it's the same man. I'd swear to it."

Rynert smiled coldly. "You might have to. Where and when did you meet him?"

"Not meet, sire. I saw him in a—with respect, sire—in a tavern brawl I got caught up in. In Radmur, that was, a couple of years back."

"A couple?" broke in ar Korentin. "How many exactly?"

"Well, three, captain. Three last autumn, I think. That was when I got this." He touched his flattened nose. "They said he was just past *Eskorrethen*, but he was a rare fighter for all that. Over a woman, the trouble was, and her somebody else's lady too." Stirring uncomfortably, Aldric felt Kyrin's eyes rest on him like two hot coins laid against his skin. "Then the Prefect took us all under arrest and I got posted to the Guards in Cerdor—to give me a taste of discipline they said."

"Dewan, remind me to write to Uwin at Radmur-hold," said King Rynert; though he sounded amused, no humour showed on his face. "He must remember that the Guards cohort isn't somewhere to dump his rubbish . . ."

"Captain . . ." the soldier muttered as reproachfully as he dared.

Dewan's face twitched as he too fought down his amusement. "They aren't always rubbish, King. Mostly—but not always."

"I see," Rynert murmured, looking at the guard. "One last question, soldier. What was this *kailin*'s name?"

"Talvalin, sire. Haranil-*arluth*'s youngest son Aldric. That's the name he gave the Radmur magistrates, anyway."

"Enough. Dismissed!" After the sentry had returned to his place Rynert glanced at his captain. "Promote him, Dewan, and make sure he's paid a bounty for this. He's observant, clever enough"—his voice rose slightly—"and he stopped a miscarriage of justice. Take a seat, Aldric-*an*. I beg pardon

for what might have happened.'' The *eijo* saluted in acknowledgment, then sat down carefully, thankful to get the
weight of his armour off legs which had become very weak in
the past few minutes.

At a nod from the king, his guards wheeled and left the
room. Ar Korentin poured wine for Kyrin, Aldric and—after
a swift look out at the sky—himself. ''But you said—'' the
eijo began in surprise, then shrugged and fell silent.

''I do not drink wine? Not on holy days, like Spring-Feast;
then it's not permitted until after sunset—but it's quite dark
now.'' He took a trial sip. ''And this was worth the wait.''

''Aldric-*an*,'' said Rynert quietly, ''I sent my guards outside so that you could speak freely. I want you to tell me
what is happening in my kingdom. Leave nothing out—I
have a feeling yours is the only story which has all the details
I require.''

Aldric nodded, moistened his mouth with a little wine and
began.

*

''It's incredible,'' said Dewan ar Korentin. ''I have never in
my life heard anything so fantastic—except maybe that you
want us to believe it.''

Very softly, King Rynert cleared his throat. ''*I* believe it,
Dewan,'' he murmured. ''If he was lying it would be a
credible, well-thought-out lie, the kind of thing you've heard
in the law courts before now. Not something like this.

''And don't forget what you saw this afternoon, old friend.
How thick was the ice on that moat . . . ?'' Dewan inclined
his head a little but said nothing. ''I wondered a little when I
saw your hair, Aldric-*an*,'' Rynert continued. ''Though I've
seen *eijin* before, you're the first *venjens-eijo* I've met in my
life. The oath was taken against this—Duergar, you called
him—this Imperial necromancer, and no one else?''

''Only against him. Why do you ask, *mathern-an*?''

Rynert hesitated then and looked for confirmation at ar
Korentin. The Vreijek nodded slowly. ''Better that he hears it
from you, King,'' he said. ''For he'll hear it somehow.''

A coldness awoke in the pit of Aldric's stomach and sent

tendrils burrowing up the marrow of his spine. "Hear what. . . ?"

"Aldric-*an* . . . Aldric Talvalin, your brother Baiart told me none of this."

"My . . . brother? Baiart's alive? *Alive?*" The cold in his belly gave a sluggish heave and sourness fouled his throat. "Is he in Cerdor . . . ?"

There was a pathetic hope in the youngster's voice which made Rynert slow to answer. "No. In Dunrath. As Clan-Lord. I granted him the title myself." Aldric looked away, and the only person who saw his face before he controlled it was Kyrin. She winced visibly. "*Kailin-eir* Aldric," the king continued, his tone growing sharp, "do not assume the worst. He may be under threat—or even a spell, if what you've said of Duergar is even half the truth."

"And if he isn't? What then? The word, lord king, is *traitor*!" Slamming one fist against the wall, Aldric heeded neither the crack of a split panel nor the pain and blood of his own torn knuckles. "That oath . . . I cannot kill my own brother. I don't want to. I will not!"

"You will not," echoed the king. "I forbid it. The law—and the crime it governs—is no longer so black-and-white as that recognised by the old Honour-Codes. Leave Baiart Talvalin to the Council Court and to me. Leave your brother to my laws, Aldric. Remember that. Give him some wine, Dewan—no, better make it something stronger. And call a surgeon for that hand."

*

There was a table of black ebony. On it was a mirror of black obsidian which rested in a frame of red gold. The sorcerer who studied it was robed in scarlet cloth. Kalarr drummed his fingers irritably on the table-top and then dispelled the images drifting deep within the volcanic glass. "We underestimated him," he said bleakly. "That must not happen again. It irritates me."

"It doesn't fill me with delight either," snapped Duergar. Since the destruction of Esel he had been sulking, a condition not improved by the fact that Kalarr found it amusing. "Were those soldiers yours?"

"None of mine in Erdhaven," said cu Ruruc. He pushed himself back from the table and stood up. "The only reason your bronze *traugur* was there was your own suspicious nature. I wonder . . ."

"We don't have time to wonder." Duergar started leafing through a thick book. "He wasn't killed on the spot, so I'm assuming he'll be released."

"And what else are you doing there . . . ?"

The necromancer looked up, then tapped his volume. "I'm going to deal with that whelp once and for all."

Kalarr rolled his eyes upward and clenched both fists and teeth. Then he breathed out slowly. "You had your chance to do so and you failed. This is my turn." He smiled, both at the childishness of it all and at the thought which had just struck him. "You couldn't send a spell after him anyway."

"Why not?"

"Not unless the old limit on the range of spells has been overcome—and I don't think it has. At best you'd raise a storm over Erdhaven; at worst the magic would be over-extended and would snap back here. You know what that would do, don't you?" Duergar did. "All you can do is form a plague-sending and that's too slow for this game."

"Game?" shrilled Duergar. "It's a game, is it?"

"Of course—and a most stimulating one. You Imperials treat everything too seriously. What's the boy likely to do now, eh?"

"I have no idea," Duergar retorted pettishly.

"After going to a sea-port; after risking his neck to earn money; and you have no idea . . . Then I suggest you try to find out. Now I, I intend to do something about it—and I intend to watch that something happen."

"At sea?" scoffed the Drusalan necromancer. "And you just after mocking me for forgetting about distance. Do you ever listen to yourself, cu Ruruc?"

"At sea," repeated Kalarr calmly. "With a flying eye." Duergar stopped in mid-laugh and stared at his colleague. *What*, he mouthed, but no sound came out. Kalarr dipped one hand into his belt-pouch and threw something at Duergar, who dodged. The missile did not fall, but fluttered round and round his head on silent wings. When he got a close look he gasped in disgust and regretted ever raising the subject. It was, literally, a flying eye: an eyeball the size of a cat's head, bloodshot across the white with tendrils of muscle from its moth-like wings. It circled him like some repellent insect, then returned to Kalarr's pouch with the same movement as a swallow entering its nest. "I'll send this to Erdhaven at first light tomorrow."

"Why not now, tonight?" Duergar wanted to know.

Kalarr glowered at him, then diluted the look with a sardonic grin. "Owls," he said.

*

King Rynert was not in Erdhaven simply to enjoy the festival; no monarch would let an event which gathered scores of *kailinin* in one place go unobserved. Scattered through the town in disguise and camped plainly outside it after a "training march" was almost a full legion of soldiers. Just in case. And there was a ship to be despatched, its cargo of sufficient importance to require Rynert's personal sendoff. That would have been of great interest to the Empire, had its presence not been concealed better than even the best-disguised soldiers.

The King had not forgotten that young Talvalin had mentioned Kalarr cu Ruruc and though he was courtly, sophisticated and cynical, Rynert had never adopted the disbelief so fashionable among his lords. He had been a sickly child, afflicted with some wasting disease which left him lame and crippled, in a body too frail for a warrior. Instead he had strengthened his mind, reading, absorbing knowledge wherever he could find it, learning both military and political strategy—in short, becoming the kind of king who needed no strong arm to rule well. He knew as much about the theory of magic as any lesser wizard and was aware of the power which practical sorcery brought. Rynert had no desire for that power; it soiled the soul like black pitch and made the thought of cu Ruruc a frightening one.

Dewan had called the place *his* house, even though the king was living there. It was somewhere restful away from court, where private councils could be held and where at present the champion's wife was living. Ar Korentin had deserted from his regiment when the Empire annexed his home province some ten years before, and though a storm of protest in the Senate had revoked the annexation only a short while later, by that time Dewan had neither the need nor the desire to return.

"A ship will be leaving port in two or three days time," said Rynert as he rose to go. The others rose as well, bowing politely. "You two will be on board; the cargo is not so urgent that the shipmaster can't make a small diversion on your behalf. Have your adjutant take over, Dewan—you'll be going with them. Convey my apologies to your wife. Good night." The door clicked shut behind him.

"Well now . . . " Ar Korentin released a held-in breath through his teeth. "Lyseun won't like this—or you, *eijo-an*." Aldric did not trouble to ask why; he guessed that he would find out anyway. "By the way," the Vreijek continued, "how long do you practise *taiken* daily?"

"Two hours—one in the morning, one at—"

"I thought so. To the exclusion of all else. Then I've got two or three days in which to sharpen up your archery. That exhibition today, *kailin* Talvalin, wasn't worth a damn in combat. Now, follow me."

Another bloody expert, Aldric thought bitterly—something I could certainly do without. The champion's wife could equally well have done without Aldric; she did not say so, but her disapproval was plain despite the presence of King Rynert's wife Ewise, just across the gaming-board at which they sat. To Lyseun this young *eijo* in the sinister black harness was just another in the series of armoured young men who came with various reasons to take her husband from her side. Lyseun hated them all, for she could see the day when only the young man would return, making some insincere noise of grief about her husband, and then she would be left all alone. She had begged Dewan to stop taking risks and settle down, so he had eventually learned the practice of Alban law. And now here he was with another ice-eyed warrior at his heels, excuses on his lips and that old, familiar inability to look her in the face.

Neither Aldric nor Kyrin liked that room, even though Lady Ewise was a kind and gentle woman who did her best to make them feel at ease. The air was as taut and tingling as an overstretched harpstring, and just as likely to snap with painful consequences. They were both grateful when a servant offered to show them to their rooms.

*

Charcoal-burners stood at apparent random across the peak of Dunrath-hold's great donjon tower, while Kalarr cu Ruruc joined them together with lines of chalk drawn with the aid of a diagram. When he had finished he stood back with a grunt of satisfaction and surveyed his handiwork. The chalk-marks writhed with such complexity that in places they seemed to sink into the stone floor or vanish up into the night sky. Incense-laden censers fumed above certain angles, bowls of clear water rested on others.

"Now," muttered Kalarr, dusting his hands. He laid a heavy book on a lectern and thumbed through the pages until he found the one he had marked with a strip of ribbon, then read the spell through once in silence, his lips moving as they worked out words more outlandish than usual. At last he cleared his throat and pronounced the Summoning aloud.

The charcoal-burners ignited by themselves with small flurries of sparks, and the water started to steam and bubble. A breeze came whining out of the still, silent night and whipped the incense smoke into grey threads whirling across the floor. They spun together, crossing and recrossing until they had woven a great inverted cone which seemed almost solid in the faint starlight. The air throbbed, fluctuating between cold and sticky heat. A glow sprang into being within the shroud of smoke and the charcoal-burners roared as all their fuel was consumed in a single burst of heat that Duergar felt at the far side of the tower. From within the cone he could hear a sound like something huge, shifting and breathing. Then it split from base to apex, spilling out an amber light which made the stars grow dim.

Kalarr stepped forward with his shadow stretching out long

and black behind him and raised both hands in a gesture of invitation. He voiced a soft, ululating call and the being in the cloud emerged.

It hung above the magical symbols on motionless wings, black scimitars like those of a swift but thirty yards from tip to tip. The thing's breath moaned through great vents where the wing-roots joined its bulging triangular body, vents guarded by sweeping arcs which resembled horns and yet, growing from its shoulders, were no such thing. The head was vaguely like a wasp's both in shape and in the positioning of two bulbous yellow eyes; but no wasp ever possessed eyelids, even lids which closed horizontally. The nightmare was completed by twenty feet of whiplash tail writhing with boneless flexibility behind it.

"An isghun," breathed Duergar in horror. Kalarr nodded, then spoke to the creature in a rapid monotone of inhuman syllables. "An isghun," the Drusalan repeated. "You're insane! You don't know what you're doing . . ."

"I do—and I also know the Masterword which controls these things." Otherwise no man in his right mind would have gone anywhere near the being, and Duergar had no intention of approaching it even now.

He shrank back against the cold stones as the isghun drifted lower. Though he could not hear what reply it made to Kalarr's words, he felt the air vibrating with the cadences of its speech and wondered what it might be saying. The baleful eyes closed to vertical phosphorescent slits and then winked out as their owner slept. Even then its body did not settle on the floor but remained suspended, immobile on those rigidly outstretched wings.

"You call this a game?" Duergar demanded after an apprehensive glance towards the vast, hovering bulk. "Then, my friend and sworn ally, you'll not face me across a board. Your play is far too rough."

"Rough? An isghun, rough?" Kalarr spat the words contemptuously. "If the boy had stayed landbound I'd have given you cause to think my play was rough—I'd have summoned up a shri."

"A . . . shri?" Duergar whispered, his face turning the colour of meal. The necromancer's voice trembled. "You dare to even think . . . You *are* mad!"

Kalarr smiled: a slow, infinitely cruel smile. "Perhaps I am. Drusalan. Perhaps I am."

*

Kyrin had watched Aldric's first archery lesson under ar Korentin's tuition for only a few minutes before walking away. She felt genuinely sorry for him as the echoes of Dewan's parade-ground bellow followed her from the butts. When next she saw the young *eijo*, late that evening, he was sour-tempered, sore-fingered and very poor company, although he brightened considerably when she caught his eye with a sympathetic smile—until Dewan's voice cut across the general dinner-table chatter. "You're getting better, Aldric-*an*," he said kindly enough. "Another full day of shooting and you'll be almost quite good." Though Aldric laughed dutifully, Kyrin could see his heart was not really in it.

The following night he was not at table and Kyrin retired earlier than was usual for her. When she reached her room the windows had been shuttered, the lamps lit and the thick down quilt on her bed turned back. The Valhollan girl smiled; if this was how high-clan Albans lived, she approved wholeheartedly. Kicking off her boots, she dropped them with a muffled double thud onto the thick rug, then poked at the scuffed doeskin with her foot.

"Hardly ladylike," she mused, then lifted the *estoc* from its harness across her back. The sword rattled faintly and she stared at the giltwork on its hilt before tossing the weapon into a corner. "Not ladylike at all," she decided; then her eyes strayed to the wardrobes set into the bedroom walls and speculation gleamed in their blue depths. Five Kyrins blinked at her from under five fringes of tousled pale-blonde hair and wiggled their bare toes in five rugs, all reflected in the mirror-faced doors. She had already looked inside them, of course, but the garments within had been so fine and delicate that she had not dared to touch them.

"And why not?" she said aloud. Sliding one wardrobe open, Kyrin gazed longingly at the peacock fabrics. Silk, satin and velvet rustled seductively as she ran her fingers through them and then pulled one gown free, with a guilty glance at the bedroom door as she did so. It stayed shut, and she slithered hastily out of her everyday clothes before draping herself in the sendal over-robe. It was clinging, soft and heavy, pure snowfall white shot through with rainbow lustres which shimmered as she moved. Kyrin neither knew nor cared that it was meant to be worn over a contrasting mantle, but luxuriated in the sensuous feel of the stuff against her skin, twisting and turning before the mirrors in what was almost a graceful dance.

"You look very well," said Aldric softly. Kyrin spun, one hand flying to cover her mouth. The *eijo* smiled, but remained where he lounged elegantly in the doorway. She recoverd quickly and nodded at his compliment.

"I'd almost forgotten I was a woman," she explained shyly.

"I never have," he replied with the beginnings of gallantry, then shook his head as if to clear it of a momentary dizziness. "Kyrin, what I . . . what I came to tell you was that the ship sails tomorrow. It's one of Rynert's fleet and he says—asked me to tell you—that he'll put another vessel at your disposal if you wish to go home."

"And you want me to go . . . ?"

"Light of Heaven, no! That is . . . it's your choice now. You don't have to keep following me to find your passage back. Unless you want to . . ."

"What do *you* want?" she responded. Aldric blinked rapidly, swallowed down a dry throat and avoided Kyrin's steady gaze. "Tell me, Alban."

He was unprotected; out of armour and not even wearing the sinister black which had been his unfailing custom until now. Instead he was dressed simply in a white shirt nipped at the waist by a belt to hold his *tsepan*, and blue boots and breeches worked with silver along the seams. There was a clean-scrubbed look about his face which, when the scar was not visible and his haunted eyes were shadowed, made him seem almost innocent. The pinkness of his skin did not come from washing, however—more from embarrassment.

"I . . . want you to stay. Not just stay here, but stay close to me. Please . . ." He drew in a deep breath and in that instant Kyrin realised just how very scared he was. Her half-formed smile evaporated in case he thought it mocked him, to be replaced by a solemn expression more in keeping with the moment.

"You aren't real, Aldric. Not enough for this harsh world. Keep it that way if you can," she said, then leaned over and kissed him gently on the mouth.

"Kyrin, I—" he began to say. Then he dismissed the words and put his arms around her. Kyrin's lips parted under his and he felt the intimate touch of her tongue entering his mouth, exploring. Her breath, her hair, her body all smelt bright and sweet, like apples in sunlight, warm and firm and curved. As his head bent forward, mouth opening over the soft hollows of her throat, Aldric closed his arms gently, drawing her tight against his chest and the pounding heart within.

*

They lay silent for a long time, arms entwined, still, peaceful and content merely to be together. Then Aldric rolled slightly and raised his head to look at her, fingertips delicately caressing the curve of one breast. She opened sleepy eyes and watched the silver at his throat glinting in the lamplight. "Did I hurt you?" he whispered hesitantly. Kyrin smiled at his concern, stroking the dark hair on his chest as she might have stroked a cat.

"No. Don't worry. I . . . I wasn't a virgin." She felt his silent laughter against her cheek. "What's so funny?"

"Because I was!"

"You were . . . ?"

"Yes. Thank you." He kissed the palm of her hand; but there was something in his voice she did not care for and she sat up in order to see his eyes. They were hooded, languorous and as she leaned closer something flickered in the jade-green depths. An instant later it was masked by his long lashes, but Kyrin breathed out very slowly through her nose.

"Aldric . . . don't get involved. It won't work." She cupped his face in both hands and kissed him lightly on the forehead, smiling at her own restraint. "You can stop pretending to sleep."

His eyes snapped open. "What won't work?" She could feel the words growling low in his throat.

"Anything between us. Behind that cynical mask you're a romantic, Aldric-*ain*. I'm a realist—and a foreigner." Kyrin felt a spasm of something—anger perhaps, or awareness of what she meant—tense the *eijo*'s muscles. "You can't fight tradition with a sword."

"Oh no . . . ?"

"No. Because you're an Alban *kailin-eir, ilauem-arluth* Talvalin, heir to lands and ranks and titles."

"What the hell difference does that make?" His voice was quiet, but it thrummed with controlled rage for all its softness.

Kyrin laid one finger across his lips to still whatever outburst was building up behind them. "Enough," she said.

"But your father Harek—you called him *ur'lim*. That means 'lord'."

"It means 'chieftain'," Kyrin corrected flatly. "He can reckon his lineage back for six generations. Two hundred years. He's very proud of that. How far does your clan go back, Aldric?" The question seemed artless.

His mouth opened and then closed again over clenched teeth as he realised the true significance of what she had asked him. Six generations—two centuries perhaps. But there had been *yrloethen* Taelvallyn, the brothers Shar and Hachen, with the Horse Lords almost two thousand years ago. More than fifty generations past. His Elthanek ancestors went beyond even that into an age almost impossible to comprehend, where written records mingled with stories and legends until they were no longer told apart. Aldric turned his head away, mind reeling under the weight of uncounted years.

"It goes back . . . far too long," he answered thickly.

"You see. What does a line of six chiefs count for now?"

"It counts. I'd make sure it counts."

"Don't be foolish, Aldric." She lay back and their fingers

slid apart. "Hush now. You and I have said enough. Go to sleep."

Although she slept almost at once, Aldric stayed propped on one elbow and wide awake for a long time. The creases of a frown smoothed from his face eventually and a thin, wistful smile took its place. Very, very gently he touched her white-blonde hair, letting each silken strand drift across his honourably scarred left hand. "Perhaps you're right," he murmured, drawing the quilt up and across them both. "And perhaps I am. Perhaps . . ." Curling up close to Kyrin's warm body, he looped one arm tenderly about her waist, then closed his eyes and slept like a child.

*

The vessel, *En Sohra*, was an Elherran galion, a big, burly ship with a complicated rigging. Her crew were also Elherran, folk of a trading nation which had so far kept its balance on the tightrope of neutrality, and while they looked askance at Kyrin—disapproving perhaps of her wearing men's clothing—they made no open protest.

The galion was towed early into deep water and was well under way by mid-morning, bowling along down the Narrow Sea before a stiff north-easterly breeze. Though her cargo of roofing-lead ballasted the ship and made her ride low and steady, Aldric was unsure whether he liked sailing very much. Not that he was sick . . . just not terribly interested in food.

The queasiness lasted only for a day or so and once he recovered and learned to cope with the rolling deck, he and Kyrin spent much of their time on the poop, screened from prying eyes by sails and rails and cabin. Dewan, who by his profession noticed things, found the way they were always holding hands rather amusing, in an innocently romantic way—but he remained, for a foreigner, honourably discreet.

For the first two days of open sea they encountered nothing but several fishing dories and the usual circling gulls; but on the third morning breakfast in the great cabin was interrupted by a yell from the lookout, in tones of such urgency that the meal was abandoned without a second thought. With her sails taut and filled by the wind whistling in over her stern rail, the galion was making excellent speed, but breaking the grey horizon on the port quarter was a sail.

"What is it?" Dewan demanded when he reached the poopdeck. Somebody passed him a long-glass and he stared through it long and hard, but no matter how much he hoped the image would change his first impression remained the same. The sail was red.

"Well?" asked Aldric, squinting a little in what promised to be a bright, clear day.

"Red sail," the Vreijek said shortly. "That means the Imperial Fleet."

"There's always the possibility it's just a merchant captain who likes the colour red," suggested Kyrin hopefully.

Dewan favoured her with a withering glance. "Maybe so . . . but given the price of that red dye, I wouldn't bank on it."

Within an hour the other vessel was running slightly astern, close enough for them to see an occasional flash from her deck as someone turned a long-glass on the scudding galion. She was a warship; that much was all too clear. What remained obscure was why, no matter what manoeuvres she executed, only her masthead pennants shifted to match the changing wind; both big sails remained square-set and full.

The Drusalan ship was armoured; sheets of steel covered her upperworks and hull almost to the waterline, and by now even unaided eyes could discern where seven turrets rose from her main deck and her bow. The mainsail was vivid red and displayed the Emperor's silver star-with-streamers, but the black sprit-sail bore a white-outlined four-pointed star: the Grand Warlord's badge. A long ram broke surface now and then, although the ship was no galley; the rakish sides towering above *En Sohra* were smooth, unbroken by ports or oarlocks. Still the galion retained her lead.

Then the impossible happened. Under full sail, with no more room on her yards for even a silken kerchief, the warship accelerated. A white bone of foam surged up between the teeth of her ramming gear and in a matter of minutes she scythed past *En Sohra* in a hiss of broken water. The galion's people could hear a clang of gongs sounding battle-stations and then a voice amplified and distorted by a speaking-trumpet. "This is the Imperial Battleram *Aalkhorst*!" it blared. "Heave to and prepare to be boarded!"

Leaning over the galion's waist-rail, Kyrin glanced up at an outburst of sharp words on the quarterdeck above her. Aldric had given orders to *En Sohra*'s master which the sailor seemed reluctant to obey; then the *eijo* put one hand to his *taiken*'s hilt and the captain hastily did as he was told, addressing a string of Elherran to his helmsman. Kyrin knew only two words: "turn" and "run". Consequently she was one of the few people not taken by surprise when the galion heeled over and away from the battleram. Her clumsy-looking lugsails allowed her to sail closer to the wind than almost any other rig, and by rights the big Imperial ship would now be reduced to sluggish tacking. In theory.

Aalkhorst's steersman had not been watching as closely as he should have been, for the warship stayed on course for almost three ship-lengths—in her case a considerable distance—before anything happened. Then she leaned over in a skidding, gunwale-submerged turn which brought her head straight into wind. There her sails should have gone slack and useless—but after a momentary flap they bellied out, ignoring the wind of the world. Then she came boring in at them, faster even than the first incredible dash which had brought her level. For a terrifying instant the spikes of the black star reared high above *En Sohra*'s stern lanterns, and the ram slopped cold brine across the galion's deck as it lifted on the swell and then came crashing back in a shower of spray.

Sliding back into place on the starboard beam, *Aalkhorst* blanketed the merchantman's sails so that they hung limp and her pace faltered. Two of the armoured cupolas on her portside revolved until their shuttered slots faced *En Sohra*, and then the shutters snapped open. Across the narrow strip of salt water Aldric heard a crackle of orders in the guttural Drusalan speech, just before ar Korentin grabbed his arm and jerked him under cover.

There was a clatter and the deck where he had stood sprouted catapult bolts and splinters of chewed-up planking.

A moment later the galion's master had struck his colours

and lowered his useless sails. Part of the battleram's armour opened and a small boat was winched down into the sea. Shortly afterwards four soldiers in the red-and-green of Imperial marines clambered up *En Sohra*'s boarding ladder, with their officer following at a more dignified pace.

He was tall, lean, his eyes startlingly blue in a face tanned by wind and sun. The man took off his rank-barred helmet and cradled it under one arm, passing a hand over his close-cropped scalp as he studied the damage his salvo had inflicted. Then he called for the captain.

"You disobeyed my direct command," he accused. "Why?"

"I . . . that is, we—" the sailor floundered.

"I ordered it," interrupted Aldric.

The officer's arrogant stare switched to him and one of the man's eyebrows lifted quizzically. "I am *Hautmarin* Doern," he rasped. "Who are you?"

"A . . . mercenary. Between employers—not that it's your affair," the Alban retorted frostily.

Doern laughed at him and swept a pointed gaze over the galion's grimy finery. "Indeed. Not a very successful one, if you have to sail on a tub like this. Why did you run?" He barked the question, hoping to startle an admission from somebody.

"I made some enemies," Aldric drawled smoothly. "Powerful enemies. Using an Imperial warship isn't beyond them. So I took no chances." He turned his back and kicked at a hatch-cover. "But since you're real I suppose you'll want to search the bloody ship, so get on with it. I'll not stand in your way. There's been enough time wasted already."

Kyrin was the only person who saw the glance Dewan exchanged with the galion's master at Aldric's words. With a nasty start she realised there was more to *En Sohra* than either she or the *eijo* had been told. Much more.

Doern missed the by-play, which was just as well. He was studying Aldric as if trying to interpret something from the warrior's expression.

"So," he muttered. "You seem honest enough." He turned to his men, gestured at the hold and issued orders. All four marines went below and by the noise they made carried out a most thorough search. There was a sudden clatter and the enraged neighing of a war-horse; Aldric grinned wickedly at the burst of Drusalan swear-words which followed. Then a marine half-emerged from the deck gratings and said something which brought Doern across the planks in two noisy strides. When he straightened there was a helmet like his own dangling by its chinstrap from one outstretched hand. "Whose is this?" he demanded in a low, dangerous voice. *"Whose?"*

"Mine," said Dewan.

The *hautmarin* glowered at him. "There is a full harness down there," he grated. "Our cavalry pattern. Where did *you* get it?"

"As standard issue," ar Korentin replied crisply, lapsing into fluent Drusalan, "when I served with the Bodyguard in Drakkesborg." He paused just long enough for his words to sink in, then went for the kill. "Holding *eldheisart* rank."

The pine deck boomed as all five Imperial soldiers crashed to attention. "My apologies, lord-commander," muttered Doern. "You should have made yourself known at once."

Ar Korentin cleared his throat but said nothing, letting them stew for a little by taking a short walk around the deck. The *hautmarin* and his marines stayed where they were, heels together and eyes straight ahead. Thus they missed the small wink which Dewan directed at Aldric and *En Sohra*'s captain.

"*Hautmarin* . . . Doern, wasn't it?" said the Vreijek at length, not looking round. "I didn't . . . make myself known to you at all. There was no Imperial armour aboard this vessel. You encountered nothing out of the ordinary." He strode up to the officer and stared at him. "Do I make myself perfectly clear, *hautmarin*?"

"Sir!" Doern slammed once through the rhythmic sequence of a full salute and then looked through ar Korentin as if he was not there. "Re-embark!" he ordered. "There's no contraband here. Good day to you, shipmaster."

"One question only, *hautmarin*," Dewan said quietly. "Doing . . . what I do, I hear little news from home. How can your ship sail against the wind?"

Doern glanced sideways. "I shouldn't tell even you, sir, but—call it an exchange of confidences. Grand Warlord Etzel paid a sorcerer to lay enchantment on the *Aalkhorst*—to charm a witch-wind into the sails. We can go where we please. But—but I don't like it, sir; magic's been proscribed for years and now to make so free with it . . . Something's wrong.''

"Hautmarin," Dewan cautioned, "I didn't hear you say that. And don't let—" His insincerities broke off as Kyrin shouted, pointing at the sky. She had whiled away a conversation which she could not understand by peering through a long-glass at whatever caught her attention. One such distant speck had seemed to be a gull at first, but closer scrutiny and her own suspicions revealed it to be nothing of the sort. Crossing the quarterdeck in two long strides, Aldric seized the glass and raised it to his eye, then flinched visibly and muttered something savage under his breath. "What the hell is *that*?" he heard ar Korentin gasp.

Aldric's mouth was dry and he could taste the acrid bitterness of fear under his tongue. So soon after Esel, he thought, and felt an ill-suppressed shiver crawl along his spine. "I can't give you a name," he answered very softly, "but I think it's looking for . . ." His voice was drowned by a thin whistling shriek of exhalation as the isghun passed high overhead, and *En Sohra*'s deck blinked dark as vast wings slid across the sun. The spellbeast turned, spiralling on one wingtip with heavy, ominous grace, and came back low and fast.

It skimmed past the galion's portside just above the waves, the banshee scream of its breath slapping back from whirling disturbed water in its wake, and for just an instant Aldric met the demon's eyes. The force of that unhuman gaze was like a blow and, horribly, there was recognition in it. Then the isghun was gone, soaring into the hard blue sky while the storm-wind of its passage flailed across both ships.

Aldric laid one hand to *taiken*-hilt, sickly aware of how small both he and Widowmaker were beside the monster's bulk. He was conscious too of other things; of how the hand had trembled before he clenched it tight, of how wind-blown hair and clothing stuck to skin already chilled by sweat, of how he felt more alone than ever in his life. And more afraid.

Esel had at least been manlike and familiar, no matter what his shape concealed. But *this* . . .

The *eijo*'s last rational thought was one of disbelief that anything so big could move so fast, as the isghun swept around and dived like a falcon on a mouse. Then he flung himself clear of the quarterdeck. A shadow flashed across *En Sohra* and there was a rending crash right at his heels which made the galion vibrate from stem to stern. Though he landed heavily and barely kept his balance, Aldric was still able to glance up in time to see what might have been his own fate.

The isghun's tail had whiplashed round the companion-ladder where he had been standing and had wrenched it clean out of the deck without apparent effort. Emitting a deep, disgusted grunt, it let the false catch drop more than three hundred feet in a slow end-over-end tumble until the stairway smashed to matchwood against *Aalkhorst*'s armoured stern.

Aldric could hear the sonorous howl as air pumped through great vents in the creature's wings, driven by rippling contractions of muscle to thrust it forward. Its mode of flight gave his racing mind a clue to what might well prove weakness. If only he was able to—

It broke off its lazy circuit of the ship and plunged straight towards him, body rearing high so that its tail was free to clutch. But the tail did not even come close. Over-eager, perhaps impatient, straining to reach its victim, the isghun slammed into *En Sohra*'s mainmast with an impact that sprang timbers all over the merchant vessel and then slewed across the deck fighting to stay airborne. As its hideous head came lurching closer Aldric yelped, rolling aside and upright. Isileth Widowmaker blurred out of her scabbard.

Behind the spellbeast sailors lunged with boarding-pikes, only to be hurled aside by its thrashing tail. An arrow ripped through its wing and acid-smelling fluid spurted out of the wound. More missiles drove into its body, penetrating with an ease that betrayed the monster's fragile flesh, if flesh it was. Suction dragged at Aldric's body as air rushed into the isghun, expanding its body even as he watched; none was released and, guessing what was about to happen, the *eijo* gripped something solid and held on tightly.

Muscles contracted, fleshy valves snapped open and what air the demon had drawn in came shrieking out, blasting its body upwards and hurling three men overboard. Aldric, though unsteady on his feet, was not one of them. He slashed Widowmaker deep into the swollen belly passing just above his head.

A bellow of agony all but deafened him and the isghun lurched uncontrollably sideways as half its body underwent a violent deflation. Then it struggled skywards and Aldric cried out in shock, for the demon's tail had looped around his legs and he went up as well. Somebody shouted incoherently in panic. Himself? The brutal grip was crushing both his knees and as he was jerked upside-down his shoulders crashed first against the deck and then against *En Sohra*'s sterncastle. It was impossible to use the *taiken* now, because his legs and the isghun's tail were so entangled that to cut one would almost certainly wound the other. Unless . . . Aldric closed both hands around his longsword's hilt; the loss of a foot was preferable to what Kalarr and Duergar had in store for him.

The inverted deck jumped up as he abruptly dropped towards it, but his only pain was in the skull he cracked on landing. A length of severed tail uncoiled from his kicking legs, the vinegary stench of isghun blood was in his nostrils and it was dripping from Kyrin's sword-blade as she clattered down the remaining stairway from the quarterdeck. If my face is as white as hers . . . Aldric thought grimly, somehow dredging up a feeble smile of thanks. "Where is it now?" he demanded, following Kyrin as she ran towards the poop. The girl raised her arm in silence and Aldric knew he had been right about the isghun's vulnerable spot. Injured and unbalanced, it could only fly in sluggish oblique swoops while the *Aalkhorst* closed at flank speed with white water boiling from her prow.

Dewan and *Hautmarin* Doern, bearing crossbows, were both at the starboard rail, and as Aldric drew level with him the Imperial officer clenched his fist and muttered "*Now!*" As if in response the warship loosened a ranging volley; then unleashed a salvo from her forward batteries that made the isghun shudder in mid-air. Right from the start, when only two turrets had been enough to fill *En Sohra*'s deck with darts, Aldric had suspected that the battleram was armed with something out of the ordinary. He was right. Her first three turrets carried quick-firing catapults both wound and triggered by the same geared mechanism; they could shoot as fast as crews could crank them.

With its wings shredded and its body punched full of gaping holes, the isghun fell towards the waiting sea. And just before it struck, it vanished—winked out of existence as if it had never been; although *En Sohra*'s condition gave the lie to that suggestion. Doern watched his battleram swing back towards them and drew a long deep breath before settling his helmet back in place. "That was . . . ?"

"Sent by my enemies, *hautmarin*," Aldric returned unsteadily. He felt very tired. "I told you they were powerful."

"Quite . . ." The officer cleared his throat and spat across the rail. "I know now what I dislike about sorcery. Every hell-damned detail! Good luck to you, mercenary." He swung outboard and down towards his waiting cutter, then paused and looked back. "I fancy you may need it."

The witch-wind filled *Aalkhorst*'s sails and with a rustle of canvas she drew away from the galion before turning leisurely, a wide, arrogant sweep which flaunted her armoured, destructive might to all aboard the merchantman. As she swung onto a parallel course the warship's bow rose and foam creamed from her ram as she came slicing past. A surge of wash made *En Sohra* roll heavily; then the battleram was gone, dwindling towards the horizon at the tip of an arrow-straight wake.

As they began to put their damaged ship to rights, the Elherran crew avoided Aldric, tacitly blaming him for what had happened. The young *eijo* did not care. He slumped down in a quiet corner of the deck, knees drawn up, head resting on his folded arms, weak and shaking with reaction. Kyrin sat crosslegged beside him, polishing her sword. "Aldric-*ain*," she said, "there's something odd about this ship."

Aldric glanced at her and grimaced slightly. "It's not the ship," he muttered, reluctant to talk. "And it's not my business."

"I think it is." She told him briefly of the look she had seen pass between the captain and ar Korentin, and of its circumstances. Aldric realised that the girl was right: this affair had become his business.

Dewan was not disturbed by the interrogation which followed; he was more surprised by the Alban's calm, not knowing that its source was simply weariness. Aldric was too exhausted to be angry. "It isn't that we didn't trust you," ar Korentin told him, "but the fewer who know of this, the better." Aldric settled back into the captain's chair and let the Vreijek talk. "Your ignorance meant that you told Doern the truth—as you knew it. And he was convinced. He didn't really expect to find anything aboard, much less the gold we—"

"Gold . . . ? What gold?" There was an edge to Aldric's voice that Dewan disliked and he chose his words more carefully.

"To finance another thorn in Warlord Etzel's side. Just as he financed Duergar Vathach."

The *eijo* stared at him, his grey-green eyes devoid of all expression. "Ignorance," Aldric repeated, as if tasting the word. A faint smile twitched his mouth. "You are a devious bastard." Dewan acknowledged the compliment with a slight bow.

"One of my varied talents," he retorted blandly.

Down on deck Kyrin listened, appreciating the trick. Then she stiffened and gripped her *estoc*'s hilt more firmly. There was a soft fluttering noise behind her—and its source was moving. The girl half-turned and bared her teeth disgustedly at the ball of jelly hovering on small wings beside the rail. Without thinking she chopped the thing in two and watched the pieces drop into the sea; then, very carefully, began to clean her sword again.

*

Kalarr jerked back from his magic mirror and spat an oath. "Bitch!" he finished with feeling.

"You've lost them now," Duergar pointed out unkindly. "What will you do?"

"We," Kalarr emphasised the plural, "will wait. He'll

come back. For you, if nothing else." The Drusalan flinched, but Kalarr still knew he had lost face. Rising suddenly, the sorcerer turned to Baiart who was watching from the shadows by the door. "You said one was the king's man. Do you know what that means?" The clan-lord shook his head. "It means, my friend"—and that word dripped vitriol—"that your brother has been speaking to King Rynert. From now on, you don't go back to Cerdor."

"But—" Baiart started, before he was silenced by a glare from eyes as cold and black as the spaces between the stars.

"You will never leave this citadel again." Kalarr's lips thinned above his teeth. "Not even to go to your own execution. And that, dear Baiart, is final."

SEVEN

Lair of Dragons

Lying on his back, Aldric made complicated patterns from the dappled sunlight reflected on to his cabin ceiling by the sea. As *En Sohra* rose on the slow deep-water swell, golden blotches chased one another across the planking and down a panelled wall. He had woken at sunrise with a feeling that the ship was no longer moving, but lying at anchor in calm water. Even so, at such a time of the morning he had no intention of leaving his bed—or rather, bunk. It was uncomfortable, narrow and hard, with sheets of linen cloth instead of the usual quilt, and not really big enough for two to sleep in. All the same, he and Kyrin had managed fairly well.

She was still draped across him, head cuddled against his shoulder so that he felt the warmth of each tiny, purring breath, their limbs all tangled with each other and the sheets. Moving one hand up the smoothness of her back, Aldric twisted to kiss her gently on the cheek. "Mmm . . . ?" Kyrin ventured drowsily, and the young *eijo* felt her eyelashes flutter against his throat. She stirred a little in the crook of his left arm, almost awake now.

"I love you, Kyrin," he whispered, touching her face with his lips. They were words he knew she did not want to hear, but equally he felt they had to be said. The girl breathed in deeply, raised her head and opened her eyes wide, then she thought better of it and half-closed them again. Aldric realised she had not heard him—and with that heavy-lidded sapphire gaze resting on him, he lacked the courage to repeat himself. Coward, he thought. Or over-gentle gentleman. . . ? "I think

151

we've reached our destination," the Alban ventured in a louder voice.

"Is it morning, or could you put that light out?"

"Morning. Sorry, but I can't do anything about it."

Wriggling experimentally, Kyrin succeeded in working her feet free of the knot of bedclothes and sat up. "You could pull the shutters over," she suggested.

"I could," yawned Aldric, making no attempt to do so. "But since you're now closer to them . . ." Kyrin considered this; then she hit him with a pillow.

Somewhat later, as they dozed in a cooling breeze from the still-unshuttered port, ar Korentin rapped loudly on the door. Being an officer and a gentleman—and no fool—he did not open it, but called, "Breakfast, if you want any," through the timbers. Aldric was fairly sure he heard a muted chuckle as the Vreijek walked away, and tried to calculate just what time it really was. Indecently late even for lovers, he guessed, and with a wry grin swung his feet to the floor.

*

Thanks to the weather they were able to eat on deck under an awning, though Aldric seemed disinterested in his food for once; he spent much of his time leaning over the stern-rail with an untouched cup of something cradled in one hand, staring at the green bulk of Techaur Island. It was certainly worth staring at, especially for someone who had never seen anything bigger than a lake-eyot before. Quite apart from the other things he knew about Techaur, about the Dragonwand . . . and about the dragon.

Most of the island reared sheer out of the water, and there surf crashed ruinously against rocks which jutted from the sea like menacing teeth; but the cove in which the galion lay was protected by cliffs on one side and a sloping headland on the other, with a sweep of gravel beach between. Even so, *En Sohra* tugged now and again at her cable when a current drew oily curves across the surface of the little bay; a shift in the prevailing wind would turn this natural harbour into a scoop for waves which would hurl anything—whether weed, driftwood or ship—in ruin on the fanged rocks. Many of the so-called Thousand Islands earned their title only at low tide, spending the rest of their time awash; covered by an impenetrable shroud of green from the beach to the slopes of its single small peak, Techaur was not one of them. But a visible, tree-clad island could rip the bottom from a ship as easily as any crusted with barnacles and hidden by the sea.

Aldric had watched his destination since starting his meagre breakfast, and liked it no more at the beginning than when he had finished. "Lower a boat, shipmaster," he heard Dewan say behind him, "and tell off some sailors to come with us."

"I will not," the captain answered. Aldric glanced round, half-expecting something of the sort and the captain saw him turn. "No man of mine would go with you to—to that place," he said, as much to Aldric as to Dewan. "Not for all the gold we carry. It is accursed, a haunt of demons. Ask that one"— his finger jabbed at the *eijo*—"if he feels the evil in the air. Ask him! He knows."

Though he could indeed sense something, probably more than the shipmaster would have believed, he had no intention of admitting it. Not after the isghun. Instead he smiled, appearing cool and unconcerned. "Why then did you bring us here, if Techaur is—," Aldric purred the word viciously, knowing how it would sound, "—haunted?"

The sailor's swarthy features darkened at any imputation of cowardice on his part. "I pilot this ship for your king!" he snapped. "He says, bring these three to Techaur Island. He does *not* say, land there yourself. So we will stay on board."

"Then get someone to row us in," Aldric grated, "and we'll wade ashore. That should keep your crew content." The young Alban was unused to having his orders questioned, especially twice by the same man. He began to lose his temper, and the shipmaster made no attempt to help him keep it.

"We stay on board *En Sohra*," he repeated flatly.

Aldric drew in breath and took a step towards the Elherran with one fist clenched; then Kyrin caught her lover's half-raised arm and smiled a little when he turned on her.

"Have you ever rowed a boat?" she enquired pleasantly, refusing to be disturbed by what she saw in Aldric's eyes.

The *eijo* shook his head, slowly, clearing the heat from his brain as much as answering her question.

"Well, I have. So come on."

*

They dragged the little rowboat up the beach and for safety's sake made its painter fast around a boulder before setting off into the undergrowth. Within half-a-dozen strides the sea was lost to sight and almost inaudible through the rustling of leaf-heavy branches and the crackle of dead wood underfoot. Birds were calling somewhere.

"Dewan, is this common on islands?" Aldric wanted to know.

"Depends on the size. I'd say this place is big enough to weather most storms without being drenched in salt water, but even so, I see what you mean."

"It's uncanny, that's what you're saying," Kyrin put in. "Look at those trees; they shouldn't be half that size and you know it."

Dewan made no reply; there was really nothing more to say, because all three were fully aware of the strangeness of this island, made eerie by being subtly half-hidden until they looked for it and then appearing to be all around them.

Once they startled—and were startled by—a sounder of wild pigs, not boar but smaller, patterned with brown-and-buff streaks not altogether unlike common farmyard swine. Dewan saw a pair of goats which he swore had ram's horns, and then Kyrin found the spoor of some animal's feet in soft mud near a stream: feet with paws, not hoofs, which Aldric recognised at once as the pad-marks of a *kourgath,* the same wild lynx-cat which he wore as a crest. Except that this *kourgath* was twice as big as it should have been, easily able to prey now on pigs, goats—or indeed, any human unwary enough to let it get too close. It made them realise that when Aldric had insisted that all three wear armour, he had not done so as a joke. Though the hot, still air made them sweat just as much inside their battle harness, its weight no longer seemed an unnecessary burden.

Abruptly the trees thinned out, revealing a sheer crag which peaked almost a hundred feet above them, naked rock as seamed and fissured as pine-bark, impossible to climb and, by the flaky look of it, dangerous to stand near.

"Where now?" Dewan asked, leaning back to see where the wall of stone went and then glancing at Aldric for an answer. "Up, down or around?"

"Around," the *eijo* said confidently. "There's a way up somewhere, so we'll go . . . this way." As he walked off, Kyrin looked at Dewan. They both had a fair notion that the young Alban was bluffing, though neither was quite sure to what extent.

"Better get after him," said Kyrin after a moment's pause. "He might—just might—know what he's talking about."

"Care to put some money on that?" grinned Dewan. "Say twenty in gold?"

The Valhollan hesitated, listening to Aldric whistling through his teeth, thought for a moment and then nodded. "Make it in silver," she amended carefully.

"Done! But I'd have thought you more confident than that, my dear."

"I am confident—just not *that* confident, or that wealthy even if I was. And I'm not your dear."

Then, quite suddenly, Aldric's whistling stopped.

When they reached the spot, swords drawn, there was no sign of him at all. No blood, no crushed grass, no trace of a struggle—not even somewhere he might have gone "You don't think—" Kyrin began, then jumped backwards with a cry of fright as something black and gleaming heaved out of the turf almost at her feet. Dewan lunged forward and his heavy sword came down with all the Vreijek's muscle behind the cut. It crashed into Aldric's helmet hard enough to cause a shower of sparks, and the *eijo* vanished again without a sound. Kyrin dropped on to hands and knees and peered into the dark hole from which he had appeared and into which he had abruptly been returned. There was a small, anguished groan from deep inside.

"Aldric . . . are you all right?" The Alban's steel-sheathed fingers reappeared and gripped her wrist less gently than she would have liked. Aldric's face was pale under his dented helmet when it came back into view, and he glared at Dewan in a way the Valhollan girl hoped she would never experience. But then, he had good reason to be angry.

"No, my lady," Aldric said between clenched teeth, "I am not all right. I hurt at both ends, thanks to this bloody over-eager fool."

"I nearly split your skull!" barked ar Korentin, hiding his relief with irritation. Aldric stared up at him balefully.

"Must you always state the painfully obvious?" the *eijo* snapped.

"Shut up, the pair of you—this is no place for bickering over accidents." Kyrin's voice cut through their argument and silenced them more through surprise than anything else. "Better!" she said. "Now, what is that hole in the ground anyway?"

"Give me some light and I'll tell you," retorted Aldric, still annoyed and sore. Dewan lit one of the ship's lanterns they had brought, then lowered it into the pit. After only a few minutes Aldric's head reappeared; there was a smile of sorts inside his war-mask. "We go down from here on," he said quietly.

The other lamps were lit, and all three descended out of sight. Nothing moved in the clearing for a while after they had gone, until a small bird landed and began to peck through the soil turned up near the tunnel mouth. Then it looked up, twittered nervously and flew away just as one of the nearby branches rustled, very slightly. Then the branch was slowly pulled aside.

*

Dewan and Kyrin speculated quietly as to who might have made the steps down which they walked. There was no reason to speak in hushed voices, but like a religious house or a funeral crypt, this place discouraged loud talking.

By the sound of ar Korentin's voice, he was feeling uncomfortable, almost frightened, though he concealed it well. Aldric smiled mirthlessly into the darkness; even champions have their weak points, he reflected, not thinking any less of Dewan for proving human after all. Having spent the past three years in just such a subterranean complex, the young *eijo* was more at home than his two companions; even so, after having the sky and sea around him he felt cramped and uneasy, though the passage was unnaturally spacious and dry.

Then he hesitated as a movement of the air stroked his face; it was warm, spicily scented and totally unexpected in a tunnel. Light and shadow danced across the walls as he raised his lantern high. It revealed nothing, but from somewhere impossibly distant he could hear a tinkling like windblown crystal bells, mingled with the sweet chattering clash of finger-cymbals.

"Can you hear it?" whispered Kyrin. Metal scraped as the two men nodded armoured heads. Remote sounds as of flute and strings formed unbidden inside the girl's head, a tenuous thread of melody bringing visions of seductive elegance, of sinuous grace. There was a vague suggestion of amber light rising from far below, growing more clearly defined with every downward step.

"Douse your lanterns," Aldric hissed. As they did so the ruddy glow swelled and brightened much more than the fading lamplight seemed to justify, and they shrank back against the wall, each with a mental image of something searching for them with luminescent fingers. There was a creak of leather and a slithery sound as Aldric released the crossbelt supporting Isileth Widowmaker across his back, letting the *taiken* drop into place on his left hip before moving on down the steps. Though he reached out with every sense, stretching them to their limit, he could detect nothing alarming or hostile; only a barely perceptible feeling of . . . awareness.

Hand on hilt, he eased carefully to the stairway bottom and loosened Widowmaker in her scabbard. The steel-scrape was harsh and jarring against the background of soft musical tones—a stark, unequivocally brutal noise which did much to relieve the curious lassitude which he only noticed as it left him. Then he looked out of the tunnel.

Bales of rich fabric, fine garments, precious metals both raw and exquisitely worked, jewels and crystalline bottles; all were littered carelessly along the walls and around the pillars of a great vaulted hall. Piles of coins formed tempting snow-drifts wherever there was room for them—and there was certainly plenty of room. The whole vast chamber was lit by live flames which spilled from the mouths of dragons carved around each pillar, and by a great orange-red glow which pulsed and shifted at the farther end of the hall. Aldric caught his breath at the unimaginable riches piled here, and at the monstrous magnificence of it all. It was . . . glorious.

"What is this place?" Dewan's voice was gruff and he tried hard to keep it matter-of-fact as befitted a man of his rank and station. Aldric could have told him that rank was no defence against the arrogant splendour of a sorcerous hold like this one, but he could tell just by looking at the Vreijek's face that Dewan had already realised as much.

"This," Aldric said quietly, "is the Cavern of Firedrakes, the lair of Ykraith, the abode of the dragon." Dewan stared at the younger man, then unaccountably felt himself shiver.

Sight, hearing and smell were all dazed in that hall: by the dance of flame on gold; by thin, eerie chords of music; by rare and costly fragrances. Touch and taste begged to be indulged by an insidious compulsion to run fingers through the precious things, to broach the crystal jars which doubtless each held wines of noble vintage. . . . This was not mere avarice, something which might have been expected, but a headier sensuality which amounted almost to a lust. Hands were already reaching out as Aldric remembered the half-forgotten words he had been sifting for at the back of his mind. Gemmel's words, then just one instruction among many but possessed now with a terrible significance: ". . . remember, don't touch anything but the Dragonwand, no matter how tempting . . ."

Against the humming music, Aldric's best modulated voice would have sounded coarse; his incoherent yell of warning rasped hideously. The others jerked as if stabbed by pins and a frightening blankness slowly vanished from their faces. The *eijo* allowed himself a sigh of relief. "I think I said before, don't touch." He made no attempt to hide the tremor in his voice. "Better not, or else . . ." His helmeted head jerked meaningfully at the gaping jaws of carven dragons and at the fires which fumed in each.

Aldric began the long walk down the Cavern all alone, but

before he had completed three strides Kyrin had pattered level with him. He made a gesture which if completed might have been one of dismissal; but then smiled and lowered his hand before its movement was two-thirds finished. From where he stood to the throbbing fiery glow was a long and lonely way, and he was grateful for her company.

Dewan ar Korentin watched them both dispassionately, then leaned his weight slightly on to his scabbarded sword as he had learned to do on parade in Drakkesborg years before. He did not relax, despite the comfortable warmth of the great hall; it was not a place in which any sane man could ever relax.

As they walked closer, both Aldric and Kyrin could see how the cavern ended in a lofty plinth, massive and conical, a flight of steps cut into its side and its whole surface scored with runes and signs of power. The hot, misty glow welled from its peak and splashed reflections of flame-coloured light across the ceiling, countering them with deep, dark shadows on the floor. Then Kyrin seized Aldric's mailed arm in total, terrified silence and pointed towards the deepest swathe of gloom with a trembling finger.

The Alban's eyes dilated and heat-born redness ebbed from a face in which the mouth opened but emitted not even an expulsion of breath. He found his feet were rooted to the spot, making flight impossible even if it was not being pushed from his mind by an overwhelming sense of wonder.

It slept in the darkness around the base of the plinth: hunched, huge, lean, undulant and elegant. A firedrake. A dragon. Its wings were folded along its spiked back, its monstrous head rested on slender claws and a coil of armoured tail wrapped across its nose, giving a momentary image of some colossal cat asleep by the hearth. There was no trace of life anywhere about it; no breathing moved its scaled flanks, none of the legendary smoke drifted from its half-hidden nostrils. Aldric was almost disappointed that all seemed dark and still and dead. He took a single quiet cat-step forward.

Then he laughed, briefly and harshly, with more disgust than mirth in his voice. That step had been enough to reveal a platform underneath the firedrake's body, carved from onyx, agate and lapis lazuli, inset with turquoise and gold. No wonder the creature seemed dead. Statues were often like that. It was metallic, all polished steel and beaten copper, a lifelike, life-size conversation piece which was worth a great deal of money and had, with the pillars, given the Cavern of Firedrakes its name. But . . . "It's not real!" There was more than a little indignation in his voice.

"You mean—you wish it *was* . . .?" Kyrin's voice held simple disbelief.

"I'd half-expected that it would be," the *eijo* responded. "Even so . . ." He was remembering Esel now, and recalling that statues were not always as immobile as they should be. It was several minutes before he risked going any closer to the firedrake and Kyrin stayed where she was.

The creature's body rose to more than twice Aldric's own height and was covered in fine scales like lizard-mail—another uncomfortable reminder of Esel—which were complete in every detail. The unknown sculptor who had made the dragon had been a true artist in every way; he had possessed the imagination to create such a fantastic beast and the skill to portray it with such realism that it could almost have been taken from a live subject. Silently saluting its creator's genius, Aldric turned away from the firedrake and walked back towards the stairs.

Gemmel had told him what ritual he would have to follow, but typically had refused to divulge any explanation of the whys and wherefores. In the old enchanter's opinion Aldric's interest in—and aptitude for—the Art Magic was unhealthy and not to be encouraged. Even so, he had had no choice but to teach the young man certain charms for his own protection; this had been done reluctantly, but as was Gemmel's way, when in the end it became essential it was done thoroughly.

"You'll have to stay here, I'm afraid," he told Kyrin, hiding nervousness with flippancy.

"I'm afraid too—so I'd rather come with you."

Aldric tugged off helm and war-mask, coif and wrapping-scarf, then shook his bared head. "You can't. But Spiny-tail over there will keep you company until I come down again."

He gave the helm to Kyrin, who took it with an air of resignation.

"I've told you this before, Aldric," she said. "Please . . . take care."

The *eijo* nodded, without his usual sardonic smile, and kissed her gently. There were no longer any words which needed saying between them; but in that brief, tender touching was much more than speech could ever convey. Then he turned to face the plinth, drawing Widowmaker and his *tsepan*, and went down on one knee with the weapons raised before him.

"I swear now by the Low and by the High and by the Ancient Powers that this thing which I must do is not my wish or will, nor is it by my choosing, and I call upon these Powers to witness that my oath is true. I, *kailin-eir* Aldric of the Alban clan Talvalin do swear it by the name which is my own and by the blade which guards my honour and by the blade which guards my life."

As he rose the young man sheathed both sword and dirk, then went up the stairs slowly and with dignity—even though his impulse was to run, to get this thing over with as quickly as possible.

The tapering plinth lacked a point, as if it had been neatly sliced away. If Aldric had realised how much it now resembled a volcanic cone, he might have had some inkling of what to expect. As it was, the discovery came as a most unpleasant surprise.

Instead of a flat platform at the top there was only a narrow rim, and beyond that a sheer drop into the hot embrace of a pool of molten rock. It was from this magma lake that the red-gold light came throbbing up, and with it came a shrivelling blast of heat which struck the *eijo* like a blow in the face. The air danced and shimmered, making it hard to distinguish outlines even though something rose dark and dense in the very middle of the burning haze.

When at last he saw what it was, his already-churning stomach cramped savagely and then turned right over with pure, undiluted fear. There was a slender column of granite rising from the centre of the seething crater, its uppermost part carved into the likeness of a warrior in antique armour. Its outstretched stone hands bore a darkly glinting staff.

Aldric recognised the Dragonwand at once . . . but the only way to reach it was by a causeway which ran, without parapet or rail, from the topmost step just at his feet straight to the statue's base. This too was stone, polished to a gleaming, treacherous smoothness—and it was less than a foot in width. Even given such narrowness, the twenty paces out and back would normally have been a matter of little account. But not with another twenty paces to consider: the distance straight down, to where bubbles burst with obscenely hungry belches in the liquid rock. While sweat formed and trickled on his shuddering skin, Aldric closed his eyes and expelled horrific images from the conscious part of his mind.

Heat and awestruck terror had dried his mouth so much that his first attempt to speak was little more than a rasping croak. The Alban's eyes opened, narrowed by concentration and against the glare. He worked his jaws briefly to produce a slight moisture around his tongue and rearmost teeth; it was a paltry effort, but enough. When he tried again, his voice was still hoarse but at least audible now above the gurgling mutter of the earth's hearth-fires. Without feeling self-conscious Aldric raised one arm towards the statue in a full salute, then kept that arm outstretched, hand open and fingers spread apart.

"*Abath arhan*, Ykraith," he said quietly. "*Echuan aiy'yan elhar, arhlath ech'hil alauin.*" He could hear his own heart beating, the sound of his breath and the rush of blood in his ears—but the soft, eternal magma-roar had fallen silent.

And the heat had died away.

Aldric put one booted foot on to the causeway, paused for a downward glance into the furnace maw and then walked quickly to the statue.

Although its hands were tightly closed around the Dragonwand, when Aldric grasped it the stone fingers suddenly relaxed. So suddenly that he took a staggering pace backwards before recovering his balance with a frantic spinal jerk on the very brink of the pit. Flakes of granite crumbled from the edge beneath his heel and were swallowed up.

Aldric's lips stretched thinly over the clenched teeth bared by his grinning snarl. Firelight tinted their enamel a bloody red. Trembling all over, he returned along the narrow bridge, sank down crosslegged on the safety of the plinth's top step and stared at nothing for a long, long time. His racing heartbeat slowed at last to something almost normal and his sodden clothing dried a little, but only when his breath once more was coming slow and deep did he lower his eyes and focus them on the prize which he had won.

It was the height of a man or the length of a good straight spear, heavy, but balancing well in one or both of his hands. Its shaft, so Gemmel had told him in a rare expansive moment, was of the mineral called adamant: a translucent stuff, glinting greeny-black like obsidian glass but shot through with tiny filaments like spun gold. A dragon with scales of greenish gold wrapped its serpentine coils around the shaft, seeming less an inlay of metal than something which had grown from the surface. The dragon's tail, tipped with blued steel, formed the staff's spiked butt, while a green-gold dragon-head with one sapphire eye capped its other end. The empty eye-socket looked less like a hollow from which the stone had been prised loose, than a cavity waiting to be filled for the first time. A flame-shaped crystal, clear as quartz, writhed from the open mouth. It seemed fragile, but when Aldric idly scraped its point across the step under his knees, the delicate-looking substance gouged stone like a chisel in soft wood.

His daydream was interrupted by a piercing scream from Kyrin in the hall below. Springing to his feet with dignity thrown aside, Aldric came down the stairs in clattering bounds of four at a time. Even above the noise of his descent he heard a slithering like a thousand swords all drawn at once.

The firedrake lived!

Aldric jumped the last short distance to the cavern floor and landed with a crash of harness, skidded wildly, steadied himself with the Dragonwand and ran to Kyrin's side.

After that single shocked scream she had reacted more in the way he had expected, and half-crouched now in a defensive stance, her *estoc* drawn and poised. The slender thrusting-sword had always reminded Aldric of a needle, but against such a being as they faced together, it shrank to the merest pin.

Iron coils slid together with a grating sound as the dragon stirred. Iron talons stretched out, clicking on the agate of the platform. An iron eyelid lifted. Aldric wrenched his own eyes away and made sure Kyrin did the same—he had not listened to so many old stories without learning something of the lore concerning firedrakes. One did not meet them stare for stare.

Somehow knowing it was the wisest thing to do, Aldric raised the Dragonwand in both hands. He was painfully aware of how it looked—more a twig than a talisman of power. Then the words came; like those Gemmel had taught him for the Claiming of Ykraith and in the same language— but these were not words he had ever been taught.

"Ymareth!" Scales rang with a steely music and he felt the vast, brooding presence of the dragon leaning over him, an unimaginable intelligence considering him, a shadow like the shadow of death hanging right above him. "Ymareth," he said again, without the first desperation but with more respect; and then a third time. "Ymareth . . . *sachaur arrhath eban Ykraith, aiy'yel echin arhlathal Gemmel pestreyr.*"

The firedrake's movement ceased and Aldric risked an upward glance, sliding his wary gaze across its armoured, eerily beautiful head but always avoiding those pupil-less, glowing amber-green eyes. He wondered about the old tales, especially those in which a dragon spoke. It seemed unlikely now that such a thing had ever happened, faced as he was with the reality of a lipless mouth and thin forked tongue which could never form the sounds of any human language. Yet the firedrake was intelligent—he was sure of that—and had understood whatever he had just said. Which was more than he had done himself.

Then it spoke.

The creature's voice was not loud, but it was huge, a rustling metallic hiss like cymbals brushed with wire. Aldric could never have pronounced the sibilants—at least, he realised with a touch of irony, not without a lipless mouth and a thin forked tongue—but their meaning was somehow clear, in an archaic, formal mode which seemed entirely right and proper.

"I give thee greeting," said the dragon. "I am Ymareth. Know me, and know that I am lord. What do ye here in mine abiding-place?"

Aldric knelt, bowing forward to give the courtesy of Second Obeisance that was due to any lord in his own hall, then sat back on his heels, hiding his pounding heart behind a mask of elaborate high-clan politeness. "I ask a favour, Lord Firedrake," he responded.

"Speak, man," it said, "that I may judge."

The *eijo* gathered his courage and lifted the Dragonwand above his head. "I ask to borrow this talisman, Lord Firedrake."

"Upon what cause?" Ymareth rumbled. Grey smoke curled briefly from its jaws, token that its wakening was complete now, even to its banked and glowing inner fires. "Wherefore desire ye Ykraith only and not the many treasures of mine hoard, Aldric Talvalin?"

A muscle twitched involuntarily in the Alban's face, both at the implications of the smoke and at hearing his name issue from such a throat. Yet the dragon had already given its own name quite freely, proof of a colossal self-assurance which Aldric did not share. Gemmel had told him a little about dragons, a year or so past; it had sounded boring and like a fool he had paid small heed. But one thing he recalled quite clearly. "Firedrakes," the enchanter had said between puffs at his pipe, "are no more wicked than the normal run of people; it's just that their notions of good and evil are . . . well, flexible would describe it best. An over-honest man could be easily deceived—but you, I suspect, would be in little danger." The *eijo* managed a small, sour smile at the memory.

"I have no need of gold, Lord Firedrake," he answered. "But I seek revenge on my enemies, and Ykraith will help me. I ask you for it, and do not touch your treasure, because I am an honest man and not a thief."

Ymareth snorted, so that smoke and a few sparks billowed from its nostrils. Aldric could have sworn the huge old thing was laughing at him and perhaps it was. "O prideful!" hissed the dragon softly. "Do I touch too closely on thy honour? So, and so, and so. Now verily this is true, for were ye not an honest man I should not have spoken, save to taunt thee ere thy most assured death.''

Aldric raised his eyes slightly. As if expecting him to do so, the dragon opened its mouth fractionally. There was no more blatant menace in it than in any panting dog, but the action gave a glimpse of nine-inch fangs, of great cheek-teeth big enough to shear an ox in two—and a slight, almost accidental but certainly deliberate exhalation of yellow-white flame. Though he cringed within himself, Aldric did not move. Ymareth seemed impressed, if such a word had any meaning to it.

"Speak and say, what foes do so concern thee, that fear of my wrath does not deter thee?"

"One is the necromancer Duergar Vathach," Aldric replied, "and the other is Kalarr cu Ruruc."

There was a coughing sound within the firedrake's throat and tongues of flame licked from Ymareth's jaws as its ruffed head shook with amusement. Aldric began to choke as smoke enveloped him, and when it cleared he saw through streaming eyes that the dragon was leaning towards him, mouth agape. He felt the wash of a great hot breath and the icy stab of the fear of death.

Ymareth unleashed no blast of fire, and when Aldric opened his eyes again—carefully avoiding those of the firedrake—he found the creature wore a tongue-lolling grin like that of some vast fox.

"I compliment thee on thy choice of enemies, *kailin-eir* Talvalin, if there was choice at all." The dragon's voice became quiet and deadly. "Cu Ruruc of Ut Ergan is a creeping viper and made essay to dominate me many lives of men ago. He was most wise and cunning, well versed in words of power, but he knew not that Masterword which has governance of dragonkind. Verily it was his great good fortune to get from here alive that day." Aldric heard the susurration of a scaled neck, the bright, ringing clank of a talon laid on the floor and saw the shadow of the dragon's head move as it leaned down to study him more closely. He stared hard at his own gloved hands and tried to ignore the colossal wedge-shaped head which hung less than an arm's length from his own; even then he could feel Ymareth's gaze probing at him, searching for what a firedrake might term falsehood.

"I did hear thee speak the words of swearing and of summoning and of claiming. What of the words to master such as I, *kailin* Talvalin?" The voice reeked of heat, of the clean stench of fire—and of suspicion.

Aldric felt panic welling up inside him; if Ymareth thought for one instant that its own mighty person was in danger, it would obliterate him before he could draw another breath. He took a desperate chance, bowing with proper respect for the dragon's power before raising his head to stare not at, but between Ymareth's eyes. Even then that blank, phosphorescent glare glimpsed only with the edge of sight was enough to set his senses swaying. It required an effort of which Aldric had not known himself capable, not to gape in helpless fascination at the golden orbs and let the peace, the stillness, the terrible tranquillity of the dragon-spell take him where it would, even to walking down the firedrake's throat. He could feel runnels of perspiration tickling his back and taste salt droplets forming on his upper lip. The eyes enticed, but Aldric managed to keep his gaze fixed on Ymareth's crest and let it wander nowhere else.

"Lord Firedrake," he managed at long last, "I have few words of any power, and none that might impose my will on you. The strongest word controls myself alone. It is my Word of Honour, and one I try always to keep—but it is often far from easy."

The spell was withdrawn so abruptly that Aldric cried out like a man in pain and fell forward on to his hands, forehead almost touching the ground. "Those who speak with dragonkind make use of twisted talk and riddles," said the great voice. "Always until now. It is passing strange that thee of all men should be forthright. Take Ykraith, *kailin-eir* Talvalin, and may it give thee power to visit vengeance on thine enemies that they may be consumed with the heat thereof and entirely eaten up. But when all is accomplished, I would have thee and none other bring it back."

Aldric bowed gratefully, extending deliberately now to the full obeisance which he had reached only accidentally before. Ymareth seemed to ignore him; it was coiling up again on the platform where he had first seen it, slow and sinister grace in every movement. Then its head swung to regard him once more. "The Charm of Understanding wearies me, and I would sleep the long sleep once again. Ere then I would tell thee that which may prove of some purpose. If perchance ye should *possess* a thing sought after greatly by cu Ruruc, make pretence of its destruction and await what follows . . ."

The *eijo* had no idea how Ymareth had gained such knowledge, but its advice seemed sound enough: if Kalarr thought the spellstone was destroyed, then he would also think himself free of any challenge to his own ability and might . . . just might . . . do something stupid. Unless what the dragon really meant was . . . Aldric's head began to pound, what with the unremitting heat, the air stiff with enchantments, and the strain of talking to an old, wise, crafty and—hide it how he would—frightening firedrake in awesome full maturity. The convoluted workings of sorcery and dragon-minds were enough to give anyone a headache.

Scales clicked and grated as Ymareth settled on the plinth, and its eyelids slid down to shutter the glow of those terrible hypnotic eyes. At his side Aldric could sense Kyrin stirring; despite his warning she—and probably Dewan who had been too far away to hear him—had looked full at the dragon's gaze and had been snared, subject only to the firedrake's will. If it had bidden them walk up to be devoured, they would have done so without resistance. The smoke-plumes drifting from Ymareth's nostrils ceased as some internal process slaked the fires in its belly. There was a heavy silence.

In the shadows at the entrance of the hall, something glinted as it moved.

*

When the dragon fell asleep Kyrin shivered violently, glanced from the corner of one eye at Aldric, then threw her arms around him and clung there tightly. After only a few minutes she released him and backed away, her glazed sleepy look rapidly becoming one of disbelief as the spell faded and understanding took its place. "Aldric-*ain* . . ." She faltered, glanced at Ymareth and then looked him full in the face. "You were talking to . . . that thing . . . as easily as you talk to me. Who are you? *What* are you?"

"I'm Aldric Talvalin and I'm scared." The *eijo* smiled, a sour twist of thinned lips, but he was not being funny. Under his black metal carapace he was trembling with reaction, and there was something with big, soft wings flapping around the pit of his stomach. "Which I expected to be. And I'm still alive, which I didn't expect at all. Speaking to firedrakes is. . ." he laughed weakly, " . . . rather a strain."

Ar Korentin came sprinting up with a clatter of armour, but when they turned to look at him he slackened his headlong pace and approached more sedately, as befitted a captain-of-guards—even a thoroughly shocked one. His eyes rested briefly on Aldric, then slid past him to the dragon. The *eijo* could tell there were many questions dammed up behind Dewan's impassive features; questions which he would be well advised to answer. But not just yet.

"Are you both all right?" was all the Vreijek asked, and Aldric nodded.

"Yourself?" he returned.

"Well enough," said Dewan, shrugging off the languorous heaviness in his limbs as unimportant, and showing some teeth in what should have been a grin but fell rather short of the mark. "Though I have felt better."

"So have I," Aldric conceded. Laying the Dragonwand carefully by his feet, he wrapped head and chin in the heavy silk scarf he had taken off earlier, then settled the comforting weight of coif, mask and helmet over its padding and laced them in place. As he straightened with Ykraith in both hands, he saw ar Korentin watching him thoughtfully. Aldric's mouth twitched into a little smile. " 'In strange places, when all seems still—look to your armour,' " he quoted. "I've got what I came for. Let us leave."

They walked up the hall together, with that strange attraction of the treasure still tugging at them—but after having seen its guardian, resisting the urge to steal was easy. Even though hidden now by shadows at the far end of the Cavern, Ymareth's ominous bulk was an ever-present deterrent.

Perhaps his senses had been dulled by the proximity of the firedrake's spell-binding gaze, perhaps his mental faculties were not operating fully in this place of sorcery. For whatever reason, when two swordsmen sprang at him from the stairs Aldric was taken completely by surprise.

Unbalanced, he could not sidestep the nearest man fast enough, and like most *kailinin* he seldom carried a shield when out of the saddle. But he reacted with the speed of training that had become almost a reflex action, blocking the closer cut with the only thing to hand—the Dragonwand. As the sword came slashing down on to his head he flung Ykraith up, braced like a spearshaft in a wide double grip. Steel and glassy adamant met with a harsh belling clang and sparks flew. Splinters also, as the sword-blade shattered.

Aldric twisted at the waist and lunged towards his second enemy with the long, sharp crystal tip, using only his right hand—lower down the staff—to give a longer reach. It was an old trick of straight-spear fighting.

Like so many old tricks, it worked. Ykraith's crystal flame and its dragonhead slammed into the swordsman's throat just where neck joined collarbone, tore through everything in their path and burst from his spine with sufficient force to nail him to the wall. With his neck uncleanly but completely snapped, the man was dead almost before he knew that something was wrong.

Long before that Aldric had released the Dragonwand. His left hand had already freed Widowmaker's safety-collar from her scabbard's mouth and tilted the longsword's hilt forward. His right hand crossed, gripped and drew.

Dewan had already noticed how fast the young *eijo* could move, but he was two hundred years too young to have seen this form of draw before. And his eyes were hardly fast enough to see it now.

With a bright, brief *sring* Isileth blurred from her scabbard in an arc of light. Dewan heard a noise, a thud blended with a moist, ripping crunch; and then Aldric's arm was fully extended after its horizontal sweep, the longsword gleaming in a hand which had been empty one-eighth of a second before. There was a dark, wet smear on the last six inches of its blade. Aldric whirled the *taiken* up behind his head, left hand joining right prior to a vertical cut. It was not needed.

The Alban's opponent made a wheezing sound, not from his mouth but from his chest, and his eyes glistened white as they rolled up and back. Though the man wore a bullhide jerkin, *taikenin* in hands little stronger than Aldric's had cloven armour. Mere human bodies were no obstacle. Isileth's backhand cut had sliced through breastbone, heart and lungs, and as the man collapsed a bubbling spew of blood erupted from his gaping ribcage. Both legs kicked in random jerks and then, as the body accepted it was dead, they quivered and were still.

From beginning to end the thing had taken seven seconds.

With a slow, sweeping movement, Aldric brought the poised longsword over and down into a posture of readiness and drew in a deep, rather shaky breath. The breath whispered softly out between his parted lips as he relaxed, then stepped back, fastidiously avoiding the mess which oozed across the floor. Light and shadow moved within the trefoil opening of his war-mask as he turned his head away. There were spots and trickles of blood on his face, but no emotion; it was cold, immobile as if graven of grey metal, with a flawed imperfection scarring one cheek under the curved black armour.

Kyrin stared at his dispassionate features and an over-whelming sense of unreality filled her mind. This was not the Aldric she knew, the one who smiled and had gentle hands. This *eijo*'s face was that of a stranger who had felt no tenderness in all his life. Her Aldric would not have . . . Would not have done what he had just done without showing some trace of feeling.

Then she met his eyes and saw the pain in their grey-green depths. Aldric was skilled in the art of *taiken-ulleth* and would kill without hesitation. But not without reason. And not without remorse. Not yet.

Dewan, perhaps unfairly, had seen nothing of that brief, wordless exchange; he was impressed merely by the speed and near-surgical precision of Aldric's fighting style. He was not an Alban. "Who were they?" he wondered, half to himself.

Widowmaker, cleansed and sated, hissed softly like an angry cat as she slid down into her scabbard. She had tasted human blood again, for the first time in three centuries and her thirst was quenched once more. Until the next time. Kyrin remembered all the stories she had heard of Alban named-blades and remembered, too, the sense of icy menace she had felt on the only occasion she had drawn the star-steel sword herself. Then she had been unsure of the feeling's source; now she was quite certain. Yet the *taiken* was not evil in itself, no more than men or dragons were—but it had been forged and named with one purpose in mind, and though she could not blame either Aldric or his blade, it did seem that Isileth Widowmaker fulfilled that purpose all too eagerly.

The young *eijo* jerked Ykraith from the stone wall, lowered his second victim to the ground, then eased the Dragonwand's deadly crystal point out of the corpse's neck and brought it round for cleaning. He blinked; the talisman was unblemished by any trace of blood, as if the fluid had refused to touch its surface. Or had been absorbed.

"I said, who were they?" ar Korentin repeated, more loudly than before.

"Your guess is—" Aldric began; then his eyes narrowed and he jumped almost six feet backwards from the entrance to the stairway, Ykraith tucked spearwise close into his right hip. That sixth sense of his had begun to operate again, like a lantern being unshuttered—and not before time, he thought viciously. It was weak, a premonition, a mental tickle rather than the usual full-throated yell of alarm, but it was undoubtedly there. The scuff of his soft-soled boots and the faint rustle of his armour sounded very loud in the stillness his movement had engendered.

Much louder than the suave voice which drifted down the stairs towards him.

"No need to guess, gentlemen," it purred. "They were once my colleagues. Rash fellows both—if I warned them about startling people once, I warned them a thousand times." The voice took on a world-weary, paternal tone. "And now see where such foolishness has brought them. Most regrettable . . .''

The speaker sauntered into view; he was a tall, thin, wolfish man with an overly-precise moustache which looked as painted as a woman's brows, dark, roguish curls rather at variance with the predatory gleam in his grey eyes and a solitary pearl-drop in the lobe of his right ear. His clothes were equally dashing—black breeches with silver medallions down the outer seams, glossy boots worked with gold around their fringed tops, a fine white shirt and a blue coat over all, worked with more gold and embroidery, caught at the waist by a scarlet sash through which were thrust two curved shortswords and a fancifully carved *telek*. It was this individual's stylish—if eccentric—mode of dress which told Dewan what, if not who, he was.

"Pirate," the Vreijek growled, putting all the distaste a king's officer could summon up into that one word.

A flicker of annoyance crossed the other's saturnine face and his lazy smile became momentarily somewhat stretched. "You're over-blunt, my friend," he reproved. "That is not a word I like. I prefer to regard myself as an adventurous businessman, a dealer in the transfer of expensive commodities." He smiled broadly and snapped his fingers. "Now *these* are pirates."

Feet clattered on the stairs and seven more intruders joined the first. They were a motley group, ill-favoured and villainous; some, in ill-fitting and ragged finery, tried to ape their leader's romantic attire, but without taking his painstaking care succeeded only in looking faintly ridiculous—although neither Aldric nor his companions felt like laughing at the spectacle. The remainder dressed—or to judge by the amount of scarred, weatherbeaten flesh on view, did not dress—much as the fancy took them, in leather war-harness and furs, or in grubby jerkins and pieces of cast-off armour. Their threatening growls and curses fell to silence as they saw the heaps of treasure strewn about the Cavern of Firedrakes.

Aldric paid them no heed, apart from the germ of an idea in which Ymareth the dragon played a leading role. His attention was focused on their lord, chieftain, captain or

whatever he chose to call himself—and the pirate's attention
was focused on Tehal Kyrin. Any Valhollan woman could
take care of her own virtue, as the *eijo* knew quite well—
Kyrin perhaps better than most—but he was still a *kailin-eir*
and honour was still something to be upheld.

"Gentlemen, and of course the lovely lady," the pirate
murmured in a caressing voice calculated to provoke, "let me
explain this delicate situation. Techaur Island is our . . .
cashbox, if you like, where we deposit the profits from our
various . . . transactions. In such circumstances you must see
that your presence here is less than welcome. Apart, of
course, from you, my dear." He bowed elaborately to Kyrin
who, Aldric was pleased to see, failed to appreciate his
courtesy.

"I am not your dear," she snapped, drawing her *estoc* for
emphasis.

"For the moment," returned the buccaneer, not one whit
deterred by her rejection. "We'll see what more intimate
acquaintance produces. You see, gentlemen, we usually feel
obliged to execute trespassers but on this occasion I think a
fine would be more rewarding. The girl and twice her weight
in gold, in exchange for your lives. Agreed?"

"Not agreed." Aldric drove the Dragonwand into the floor
with as much ease as piercing a fresh loaf and left it embedded in the flagstones. "Leave my lady right out of your
calculations, *pirate*. Consider: there are three of us, eight of
you." He was talking now not to the captain but to his
common sailors, those with most to gain and lose from a
good bargain or a hard fight.

"The odds are not good—but enough to ensure somebody
will not live to enjoy whatever the survivors win. All for a
girl. Whereas if your captain leaves his own lechery aside,
you'll all get gold enough to buy the favours of twenty
first-rank courtesans and never a scratch to show for it. So
there's my offer. Gold." Widowmaker sang as she slowly
left her scabbard. "Or steel. And a death I'll make as painful
as my skill allows. Choose."

As a growling mutter rose behind him, the captain looked
narrowly at Aldric, then at Kyrin and ar Korentin. All had

now drawn blades and the firelight in the hall reflected from their weapons like molten copper—or fresh blood.

"How much gold?" the man asked, much of his mocking good-humour dissipated by the possibility of his own violent death.

"As much gold as each man can carry out unaided in one journey. But I want some word of honour that you won't come back again." Careful, Aldric reminded himself. *If you sound too naïve, they will suspect you're up to something.* He deliberately sneered at them. "Assuming scum like you use oaths for anything but foul language, of course. Well?"

"By the sea on which we earn our living, I swear we will not return once we have taken what we can carry," the pirate chief said primly.

Dewan guessed that both men were hiding smiles; the buccaneer for his ambiguous oath, which would change with the tide, and Aldric for his devious trick which seemed to be working well. Ar Korentin did not approve of such a scheme, but the circumstances were desperate enough to require harsh measures.

"And my lady?" the Alban persisted.

"You can keep her. I'll settle for a willing woman."

"But *I* will not!"

The bull-bellow startled everyone and almost precipitated the fight which Aldric was trying to avoid. Then he stared at the man who was forcing his way to the front of the bucca-neers' ranks.

"I am Khakkhur," the huge figure rumbled. "I want *your* woman, now. And what Khakkhur wants, he takes!" The man was a barbarian from the far north, but totally unlike the fair, ruddy-featured big men Aldric had seen on the docks at Erdhaven. Where they had been stern and grim, Khakkhur's heavy features were set in what looked to be a permanent scowl. A mane of coarse black hair hung to his shoulders and his massive body was clad only in boots, swordbelt and a length of bearskin strapped around his hips as a kind of kilt.

The Northrons at Erdhaven had dressed in much the same way, proud of their sleek muscles and showing them off adorned with gold bands and ornaments of bear-teeth. In

Aldric's opinion, Khakkhur would have been wiser covering himself up. The man was overdeveloped to the point of grossness, his biceps as thick as the Alban's thigh, the ponderous muscles of his chest like a woman's breasts.

A barbarian, to Aldric, had been one who neither spoke Alban nor lived in a land with permanent towns. He saw now that there was a third, more bestial type, who had left his tribal customs behind but who called civilised laws weak and in consequence did what he pleased. Even the wolf in the wood obeyed the rules of his pack. But not a wild animal like Khakkhur.

"Give me the girl, little black-beetle," the barbarian growled, and drew a heavy broadsword from its sheath at his belt. "Give her to me, or Khakkhur will crack your shell apart and eat your liver raw."

He probably would at that, Aldric reflected sombrely, then wrinkled his nose as a whiff of unwashed body reached him. Not all the big man's bronze skin came from sun and wind; it seemed he had decided soap and water was a mark of civilised decadence, along with manners, morals and the rest. Then the young *eijo*'s teeth showed in an ugly grin. Shell—Light of Heaven, of course! Bare muscles were just meat, no matter how powerful, and Isileth Widowmaker was the ultimate carving-knife. "Captain," he advised, "call your henchman off if he's of any value."

"I cannot do that, my friend," said the pirate with totally false regret. One fewer opponent would bring the odds even more into his favour. "My promise concerned gold. Killing is something else entirely."

Aldric looked at the massive blade in the barbarian's fist and swallowed hard despite his own confidence. His *tsalaer* was full battle armour, but it wouldn't keep such a weapon out without being so heavy he would be unable to move. Long ago the *kailinin* had struck a balance in their armour: thick enough to turn chance arrows or glancing blows, but light enough to give them speed to dodge anything more deliberate. *Tsalaerin* were not impenetrable and Aldric's mind's eye had seen—was still seeing with hideous clarity—what that huge sword would do to him if it struck home squarely.

So keep out of its way, he thought, and roll with what you cannot avoid in time. Duck and sidestep, then cut straight.

The slightly stylised look of *taiken*-fighting had a purpose; it demanded accuracy, not brute force, aiming as it did for the vulnerable points of a fully armoured warrior. Khakkhur had no armour whatsoever, but his unknown strength and skill were as much a threat as any hidden blade might be.

"If you want my lady, you barbaric ox," said Aldric pleasantly, "you will have to come and take her."

Steel rang as the blades met in a tentative probing of defences, then parted with a little slither. Khakkhur chopped suddenly at Aldric's eyes but the Alban sidestepped like the beat of a swallow's wing, just enough to avoid the blow with deft, disdainful ease. He did not parry. There was contempt in the movement, and it looked to Kyrin as if the barbarian should have died at once.

Without knowing how fast his opponent could recover, Aldric was not going for a quick kill—that was the way to risk his own death. Instead he watched even as he jerked aside.

Khakkhur's muscles tensed and he grunted slightly as his sword came out of its swoop. One of Aldric's questions had its answer: the barbarian could swing his weapon with ease, heavy though it was beside an ordinary blade—but sheer momentum made it hard to stop if his weighty stroke should miss and against someone skilled in the disciplines of *taiken-ulleth*, this would usually happen.

The pirate cut back-handed at thigh and was blocked, both swords ringing like bells and his own, deflected, throwing up sparks as its point gouged the floor. The blades met again with a double clash and a sound like monstrous shears, sprang apart and clanged back. Aldric thrust and was parried by the heavier blade, spun and cut, was blocked and darted away.

There was a pause when the scuff of feet and the panting of breath were the loudest sounds in the whole of the cavern, as both men glided along the perimeter of a circle only they could see. The barbarian was good, tutored in the violent school of experience where failure meant death, but Aldric's tuition, even if not so fatal towards error, had been every bit as rough.

Then a cut went home.

Aldric whirled across the floor and crashed into a pillar, slid down it into a crumpled, untidy heap of black metal and lay very still.

Kyrin bit her knuckle until the blood flowed. She did not cry; she simply did not believe what she had seen. Aldric had said once, in a gloomy moment, that there would be someone, somewhere, stronger or better or faster than he was, and that on the day they met he would go out into the darkness. Now it seemed this had happened.

Dewan seized her by the shoulder and pulled her round to guard his back, knowing that when their surprise had worn off the pirates would surely attack. He was right.

"I think my promise is null and void, don't you?" said their captain cheerfully. He gestured with both hands. "Kill the man, but keep the woman for later."

"Not—so—hasty—friend . . ." Aldric gasped hoarsely. He dragged himself upright with the aid of the firedrake carved around the pillar, then leaned against it and fought for breath.

"You are *dead*!" choked Khakkhur, his face going as pale as his grimy skin allowed.

Aldric coughed on a laugh. "Not quite. I merely look . . . and feel . . . that way." Straightening up, he dragged air into his lungs as the crushed sensation in his solar plexus faded to a queasy throbbing, and almost managed to conceal a slight wince when at last he got all his breath back where it should have been. "I don't wear all . . . this metal . . . without good reason."

Khakkhur's superstitious awe died away as he realised he was not facing a living dead thing, one of the *traugarin* of Alban legend, and he shambled forward to finish what he had started. The barbarian was not to know that an *eijo*—and especially this *eijo*—was far more dangerous than any *traugur* in a story. Isileth was not fiction; she was hard, razor-edged fact.

Aldric did not wait for his enemy to attack. Instead he came to meet him behind a low, vicious lunge which made the pirate parry wildly. Their blades crashed together half-a-dozen times with blinding speed, near-invisible blurs of steel with enough power to sever heads and arms and legs if they ever had a chance to strike their target. The hall echoed like a bell-tower. Then Khakkhur saw an opening and slashed double-handed at the Alban's neck.

Ducking under that wild swing, Aldric thrust his *taiken* out and through the barbarian's nearest bicep, then sliced sideways and peeled the muscle off its bone with obscene ease. The man screamed harshly and made a frantic attempt to hold his arm together, then shrieked on an impossibly high note for such a bass voice when the young *eijo* laid a forehand drawing cut across the corded sinews of his exposed belly. Mighty muscles—but only so much meat. They parted and everything spilled out in a foetid gush.

Khakkhur folded over the stench of his own ruptured intestines, and with a graceful sliding half-turn Aldric took up position at his side. Isileth swept up in both the Alban's hands, paused momentarily and came whirring down.

"Hai!"

As if propelled by its own long spurt of blood, the barbarian's head flew out of sight, while his body flopped like a puppet with its strings abruptly severed. It gave a single tremor and lay still.

Setting his foot between the corpse's shoulders, Aldric surveyed the buccaneers with all the arrogance at his command. There was blood on his face, running sluggishly from one nostril in a darkly crimson stream. The unblemished glint of his *tsalaer* covered what he guessed to be at least one cracked rib, and it hurt to breathe. Even so, he tried to hide the jabs of pain in case it gave some pirate bold ideas. Better that they think him made of iron, even if he had to drive his nails clear through his palms to convince them fully.

"Are there any more like this one?" he snarled. Nobody spoke. "Very wise. Then we'll be going, captain. Don't try to follow."

As they retreated up the stairs, Aldric leaning on the Dragonwand and trying not to show it, all three kept their swords drawn in case of treachery. There was none—three bloodstained bundles were sufficient warning. Only the pirate captain took a step forward, his eyes fixed on Aldric until the Alban was lost to view. "I'll remember you, swordsman!" he yelled at the darkness.

"Probably for the remainder of your life," somebody replied. The pirate wondered what that meant. He did not see Aldric look back, good sense wrestling with honour-inspired guilt over the cunning trap he had laid. The young man was having second thoughts. Dewan sensed his change of mood, perhaps from some slight hesitation half-glimpsed in the glow from the hall below them, and grabbed one armoured shoulder before the *eijo* could do anything stupid. Such as shout a warning. He regretted his own comment which had caused this change of heart; one did not mock those condemned to death.

Then one of the pirates must have run his fingers through the treasure, for there was that musical chiming sound unique to minted gold and a burst of raucous laughter. Both noises then stopped abruptly and a vast steely grinding took their place.

Ymareth, Lord of the Cavern of Firedrakes, was awake once more.

Perhaps some trace of the charm of understanding remained with him even out of the dragon's gaze, for Aldric found that he still understood the hissing speech which filled the silent cavern. As its meaning penetrated his brain, he cringed inside his armour and began to back away.

"Hear me," said the huge, ominous voice. "Hear my will. Thee shall do only as I bid thee do. So. Forward all, one step. And again. Now. Tall man, thee alone will come a little closer . . ."

Aldric's mailed hands flew to his ears, but could not reach inside his helm sufficiently to block the nauseating sounds which floated up the tunnel after him. Overwhelmed with revulsion and shame he sank on to the steps, racked by shudders which made his teeth chatter like those of a man with the ague. When Kyrin put one arm around him and helped him to his feet, warrior or not he came very close to breaking down. Dewan retired a tactful distance.

"Only a barbarian would not care," the girl said; then, after a glance at the unmoved Vreijek, added, "or a professional. You are neither. But what you did was necessary."

Aldric's face went cold and bitter. "How much will that excuse away, do you think, before the world dissolves in fire? And some power calls *that* necessary?"

Kyrin stared at him for a long time, then shrugged expressively. "Who can say? I hardly think it matters now, do you? Lean on me a little, Aldric-*ain,* and we shall all get out of here."

EIGHT

Desires and Excuses

En Sohra's master had never laid much claim to being very brave, but he was a skilled and crafty seaman. After momentary panic when he discovered that he sailed the same stretch of ocean as a shipload of pirates, he did not waste time in tacking laboriously out to open water. Instead he put off the galion's longboat, secured with a towing-line to *En Sohra*'s bows, and filled it with irritated sailors before ordering them to "Row!"

There was a brisk south wind beyond the lee of Techaur Island, and after little more than two hours under full sail their anchorage had slipped away below the horizon. There had been no pursuit, but as the afternoon turned into evening a new problem appeared as the wind grew ever stronger. By nightfall the ship's full sail had been stripped to a single topgallant on otherwise bare masts, and still she heeled ponderously as each comber smashed against her side.

At least the bullion in her hold made good ballast; though after every lurch the Elherran captain strained his ears to catch the first rumble of his cargo coming adrift. Not that he expected this to happen, having supervised the loading himself, but ignoring such a possibility would have been foolish in the extreme.

The storm began to die as swiftly as it had risen and stars appeared through rents in the flying clouds. Such sudden gales were common in Alban waters around spring and autumn and the captain had experienced them before; however, familiarity had not increased his liking for them. The sea took longer to calm down than the wind, and as *En Sohra* settled into an evil corkscrewing motion her master glanced towards the master-cabin and wondered how his passengers were faring. One of them, besides being wounded, had already looked sick when he came on board; the captain preferred not to contemplate how he must be feeling now.

*

Aldric felt sore.

Ignoring a constant and rather monotonous stream of abuse which flowed about his uncaring ears, Dewan probed the Alban's wounded side as gently as he could. The galion's irregular pitch-and-roll—something impossible to balance against—meant that this was not really very gently at all, as a gasp and a series of quite original oaths seemed to prove. Finally he straightened and cleaned his hands on a wet towel, since water poured into basins spilled over almost at once in such a sea.

Aldric whimpered softly, unclenching fists and teeth. "You are not much of a doctor," he managed at last.

"I only know some rudimentary field medicine, so what do you expect, comfort?" the Vreijek retorted waspishly. "Not that you're much of a patient. It's a mercy I won't have to nurse you back to health."

"Meaning what—and can I put my shirt on again?"

"Meaning there's less wrong with you than you think or I feared—and no, you can't; I have to bandage that mess first."

"That mess", as Dewan accurately described it, was the bloody purple welt where Khakkhur's sword had landed. It ran across the *eijo*'s ribs from left armpit to mid-chest and, though there were no bones broken underneath it, there was plenty of *tsalaer*-patterned broken skin above. After ar Korentin's peeling away of armour and clothing, even without his subsequent accidentally-rough handling, it was bleeding quite impressively.

The Vreijek knew that Aldric would lose more blood from a clumsily-pulled tooth, but he knew also that the young warrior was suffering from shock as much as anything else. There was no doubt that the injury was painful, but when he

started to think about such things Aldric would realise that
had he not been already twisting aside he would have been
split open like a lobster, armour or not. That was rough
comfort, of a kind.

Ar Korentin, of course, had been punctured, slashed and
dented many times in his career and regarded Aldric's wound
as slight. He had said so to Kyrin, only to be informed that
some people would call a severed limb a flesh wound and that
if he could find nothing more constructive to say, would he
please shut up or get out or preferably both. Tehal Kyrin,
Dewan had thought both then and afterwards, was quite a
woman—even if not quite a lady.

"Your problem," he continued sagely but unsympathetically,
"is that on top of everything else you're a dismal sailor."

Aldric went slightly pale at the recollection of being sick
that last time, long after his stomach had emptied; his side
had felt as if it was tearing away from his body. "You don't
have to remind me," he snapped. Then hiccupped and groped
miserably for a bucket. The pain of Dewan's surgery had
diverted his mind and stomach for a while, but now *En
Sohra*'s heaving was making him heave again in sympathy.

"I think if you could try to eat something you'd feel much
better," Dewan pointed out. The *eijo* doubled over his bucket
and retched dryly, wincing as he did so. "At least if you had
something to bring up, it wouldn't hurt so much."

"Dewan . . . " Aldric paused, then spat. "Dewan, for a
King's Champion, you make a first-class bastard."

The door opened and Kyrin came in with an armful of
bandages and several bottles balanced atop the heap. "Feeling better?" she asked pleasantly, then saw the bucket between Aldric's knees. "Oh . . . Probably not. Still, the gale
has blown itself out and those waves are getting smaller at
long last."

"I'm glad to hear it," Dewan grinned, "and Aldric's *very*
glad to hear it."

The Alban laughed without much humour. It hurt.

"Most amusing. Kyrin can put these bandages on—so you
go below and make sure the horses are all right. Dewan . . .
at once, if you please. Out."

With a mocking little bow, ar Korentin left.

Aldric sat quite still until the door was firmly closed, then got to his feet and locked it. As he gazed curiously at Kyrin, the girl looked away. "What's wrong with you, Kyrin-*ain*?" he wanted to know.

"I'm just tired, that's all."

"You must be . . . that's a very lame excuse. Now Dewan's gone, we can talk quite freely. So why won't you?"

"Lift your arm and let me at that wound," she said briskly, picking up a roll of bandage to avoid both his question and his eyes. Aldric sighed, then submitted to her ministrations with as much good grace as he could muster. He knew that anything but the most banal conversation would be impossible now, just so long as Kyrin had some other activity to hide behind.

By the time she had finished the young Alban's torso was wrapped from neck to navel in strips of linen drawn so tightly that they made it hard to breathe. Even so, this did not stop him trying again to get an answer. "Kyrin—what's the matter?" His voice, perhaps unconsciously, took on a sharper edge.

At that point the Valhollan took his breath away—and effectively stopped his questions—by sprinkling what felt like molten lead from a small bottle over his dressings. "Twice-distilled grain spirit," she said by way of explanation. This was not what he wanted to know, but it did at least tell him why his ribs had just caught fire.

"You said once—" Kyrin began, her back towards him. She hesitated, set the bottle down and absently caught its sideways slither when the ship rolled. Then she turned and the words came pouring out.

"You said once that you'd tell me whatever I needed to know, however little that might be, but you've somehow told me hardly anything. Even when you were talking to your king, half of what you said was masked by hints and vagueness. I thought that this was a simple thing, a bloodfeud; I thought I knew what you were doing, and why you had to do it.

"I'm Valhollan. Tehal *ur'lim* Harek's daughter. I don't

usually need to talk like this. But now . . . Aldric, I'm not
sure of anything any more.''

The *eijo* was silent, eyes hooded by his long lashes so that
the thoughts which drifted through them were unreadable.
Aldric was aware that what the girl said was true. He explained events quite clearly up to when he met Gemmel, but
after that became reserved and taciturn. No, he corrected
himself sharply: the word is secretive.

Of course there were obvious aspects to his situation.
Venjens-eijin were permitted, indeed expected, to use any
means which would further the completion of their oath. But
they were not supposed to employ sorcery with anything like
the freedom Aldric had already used, much less to the degree
which he intended.

The fewer people who were aware of that, the better for his
reputation.

He had caught something in King Rynert's voice which
seemed to imply that he, Aldric, was likely to be the next
Talvalin clan-lord. Kyrin had noticed it too; she had actually
called him *ilauem-arluth* on one occasion. Now while an *eijo*
could take certain liberties with the honour he had deliberately set aside, it was always with the view that he should
never do anything which would shame his clan if and when
he rejoined it as a *kailin*. Any high-clan *arluth* displaying
Aldric's fondness for the Art Magic could well find himself
under uncomfortably close scrutiny from both Cerdor and his
peers. It was a delicate, devious business, doing what was
required by Gemmel while appearing to do what was expected by tradition and the Honour-Codes.

As far as Ykraith the Dragonwand was concerned, Aldric
had taken a deep breath and had half-lied about why he was
fetching it from Techaur. The excuse sounded convincing—
that he had foolishly offered anything in repayment to the old
sorcerer who had healed him, and that when told to bring
back the talisman he had been honour-bound to do so. Dewan
had looked sceptical then and still seemed more than a little
dubious now.

''If I remember rightly, Kyrin, you said you would accept
whatever I chose to tell.''

"But you've told me nothing."

"I made no promises one way or the other."

"Then what . . . ?"

"I think that after all you've been through, you have the right to hear a little about what's going on. More at least than ar Korentin; I wouldn't consider giving him too many details."

"Why?"

"Because I don't trust him."

"Don't trust your own King's Champion? Then who can you trust?"

"Kyrin-*ain*, it's because of what Dewan is that I cannot trust him with the whole truth. He's a crown officer—what I have in mind goes against everything he represents, and I don't know that he would act sensibly. Or rather, with my best interests at heart. The law can be very inflexible sometimes."

"And what about me?"

"You don't have the authority to have me jailed or worse without trial." Aldric smiled thinly. "Help me here, will you?" There was a fresh shirt in the loose-cut Alban style laid out over a chair, and with Kyrin's assistance he managed to wriggle into it with a minimum of discomfort and close it in front with his weapon-belt. "When I've put on something warm we'll go up on deck to talk—it attacts less attention than staying behind a locked door."

"You are so suspicious . . ."

"Call it cautious." He put out one hand and touched her gently under one ear with his fingertips. "I'm a man with a blade at his neck, Kyrin-*ain*. In such a circumstance, can you blame me for avoiding sudden movements?" The Alban donned an overmantle and unlocked the door, then bowed as deeply— and as sardonically—as his wounded side permitted. "I know it is not good manners, lady, but I will follow. If there's anyone standing about doing nothing, let me know. Anyone at all." He allowed himself what was almost a mischievous grin. "Apart from what I have already said about not wanting Dewan to know, I think I owe him something for being so quiet about this thing's cargo. Eh?"

*

Kyrin stared out over the dark water for a long time when Aldric had finished speaking. There was a slender waning moon hanging near the horizon, and stars glittered in a sky which seemed to have been washed clean and clear by the tempest. There was still something of a choppy sea, and the occasional glimmer of a white-capped wave slid past *En Sohra*'s hull. Finally Aldric broke the silence.

"You see now why I wasn't making free with that sort of information," he said quietly.

"Oh, indeed." Kyrin's voice sounded as if she had to summon up the words from a great distance. "I see a great many things now that I was unsure about before." She moved a little closer and the *eijo* slipped his arms about her waist. "I'm cold, Aldric. The whole world's becoming cold, and harsh, and brutal." The girl turned away from the sea and embraced him tightly. "It's growing so very, very dark. Where will the light come from, when the darkness covers everything?"

"From the sun, as it always has," Aldric replied, and kissed her. He draped a fold of the long overmantle across her shoulders and they watched the moon set, Kyrin with her head snuggled back against his neck and the body-heated silver of his crest-collar pressing warmly on her cheek. There was no passion in the contact; only a tender caring which Kyrin recognised reluctantly as the love she did not want. She shivered and Aldric held her closer. "You are cold," he muttered. "Better go below and get some rest."

"What about you?"

"I'll stay here for a while. I doubt if I could sleep anyway."

Kyrin glanced at him; his words had lacked all inflection, as if he was thinking about something else long ago and far away. "There's something troubling you," she said, not asking but telling. "What is it?"

"I was remembering. Right now, that's not a good thing to do."

"Because of those pirates? Aldric, I mean no insult to ar Korentin, but if it hadn't been for you—*you*—we would all be in pieces now. Or worse."

"The men I cut down don't concern me. Much . . . They

had an even chance to do the same to me. Even though that brings my tally up to six—and I'm not yet twenty-four.''

"Those swine deserved to die.'' Kyrin's voice was flat and vicious.

"Perhaps. But honourable death by the *taiken* is a part of my heritage. A firedrake is not. That was too deliberate, too well-thought-out for me to feel any pride in my cunning. Your lover's not a warrior any more, Kyrin-*ain*. He's just a calculating killer—a deathbringer. That's a fine, dramatic title, but it makes me feel dirty. I wish there had been some other way.''

"There wasn't. Forget it. If the tables were turned, would your death be preying on Khakkhur's mind? I doubt it very much.'' Kyrin pulled free of the clinging mantle and walked away, then glanced back at him. "My father's a bigger, fiercer man than you, Aldric, but he told me once that nobody should laugh if they don't know how to cry. Think about that.''

The *eijo* did, for a long time.

*

Kyrin was scarcely undressed and into her bunk before the expected knock came at her cabin door. Pulling the sheets modestly high, she said: "Come in.''

Dewan ar Korentin slipped inside, closed the door behind him and sat down with the muted rustling click of a man wearing armour under his outer clothing. Mail-rings sparkled momentarily at his collar. Kyrin looked, listened and raised one eyebrow, but the Vreijek paid no attention. Instead he removed the stopper from a wine-jar, filled two cups and offered one to the girl before taking a thoughtful sip himself.

"Well? What did he tell you?''

Kyrin tasted her wine before replying. "Little enough. The Dragonwand staff is, as he said before, a gift for Gemmel-*altrou*.''

"His foster-father. And a wizard.''

"So it seems.''

"That young man asks a lot of questions, or simply stands quiet and listens—but have you ever noticed how seldom he volunteers any answers?''

"Of course I have. It doesn't match the rest of his character— about which, I would remind you, Lord-Commander ar Korentin, I know much more than you do."

"I wasn't about to question that fact, my dear."

"I told you I'm not . . . but let it pass. This time."

"So then, his secrecy seems to you more like an assumed habit; one he has acquired from somebody. The wizard, maybe?"

"Maybe. Some more wine, please."

The Vreijek poured a second cupful for them both, then rose and walked quietly to the cabin door as footsteps approached down the passageway outside. They passed and receded and Dewan smiled to himself before returning to sit—this time on the foot of Kyrin's bunk. She jerked her own feet aside just in time.

"Aldric . . ." mused Dewan softly, then shook his head. "No, not yet. Much as I'd like to, I cannot trust him until I'm sure." Kyrin tried without success to stifle a snort of ironic laughter. "And what do you find so funny?"

"Just a coincidence, that's all." She did not elaborate further.

"Indeed? Kyrin, be careful. Don't let your emotions into any relationship with him. You're only an observer, after all."

"Just because you persuaded the king to grant me use of a ship doesn't give you permission to take liberties with my private life, ar Korentin."

"In exchange for which you agreed to help me keep an eye on him."

"That was only to prove what I thought—your suspicions were groundless."

"It depends rather on whose viewpoint you take, Kyrin-*ain*. Oh yes, I've heard that lover's endearment before. I warned you not to get involved too deeply—it affects your judgement."

"Is that jealousy I hear . . . ?"

"There are high-clan *arluthen* who would be very dubious about how nonchalant he is where magic is concerned—"

"And others who would wonder at how friendly you seem to be with an Imperial ship-captain of the Warlord's faction.

To say nothing of what your dear, so-possessive wife would say if I told her—''

''—What? There's nothing to tell!''

''You're a man, I'm a woman. I've seen you watching me. Oh, there's no harm in looking, but if I gave you the chance to do more you'd take it, wouldn't you? Lyseun would think so. All I need to do is substitute your name for Aldric's and you wouldn't be done explaining this side of the grave.''

''Now let's not be foolish . . .''

''Get off my bed!''

''You are in love with him, aren't you?''

''No, I'm not.''

''What?'' Dewan got off the bunk as if he had been kicked. ''But I thought . . .''

''Quite clearly, you did not.'' Kyrin favoured Dewan with the sort of smile he had not received from anyone since he was about ten years old; a smile which said ''amusing simpleton, aren't you!'' with altogether too much clarity. The Valhollan girl had regained some of her good humour now, thanks to the way she had succeeded in bringing ar Korentin down to a more manageable size. With the threat of his wife suspended like a battleaxe over his head, he was less inclined to bluster and hide behind his rank.

''Then what exactly *is* the situation?'' He asked the question rather than demanded it.

''I'm four years older than Aldric. I like the boy—he deserves that much—but for several reasons I cannot and do not love him. Nor does he love me, though he thinks he does. Infatuation describes it better. Dewan, he was a virgin before we met.''

Ar Korentin blinked, started to laugh and then thought better of it. ''I was thinking such a claim would be easy to make and hard to disprove,'' he explained. ''But he would have no reason to lie. And I remember his brother Joren. He was a very moral gentleman, one of the old type you seldom meet nowadays. I think Aldric told you the truth . . .''

''And I'm sure he did. I won't see him hurt, King's Champion; not simply because you're suspicious of the way he behaves. So long as we understand each other, Dewan,

your wife will hear nothing but good about you. You do see
what I mean, don't you?''

"In every detail, lady. But remember what I told you and
discourage Aldric from any romantic thoughts he might be
entertaining. You'll be going home within the month, and
. . . well, he is a Talvalin, after all. Very shrewd, very
clever—and very dangerous.''

"I said I did not want him hurt. Especially by me. I'll
manage somehow.''

"I hope so, Kyrin. For both our sakes.''

The Valhollan stared at him as he gathered up wine, cups
and the cloak he had used to cover them, then smiled carefully. "I didn't have the pleasure of meeting Joren Talvalin,
but I can tell you this, distrustful Captain-of-Guards ar
Korentin,''—she pronounced the title as if it was some
obscure and subtle insult—''his brother is as much an honourable gentleman as Joren ever could have been.''

"That's as may be—but Joren had the devil's own temper
when he thought he had good cause. Remember that when
you start explaining things to Aldric—and choose your words
with care. Good night, lady.''

The door closed behind him with a solid, final click.

*

Kyrin awoke to the sound of more clicks. She rubbed the
sleep from her eyes and opened the shutters on her cabin's
port, blinking as the newly-risen sun shone full into her face.
As she washed and dressed the sharp, brittle clacking noise
continued intermittently, although she was sure that nothing
was wrong with *En Sohra*; the galion was sailing easily
through a gentle deep-sea swell, and the creak of structure
and cordage sounded as it should.

Tying back her long hair with a ribbon, Kyrin walked up
the companionway and on to the ship's main deck, thinking
deeply. There was a familiar quality to the clicking, an
irregular rhythm reminiscent of something other than wood.
Awareness came an instant before sight.

The sound was that of a duel.

Aldric and Dewan faced each other across the deck, both
unarmoured but carrying long staves of polished oak. Kyrin

recognised the weapons as *taidyin*—staff-swords—which were usually rolled in a bundle among Aldric's gear, hardwood foils with which he practised daily before exercising with Isileth's live blade. He had never used them against an opponent until now, something which the girl found suspicious in itself. What if he had overheard last night's conversation? Or only a part of it? What if . . . ?

Her thoughts were interrupted by a stinging crack as Dewan blocked a vicious cut at his leg. Aldric darted past him, half-spinning to slice again at the Vreijek's face and Kyrin winced as the *taidyin* crashed together; there was an awful ferocity in that assault, more than seemed justified by a mere training routine. Ar Korentin assumed a defensive attitude and Aldric glided sideways, analysing his opponent's stance before launching another attack.

"Stop this, both of you!" shrieked Kyrin in a mixture of rage and fright. "Stop it at once!" The duellists moved apart, Aldric lowering his *taidyo* to regard her with open astonishment while Dewan, realising at once what she thought had caused the fight, favoured her with a wicked smile.

"What's wrong with you?" Aldric snapped. He had just succeeded in getting ar Korentin where he wanted him and considered the intrusion ill-timed to say the least. "You've seen me practising before, haven't you?" he demanded irritably, then winced a little and pressed one hand to his side.

Kyrin noticed the movement and allowed herself a frown. "I didn't think you were . . . that is, I didn't think you would be training this morning."

"Not without good reason, my dear?" purred Dewan. The Valhollan's frown deepened and Dewan's grin became if anything wider still.

"The reason, Kyrin-*ain*, is just that I don't want this to stiffen up," said Aldric quietly. He tugged up his shirt. "See—no bleeding. The skin's just badly grazed, but all that bruising is going to ache if the muscles are not kept working." He paused, considering, then smiled crookedly. "Not that it doesn't ache whatever the hell I do . . ."

"I thought last night you wouldn't be moving for a couple

of days," Kyrin pointed out, tucking the shirt carefully back through his belt.

"Last night somebody had just drenched a raw wound with neat grain spirit!"

"Oh . . . Well, at least it seems to have done some good."

"Some . . . but that wasn't the only thing to make me feel better. You did. You helped me get some sleep. Thank you."

"Then let me help again. Put those sticks aside; rest; take some food."

"Not just yet. There was someone long ago—I've forgotten his name—who claimed there are two sorts of people, the quick and the dead. He was wrong. There are three: the quick, the dead—and the very, very lucky." He grinned and touched his bandaged side. "Like me."

Kyrin smiled a wan little smile and stepped back to watch the next exchange. They were using two *taidyin* each this time, in the *dyutayn* or two-blade style of fighting. It was a complex blend of sidesteps and gliding turns, spinning displacements of the body and circular cuts with the swords.

Aldric was sensible enough to avoid the more vigorous waist-twisting moves, but taking such care slowed him down more than either he or Dewan realised until it was far too late. Halfway through the horizontal double-cut called "interlaced windmill," ar Korentin found that Aldric was a foot closer than he should have been.

His discovery and the crisp snap as his backhand cut struck the young Alban's ribs were almost simultaneous. Aldric cried out and dropped both swords. Oak clattered on pine as they fell to *En Sohra*'s deck. The *eijo*'s face had gone stark white; as white as the shirt now disfigured by a wet, dark-red blotch spreading all over its left side. Aldric put the flat of one hand to where he hurt, trying not to breathe. "You said there were no ribs broken," he said thickly, trying to sound dryly amused. Something like a piece of splintered wood pressed into his palm through the shirt and his senses swam. "I think . . . there's definitely one . . . gone . . . now. . . ." He swayed, feeling giddy, then with no other warning than a little sigh followed his swords to the deck. Soft-edged dark outlines crossed the blue sky above him, bent over him, lifted him gently. The galion was pitching alarmingly and it was getting very dark . . .

"This time he's staying in bed if I have to tie him down," said a voice, half-angry and half-concerned.

"Don't be so drastic," said a second voice. "I doubt if he'll want to move about much anyway."

"You thought that last night too, didn't you?"

"I was wrong; I'm sorry."

"Still, forget the ropes. This ship's medicine-chest holds enough soporific drugs to make him sleep for a week. Satisfied?"

"Where did you learn how to use things like that?"

"Misuse them, my dear. The Imperial Court in Drakkesborg opened my eyes to a lot of . . ."

Aldric did not learn what Dewan had found out in Drakkesborg. The words he heard slurred into a buzzing noise and thence to a silence as absolute as the blackness clouding his vision beyond his leaden eyelids.

*

Aldric's eyelids snapped back and he was awake at once, with no intervening period of drowsiness. He stared straight ahead, not daring to look right or left in case it brought back the dark. There was a flat surface above him, dark planks criss-crossed by adzed red-oak beams. A ceiling . . . ? Not the honey-coloured pine of his cabin, though, and his bed had a proper quilt now, not those foolish sheets. Rain pattered gently on the small panes of a draped window. There was somebody else nearby; he could hear the rustle of a book's pages being turned.

With teeth clenched against any pain which might accompany the movement, Aldric sat up. There was nothing wrong at all; he might as well be waking from a refreshing night's sleep. And there were no bandages either . . .

"Good morning, Aldric," said a familiar voice.

The *eijo*'s head jerked round. "*Altrou!*" he gasped in disbelief. Gemmel nodded, smiling, and after marking his place set down the book and closed it. "But how did you get here? And where is here anyway?"

"Just as before—questions, always questions. I should

have expected it and let someone else wait for you to wake up. Still . . .'' The enchanter got to his feet, crossed to the window and opened its curtains. "I came here with your king—having rightly assumed after that episode at Erdhaven Festival that he'd appreciate a word with me—" the old man chuckled; "which he did to the tune of three hours' talking without a rest. And this is the port of Kerys, in Cerenau.''

"What happened to me, *altrou?*''

"From what I gather, you were being stupid again,'' the wizard said without rancour. "Trying *dyutayn* with any sort of injury is foolish enough, but with a damaged side of all things, it plumbs the depths of utter idiocy. Fairly typical behaviour, really. Ar Korentin—who knows more than seems quite proper about drugs—kept you asleep until the ship docked, knowing that there would be better doctors ashore. He was right. I was here.''

"And you healed me?''

"Of course. A simple enough process with the right equipment—which I had the good sense not to leave behind on this occasion. Now, what about the Dragonwand? I gather you had some small difficulty from various sources.''

"Your understatements are showing, *altrou,*'' Aldric grinned. "Yes, we did have some trouble—though none of it was connected with *them.*'' Gemmel nodded, knowing quite well who *they* were. "I can't understand why, because they found me easily enough in Erdhaven.''

"Don't look for reasons—just consider yourself lucky. By the way . . . how do you find talking to firedrakes?''

Aldric made a face. "Hard—very hard. They don't have much in the way of small talk. I'm glad you taught me what you did, because Ymareth doesn't seem like a being that would listen to excuses.''

"It isn't. Where is Ykraith now?''

"I gave it to Dewan—he has a sheaf of javelins on his saddle, and the Dragonwand's hidden amongst them. How are the horses, by the way?''

"Quite healthy. Lyard's probably a better sailor than you, by all accounts.''

"Not very difficult. Gemmel . . . I'm always asking questions and now I've got two more. Important ones. What does the Dragonwand do? And how do you plan to use it? I'd like a proper answer to each, please.''

Gemmel combed his beard with his fingers, neatening it, then stood up and bowed with mock-politeness. "Of course, my lord," he said. "But not at once, my lord—because I'm telling King Rynert and part of his High Council almost exactly what you want to know, and if you're at the meeting you will find out. Of course, since you're still in bed . . .''

"Not for long. I shall want a bath and something to eat before . . . what time is it, anyway?"

"Dawn, on a wet, windy, thoroughly miserable midsummer day. Well, it's not actually midsummer, but the alliteration pleases me."

"Oh Heaven," Aldric moaned in feigned horror, "what you do to our language is probably illegal."

"Come on, Bladebearer Deathbringer—Rynert expressed a particular desire to see you, and if he doesn't you will be in more hot water than your bath can hold. But afterwards you and I shall have a private little talk concerning the spell-stone of Echainon. Good morning once again." He turned and left the room.

"What was that you called me?" Aldric asked an instant too late. Then he shrugged, yawned, stretched and slithered out of bed, shivering in the unaccustomed cold air. As the young man wriggled hastily into a robe he glanced out of the window at the wet rooftops, grimacing as a gust of wind slapped raindrops against the glass. "Fine summer weather," he muttered, and turned away.

He did not notice the crow huddling for shelter under the eaves of an opposite house, even when the bird's head lifted with a jerk as he appeared at the window. Its beady eyes fastened on his face, and its pickaxe beak opened to utter a croak of surprise even as it shuffled further into the shadows. Once Aldric had gone, the crow gurgled to itself in a most uncrowlike fashion and performed a triumphant little dance on the narrow ledge. Then it launched itself into the rain-slashed air on wide black wings and glided silently off across

Kerys, heading north-north-west for Dunrath six hundred miles away.

As the crow flies.

*

Lord Endwar *ilauem-arluth* Santon reined in his charger atop the same ridge where Aldric had once sat and, like the younger man before him, gazed at the brooding might of Dunrath-hold. There was an army camped before the fortress, six thousand men in a ring of steel through which nothing passed unchallenged. Santon dismounted and went to sit on a camp-stool under the shade of his blue and purple standards with their white lettering. Not that he needed shade, even though the sun shone brightly from a cloudless sky; there was no warmth from it at all and the wind which tugged the snapping banners overhead was icy cold.

Endwar-*arluth* took off his helmet and scowled. It had taken eight days' hard marching to bring his legion up from Erdhaven; two hundred-odd miles, and somewhere along the road they had passed from one season to another, leaving the Spring Festival far, far behind. Santon had seen with his own eyes a brief but unmistakable scudding of snowflakes across the open moorland. Snow—and summer air like the breath of an underground crypt. He shivered with more than the cold.

Dunrath had been grey when last he saw it, blue-grey stone from the Blue Mountains under a blue-grey autumn sky as he rode to young Aldric's *Eskorrethen* ceremony. Now, perhaps by some trick of the light, the fortress was red. Red with the rustling vermeil silk of Kalarr cu Ruruc's war-flags hoisted over every wall, and red too as if every stone, every tower and every turret had been dipped in some great pool of blood. The crimson hue shifted and changed like the folds of a shaken cloth and only one thing remained constant: the ominous, glistening scarlet of the citadel's donjon, which drew and held the gaze with an awful fascination. It reminded Santon of an Imperial prison he had once seen in the city of Egisburg, the sinister Red Tower whose gates had never yet released a living prisoner.

The lord drank wine offered him by an armed retainer and wondered how long it would be before King Rynert and the other legions joined his leaguer. The men he commanded here were not—save for two thousand foot—regular troops, but levied vassals, *kailinin* of lesser clans who owed him service for their lands and those warriors of his household who had come with him to Erdhaven. Four thousands of foot and two of horse—not enough to take the fortress by either siege or storm, but quite sufficient to bottle up its occupants behind the high, strong walls and put all thought of open battle from their minds.

Dunrath was widely regarded as the mightiest fortress in all Alba; true, it was not so large as Leyruz-*arluth*'s citadel at Datherga, nor as modern and complex as Santon's own hold of Segelin, which he called a "castle" after the Drusalan word—but Dunrath had never fallen to any foe in war. It had changed hands twice during the Clan Wars, leaving and returning to Talvalin possession within the space of two months, but both occasions had been by treachery. And now it had been taken by treachery again. Santon drained his cup and rose, glaring towards the blood-red tower. Why was it so cold? he wondered silently, rapping his commander's baton against one armoured leg. What purpose did it serve? And was the answer one a wise man would want to hear . . . ?

*

After a leisurely bath and a meal which by its size deserved a better title than merely breakfast, Aldric walked back to his room to collect his weapons and put on the only formal *elyu-dlas* he owned. Custom and protocol required that he wear only a *taipan* shortsword with the Colour-Robe, but in the circumstances he felt a *taiken* of Widowmaker's lineage would make an acceptable substitute.

It would have to serve.

The building, indeed the whole town, seemed aswarm with *kailinin*, lesser lords and legion officers, and Aldric had bowed or saluted more often since leaving his bed an hour before than he had done during the previous fortnight. He had also been the source of considerable speculation—the anomaly of a young, short-haired *venjens-eijo* in combat leathers, who yet wore a high-clan crest-collar at his throat and the colours of Talvalin on his *tsepan*, had caused more than one dignified head to swivel in a most undignified manner.

Then Aldric turned a corner and stopped with one eyebrow arching quizzically. Tehal Kyrin was standing a little way from his bedroom door, holding a letter in the fingertips of one hand as if it was a noxious insect, with a distracted expression on her face and her lower lip nipped between her teeth. When she saw the Alban she started slightly, made as if to say something and then instead twisted the letter into an untidy cylinder which she pushed through her belt.

"You look rather better than when I last saw you," she said, venturing a smile which fell rather short of the mark. Aldric failed to notice anything wrong even when he tried to embrace her and found her slipping nervously aside.

"It's surprising what hot food, hot water and a sharp razor can do," he grinned. "Have you eaten yet?" She nodded, toying with the rolled-up letter, and seemed once again on the point of telling him something important when he continued talking. "It looks as if I'm finally going to get some answers out of Gemmel about the Dragonwand. Usually he listens politely to every question you ask and then equally politely avoids giving a reply."

"Sounds familiar," the girl murmured. Aldric let her comment pass.

"He called me Bladebearer Deathbringer. Why? I don't like the title."

"You'll have to get used to it. *En Sohra*'s gone, but her crew did a lot of talking during the few hours they spent in harbour. You're quite a hero."

"Hero!" Aldric laughed without much humour. "I've heard some unlikely things in my life, but that really—" He stopped and reached out one hand to the girl's face, turning it towards the wan daylight from the window at the end of the corridor. "Why are you crying, Kyrin . . . ?"

She pulled away from him, wiping her face with the back of one hand, and with the other drew the letter from her belt and pushed it at him. Aldric unrolled the parchment and scanned it quickly, his gaze flicking once or twice from the writing to her face and back again. Then he took several deep breaths before trusting himself to speak.

"The characters are Alban—but the language is Valhollan, yes?" Kyrin nodded her head sadly. "And this name, Sijord—"

"Seorth," she corrected.

"Seorth, then. That's the man who was to marry you?" Another nod. "I can't read this, but let me guess; Seorth has come looking for you, am I right? And you will go with him, of course." This was not really a question, more a statement.

Kyrin studied her lover's face for a long time before she replied, gently touching the white scar under his eye with her fingertips.

"Yes, I will, as I think you expected all along. I've tried to tell you often enough . . . But it's not a duty—I do have the right to choose—"

"And you choose the man you've known for longer than two weeks. I can't blame you." The look in his dark eyes said differently and Kyrin knew it.

"You put a great deal of living into those two weeks, Aldric," she said. "I've come to know you very well and like you very much—but I have loved Seorth since I was little more than a child, and from this it seems he loves me too. That's why I'm going. Believe me, Aldric-*ain*, you will understand . . . eventually."

"Will I? Tell me why?" He fought to keep the harshness from his voice, knowing that to be *kailin-eir* was of necessity to accept ill-fortune with the same courteous equanimity as the most splendid victory.

"You should know." Kyrin's voice was very soft. "You've come to terms with a greater loss than my going away."

"I . . . I had no choice then. I have now—and the power to alter it. You said yourself I was heir to lands and ranks and titles. So . . . What I want, I take, and no man—or woman— can gainsay me." The girl stared at him in disbelief, then stepped over to his bedroom door and threw it open. One corner of her mouth tugged down as she tried to summon up contempt and failed. "You're crying again," he said, not caring that the words came out like the crack of a whip.

Kyrin flinched as if he had indeed lashed her across the

face, and still the tears welled silently from her eyes even when she scrubbed at them with her knuckles in a gesture almost violent enough to bruise the sockets. There were no sobs, and when she spoke her voice was without a tremor though it was faint and desolate. "Yes, I'm crying. Crying for you—for whatever spark within you that must have died last night. Because you aren't the man I knew any more. I'm crying for you, Aldric. Because someone must." She entered the room and returned seconds later with Widowmaker in her hands. "Here, *kailin-eir* Aldric *ilauem-arluth* Talvalin. Wait for Seorth and my father. Justify your *taiken*'s name and kill them both, then take me to your bed by force. Because you're not a naked barbarian makes all the difference to rape and murder . . ." She flung the longsword at him.

Aldric caught the weapon without thinking, his gaze fixed on the girl's face which still held more of sorrow than of rage. Hard to hurt an enemy, he thought sombrely, easier to hurt a friend—and easiest of all to break a lover's heart. Perhaps it was as well, to make their parting easier. Then his fingers clenched spasmodically around the *taiken*'s hilt. He wanted to shout, to rave, to smash things, to . . . Yes, to kill . . . something, anything, himself. To behave as not even the lowliest of lordless *eijin* should behave.

Then it was as if a sheet of ice closed over the anger boiling in his brain, and he became abruptly calm again. Why so angry? he asked himself. Especially with Kyrin, who had done nothing except react the way any right-minded woman would to his vile temper and grossly dishonourable suggestion. The whole foul episode was his own fault and no one else's. His thoughts touched briefly on the *tsepan* pushed with meticulous nonchalance through his belt, then dismissed it with a mental shrug. Why bother, when at any time within the next three weeks he could be flung into the Void. If he survived beyond that, perhaps his formal suicide might recompense many people for many things, but first and foremost were Kalarr and Duergar. Their deaths, whether formal or otherwise, were long overdue.

Aldric went down on both knees and laid the *taiken* at Kyrin's feet, then bent forward and pressed his brow to the cool, lacquered scabbard. "Tehal Kyrin-*an*," he whispered huskily. "Lady, forgive the words I spoke in anger."

She knelt too, so that their faces were once more level; so that she could watch his eyes and see if they truly mirrored what he said, or gave the lie to his courteous phrases. What she saw was an expression disturbingly like that he had worn after learning of his brother's apparent treason, except that this time it was directed at himself. It was shocked, haunted, unwilling to believe how easily mere words had soured their relationship. A face which should have wept, but where any tears had frozen in eyes like obsidian, or flint, or jade. The same bone-chilling grey-green as a winter sea. A widow-maker's eyes.

"I am truly sorry, Kyrin."

"I believe you."

He bowed forward slightly, as much to hide his face as to acknowledge her acceptance of his apology. Kyrin hesitated, then leaned towards him and touched her lips against each eyelid, then to forehead and mouth. The movement was less a kiss than a valediction, and Aldric knew it.

"Go now, Kyrin-*ain*," he muttered. "All the words were said long ago."

She rose and walked away, then stopped and took a few steps back towards him. "I cannot just leave like this," she said firmly. "Aldric-*eir*, the quarrel's already been forgotten. You acted honourably towards me at all times, and I shall tell Seorth of it. Any house of ours is yours, Alban, fire and food and safety if you ever need it. I promise." Kyrin bowed slightly, the way she had seen Aldric do so many times. "Go with God, Aldric—and may Heaven grant you long life."

"Long life is often no great gift," Aldric murmured, "and can sometimes be a curse." He thought for a moment, staring into space with narrowed, frosty eyes, then half-smiled and said:

> " 'What is life, except
> Excuse for death, or death but
> An escape from life?'

"Recall my name with kindness, lady, now and then."

As she left him kneeling there, a black figure with a black *taiken* before him, Kyrin thought about his poem and as she did she shuddered.

*

From the balcony of Dunrath's donjon Lord Santon's legion resembled a child's toy soldiers, set out in little blocks of men around the fortress walls just out of arrow-shot. Duergar Vathach leaned on a parapet and surveyed them dispassionately, aware of the impasse which had caused the siege. With another thousand picked troopers of Grand Warlord Etzel's guard he could pulverise the small Alban host, while without them he merely stood up here and wished. Fabric rustled behind him and he turned as Kalarr cu Ruruc stepped out on to the balcony, wind whipping at his forbidding vermeil robes.

"Have they altered their disposition?" he demanded.

"Not since dawn. Why? What difference would it make?"

"Enough to annoy me greatly. I've spent the night preparing a spell based on the siege positions they assumed when they arrived last night, and while it's effective it's also inflexible. What about the *traugarin*?"

"The putrefaction stopped once the air cooled—it has not returned."

"Good. One disadvantage about using corpses as soldiers, little necromancer, is that you can resurrect the bodies, but you have to keep fending off the natural processes which follow death. Awkward if you don't want your army rotting away before you can put them to use."

"But having set the Charm of Undeath on them, I have to keep them in that state. The spell will not affect a cadaver more than once."

"Isn't life awkward for the workaday wizard," Kalarr observed drily. "Why you didn't think of weather-magic before, I cannot imagine. After all, even the Drusalan Empire must know that killed meat keeps better when it's cold."

"I don't like nature-magic; it's slow, clumsy, crude—and hard to control safely."

" 'Like!' " scoffed cu Ruruc. " 'Safe!' Those are not words a true sorcerer should have in his vocabulary."

Duergar sensibly did not argue with him and the issue was tacitly dropped. "It seems," Kalarr continued, "that yonder lord has sent me his defiance." He grinned with sinister relish as he used the old term. "Therefore I feel justified in giving him a demonstration of the power which he has challenged—making sure, of course, that enough are left alive for the warning to be noted." Though his lean face remained devoid of all expression, there was an ugly purr of eagerness in his voice as it shaped the prolix phrases.

Duergar looked at Santon's army, the scales of their *tsalaerin* twinkling in the chilly sunlight, then turned to his companion. "What do you intend?" he ventured carefully, knowing from previous experience that with this mood of fierce exuberance on him, it was unsafe to be near Kalarr.

"Once, long ago," cu Ruruc said, "someone called me the slayer of hosts. It is time, I think, to reaffirm that title. There's a spell known to few sorcerers and seldom written in grimoires. I know that spell, and have spent the night preparing it. Now it merely needs priming and direction before I can unleash it."

"But . . ." Duergar began, reluctant to raise an objection, yet knowing it had to be done, "but surely they have some protection—otherwise they wouldn't have dared to come so close."

Kalarr allowed himself to smile with a slow, evil unveiling of his teeth. But he was not angry, merely amused. "You're very sharp today, my friend," he observed. "Such a theory crossed my mind earlier this morning, so I tested it. Lesser enchantments only, mere probes, extinguishing fires and the like—but nothing so dramatic that it might remind them they're besieging a sorcerer's fortress. They'll learn that soon enough.

"That army's as helpless as a tethered goat, thanks to its commander's pride. I know these high-clan *kailinin-eir*, though they ignored me until I persuaded them otherwise. A haughty, stubborn breed, who can't see further than their long patrician noses. Magic's something from a story to them, and wizards are less than dirt.''

"Not to all of them." Neither sorcerer had heard Baiart emerge on to the balcony behind them until he spoke. "My brother understands you well, cu Ruruc. That's why he's going to kill you."

The wizards glanced at Baiart, then at each other. Kalarr's nostrils twitched and Duergar broke into a high-pitched bray of laughter. "Your brother," spluttered the Drusalan necromancer when he had regained a little composure, "is still floating about on the high seas, prey to everything we choose to throw at him."

"My brother," corrected Baiart with a hint of his old suavity, "passed from your reach when that flying eye was destroyed. I was there. I saw it happen and heard how you reacted. You don't even know where he is any more, much less have any power to harm him."

Kalarr's saturnine face darkened. "Maybe so, Talvalin," he hissed. "But if you stay here a little longer, you will get some inkling of what awaits bold clan-lord Aldric"—he sneered the words—"if he has the courage to come back."

"You're scared of him, aren't you?" Baiart jeered. "He killed the monsters that you sent to get him and now he's escaped you. And you're afraid!"

"If death is what you want . . ." Duergar snarled, lifting his open hand only to have it seized by Kalarr and forcibly lowered again.

"Then it's the last thing that we'll give you," cu Ruruc finished. "However much you may deserve it—or desire it."

NINE

Bladebearer

When Aldric eventually stood up, after several minutes of utter stillness, he walked quietly into his room and began to don his armour, dismissing the servant who would have helped him so that he could concentrate completely on the task and so prevent his mind from dwelling on . . . other things. *An-moyya-tsalaer* was difficult to put on without assistance; its complicated design required each part to be fitted in a certain sequence, although once that sequence had been mastered an agile warrior could scramble into his battle harness with remarkable speed.

Aldric could do so in a matter of minutes, but on this occasion he moved slowly and methodically, letting himself become totally absorbed by the precise, almost ritual care needed when a man sheathed himself entirely in metal but wished to remain flexible enough to move. The *elyu-dlas* and its matching wing-shouldered overmantle were both padded to mute the rustling scrape of lamellar armour, and both were marked with the spread-eagle crest of clan Talvalin embroidered in silver on dark blue. Once he had put on both these and arranged the high collars properly, Aldric changed Widowmaker's braided combat hilt for a ceremonial grip of etched silver which someone, probably Gemmel, had left on the low bedside table, and slung the sword horizontally so that hilt and scabbard protruded through the slits cut in his robe for that purpose. In what amounted to court dress, the wearing of *taikenin* slung *eijo*-style across one's back was definitely not encouraged.

Belting his Colour-Robe with a sash through which he slipped his *tsepan*, Aldric picked up his helmet and, methodical care now set aside, hurried to the council room. From what he had seen of the building, it was constructed in the usual fashion of Alban town houses: the bath-house and the eating-hall had been in the usual places and he guessed the meeting-chamber would be too. On that assumption he felt able to take a short cut through one of the upper galleries.

Someone had laid down thick mats of woven straw to protect the fine wood floors from many feet in military boots. Since Aldric was wearing his own long, soft-soled moccasins he made virtually no noise as he hastily strode along the corridors. Had he given the matter any thought, he might have realised that walking so quietly through a houseful of high-ranking lords could lead to his being somewhere he was neither expected, wanted nor supposed to be. He gave such a possibility no consideration at all until he crossed a high balcony and by then it was too late.

There was a clear view through its carved screen into a narrow hall well-lit by several tall windows, and from the corner of his eye he caught a glimpse of something which made him pause for a closer look. Glancing down without thought for the consequences of his action, Aldric went suddenly pale and stifled a gasp as he flattened against the wall.

There were three men in a tableau below him: King Rynert sat at one end of the hall, a fully-armoured Dewan ar Korentin stood in the centre with his arms folded so that his drawn sword rested threateningly on his left shoulder, and a third figure knelt politely on one knee in the dark area between two windows. Not that he needed to take such trouble, for he was dressed from head to foot in black with only his eyes and a thin stripe of face visible. In the shadows he was almost invisible. He had no obvious weapons, but the mere reputation of the *tulathin* was reason enough for ar Korentin's caution. Sudden violence and a *taulath* went hand-in-hand.

Aldric could hear the soft murmur of voices, but not enough to make sense of their conversation. He did not really want to know anything about it, and indeed wished most heartily that he had gone another way. It was too late now to creep away; getting in unnoticed had probably used up all his luck for the day on that score at least. Why King Rynert was having any dealings at all with a *taulath*—a shadow-thief— was beyond Aldric's comprehension. *Eijin* were men who, willingly or not, had lost their honour. *Tulathin* did not know the meaning of the word. They were mercenaries; spies, kidnappers, assassins . . . any task at all was performed without question, just so long as their price was met.

There was the muffled chink of a moneybag and then the *taulath* was gone as if he had never been—like a shadow banished by sunlight. Aldric breathed a little more easily, but his heart did not begin to slow down until Dewan and the King had also left the hall. When they did his mouth stretched into something which did not really succeed in being even the wryest of smiles, and he became uncomfortably aware of the light film of sweat which covered his skin.

Today was a day for shocks, it seemed.

*

Lord Santon studied Dunrath from his position on the ridge. For an hour now the uppermost part of the donjon had been veiled by a strange azure mist. There was a dull, sonorous humming in the air, like the sound made by a swarm of bees but deeper, as much felt through the ground a heard in the air. Santon did not like it. Trying to push the mystery from his mind until he was more able to give an answer to it, he opened a chart and tried to concentrate on the lists of figures set out neatly beneath each diagram.

He had barely begun to read when someone shouted.

Endwar-*arluth* Santon wasted no time in idle questions—he knew instinctively where to look. Dunrath's citadel was now wholly shrouded in a globe of coiling blue vapour lit from within by a pale glow. Now and then streaks of brilliant white light spat like shooting-stars from the cloud, dragging long bright tails through the air behind them as they curved down to splash in frosty extinction on the ground before the fortress. The dull hum became more intense, a harsh drone which set the teeth on edge and ground into men's skulls like a rusty drill-bit. It became steadily colder.

Santon stared at his own breath drifting smokily in front of

him and then at the perimeter wall of Dunrath's outermost
defensive ring. The reddish stone was inches deep in sparkling white crystals, as if snow had fallen and mingled with
powdered diamonds as it fell. He swore in disbelief and
stooped to lift his helmet, then yelped, swore again more
viciously and sucked at fingertips which had left their skin on
the icy metal. There were four little blots of tissue on the
helmet's neck-guard and even as Endwar looked at them they
became hard and bluish-white, like the flesh of a man with
frostbite.

The entire fortress was lost now in a blinding, frigid light,
and long filaments of bitterly cold energy came whispering
through the ranks of his army. "Sound the retreat!" snarled
Santon, trying to smother the fear in his voice with an overlay
of anger. The nearest trumpeter set his instrument to his lips,
then released his breath not in the ordered signal but in a cry
of pain as the bronze mouthpiece froze against him. Blood
trickled from both lips after he finally wrenched the thing
away, ran down his chin but, instead of dripping there, it
congealed in crackling cherry-red icicles.

The orderly regimental blocks bulged, heaved and broke as
the men in those formations began to run, screaming as they
flung away shields, helmets and weapons which had become
too painfully cold to touch. Their cries mingled with the wind
which rose from a sullen moan through a howl to a shrieking
gale, tearing flags from their poles in long shreds of fabric,
pavilions and bivouac tents in tatters from the ground and
breath from the lungs of men too stabbed by the gelid spears
of a blast from between the stars to fight against it.

When he looked down at his armour to find it cased in
white rime, and at the faces of his generals made old by frost
lying thick on beards and brows, Endwar Clan-Lord Santon
knew himself to have been defeated without a blow being
struck. Then, with shocking suddenness, the gale died in
mid-howl. As one man the officers on the ridge looked
towards Dunrath. Some swore. Others prayed. At least one
that Santon could see fumbled his *tsepan* from his belt with a
hand leaving much of its skin on the weapon's scabbard, and
in a fit of despair or impotent rage stabbed himself through

the great vessels of the throat. Though his blood spurted steaming from the wound, it had frozen before it could splash on the ground and fell instead as crystals, like rubies crushed in a mortar.

Santon sympathised with the man: at least his death had been an honourable one and not of some wizard's choosing. He was only surprised that the sight of the fortress had not broken other men's minds or driven them to suicide.

Shimmering patterns of force crawled over the massive structure, making it seem imbued with some ghastly form of life. Crystalline rings of energy pulsed heavily above the donjon, stacked like a child's quoits, their shifting, brilliant colours impossible to watch but impossible to ignore, the thick droning pouring from them in waves of raw atonal noise. They hung there, brooding, vast, ominously waiting.

For what . . . ?

*

Aldric paused briefly outside the council chamber to get his breath back while the two guards flanking the double door watched him with tolerant sympathy. "Not to worry, *arluthan*," said one, trying to combine respect with friendliness, "*matherneir* Rynert had not really called the conference to order before he was called away. Nobody will notice you being just a little late."

"Is it war, sir, do you think?" asked the other cautiously. Aldric grinned crookedly at the soldier, who stiffened to attention at being directly noticed.

"If I hadn't been late," he observed drily, "I would probably know myself."

The first sentry smiled at his companion's discomfiture, then saluted and opened the door for Aldric. The chamber inside was laid out like most Alban meeting-halls: a row of low chairs along the farthest wall for any high-clan *kailinineir* who might be present, a more imposing seat set at right-angles for the king—something always done whether or not the monarch was there—and lesser stools—little more than elevated cushions—set in lines for everyone else. As an *eijo*, Aldric expected to sit on one of these and had in fact taken his place when a retainer in the king's colours ushered him to one of the high-clan chairs. His surprise was made complete when everyone, most of the military and political figureheads in Alba, gave him a low, formal obeisance as they would to any other high-clan *arluth*.

To hide his slight embarrassment, Aldric took exaggerated care over setting Isileth Widowmaker on her stand to the left of his seat, once a retainer had brought one appropriate to the formal, near-vertical mounting of ceremonial *taikenin*, also a small padded mat for the young man's helmet. He was not made any more comfortable by the realisation that he was the only person present not carrying a *taipan*, and that with his short hair and Widowmaker rearing like a striking snake near his shoulder he was the object of scrutiny by everyone in the room.

Then the doors were flung wide open and King Rynert came in, flanked by soldiers and preceded by ar Korentin with his scabbarded sword held free of his belt in one hand, ready for instant defence of his lord. The Vreijek took up position at the right of Rynert's high seat and grounded his blade with a single precise clank. As if at this signal, the room was filled with a metallic susurration as every man present made First Obeisance. Rynert bowed from the waist in acknowledgment and sat down, waited for the warriors to resume their places and then deliberately smiled to signal an end to extreme formality.

"Gentlemen," he said, "I have just received two communications of great interest to us all. First—" he held out one hand and Dewan set a slip of paper in it, "—news from abroad. Two days ago, in the Pleasure Palace at Kalitzim, Emperor Droek joined his far from illustrious ancestors."

Nobody actually cheered—that would have been gravely impolite—but a distinct ripple of shock, relief and pleasure ran through the chamber. Everyone knew what Droek's death meant even before Rynert went on to explain.

"Though I have no confirmation here," the king continued when his audience had settled themselves, "I feel it is safe to assume that we no longer need concern ourselves with possible Imperial interference in the current crisis. Warlord Etzel, General Goth and Prince Ioen have enough problems of their own, I very much hope.'' There was a little burst of laughter at that. ''It seems he was found dead in bed—whose bed, is not made clear.'' More laughter, the mirth of men suddenly freed from the threat of full-scale war. One man, however, did not laugh.

Aldric was remembering a black-clad *taulath* neither long ago nor far away, and the sound of money changing hands. Something twisted inside him like a knife and he found it very hard to keep contempt from his face when he looked at Rynert the King.

''My second communication is more local,'' Rynert went on. ''Lord Santon has taken six thousand men north and this'' —another fragile strip was put into his outstretched hand— ''carried by a pigeon which arrived less than an hour ago, confirms that the fortress of Dunrath is now invested and under seige. I intend to—''

Rynert's intention went unheard, for at that moment a tall, lean figure rose from the rearmost row of the low-clan seats and strode forward. Several warriors sprang to their feet, snatching up shortswords to defend the king, and Dewan's long, heavy sword came out of its scabbard with a long, sinister hiss. Aldric too was on his feet, Widowmaker loose in her sheath just in case, but there was no real need.

Gemmel had the sense to stop well out of danger. He regarded the king with cold emerald eyes and then sketched a bow which was the merest token of respect and verged very close on the insolent. Rynert glared at him, ignoring the old man's lack of manners out of consideration for his age but not through any fear of his powers. Rynert of Alba was not the strongest of men in body, but he was afraid of nothing he had yet met in his life.

''You had best intend, King,'' said Gemmel quietly, ''to have a funeral service said for those six thousand men. They will be dead before the sun sets tonight.''

In the absolute silence which followed his words, the click as Aldric sheathed his *taiken* was deafeningly loud. It was a measure of the enchanter's imposing presence that not one eye turned from him to look towards the source of the sound.

"What do you mean, Gemmel-*an* Errekren?" Rynert demanded.

"I mean, King, that Lord Santon has gone up against an enemy from whom he has no protection." Gemmel slapped the Dragonwand angrily. "I would not have put Aldric-*an* Talvalin to the trouble and risk of fetching me this talisman if it hadn't been of vital importance. Kalarr cu Ruruc, King, is more powerful than you can possibly imagine—and he has a grudge against you, against every man here, against the whole of Alba, which is five hundred years old. Never think that during that time he has learnt mercy or forgiveness."

"What, then, should we do, *pestreyr-an*?" asked old Lord Dacurre.

"March north at once. This time I—and Ykraith the Dragonwand—will be with you, to turn aside any spells the sorcerers in Dunrath might hurl."

"Can you do nothing for Endwar Santon? He is the husband of my second daughter . . ."

"Lord Dacurre, spells are limited by distance, just like everything else. With my power channelled through it, Ykraith can form a shielding dome perhaps a mile across, but that will decrease as I tire—and I will. Before then I hope your soldiers will have done something useful. But as for Lord Santon—I very much fear that he and all his men are beyond my or indeed any aid."

*

The sky above Dunrath was alive with swirling patterns of power which formed and broke endlessly like visions from a drug-dream given shape and substance. There was no wind and the collective breaths of men and horses formed a fog above and around them, muting outlines but not the eldritch colours of Kalarr cu Ruruc's sorcery.

Then the waiting ended.

The rings of energy held in check for half an hour above the citadel contracted once and then exploded outwards, fragmenting into needles of blazing white light which slashed through battle armour as if the metal scales were so much sodden paper, punching men to the ground with the shock of their impact or striking them dead on their feet. One such bolt sighed over Santon's shoulder and struck his trumpeter full in the chest, burst into a flare of splinters with a brittle cracking noise and enveloped the young man in a cloud of misty pale-blue radiance. The warrior gasped, spun half round on sagging knees and fell on to his face.

Santon leaned down to turn over the already rigid body and gasped in horror as three of the fingers snapped off in his hand. The boy's once-handsome face was now that of a corpse six weeks dead: leathery skin the colour of lead was stretched tightly over his bones, leaving his nose shrivelled into suppurating pits. His lips were drawn back clear of gums where the teeth, cased in frozen saliva, gaped in a rictus of terminal agony, and though his eyes had shrunk into their sockets they still held an expression of utter disbelief.

Death had been quick—but it had obviously been neither clean nor painless.

As if in a snowstorm, the air was full of streaks of white as the darts of sorcerous power went scything through Lord Santon's host, reaping men like ripe corn. Some errant thought in the *arluth*'s mind insisted that all this was wrong, that the slaughter of a legion should be noisier, more indicative of effort and not this near-silent erasure as if a scholar were cancelling out rough diagrams on a slate. But there was only the thin, protracted hissing as the bright streaks of energy slid through the air and the intermittent crackle as they struck home.

Quite suddenly it was over.

Dunrath was once more blue-grey stone, without any trace of alien lights or colours and only the flapping scarlet banners to indicate that the Talvalins were not in possession of their ancestral hold. The drifts of hoar-frost had vanished from its walls and a gentle breeze had scoured away the skeins of mist.

Endwar Santon's army had likewise ceased to exist. Instead there were twisted, discoloured corpses scattered over the ground as far as the eye could see. There, in a pair of dense wedges, lay the two thousand regular troops who had died in their places to a man. Straggled further away were men who had broken near the end, and almost out of sight lay the levied vassals who had been the first to run. There were perhaps a hundred men left alive out of the six thousand—and one of them was Santon.

He had stood very straight and waited for the blast of magic which would strike him down, but even when a virtual blizzard of the things had straddled his position on the ridge and smashed his staff officers into so much frozen meat, he had been unharmed. Such a thing was not accidental; Santon had already guessed as much and his suspicion was confirmed as a great voice boomed out from the sombre fortress.

"Commander!" it blared. "Commander, I know that you can hear me! I know you are alive, commander. I intended that you should be. Go back to your King Rynert, commander, and tell him of the fate which befalls any who would oppose me. And commander, I thank you for the chance to exercise my skills once again. Quite apart from the reinforcements which you have given me. Get you to your king with all despatch, my lord—you may not die till then!"

*

"That was quite a performance you put on back there," said Aldric, pouring himself a strong drink. Gemmel, intent on lighting his pipe, said nothing. "I mean," the *eijo* continued, aware that he was babbling and equally aware of the nervous tension which made him do so, "if you'd been on the stage you would have got a standing ovation at the very least for the sheer intensity of that opening speech."

The wizard stared at his foster-son through a veil of fragrant smoke, wondering just how much Aldric was covering up and how much he actually knew. "Intensity, yes . . ." he murmured. "Knowing that one's words are true does give their delivery a certain weight."

"Santon's dead then—you're certain of that?" Aldric spoke in much more sombre vein; he had not liked the saturnine lord, but had respected him as a proud, honourable, worthy gentleman of a kind nowadays growing rare.

"Probably so—or as good as dead anyway. We'll know soon enough, I fear. But Aldric, put other people aside for the moment. You heard me explain at some length about the

Dragonwand's properties and I presume you've been talking to King Rynert for the past half-hour . . ."

"Talking isn't the way I'd put it," Aldric said, with a small shiver of recollection. "There are things I did not want him to know—my use of magic, for one—but the way he can twist words around so that answering one question leaves you open for three more . . . Gemmel-*altrou*, I tell you without shame he had me scared once or twice. Rynert's worse than ar Korentin at that lawyer's crooked questioning style—and Dewan's bad enough, before Heaven."

"It's all in the degree of practice," Gemmel said drily.

"They've both had far too much of that and most of it on me."

"If you've quite finished . . ."

"Sorry! Yes, I have. Say your piece."

"Thank you. Now you'd better know at once that I was lying about Ykraith's protective powers."

"What?"

"It's a weapon first and foremost—an offensive weapon. Like a sword; you can parry with one, but its prime function is to cut and thrust. Any protection which the army receives will come from my own personal force and from this." Gemmel took a small box from his belt-pouch and set it on the table before lifting off the lid. The blue aura of the Echainon spellstone pulsed out and over the table, giving as always the impression that it must leave a stain, so intense was its brilliant azure colouration. "I haven't the time to explain why just now, but because Kalarr cu Ruruc once used this himself a simple charm will be enough to cause it to absorb any sorcery he invokes—without the usual drain on my physical and psychic strength. Duergar doesn't really concern me; I've studied his methods and it seems he's a necromancer, one skilled at giving life to dead things—and not necessarily corpses, as that bronze monstrosity in Erdhaven proved. As far as really dangerous weapon-magic is concerned, say the Invocation of Fire or the High Accelerator, he cannot be considered a serious threat."

"But why lie about it?"

"Aldric, think of the military mind. If any of those legion lords knew this was a weapon they'd insist on using it their way and that would be fatal."

"Then why—"

"I had to say something other than: 'Unfortunately, King, my personal strategy is going to leave you virtually unshielded for a while. Bad luck.' Rather than let that happen, Rynert would lock me up and throw away the key."

"Personal strategy . . . ?" Aldric wondered shrewdly. "I have the feeling that includes me."

"It does. There are certain rules which must be obeyed in this sort of business—and of course it's your duty and no one else's to kill Duergar Vathach. Correct, *venjens-eijo*?"

"Correct."

"Then we understand one another. You'll need me to prevent Kalarr from turning you to a small smear of crisped fat—"

"You have such a way with words, you know . . ."

"—and in that time the army will be without protection, other than the few charms I shall be able to lay on it before we go."

"Go? Where?"

"Use your brains, boy. Where else but Dunrath? I'm quite sure there's another way in, apart from the front gate. Mmm?"

"What if there isn't?" hedged Aldric.

"Then I have ways and means of circumventing that difficulty if such should arise. But I feel certain that it won't."

"Exactly what will you say to King Rynert if anything goes wrong?"

"There are plenty of plausible explanations—perhaps his men went beyond the limits of my spell or something like that. But if anything goes really badly wrong, then making excuses will be the least of our problems. Assuming we or the king are even alive to worry about them."

"Sometimes, *altrou-ain*, you say the most reassuring things. Just like Ymareth—now there was another . . . oh dear God in Heaven!"

"Aldric—what's the matter?" Gemmel leaned forward urgently because the young *eijo* had gone suddenly, shockingly white. "Are you ill, son?"

"No . . . No, I'm all right." Aldric smiled weakly. "Just bloody stupid."

"Don't take names to yourself without reason," reproved the sorcerer.

"Oh, I've reason enough," the *eijo* muttered. "You might think anything to do with a full-grown firedrake would stick in my mind, but I'd almost forgotten what Ymareth told me. Destroy any talisman of Kalarr's that you hold, it said, and make sure he knows it—then await events. Ymareth's words."

"You forgot that . . . ?" Gemmel stared so hard that at last Aldric was forced to look away. Only then did he nod, once and hastily. "Then you *are* stupid! Listen: if I destroy the spellband, not only will it remove any threat which Duergar might hold over Kalarr—so that once they know it, their alliance will fall apart—but cu Ruruc will think I've failed to recognise the Echainon stone. The kind of mistake a petty wizard might make. So *he* might make a mistake of his own like leaving the security of his fortress—"

"My fortress, please."

"His stolen fortress to defeat Rynert in open battle. That's how he was destroyed last time, so such sweet revenge should be most enticing."

"Well, then," Aldric finished his wine and stood up, "let's do it. Have you noticed any crows about Keys?"

"A few. Foolish; gulls would be much less obvious round a sea-port."

"Not very imaginative, are they? Come on, *altrou*."

*

The regiments were already forming up as Aldric and Gemmel sauntered innocently through the streets of Kerys, both quite aware of the black bird which kept pace with them along the rooftops. Gemmel had slipped away briefly and had returned with a sapphire in his hand. Aldric had not asked where the gem had come from, but a word from Gemmel made it glow until now it was a convincing imitation of the Echainon spellstone. The wrist-band was tucked into his belt.

"Carefully now," he said in a voice so soft that Aldric

barely heard him. "If our spy guesses that all this is for his benefit, we'll have wasted our time."

"And started cu Ruruc wondering about just why we found it necessary to go through such an elaborate deception . . ."

"Precisely so."

They were looking for some deserted courtyard which would be concealed from ordinary spies, but not from the changeling hopping cautiously in their wake. Though Aldric stopped now and then to glance about suspiciously, he always moved slowly enough for the crow to hide from view. It was more difficult than he had thought to make such a pretence seem convincing. Then Gemmel grabbed his arm and jerked him out of sight.

"In there!" the enchanter hissed in his ear and gave him a firm push between the shoulders. At the end of a narrow, sour-smelling alley Aldric found himself in an old stable, its roof collapsed and open to the sky. Something moved furtively between the broken rafters and the young *eijo* gave a small, grim smile. Gemmel appeared beside him, looking about with every sign of satisfaction. "This will do," he said, and laid the spellband down on a heap of rotting straw. Above their heads, the crow almost fell into the stable as it tried to see what the sorcerer was doing.

Using a piece of wood, Gemmel drew complicated patterns on the dank floor; only he knew they were meaningless, but they looked significant and that was enough. He mumbled nonsense under his breath and accompanied the sounds with imposing gestures. The overall impression was of a fussy, inexperienced conjuror faced for once with an important spell, and Aldric was forced to hide another smile behind his hand.

Steam billowed from the damp straw as the bronze ring began to glow; then its metal ran like wax, exposing the glow of the false spellstone for a few vital seconds before the whole thing was swallowed in a white flash of heat. Only ash and a few spark-pitted cinders remained behind.

"So much for Duergar and Kalarr," Gemmel announced confidently. Something rustled overhead—not the crow, which Aldric had been surreptitiously watching, but a large brown rat. Gemmel glanced up, catching his companion's nod of approval before shouting: "What? A spy!" and pointing his finger at the rodent.

There was a hazy flicker in the dim light and a crack like the lash of a whip. The rat squealed shrilly and its body exploded, throwing bones and internal organs all over the stable as if shot from a *telek*. Though Aldric had been expecting something of the sort, the speed and violence of Gemmel's reaction made him jump. Even so, he missed neither the crow's hasty tumble out of sight nor the rapid clatter of wings as it made a hurried exit.

"I think he's convinced we meant business," he said, forcing a laugh as he glanced towards the messily-deceased rat. "What was that trick anyway?"

"A lesser form of the High Accelerator," Gemmel replied, massaging the pins-and-needles it had caused in his hand.

"Why lesser?"

"Because I saw no need to flatten the stable, that's why."

"Could you have done that?"

"Could you stop asking questions for a while?" the wizard returned testily. His index finger, which had directed the spell, felt as always as if he had hit it with a hammer. Then he relented. "Yes, quite easily. The High Accelerator is a fierce magic, you know; it can make a man's eyeballs jump out through the back of his skull, or push his skull out of his head. Hurling down a wall isn't difficult. Satisfied?"

"For the time being . . ."

*

"He destroyed it?" Kalarr repeated softly. "Are you quite sure?"

One of the thin, yellow-eyed changelings nodded emphatically. "I saw it done, lord—and barely escaped with my life."

"So . . ." The sorcerer stood up and crossed to a window, from which he stared down at where Duergar worked his necromancy on the wreckage of Endwar Santon's legion. Since the great spell two days before, Kalarr had felt drained, exhausted—but now his weariness was replaced by a fierce exultation. "Losing the stone is unfortunate," he mused, then chuckled. It was an ugly sound. "But not so great a loss to me as the wristband is to you, Drusalan."

Swivelling, he fixed both spies with a baleful glare. "Duergar Vathach must not hear of this matter," he growled, and an ominous note in his voice made the changelings quake. Both knew the easiest way in which he could ensure their silence. Then he smiled cruelly. "Good! I see you understand me. Then remember. Now, get out!"

The spies needed no second bidding; they scuttled frantically away with cu Ruruc's harsh laughter in their ears. He settled back in his chair once they had gone and began to plan his strategy, wanting the Albans crushed and under his domination but strangely unsure how to go about it. Now that the old Emperor was dead any aid from that quarter was unlikely—Grand Warlord Etzel was too busy jockeying for real power to be concerned with abstract notions of foreign conquest.

While Kalarr intended to enjoy Duergar's death in the fullness of time, he realised now that the time would have to be deferred. He had nothing like the Drusalan's skill in the art of necromancy, and it was that art which had created and maintained the *traugur* host which garrisoned Dunrath.

Using the same type of huge spell which had annihilated Santon's army was physically impossible; Kalarr knew that it would be more than a month before he could take the physical strain of the High Magic again without hideous deformity. Besides, he knew that a military victory would entice certain ambitious lesser lords to side with him, since they would not be smirching their honour by aiding a wizard, merely a skilful general. Kalarr sneered to himself; he cared nothing for what they thought, but knew that certain proprieties had to be observed. It had been just the same before . . . the last time. Men remained human and never learned the lessons of their own past.

And defeating Rynert in battle would be such a deliciously ironic vengeance that he could scarcely be expected to forego the opportunity . . . Kalarr opened out Lord Santon's battle orders and began to study them with care.

*

Both the great army roads which criss-crossed Alba and the legions which marched along them had been created by Rynert's great-grandfather in the early days of the Imperial threat. Neither had yet been used against the enemy which had caused their birth, but had frequently seen service against Elthanek border reavers and recalcitrant lesser lords who fancied a return to the old independent days before the Clan Wars. The six legions had become little more than a huge police force with a kingdom to patrol, but that state of affairs was changing with every mile they marched further north and every man knew it, whether he was a peasant's son who had joined the Standards because he expected no inheritance or the lordliest high-clan *kailin-eir* resplendent in the plumes and crests of a commander.

Many small villages had grown up near the highways in order to benefit from the travellers and merchants passing to and fro. Most had inns and lodging-houses to make such people stay longer and market places for the buying and selling of their goods. Aldric sat bareheaded in Lyard's saddle at the centre of one such market place. The village around it might have been home to perhaps three hundred people. Once. Not now.

It had been reduced to a jumble of soot-smeared stones and shattered timbers. Greasy black smoke curled up from the wreckage, bringing with it the thick stench of charred meat. The reek was unmistakable. It was the cloying, heavy smell of houses which had burned with people still inside.

Not all had burned. There were a few corpses, two days dead and already bloating, sprawled among the rubble. The sickly-sweet odour of their corruption pricked at the young warrior's nostrils despite the scarf he wrapped around his face. It was horrible, and pathetic in its horror. Hooves had ploughed up the little gardens, pounding flowers and vegetables alike into pulp and shredded fibres. Lyard, battle-schooled, remained quite still, but schooling or not the big horse's laid-back ears signalled his unease. Aldric leaned forward to pat the Andarran charger's neck, then stopped with the movement unfinished as he saw the doll.

It was a simple thing of stitched cloth, with a long rip

across its painted face, its yellow woollen hair stiff and dark
with dried blood. Part of a child's hand still gripped one
ribboned braid. There was nothing else.

Aldric stared at it with his fists clenching until the knuckles
gleamed white through his skin, as hate and helpless rage
boiled up inside him. More than he had suffered loss at the
hands of his enemies, he knew that—but the extent of that
loss was only now beginning to sink home. He stroked Isileth
Widowmaker as if the longsword was a hawk needing to be
gentled, wondering if death by *taiken* was what he really
wanted to visit on Duergar and on Kalarr. He knew now why
his ancestors had sometimes reacted as they did—there had
been one rebel fourteen generations ago who had taken three
weeks to die; he had been a destroyer of innocent villagers as
well. War was for warriors—any man who visited its horrors
on the helpless deserved whatever ingenuities the dark and
secret places of the mind could conceive.

Then he heard the hoofbeats and looked up. King Rynert
and Dewan ar Korentin were picking their way through the
devastation and both, Aldric could see, felt the same way
about it as he did. As they drew closer he saluted and asked
simply: "Why?"

It was Dewan who answered. Once an Imperial officer, he
had seen such things before he knew the twisted reasoning
behind them. "To discourage us," he said bleakly. "It must
have been Duergar Vathach's suggestion. This is a Drusalan
tactic—it's supposed to take the heart from an advancing
army when they see their enemies care nothing for human
life."

"In the Empire, maybe." Aldric's voice was flinty. "This
is Alba."

"I've lived here long enough to know it," Dewan returned. "All this will be repaid with interest, never fear." He
watched the young man and said nothing more, knowing that
however sincere he was, his words sounded like the most
insipid platitudes.

"Leave this place, *kailin-eir*," Rynert advised gently.
"Brooding about it will do no good."

"As you wish, Lord King." Aldric saluted again, bowed

carefully and then rode Lyard towards the roads, towards the army—anywhere, so long as it was away from the village and its dead.

Rynert watched him go, then looked across at Dewan. "A young man who lives his life most intensely, I think," he said. "And he feels the loss of the girl, despite what you told me. You were wrong there, Dewan my friend."

"I did not use the word infatuation, King. She did. But perhaps we were both wrong."

"What's your opinion of him?"

Dewan considered briefly. "Whoever chose the *kourgath*-cat for his crest knew what they were doing." Rynert raised one quizzical eyebrow but let Dewan continue without interruption. "He's arrogant, more self-sufficient than I think he knows himself. He's very intelligent, well-educated in . . . in a most interesting variety of subjects. He's foul-tempered when the mood's on him, dangerous, sometimes ruthless, sometimes pitiless—"

"But not all the time, Dewan. Not now, at least."

"I noticed that. He's a strange one. My wife likes him though, whatever Tehal Kyrin was telling her. Lyseun does not usually approve of people who take me away from her, as you well know. But he can be friendly when he wants to be, I suppose . . ."

"You sound almost jealous, captain."

"I don't suffer from it, King."

"Would you trust him now?"

"With my life."

"And with your wife . . . ?" The king was mocking gently, as he sometimes did with people close enough to be almost family. Dewan and his lady were part of that very small, very select group, which was why the Vreijek felt able to grin broadly.

"I'm not a jealous, possessive husband, King. It would depend entirely on what Lyseun said. But yes, I'd trust young Aldric with her. He's an honourable gentleman." Dewan's face went suddenly very serious. "That's what makes him so dangerous."

"I'll bear that in mind. Now, Baiart: if he's taken alive, he is *not* to be permitted *tsepanak'ulleth*. I intend to execute him.''

Dewan was momentarily aghast, and seemed to find difficulty in closing his mouth. ''You intend—then you'll seize the Talvalin lands by forfeiture? But Aldric . . .''

''I don't need the lands for myself; but they will be useful as something to give or withhold. When I return them—which I'm not obliged to do—my magnanimity will perhaps engender a little gratitude in that young man. It won't hurt him to feel something more human than duty and respect.''

''If he doesn't feel it, King, somebody else will definitely be hurt. I admire your cleverness, but in this case I wish my formal objections to the scheme placed on record. Young Talvalin's already quite human enough to resent such a . . . such a trick if he ever finds out about it. Rynert . . . be careful.''

''I will be.'' The King let Dewan's use of his name go by without any comment. ''But at least it will remind him that he can't gain everything by his own efforts. I prefer such a clan-lord to be under obligation to me.''

''As you wish. I still—''

Ar Korentin broke off as three horsemen in the orange plumes of couriers came clattering towards them. All had the look of men who had ridden hard and fast, but even so the most senior of the messengers leapt from his skidding steed before the beast had halted and went down on one knee while the others dismounted in more restrained fashion.

''Sire,'' the man announced breathlessly, ''we have found Lord Santon!''

*

Endwar Santon told his tale to a ring of grim-faced, silent men, and if they looked like mourners at a funeral he looked like the corpse. His armour and weapons were gone; he had been wandering for more than a week, eating what little he could scavenge—and with Duergar's raiders out that was little indeed—while he made his unsteady way south to the road where some friend would eventually pass. And there he had waited.

Even at a forced march, the king's host could not cover six

hundred miles in less than three weeks. Santon had been a fortnight without food or shelter before the first outriders came sweeping up ahead of the army; a fortnight of brooding and of black despair, of days darkened by his memories and of nights made bright with the flames of burning cottages.

Rynert's army was now less than four days' march from Dunrath, but their strength of some fourteen thousand was no longer enough to obliterate cu Ruruc's forces—not since these had been reinforced by some six thousand additional men. Only Gemmel gained some small, grim satisfaction from what Kalarr had done; he knew that there was no longer any risk of some awesome spell devastating the entire host while he was unable to protect it. There would be small magics, inevitably, but they would do no more damage than spears and arrows could. Step by step, Duergar and Kalarr were moving up to lay their heads on the block—and neither of them knew it, he was sure.

"He said I could not die until I spoke to you, Lord King," Santon said with difficulty. "I do not know if he mocked me, or laid a charm on me—without a *tsepan* I could not find out . . ." He croaked a low, ugly laugh. "I even threw my sword away, so that I could not fall on it as they did in ancient times. I wanted to die, but I had to tell you everything myself. Now I have done so." Santon laid down the cup of fortified wine someone had given him, uncoiled from his sitting position on the ground and knelt in First Obeisance. "And now I can die, if you will permit me, Lord King."

Rynert hesitated; he had been expecting such a request and trying to work out a polite means of refusing it ever since the messenger had first spoken half an hour before. Then he realised there was only one response after all, and nodded his assent.

The preparations were swiftly completed; a modicum of privacy was granted by making screens from the great clan war-banners, and Santon was left alone with one of the priests who always accompanied the legions. Aldric and several of the other younger lords stood around in a sort of horrified fascination, though few of them knew that Aldric himself had been within a *tsepan*'s length of the same situation. Then King Rynert beckoned to him and Aldric felt his mouth go dry.

"I would ask you to act as Endwar's second, Aldric-*an*," the king said in a low, private voice, "but since he was your father's friend it would be unseemly. Dewan is acting for him instead. Might I ask that he be allowed to use your sword?"

Aldric thought sombrely that Widowmaker was once again justifying her name, but he nodded consent and unhooked the sheathed blade from her slings. Dewan approached, wearing a formal overmantle marked with the crests of his rank, and accepted the *taiken* with a deep, courteous bow before securing it to his belt. Then he backed away three paces, his face an emotionless mask, and bowed again respectfully before turning to vanish behind the makeshift screens. Rynert watched the Vreijek go, then looked at Aldric. "Do you wish to witness this?" he asked.

The young *eijo* hesitated, then forced a small, ironic smile onto his lips. "I don't *wish* to, Lord King," he confessed. "But Endwar Santon was my father's friend and a hearth-companion of clan Talvalin. My absence would dishonour us all. I will be a witness."

*

After it was over, everything went very still for a moment; then the witnesses bowed in unison, rose and departed without a backward glance. All except Aldric. He waited quietly for the various rituals which had to be completed before Dewan could return his sword, then strapped the *taiken* back in place, secretly grateful that she had not been needed after all. Like much else in his life, Lord Santon had required no one's help to leave it. Aldric gazed at the huddled form covered now with a scarlet cloth, then turned to Dewan. "What will they do with him?" he asked. "There's not enough wood to give him a proper funeral."

"There is. You're forgetting that we carry fuel for the cook-fires—but I for one will eat my food cold if I must, to do him honour." Dewan rubbed his hands together; he was not Alban, had not been brought up with *tsepanak'ulleth* and found that the rite disturbed him. "Such courage deserves more than just a hole in the ground."

"I wonder will Baiart be as brave?" Aldric murmured, thinking aloud rather than asking a question. Dewan realised that just in time to stop the words which crowded on his tongue.

"I . . . wonder indeed," he said very softly.

TEN

Deathbringer

"Lord King, I have been trying to speak to you these three days past!" King or no king, Gemmel made no effort to keep the acerbity from his voice, though fortunately for him Rynert was more disposed to amusement than anger.

"I have been somewhat busy, Gemmel-*an*. An army to command, a kingdom to rule at second hand—little things I know, but time-consuming." The enchanter simmered gently, trying hard to keep his temper in check, until Rynert decided that enough was enough and became businesslike. "What do you want, anyway?"

"This concerns your battle strategy, Lord King."

Rynert lifted his eyebrows; there were some things which he considered unwarranted interference and this was one of them. "Oh. So you're a military commander on top of all else?" he said sarcastically. "Imperial service, no doubt?"

"I am an enchanter, Lord King."

"At least we have that clear. So what business is it of yours what strategy I adopt, eh?"

"Because of what you will be fighting. *Traugarin*, Lord King—not men." Rynert said nothing, and Gemmel interpreted this—correctly—as permission to continue. "You're not dealing with an Imperial Lord-General, but with a necromancer whose army has been dead for a long time. Some were resurrected from the old Baelen battlefield, others from the destruction of Lord Santon's legion. The numbers are equal on both sides, so far as I can judge—except that Kalarr's men cannot be killed. Yours can."

"That had not occurred to me, wizard," the king said softly after a pause.

Gemmel smiled slightly. "Precisely why I raised the question in the first place," he purred with some small satisfaction in his voice.

"So Duergar must be killed before his spell is broken. Is that it?"

Better, mused the old man to himself; you are actually starting to think things out for yourself again. Aloud he said: "Aldric Talvalin is oathbound to perform that act. I'll ensure that he survives to do it."

"And what about my army? You told the council that you would protect it. Are you failing in your promise?"

What *promise* did I give? Gemmel almost snapped, but spoke differently. "Of course not, Lord King. I can lay enough protective charms over the host to turn most spells—"

"Most?" Rynert's voice was suddenly sharp and suspicious.

"The spells I cannot turn are those of the High Magic, such as the charm used against Lord Santon. Like necromancy, those must be stifled at source—but I shouldn't worry overmuch. Cu Ruruc is hardly strong enough to use them yet—not without causing himself the most appalling damage."

"I know that much." Rynert was not merely bluffing to save a little face, he knew all about the merciless rules of high sorcery, and about the warping pressures they put on mind and body—which was why the most powerful wizards were never shrivelled ancients but men who might well pass for warriors.

"Also," Gemmel put in silkily, "cu Ruruc wouldn't want to defeat you by any other means than combat if it can be managed. He'll get more Alban allies that way."

By the expression on Rynert's face this also was something he had not considered. "There are *kailinin* whom I asked to join the hosting, both at Erdhaven and since; men who made excuses though they promised support later . . ."

"Watch them, Lord King."

"Oh, I will . . . Damn it, wizard, will you stop meddling in affairs of state!"

"I beg pardon."

The apology did not sound especially sincere, but Rynert
was in no mood to press for more. "Then what is it you wish
me to do, Lord General Gemmel?" he asked, only half
jesting with the title. "Run away? Because we're less than a
day from Dunrath."

"No. Not run, anyway." Gemmel stopped perforce as
cavalry clattered past the king's pavilion, drowning his words
for a few seconds.

Rynert got to his feet and looked out through the tent's
door-flap. "Dawn patrol," he observed absently. "Riding
point for the column. We'll be moving soon." Picking up
his leather leggings he began to buckle them on himself,
deciding in view of Gemmel's conversation not to summon
any servants until he had to do so. "Well, man, carry on."

"As I said, don't run—but don't meet cu Ruruc head-on
either. Skirmish. Duck and weave and sidestep. You know
now that a set-piece battle is out of the question, so break
your troops into small formations, units of two hundred at
most, and disperse them. Your purpose should be to keep the
enemy busy—because you can't destroy him. And the busier
you keep Kalarr, the better chance Aldric and I will have of
slipping unnoticed into Dunrath."

Rynert grunted; it might have been an opinion, or just the
effort of tightening a buckle behind his knee. Then he straightened up and gazed at the enchanter. "What's to stop cu
Ruruc dealing with each small unit one at a time?" he asked,
purely as a matter of form, since it was fairly certain Gemmel
would already have an answer.

He had, of course. "Two things: first, I'm going to destroy
the spies which have been keeping us under constant surveil-
lance, and second, I'll lay a fog over the army before the
spies can be replaced. That way—to be quite brutal about
it—you'll lose two hundred men at most in any one engage-
ment."

"It is brutal. But also good sense. When will you deal with
the spies?"

Gemmel twirled the Dragonwand in a spear-fighter's flour-
ish which made King Rynert smile a little. "Your host is

preparing to break camp, so they'll be watching. Now seems as good a time as any.''

Rynert shrugged into his plate-and-meshmail sleeves and followed the enchanter outside, tightening their lacings as he went. The king could not have said whether he worked at the armour with the intention of making it comfortable, or merely because he had no desire to seem interested in the practice of magic, despite being in fact interested to the point of fascination. Gemmel was muttering something under his breath and Rynert moved a little closer in order to answer him—then realised with a slight start that the old man was actually addressing the Dragonwand.

"*Abath arhan,* Ykraith," he murmured. "*Acchuad eiya ilearath dua'hr.*" There was a deep, melodious thrumming sound, like an echo of the bass register on a zither, and a translucent shimmer enveloped the crystal in the carven firedrake's mouth. Rynert felt its pressure just as he would have felt the heat from an uncovered brazier, and was conscious of a great stillness settling over the camp. All that moved were the crows which spiralled lazily high above. Gemmel favoured them with a poisonous smile and raised the Dragonwand above his head; everyone who saw him do so instinctively ducked. The enchanter's smile grew more cheerful. "There's nothing to worry about," he called.

Then he spoke a single harsh phrase which unleashed the spellstave's leashed-in force. It lit the cold blue sky with a blizzard of orange sparks, which burst in a great expanding hemisphere from the Dragonwand's crystal tip and lashed with blinding speed across the camp, piercing each changeling-crow as if on a thousand red-hot skewers. The birds spewed smoke and singeing feathers, then tumbled from the sky to leave it cleaner than it was.

"Nothing at all," Gemmel corrected primly, "unless you are a crow!"

*

Kalarr cu Ruruc stared at his magic mirror, drumming armoured fingers on the black ebony of his table's top. The obsidian glass obdurately refused to show him anything but his own darkened reflection. He strode across the chamber floor and back again, noisy in his carapace of scarlet-lacquered steel. There was still no image in the volcanic scry-glass even when he touched it and let some of his own inner power flow through its substance. Finally he swore viciously and smashed the thing to fragments with a single blow of his clenched fist.

Duergar looked round with a jerk at the sound of shattering. "That won't help," he said reprovingly. The window behind him showed greyness and the drifting skeins of fog which had grown thicker in the past half-hour. "Not even your flying eye could see through that murk."

"I know that well enough!" cu Ruruc snarled. "But it should at least show me what it cannot see through. Something's wrong with it. Something's hurt it."

"Then make another," said the necromancer simply.

"I have already told you that I can't," Kalarr grated through clenched teeth, leaning forward pugnaciously with his fists on the table. "There is a limit to that kind of shaping-spell. It's a penalty for the thing's usefulness."

"Usefulness?" Duergar laughed nastily. "What use have we made of it? Now my changelings—"

"Yes, your changelings! When did one of them last report, eh? Not since just after dawn, and now it's almost noon."

"Can't you dispell the mist?" Duergar asked, sidestepping further argument on the spy subject. Kalarr straightened with a gusty exhalation of breath.

"No I can't! As I've already told you!"

"You didn't," Duergar insisted, seemingly determined to annoy. Kalarr refused to react, merely smiling like a shark at his companion.

"All right, perhaps I didn't," he conceded. "I've more to do than remember every word spoken. But clearing away that spell-born fog is beyond my powers at present. You know what the attempt would do to me. Unless that's what you want, of course . . . ?"

"I could try to summon up a witch-wind," suggested Duergar evasively.

"No. Put all your power into keeping the *traugarin* strong. They must not die until I've finished with them—and with the Albans."

Kalarr picked up a helmet and left the chamber, clattering down the spiral stairs with Duergar at his heels. There were none of the usual guards, either living or *traugur* undead; cu Ruruc had stripped Dunrath of men so that this time there would be no doubt of the outcome of the battle. He intended nothing less than the obliteration of King Rynert's host. Striding down the corridor, he reached the donjon's double doors and flung them open with a crash.

The noise was echoed by the stamp of feet as the army outside slammed to attention. Soldiers choked the courtyard, overflowing through its gates in rank upon rank until they were lost to sight in the swirling mist. Vermeil banners hung above them, marked with cu Ruruc's winged-viper crest, rippling sluggishly in the cold grey air.

There was a burst of cheering from his cavalry, human mercenaries since *traugarin* made useless horsemen, but heavy silence from the rest of his army even when he swung gracefully into his horse's saddle and raised one hand in salute. Kalarr grinned unpleasantly and passed the thin chains of the flail he carried as a baton through his fingers. "That's what I miss about commanding corpses," he remarked drily to Duergar. "The affection troops have for their general. These seem—"

"Lifeless?" the necromancer suggested.

"Ha . . ." Kalarr's gaze swept the courtyard and settled on Baiart, who had appeared at the foot of the stairs and now leaned heavily against the stone balustrade with a winecup in one hand and a brandy-bottle in the other. Baiart Talvalin was very drunk, and consequently very bold. "Hail to the mighty general," he slurred, and then looked pointedly from Kalarr to Duergar and back again. "Who. . . else. . . do you plan to kill today?"

The Drusalan necromancer's head jerked round to stare at him, then much more slowly turned to face Kalarr. That sorcerer's features remained expressionless while he lowered his helmet into place and laced its war-mask snugly. It was probably all the unrelieved red armour which made his cheeks seem flushed with rage, because he was smiling most benevolently as he walked his big roan charger across to Baiart and stroked the drunk man's face almost caressingly with the flail's dangling chains. Baiart flinched and shivered at the contact.

"You, perhaps," cu Ruruc purred. His commander's crest nodded above him as he leaned closer and laid the flail-haft along Baiart's nose, between his eyes. "If you're very, very lucky . . ."

*

Gemmel leaned his weight on the Dragonwand and released a long breath which smoked away from his mouth into the fog he had created. Though the air was wintery, he was bathed in sweat from the concentrated effort it had required. "That should hold for long enough," he decided aloud. "I've done everything I can."

"Such as what?" Aldric was sitting in Lyard's saddle some distance away; both were in full lamellar battle armour and the young man was additionally equipped with shield and slender lance. Though the effect was probably unconscious, Gemmel felt that his foster-son was far more dangerous than any of the just-completed spells. Menace hung about him like the fog.

"I've screened the army against death from a distance—Kalarr probably cannot cast such spells yet, but it's best to be cautious where that one is concerned. And I made sure that this fog won't lift until I do it myself, barring accidents of course."

"Accidents . . . ?" Aldric echoed warily, leading the wizard's mount across to him.

"Unforeseen eventualities, then," Gemmel expanded unhelpfully. He slapped the Dragonwand as a man might slap the neck of a favourite horse. "I should be drained of strength," he said thoughtfully, "but thanks to this I'm not even tired." He wiped one hand across his forehead and grimaced at the streaks of moisture gleaming on his palm. "Well, not very."

The old enchanter took a box from his belt-pouch and flicked back the lid, turning the mist briefly blue as the radiance of the Echainon stone spilled from its confinement. Then it dimmed, as if the stone itself understood the need for secrecy, and everything returned once more to muted shades of grey. Gemmel smiled thinly and set it into the place where Aldric had long expected the stone to go: the vacant eyesocket of Ykraith's dragon-head. Though he did no more than push it firmly home, the spellstone locked there as securely as if it had been set by a master jeweller.

"That should stop cu Ruruc causing any trouble," Gemmel muttered. A trumpet yelped and he was forced to leap aside as a small troop of horsemen came thundering out of the fog, pennons fluttering in the wind of their speed. Then he laughed. "Of course, he may have more than our whereabouts to concern—"

"*Altrou*, mount up! Move it!" Aldric's yell was not in the tone of voice which suffered questions and Gemmel obeyed instinctively, vaulting into his saddle more nimbly than seemed reasonable in a man of his years. He had barely slid the Dragonwand into a scabbard meant for javelins when four of the riders came back.

Aldric met them head-on, transfixing the nearest with his lance so that man and weapon tumbled to the ground together. A sword shrieked on his helmet as he rode through the others, bludgeoning one of them off his horse with the iron-rimmed shield as he passed.

Lyard wheeled under the pressures of heel and rein as Isileth Widowmaker came hissing hungrily from her scabbard. Gemmel was lost somewhere in the fog and Aldric hoped the old man was all right—then, as another horseman came boring in with a flanged mace in one hand, he stopped worrying about other people and became totally concerned with himself.

The mace-head boomed against his shield, driving it back against his body, and then rose to swing downwards at his head. Widowmaker licked out, sank half her length into the exposed armpit and wrenched free with a sucking noise. The mace flew out of sight and its owner sagged forward, coughing a fan of blood across his horse's neck before sliding from the saddle.

Aldric grunted thickly as a blow across his armoured shoulders drove the breath out of his lungs. He lurched, recovered, warded off another stroke with his hastily-uplifted shield and

kicked Lyard into motion, cursing the stupidity which had
allowed this man to close. Then the mace—another mace,
dammit!—smashed against the plates of his left bicep and that
whole arm went numb and useless, the shield slipping from
limp fingers.

Aldric said something savage—against himself for not keeping the shield-strap round his neck—and met the man in a
brief, vicious hacking match where his skill at *taiken-ulleth*
gave him all the advantages. It ended abruptly as Widowmaker
sheared away both the mace and the hand which held it, then
opened the rider's unprotected throat with an adroit back-
handed sweep.

The Alban wheeled his mount again just as the man whom
he had clubbed down with his shield came lunging with a
shortsword towards Lyard's head. That was a mistake; with
an outraged squeal the stallion reared and slashed out with
one steelshod hoof, smearing the attacker's features into oozing scarlet pulp. Aldric gentled the stamping, snorting Andarran
courser, trying hard to get his breath and at the same time
restore feeling to his bruised left arm. Gemmel walked his
own horse closer, looking not too carefully at the carnage—
nor very hard at Aldric either, for the moment. The old man
had never watched a *kailin*'s training put to use before, and
even from the vague and hazy images which he had seen
through drifting fog, he was sure he had no inclination to see
it done again.

Aldric stared at his expression of controlled disgust for a
few seconds, then smiled sardonically. "Yes. It's rather different from mere practice, isn't it, *altrou-ain*?" he said. Without too much mockery.

"How did you know that they were enemies?" was all
Gemmel felt inclined to ask at the moment. Aldric dismounted and recovered his shield—the lance had broken—
then wiped Widowmaker carefully and slid her away.

"I saw their armour. It isn't any Alban pattern that I know
of, so I was warned. When they attacked us I was sure." He
mounted, with a thoughtful look visible within the trefoil
opening of his war-mask. "If Kalarr has hired mercenary
horsemen, then some of his footsoldiers might be hired as

well . . ." he speculated to himself, wondering where the thought might lead. More trumpets shrilled, some distant but one or two too close for comfort, and he put the undeveloped notion from his mind. "Forget it. We'd better go—I don't know what that troop was doing here, and I'd rather not stay to find out. Follow me, *altrou*. Quietly."

"Do you know where you're making for in this fog?' Gemmel sounded dubious.

"I think so." Aldric grinned, almost, but not quite, with honest amusement. "I hope so. You'd better hope so too."

*

On a clear, bright day the citadel of Dunrath-hold could just be seen from where King Rynert set his standards on the crest of Embeyan Ridge, but on this particular mid-morning there was nothing but a wall of grey vapour into which his soldiers faded like figures in a dream. Despite Gemmel's advice he was reluctant to deploy his forces in such small units as the wizard had suggested: instead he had resorted to a troop formation culled from the battle manuals every Alban general carried on campaign, a flexible disposition of mutually supporting staggered regiments known as a "dragon's head" on the forward slope of the ridge. Whether it would be successful was another matter, because although the regular foot soldiers could be relied on to obey their orders with precision, aristocratic *kailinin* and their household warriors would tend to go their own way—which, since nobody could see more than fifty yards in any direction, was something Rynert doubted would be the right way so far as he was concerned.

There had been a brief skirmish with the enemy cavalry an hour before; scouts, maybe a tentative probing of his defences—perhaps even those village-burning raiders. Either way they had been repulsed with heavy losses. But they had been human, not *traugarin*—men able to think for themselves rather than automatons. Rynert wondered if there were more, guessing in the affirmative and not liking his conclusions. Such men where they were not expected could prove a danger out of all proportion to their numbers . . .

The legions rattled and clinked as buckles were drawn tight, swords eased in scabbards and helmets pulled down just that little further. Then the noises stopped and the silence returned, a vast oppressive stillness which proved just as frightening as the more normal sound of an enemy host taking up position.

Not that such a sound had been heard on Alban soil for long enough . . .

Rynert suddenly shuddered, just once but so violently that it made his armour rattle. He frowned, wondering why . . . and then stripped off a gauntlet, licked one fingertip and held it up. The frown deepened to a scowl and a soft, venomous oath hissed past his clenched teeth. A wind was rising. It was little more than a movement in the air, but already the threads of mist had ceased their sluggish weaving and were drifting determinedly with the breeze.

Growing thinner even as he watched.

*

"The fog's begun to blow away!" snapped Aldric, swinging round on Gemmel. "You told me that it wouldn't! What the hell is going on?"

Gemmel had half-expected such an outburst, so when it came it did not cause him much concern. "Wind," he replied coldly. "An ordinary thrice-damned wind. About the only thing I didn't cast securing-spells against."

"Why not?"

"Have you any conception of the sort of power required to hold this fragile stuff in place?" Gemmel flared. "I doubt it! So don't ask bloody stupid questions!"

"But . . . " An icy emerald-green glare from under the wizard's eyebrows made Aldric hesitate, if only for a second. "But isn't this Kalarr's work?"

"Of course not! He'd rip himself to tatters with the strain of any such attempt. And before you ask, no! Duergar's maintaining the *traugur*-charm, so it's not his doing either. This is just a breeze."

"Just a breeze." Aldric allowed himself a hollow, heavily sarcastic laugh. "So there'll be a battle anyway, despite all the plotting."

"There'll be a bloody massacre if Rynert doesn't follow

my instructions. Not that we'll be here to watch it if we're not under cover by the time this clears completely."

"That would never do, now would it." Heeling Lyard to a canter, Aldric vanished momentarily and was smiling bleakly when he trotted back. "But you don't have to worry on that score. Over here, *altrou*. Quickly!"

Gemmel did not move, but watched Aldric through narrowed, thoughtful eyes until the *eijo*'s gaze refused to meet his own. "What score are you worrying on?" he wondered softly. "The men you killed?"

The black helmet nodded, once, then turned so that the expression within its mask was unreadable. "Yes. A little. There was no difficulty, no risk to me. I was better armoured, better armed . . . It was like killing children."

"Children don't carry maces, Aldric. They don't try to break your bones. Put it out of your mind, boy."

"Easily said," muttered Aldric. His *tsalaer* creaked as he drew in a slow, deep breath, rising in his stirrups to stretch like a cat. "Yes . . . easily said. Follow me."

A clump of trees congealed from out of the fog and Aldric rode straight into their shadow, Gemmel at his heels. One coppice looked very much like another to the enchanter, and he wondered what made this one different. Aldric told him briefly: seen from north or south the tree-trunks formed a cursive "tau" for Talvalin, while the east-west outline was the uncial "hai" for *halathan*, the old name for a bird shown spread-winged on a crest. Such as clan Talvalin's eagle. Despite his tension Gemmel chuckled at the simplicity and deviousness of it all.

"What is this anyway?" he wanted to know as Aldric tethered Lyard to a branch. "Dunrath's back door?"

"Sort of. More a last-ditch exit, though. In the bad old days just after the Clan Wars, if there was any sort of risk a servant would bring horses to this area—not straight to the trees, obviously, but close enough. If he had to escape from his own fortress, a clan-lord and his family could meet here—or if necessary come up—" he leaned inside a hollow stump and pulled something with all his strength, "here!" The whole stump shifted sideways, revealing the mouth of a tunnel dropping into darkness. "Most fortresses as old as Dunrath are riddled with such passages," the *eijo* continued, "but they usually have just one like this—leading beyond the outer walls."

"Who told you about it?"

"My father, years ago. It's known only to the *cseirin*-born—the lord's immediate family."

"Then won't Baiart have known about it—and betrayed it?"

"Yes—and I hope, no. None of the retainers or vassals knew of it, so those two swine can have had no suspicion of its existence. And Baiart may have kept it secret in the hope of making his escape some day."

"*May* have. . . ? That's flimsy, Aldric. Almost reckless."

Clambering down, Aldric felt about with his feet for the steps he half-remembered, then nodded grimly. "I know that. But there's one way to be sure, and I'm prepared to risk it. Are you?" He descended out of sight with a scrape and rustle of black steel, leaving Gemmel alone with the disinterested horses.

The old enchanter looked around, hoping perhaps for inspiration, but saw only that the mist was growing uncomfortably thin. Pushing the Dragonwand's inflexible length through his belt like some oversized sword, he swung his lanky frame over and down. "I'm right behind you," he called, then grinned briefly to himself. "As if there was another choice."

*

By the sun, a straw-pale disc in a chilly azure sky, it was almost noon. Rynert sat uneasily on a camp-stool, baton in hand, and watched the flags and banners round him ripple in that accursed wind. At least now his fighting—or rather, his evading—would be that of a sighted rather than a blind man.

His troops looked neat even though they had been permitted to stand down for their midday meal; this did not reassure the king much, since by all accounts Lord Santon's legion had been equally neat—before the catastrophe.

Dewan ar Korentin, looking odd in his close-fitting Imperial helmet beside so many in the peaked and flaring Alban headgear, stood a little further down the slope, tapping his own commander's baton against one knee in a nervous, jerky rhythm. The uneventful waiting was beginning to erode even his iron nerves, and Rynert wanted to get up, talk to the Vreijek—do anything to silence the annoyingly irregular tap-tap-tap.

Then it stopped. More than one of the officers on the ridge turned to stare at the sudden silence, heard the distant, hollow muttering which had caused it and shifted their gaze to the ridge north of Embeyan. Dewan cleared his throat and pointed with his baton, a long, slow arc which took in the entire horizon. "Gentlemen, to your places," he said quietly. "Here they come."

Helmets twinkled in the sunlight all along the crest of that far ridge, becoming a line of men who advanced at a measured pace to the sound of drums until the skyline was clear, and then stopped. Another rank of soldiers followed. Then another, and another, and another, until the ridge was black with men. A trumpet blew, its notes thinned by distance, and the line contracted, splitting into wedges faced with overlapping scarlet shields and bristling with spears. Wedges which came trundling ponderously down on to Radmur Plain.

The Alban horns and drums were signalling now, and couriers were galloping down from the generals on the ridge. Each regiment shifted into more open order as the enemy approached, ready to repel attacks from horsemen they could kill or to avoid the *traugarin* they could not.

With the advantage of height, Rynert could see cu Ruruc's host take up their own formation and grinned harshly with reluctant admiration. What he could clearly see as a wide-flanked "swallowtail" encirclement would from a lower vantage-point—such as that of a regimental commander—appear to be the classic "spearhead" of a frontal assault. As simple and as deadly as a stab in the back, thought Rynert. Quite in keeping with Kalarr's reputation. It seems he has guessed I will not meet him unless he forces me to do so.

Drums thudded among the distant wedges and a solitary horn wailed dismally. The red shields began to lumber forward, slowly but inexorably drawing closer. Ar Korentin, mounted now, waved his baton towards Lord Dacurre's cavalry, unleashing them against cu Ruruc's horsemen. It would give the haughty, hard-to-control *kailinin* a chance to do something useful, whereas the likelihood of their doing something stupid increased the longer they were held in check.

Arrows flickered between the riders as they closed with one another, then the Albans returned bows to cases and twirled out their long spears in the same movement, hefted shields high and ploughed into the enemy with a great howling crash. Men were unseated or skewered on both sides in that first shock, and suddenly the two galloping ranks had passed through one another with the trumpets on both sides already screaming recall.

Rynert watched, trying to remain dispassionate as a general should be but aware of a racing pulse and sweaty hands. Other commanders gave way to their excitement with shouts and waving of batons, leaping from their seats for a better view or hammering iron-clad fists on armoured knees. The king extended his own baton, signalling his foot-regiments to fall back and concentrating on their disciplined manoeuvres in an effort to push the drama of the cavalry duel to the back of his mind. Then he heard somebody swear harshly and looked up, not believing what he had heard. Although it was true.

A troop of Kalarr's horsemen came jinking wildly towards Embeyan Ridge with Dacurre's crack household troops hard after them, bows drawn and shooting as they rode. The *kailinin* were clearing saddles at almost a hundred yards and yet still were not gaining enough.

Because these mercenaries were coming for the king.

*

A glow of fox-fire hung around Ykraith's uplifted point, mingling with the shimmer of the Echainon stone to give enough light to see by—if only just. "I'd like to see a little better myself," Gemmel replied in answer to Aldric's complaint, "but I keep thinking of others who might then see *us* as well."

Aldric did not argue further; the silent darkness had begun to play tricks on him, producing footsteps from inside his head and shapes which turned out to be no more than the witch-light reflecting off pieces of quartz, drops of water and

even once from the tips of his own eyelashes. He had been
along this tunnel only once before, and that was fourteen
years ago. In consequence his memories were hazy, and what
he did recall reminded him inevitably of the Cavern of Firedrakes. That in itself was enough to make him feel uneasy.

The passage turned a sharp corner and they stopped suddenly, their way blocked by a wall of dry-laid stone. "Your
move, I think," said Gemmel and held the Dragonwand
aloft, letting his power flow into it until the fox-fire swelled
and grew, driving back the shadows so that Aldric could see
whatever it was he had to do. "Where does this open on to,
by the way?" the wizard put in quickly. "If it's somewhere
that might now be the guardroom, I'd like to hear about it
rather than find out."

Aldric showed his teeth in a sour smile. "No need to worry
over that, at least," he said, and pushed one of the stones
back into the wall. Muffled rattling told where counterweights
were drawing down long-unused chains, and a doorway ground
slowly open. Aldric permitted himself a sigh of relief. "It
would have been my luck for the thing to have rusted to
pieces," he muttered, and made for the doorway. Then he
laughed throatily, stepped to one side and bowed low in a
bitter mockery of manners. "I bid you welcome to my house,
Gemmel-*altrou*," he said, and waved the old enchanter through
the door.

The chamber beyond was vast, lined with old supply-bins
and thick with long undisturbed dust. Cobwebs draped their
grey shrouds over everything, and there was a musty odour of
decay. Gemmel's witch-light showed traces of footprints;
they were faint, but still indicated where one large and one
small pair of feet had gone out and back in again. Aldric
stared at them. "My feet, years ago . . . and my father's." He
cleared his throat and walked quickly away, as if to leave his
memory behind. Heavy grey clouds rose in his wake and
settled again without a sound, already blurring the old footprints and the new.

There was another door at the end of the chamber, which
opened with only a slight creak from its hinges. Hesitating on
the threshold, Aldric nodded slightly and made a curious little

gesture with his right arm that Gemmel did not understand until he was inside.

Then he too made the small salute of respect which honoured generations of Talvalin dead. The crypt was filled with blocks of stone, some elaborately carved, others merely polished and inscribed. More recent burial markers were smaller, upright columns containing not coffins but the ashes of cremation, and he caught up with Aldric beside one such, knowing from the stela's shape that the cinerary urn it held was that of a woman, and guessing without being told whose was the frail-featured pretty face etched into its surface.

"My mother," Aldric said, not looking up. There was a barely discernible catch in his voice. "She died when I was born. My father's place should be at her side . . . except—." The words faltered and his eyes glistened, blinking rapidly in the soft, pale fox-fire. Then Gemmel actually saw the glisten of one emotion become the hard and gemlike glitter of another. "But that's why I've come back."

*

Rynert stared incredulously as the enemy riders came surging up the slope towards him, feeling like someone taking refuge from the spring tide atop a sandhill. This was ridiculous: such suicide charges went out with formal challenges, single combats and the taking of heads. While he did not relish death, Rynert would have accepted being out-thought and out-fought by a better general—but he seethed with indignation at the prospect of being cut down by a . . . a bloody anachronism. He remained seated, but set down his baton and put that hand to his *taiken*'s hilt. Although the blade remained undrawn.

It was not necessary. Dewan's personal troops, the Bodyguard cavalry, formed a solid wall of men some twenty feet in front of the king, knee-to-knee and four ranks deep in the Imperial manner. They poured down on Kalarr's men with the irresistible shock of a flash flood, breaking what little formation remained and sweeping them away in a swirling mellay. Which pounded them out of existence.

Rynert forced himself to ignore what was happening in order to issue more commands to his infantry, grouping some to draw a charge, scattering others away from the sluggish futile assaults of heavy *traugur* wedges. The Deathless Ones would roll right over any men they came to grips with—but had found the Alban soldiers quite impossible to catch.

Dewan trotted up, dismounted, saluted and bowed. Rynert looked at him, at what he carried, and asked himself what was happening to the modern warfare he was waging. Ar Korentin went down on one knee and laid a severed head at the king's feet. "Their captain, King," he said. "There were no other illustrious personages in that attack." Rynert scratched his nose with the end of his baton, wondering if he was involved in a dream or perhaps some overly-elaborate joke. He stared at the head. Yes, its hair had been combed before presentation, as the old books said it should be. Illustrious personage, thought Rynert with a small tremor at the out-dated mode of address, if this is a joke I cannot see how you can possibly find it funny.

"Very well done, Captain ar Korentin. My congratulations on your war-skill." He had to force the words out past the questions clustered on his tongue. Then yelling resounded from the plain and he turned hastily from unreality to fact, grateful for a genuine excuse to do so. Beside him Dewan rose to see what was happening, and Rynert heard him curse savagely between clenched teeth. The king felt near to rage himself.

There had been at least one wedge of human foot soldiers among cu Ruruc's host, and they had indeed been thinking for themselves. Clad like the rest of the wizard's army, they had moved at the typical slow pace of the *traugarin* around them until they were close enough to one of the Alban regiments, and had then charged home with unavoidable un*traugur*like speed. That regiment was now locked in combat, unable to manoeuvre, while on either side real, deadly corpse-troops wheeled and came marching in like so many wasps to a honeypot.

Worst of all, instead of leaving the solitary regiment to its inevitable fate as Rynert had commanded, someone—the king suspected young Lord Andvar, who had objected with great vehemence to such a ruthless attitude—had sent four more regiments jogging down the slope as reinforcements.

Reinforcing a broken tide-wall with a bucket of wet mud, Rynert thought viciously. He glanced up at the cluster of vermeil banners along the distant ridge. This is just what you've been waiting for, isn't it? he demanded silently. From the distant yelp of trumpets and the waving signal flags, cu Ruruc's answer was a stark and simple *yes*.

*

"You see, Lord," the mercenary captain told Kalarr. "It is much more difficult to hold an army back than to send it forward." He could almost feel the glow of satisfaction welling from the scarlet-armoured figure at his side.

Cu Ruruc's steel-sheathed fingers opened wide like a clutching metal talon, then closed slowly to a fist. "I have you, King of Alba," he hissed. "I have you now!" Rising in his stirrups, he made a great sweep through the air with his flail. Drums rolled and all across the plain his uncommitted wedges broke, reforming in a crescent which moved forward to outflank the Alban host, to buckle its formations and encircle it. Before annihilation.

"Good," Kalarr purred softly as he watched. "Very, very good. Now, my dear captain . . ."

"Sir?" The mercenary stiffened in his saddle.

"These are your final orders. I need no prisoners, since all who fought here are my enemies—so kill them. Kill them all!"

*

"Where is everyone?" Aldric whispered. "No guards, no retainers, no servants. Nothing."

"All gone to the battle," Gemmel replied just as quietly. "Cu Ruruc has stripped the fortress. He wants to make absolutely sure this time."

"He should have made absolutely sure that nobody would be creeping about behind him . . ." Aldric lowered Widowmaker from across his back and made her scabbard secure on his weaponbelt. "But where's Duergar?"

"Somewhere with a lot of floor-space. He's keeping thousands of *traugarin* on their feet—that means he'll need room for a gigantic conjuration circle."

"Then I know exactly where to find him. In the feast-hall."

Follow me." Aldric made off at a quick, stealthy pace, flitting through the dim, familiar galleries in his black armour like some ominous shadow from the citadel's past.

Gemmel followed, not too closely, for his sorcery-honed senses had already warned him about the brooding violence which hung about the *eijo* now. The enchanter's fondness for his foster-son was tempered by a wary respect for Aldric's well-schooled viciousness, and he had no desire to be within the arc of Isileth's blade should the *taiken* suddenly be unsheathed.

Gemmel remembered thinking the young man was frightening when they had first met. Now he was sure of it.

Aldric stopped at the foot of a flight of stairs and nodded towards the door at the top. "There's the hall," he murmured. Then his helmeted head jerked slightly. "Can you sense anything?"

"No," said Gemmel softly. All I sense is the leashed ferocity which you wear like a garment, my son, the wizard thought to himself, but aloud he said: "Why, is anything wrong?"

Aldric's frown was lost among the shadows shifting within his war-mask. "I thought I felt, heard, saw . . . something." Gemmel heard him suck in breath between clenched teeth. "No matter. Come on."

He was half-way up the stairs when a *traugur* lurched at him from a side-passage. Aldric jumped back with his nose wrinkling at the thing's faint charnel stench—and then gagged with disbelief and horror. It was inevitable that such a thing might happen, but anticipation was no defence against the queasy shock of recognising bloated, undead features.

He had known this man long ago in Radmur; a trooper in the City Watch and a drinking companion who had often talked of joining the army in order to look fine in plumes and metal. He must have done so—joined Lord Santon's legion— and come to this.

There was rage in the sweeping stroke which Aldric put through the *traugur*'s chest; rage, and great pity. Isileth Widowmaker clove the rotten flesh like cheese, releasing slimy foulness and a dreadful reek, but the corpse refused to fall and instead chopped Aldric with its own big axe. The *eijo*'s stomach heaved with the stink that filled his nostrils, but he ducked the axe-blow and cut through the creature's nearest knee, toppling it with a sodden thump. Even then it tried repeatedly to rise, while loops of wet intestine bulged greasily through the hole torn in its body.

Aldric was almost sick at the sight and smell and sound of it all. He waved Widowmaker at Gemmel, who was standing near the bottom of the stairs, and snarled, "Finish it, for pity's sake!" in a voice made thick and hoarse with revulsion.

"Duergar might sense it if I—"

"Don't argue with me, *altrou*! Do it!"

Gemmel sighed and shrugged, then reached out with the Dragonwand and, muttering something under his breath, pressed its crystal point against the *traugur*'s neck. It flinched back from the contact, twitched once and flopped head-downwards, already beginning to sag as its flesh commenced a dissolution which sorcery had held at bay for almost a month. The enchanter fastidiously stepped across the wide dark stream of fluids trickling down the stairway and drew level with Aldric, noting how white the young man's face had gone against the black armour which framed it. The Alban said nothing, but turned quickly and all but sprinted up towards the door.

For just an instant Gemmel thought that he had put all sense aside and was going to burst into the hall, but then the *eijo* stopped, listened and very gently eased the door back just enough to let him through. Gingerly the wizard followed.

Inside was dark, the daylight kept at bay by curtains over every window, and the air was heavy with the smell of incense. It tingled with enchantments, a crawling shudder-some sensation which raised the hairs on Aldric's neck and at the same time made him start to sweat. There was the sound of chanting from the lord's dais at the far end of the hall, one sonorous phrase punctuated by the striking of a gong. After a brief glare of greenish light and a pause in which the threads of scented smoke grew thicker, the chant began again and the gong chimed its single note.

Gemmel recognised the spell; he had broken it not two minutes past, back there on the slimed and stinking stairs. It was a spell which held charmed undeath in *traugarin*, keeping their cold flesh from corruption, and it was a spell which would fade entirely if Aldric's mission was successful. If . . .

Duergar's unmistakable silhouette was plainly outlined by the glow of a charcoal brazier. Short, bald—and a perfect target. Aldric's left hand dropped towards his hip, then clenched in a spasm of black rage as he remembered that he carried neither bow nor *telekin*. All were still cased or holstered in their places around Lyard's saddle—and might as well be on the far side of the moon for all the good they could do him.

Sliding along the shadows which connected each tall pillar to its neighbour, Aldric drew slowly closer until a single leap would bring him within lunging range of Duergar's back. This was one instance where he had no scruples about a thrust between an unsuspecting victim's shoulders . . . The necromancer had noticed nothing amiss; still chanting, he walked slowly to one side of the dais and returned with a slim rod, using it now to strike the gong, now to sketch an outline in the air. Aldric's hackles rose, but he tensed, moving a little clear of the sheltering pillar to be ready for the instant Duergar turned away.

The necromancer turned—then kept on turning, right around, his left hand thrusting out and the syllables of the High Accelerator tumbling from his lips.

Already gathered to spring forward, Aldric threw himself wildly down and sideways as the destructive shock whipcracked through where he had stood and punched a gaping tear right through the wall. Duergar looked down at the sprawling armoured body and began to laugh.

"You should not have destroyed one of my children, Talvalin," the wizard grinned. "Like any good parent I knew at once something was wrong." The *eijo* said nothing, trying to anticipate which way to roll if he was to avoid the inevitable second blast of power that would otherwise smash him to a pulp.

Something flared like midsummer lightning and a monstrous detonation shattered every window in the hall. Burnstench swamped the sickly incense odour and when Aldric raised his face from the floor he saw a smoking gash ripped across the dais. It looked as if the very basalt had charred like dry wood.

"Why not test your skill on mine?" Gemmel's hard-edged voice was an arrogant challenge, a verbal slap in Duergar's face, and the Drusalan reacted accordingly with a throwing movement of one hand. Something invisible tugged at the curtains and the door against which Gemmel had been leaning exploded into kindling. "Impressive," the old enchanter observed sardonically from some feet beyond the target. "But slow. Very, *very* slow."

Duergar snarled wordlessly and levelled his wand. The end of it glowed orange-red like the mouth of a furnace. Then the thing belched death.

Gemmel replied with the Dragonwand and the smoky air of the hall was suddenly laced with streaks of flaring light and heat. Pillars erupted fire-cored smoke, fabrics flashed to crumbling ash. All was searing flame and noise and colour.

Aldric pressed flat and shut his eyes.

*

"If Aldric and the old man are going to do anything they had better do it soon," Dewan muttered to the king as he stared at the encircling shields. Rynert mumbled something under his breath. "What I wouldn't give for a clear charge across the plain," the Vreijek went on. "I'd scour that far ridge clean of Kalarr and—"

"Dewan, old friend, stop dreaming." Rynert's face was grim. "We're finished, and you know it. If the fog hadn't blown away . . . if Andvar hadn't broken ranks . . . if—"

"*If* you give up now, you might as well use your *tsepan*, King. And you're too modern in your outlook for such foolishness. We'll not be beaten until cu Ruruc can ride across this slope without fearing for his dirty life. And he can't do that just yet."

The ranks contracted a little more, swords and spears flickering about the iron-rimmed shields. Arrows slashed spasmodically through the air, and Kalarr's host drew their noose another notch tighter. More of the king's men died.

Rynert settled his own shield on his arm, then drew his *taiken* and made to throw the scabbard away. Instead, with a wry grin, he set it carefully across his camp-stool. "I'll collect this later," he told Dewan. "I wouldn't want the lacquer to get chipped . . ."

*

The mercenary captain's smile evaporated as he turned to look for more approval on Kalarr cu Ruruc's face. His master's features were pale and pinched like someone sick or starving and the sorcerer's mouth moved soundlessly. "My lord . . . ?" the mercenary ventured. "My lord, are you unwell?"

Kalarr jerked like a man awakening from nightmare and stared at the soldier with wide, wild eyes. "Something's wrong," he breathed. "I can feel it. Finish them off! Hurry!" His voice rose to a scream of fury. "I won't lose this time! Not again! I *won't*!"

Trumpets shrilled and war-drums thundered while messengers galloped across the plain with orders to hasten the killing. Kalarr watched them—at least his eyes followed them, though by their glazed dullness they seemed to see other things and other places. Then he reeled in the saddle, recovered himself and twisted round to glare towards Dunrath. "Talvalin . . ." he hissed. "So there you are! Trying to cheat me . . ." An imperceptible shiver passed through the *traugarin* and they seemed to falter momentarily. "No. . ." cu Ruruc moaned, swaying as his charger fretted.

"My lord!" The mercenary captain grabbed his arm, thinking the sorcerer about to fall, then flinched back from the snarl of feral rage which bared his master's teeth. "My lord," the man yelled hoarsely, "what in hell's the matter?"

Kalarr ignored him. He rode unsteadily to the crest of the ridge and stared at the distant spike-edged shadow of the fortress. "The chant," he mumbled. "Continue the chant. The charm is failing, damn you! Ignore Talvalin . . . Duergar, you are betraying me . . ." Kalarr's roan stallion reared and squealed as its rider sawed savagely on the reins, filled with a sudden need to hurt. "Renew my host, you Drusalan bastard!" he shrieked, and rode like a storm for the citadel.

*

Aldric lifted his head in the sudden shocking silence and looked from side to side before he dared stand up. Duergar stood on the dais, Gemmel in the centre of the floor. Neither moved, but both had their open hands raised before them and the *eijo* could see a dancing, shimmering haze in the air. He did not need to be told that the first man to weaken would die in that same instant.

Then Gemmel spoke. His voice was weak, almost inaudible through the high, eldritch howl of power, but Aldric heard him clearly enough. "This is . . . your fight now," he gasped. "Take Ykraith . . . use it. Knowledge . . . will come . . ."

Aldric started to protest, then looked more closely at the old man's face; thin, drawn, streaked and mottled with blood from a score of splinter-cuts, it pleaded mutely with him to do as he was told. Without any questions—just for once.

Aldric did, and as he scooped the Dragonwand from the ground where it had fallen all other enchantment seemed to stop. Duergar was able to extend his hand and pronounce the Invocation of Fire, but Aldric made an instinctive parrying gesture with Ykraith and the billow of flame splashed impotently against an invisible shield yards short of where he stood.

"Duergar . . ." the Alban said gently.

The necromancer cringed as if he had been threatened with a whip, then lowered his arms resignedly to his sides. "Aldric . . ." he replied, and licked his lips. The *eijo* stared at him through slitted, vengeful eyes and raised the Dragonwand above his head in both hands as if it was a *taiken*, then swung the talisman down in a great slow curve until its crystal flame was levelled at the Drusalan's chest.

"I bring you a gift." Aldric's voice was flat and dispassionate. "Something you have cheated and defied for far too long. I bring you death." He uttered no word of power to give life to Ykraith—but the talisman took his hate and focused it until it became a dazzling pulse of force which hummed across the hall to enfold Duergar Vathach in its white-hot embrace.

"No!" he wailed. "You cannot do this to me . . . !" And

then the energy enveloped him. His skin split and blackened, peeled away until the bones showed through, and his charring skull gaped its jaws in a soundless shriek of anguish while a tongue of living flame licked past his calcined teeth.

The fierce glare dimmed and faded into nothing. A twisted, flaking charcoal thing lay shrivelled in a puddle of its own still-molten grease. It was no bigger than a doll, and it sizzled faintly, sounding and smelling like meat too long in the pan. Duergar . . .

Aldric took a deep breath, flinching from the horribly savoury odour which clogged his nostrils as he did so. The Dragonwand dropped with a clatter to the floor. He felt drained, sick and unspeakably fouled by what he had done. The taste of revenge had been sweeter by far in the anticipation than in the event. He wondered if it was always so.

*

Radmur Plain was heavy with the silence and the stench of death. Rynert's legions were still drawn up in a tight mass at the top of Embeyan Hill, because to move from their positions would have meant walking ankle-deep in the morass of deliquescent corpses which Kalarr's army had become between one swordstroke and the next. Dewan ar Korentin tied a cloth around the gash in his left arm, then secured another over his mouth and nose.

"I thought something like this might happen, King," he said. "Kill their master and the puppets die."

"He did it then." Rynert fingered his nose tenderly, wondering if it was broken or not. The last few minutes of the battle had been a savage brawl very different from the dignified and elegant combats outlined in his war-manuals. "Something about this whole business stinks, Dewan—and I don't mean just because of that filth out there."

"You're being suspicious again, King. Aldric-*arluth* took an oath to destroy the necromancer and he has succeeded. That's all."

"Perhaps . . ." If Rynert noticed the use of Aldric's proper title, he gave no sign of having done so. "But I think we should get to Dunrath as quickly as we can. Kalarr's gone, and he's heading for the fortress. I'm sure of it." A retainer brought up the king's horse and Rynert climbed into his saddle. "Don't forget what I said about Baiart Talvalin, either."

Dewan nodded, then issued rapid orders about disposal of the carrion which fouled the hilltop; wood from Baelen Forest and oil from Dunrath featured largely in his instructions, to prevent some other necromancer at some other time from finding the same supply of raw material as Duergar had done. "If old Overlord Erhal had done this in the first place—" he began to say, then fell silent. "But he was killed, of course."

"So were many people," Rynert said. "It's a hazard of life."

*

"Aldric . . . ?" The voice was not Gemmel's and, coming from behind him as it did, made the *eijo* whip Isileth from her scabbard as he turned. "Go right ahead," said the man in the doorway. "I would welcome your edge."

"Baiart . . ." Aldric breathed, and lowered his *taiken*'s point to the floor. To his own secret shame, he did not yet feel inclined to sheathe it. "Baiart—before Heaven, *why*?" The word came out sounding like a whimper of pain.

Baiart walked forward and smiled grimly in the smoke-diluted sunlight coming from the shattered windows. "Why indeed? To tell you properly would take me far too long, little brother. But . . . I wanted to live, Aldric. They caught me when I came back from Cerdor that first time; gave me the choice of life as their figurehead or . . . Or undeath as one of Duergar's creatures. I chose life. Existence, rather. I've been dead for years, except that Kalarr never chose to confirm it. He even laid a charm on me so that I could not use my *tsepan*. I was not even able to kill myself, Aldric. He took away the only privilege that I had left . . ."

Widowmaker's blade gleamed as Aldric returned her to the scabbard at his hip; then he saw the longing in his brother's eyes and shuddered.

"Aldric," —and this time the voice was Gemmel's—"he has the right to die by his own hand. You know that."

The *eijo* blinked and shook his head. "No . . . I won't. I *cannot*. Not my own brother."

"You don't have to. Give Baiart your *tsepan*—or would you rather watch his execution?"

"His *what*? He's *kailin-eir,* and entitled to—"

"To do something you won't allow, Aldric," Baiart pleaded. "Please . . ."

The younger man had no memory afterwards of handing either the dirk to Baiart or his longsword to Gemmel. But he must have done both, for the old enchanter came back moments later with both weapons in his hands. "It's over, Aldric," he said gently. "And Widowmaker's still clean," he added when the *eijo* seemed reluctant to touch her braided hilt.

"Can I see him, *altrou* . . . ?"

"I don't think—" Gemmel began, then reconsidered. "Very well. If you wish. There can be no harm in it."

Baiart had been covered to the chin in one of the few wall-hangings to survive the sorcerous combat of . . . was it really only ten minutes before? The dead man's eyes were closed, his limbs had been straightened and his face had relaxed from whatever pains had twisted it, into something very close to peace. Aldric gazed down at his brother and knew himself to be alone at last. Utterly, irrevocably alone. The thought no longer frightened him as once it had done. Stooping, he lifted one corner of the tapestry and laid it over Baiart's face—lightly, as if trying not to waken him.

"Is everyone in this damned fortress dead or deaf?" snapped an irritated voice. Gemmel and Aldric jerked round to face this new intrusion, though neither was really sure what to expect. The speaker was a tall man, in full battle armour covered by a leather *cymar;* his helmet had been pushed back and its war-mask hung from loosened laces at his neck, revealing a heavily moustached, sweaty face: the face of a man who has been hurrying. A light flail was tucked through his belt and a *taiken* was slung across his back—which meant that something was missing, if only Aldric could remember what . . .

"Who are you, *kailin*?" the *eijo* demanded. "And where do you come from?"

"I am a courier," the warrior responded shortly, "and I

come from the battlefield. Rynert has the victory, and cu
Ruruc is dead." He smiled at that.

His news gave Aldric little satisfaction. The manner of
Duergar's passing had made him sick of slaughter, and with
Baiart's suicide following so soon after, it was little wonder
that the young man's mind was dull and introspective.

"This place is—or was—Duergar Vathach's citadel," the
courier stated. Steel rang ominously as he drew the flail clear
of his belt and looped its strap round his left wrist. "So
where is he?"

"Dead!" retorted Aldric. "I killed him. As I promised."
He felt Gemmel tap his heel surreptitiously with the Dragonwand and made a tiny gesture of acknowledgment with one
hand, knowing what was troubling the old enchanter. It was
worrying him as well; things were falling rather too neatly
into place, and the alarms were screeching in his mind. As
they had been from the moment he first saw this man. A
small superstitious shiver crawled up the *eijo*'s spine as he
realised that under his blue leather over-robe the courier wore
vermeil-lacquered armour. All the associations of that colour
fought for prominence in his racing brain, each one uncomfortably close to the reality he faced.

No horseman could have covered the distance between
Radmur Plain and Dunrath if he had left when the battle had
been won. Even riding his mount into the ground, this warrior had to have left—Aldric calculated hastily—at least ten
minutes before he could be sure which way the battle was
going. And why was he wearing that flail instead of an honest
tsepan . . . ? The *eijo* felt sure he could put a name to their
visitor now.

"You must be Talvalin," the man said as he walked
slowly up the hall, glancing from side to side at the extensive
and still-smoking damage. There was a well concealed ugly
edge in his voice which provoked a nervous whisper of
warning from Gemmel. Aldric ignored it, but braced his feet
a little wider and waited for events to develop, flicking wary
glances towards the flail swinging lazily from the "courier's"
wrist. "I've heard about you, *ilauem-arluth*," he continued as
he stopped two arm's-lengths away and bowed fractionally.

By rights the use of his full and proper title should have
drawn a much lower bow from Aldric, but nobody except
Gemmel knew the rank was his. Apart, that is, from someone
who guessed the significance of the honourably laid-out body
on the floor. Someone like the scarlet-armoured *kailin* facing
him.

Someone like cu Ruruc.

"I have wanted to meet you for a very long time, Lord
Aldric. To give you my commiserations; to give you my
compliments; and to give you—*this*!"

Though he had anticipated such a move, the flail slashing
at his face almost took Aldric by surprise. Almost . . . but not
quite. In his eagerness Kalarr had misjudged his distance and
had come too close.

Instead of ducking away from or under the stroke, Aldric
threw his full armoured weight inside its arc, smashing one
shoulder against cu Ruruc's belly. All breath went out of the
sorcerer's lungs in a single throaty grunt and he staggered
backwards, dodging the fingers which jabbed towards his
eyes by pure luck and with mere inches to spare. Even then
Aldric's hand flattened out and its steel-sheathed edge slammed
solidly below cu Ruruc's ear, where the flexible mail-and-
leather coif was no protection against percussive blows.

Kalarr was dazed and horrified. Grappling in armour was a
skill he had disdained as being beneath his dignity, and the
discovery that Aldric had no such dainty notions was a painful one. No man wearing *an-moyya-tsalaer* ever fought bare-
handed—its weight alone made the metal harness into an
impressive bludgeon, and when its plates and scales were
coupled to techniques such as the *eijo* was employing, even a
clenched fist became as lethal as a mace or blunted axe.

The wizard struck out once more with his flail, in an effort
to make his adversary back off rather than do damage, and
Aldric blocked it by catching the weapon's chains on his left
arm—his shield having been lost when Duergar first attacked
him. With that shield, or with any other weapon, the parry
would have worked, but not with this one. The chains slapped
hard against his vambraced forearm, ·curled round it and sent
their spiked and weighted tips lashing on towards his face.

Had those chains been two links longer the Alban would have lost his sight, but he escaped with bloody grazes as they got just inside his war-mask and no further.

As he flinched aside, Aldric clamped his fist shut on the two chains which had wrapped around his palm and heaved with all his strength. The weapon's haft wrenched from Kalarr's grip, hesitated as its leather wrist-strap took the strain for almost two seconds before snapping, and then whirled with a clatter over the *eijo*'s head and out of sight.

"Now, Aldric!" barked Gemmel. "Draw now and finish him!"

"Let be, *altrou*," Aldric replied quietly. "Everything in good time."

The softness in his foster-son's voice made Gemmel's skin crawl as his sorcery-trained senses read below the voice to what had caused it. What he saw there chilled him and made him take several long, slow steps backward, away from the spot where the inevitable clash would take place. And well away from Isileth Widowmaker, whose hunger had become as tangible as heat or cold. "Not too far!" It was more an order than a request, and Gemmel halted in his tracks. "Watch this one for magic," Aldric continued, "and if he tries to cast a spell, you can obliterate him with my blessing. But otherwise, keep out of it."

Kalarr's eyes narrowed, wondering if this was all just hollow bravado . . . or something more. Then his thin lips writhed into a grin and he swept his *taiken* from the scabbard high across his back. "I need no spells, Talvalin," he said, and laughed. It sounded slightly forced.

"Considering your past performance, you need something, *pestreyr*," the *eijo* observed. "Feel free to try."

The sorcerer flicked a glance at Gemmel, who smiled pleasantly back at him. "Don't interfere with this, old man," cu Ruruc growled threateningly. The enchanter shook his head.

"I wouldn't dream of doing so. But I hope that you know how to use your sword."

"Know how . . . ?" Kalarr's voice was incredulous. "I've

forgotten more about the *taiken* than this whelp could ever know. He's dead, old man. And so are you.''

"I doubt that very much," returned Gemmel calmly. "For two reasons. I have the Echainon spellstone"—cu Ruruc's slitted eyes dilated as they fell upon the glowing jewel—"and have you looked at Aldric's *taiken*? I don't think you have, somehow. Not carefully enough.''

Aldric unhooked the longsword's scabbard from his weaponbelt and pulled its shoulderstrap across so that the sheath rose slantwise to his back, well clear of his legs. He was conscious that Kalarr was staring dubiously at him, and the knowledge provoked a thin and mirthless smile within the shadows of his war-mask. Then he gripped the long hilt rearing like an adder by his head, twisted it to loose the locking-collar and drew.

The faint slither of steel as Isileth slid free of her lacquered sheath was by far the loudest sound in the hall. Louder than the beat of Aldric's heart, louder than the blood whose rushing filled his ears. And far, far louder than the tiny indrawn gasp as cu Ruruc saw what Gemmel meant at last.

"Isileth . . ." he whispered, feeling an old, long-forgotten pain begin to burn the knuckles of his sword-hand.

"Isileth," echoed Aldric. He said nothing more. The time for words was past. Instead, moving with as much care as if under instruction from his swordmaster, he assumed the ready posture of high guard centre and waited for Kalarr to make his move.

After pulling down his helmet and lacing its war-mask tightly into place, the sorcerer adopted a counter-position and slowly circled his opponent. Then he screamed hoarsely as he sprang and cut.

The blades met in a series of blurred strokes before they shrilled apart as both men glided backwards, each analysing the other's fighting style. They met again, more cautiously now, a tentative stroking of steel on steel before the single explosive clangour of cut, parry and stop-thrust which drew threads of glistening scarlet from Aldric's left wrist. Kalarr was good. Very good. But the *eijo* could still use his injured hand, so he was not quite good enough . . .

Or so Aldric hoped. The initial flare of agony had faded from the wound, leaving in its wake a sullen throb of pain which indicated no real harm was done. Though when he took up the waiting attitude of low guard left, it was imperfect, suggesting that there was a weakness in his bloodied wrist. A lesser swordsman than Kalarr would not have seen the error, and a better one would never have been drawn by the potential trap. Cu Ruruc fell between the two.

Darting forward two quick paces, he slashed viciously towards the proffered opening—only to find that opening no longer there and Widowmaker stabbing at his throat. With neither time nor room in which to dodge, he charged right on to the waiting point and jolted to a stop as it took him squarely underneath the chin. Clawing at the blade, Kalarr went lurching sideways as it withdrew.

Then he regained his balance and lunged in turn, so fast and so ferociously that Aldric did not block the stroke in time. Gritting his teeth against the wave of black and crimson anguish threatening to swamp his senses, the *eijo* jerked himself away from Kalarr's sword. It had jabbed between the joints of his *tsalaer* and gouged a long groove in his hip-bone. Had it not skidded there, he knew the blade would have transfixed him—small comfort in that knowledge, true, but comfort of a kind. He was not dead yet, at least . . .

As for cu Ruruc's mangled throat, Aldric could see it closing up before his eyes, ripped flesh running like hot wax until in seconds there was only the torn coif to show a thrust had ever been received. Some healing-spell at work, he guessed; made by Kalarr himself. Did you really expect a sorcerer to rely on armour by itself? Not in your heart, no. So start to think, man! Quickly!

Kalarr laughed harshly at the shock on Aldric's pain-blanched face, then pressed home his attack. More blood spurted on to the black-lacquered armour and smeared the tiled floor underfoot. It came from small cuts, wounds without importance in themselves—but the very fact that Aldric suffered them was like a premonition of the end.

It seemed to Gemmel that his foster-son was fighting in a dream, his reactions automatic and often far too slow. Spells began to fight for precedence within the old enchanter's mind, but none were selective enough; all required at least some space between the duellists if both were not to share the same fate. Then abruptly Gemmel realised what it was he had to do. "Ykraith, Aldric!" he yelled above the clamour. "Use the Dragonwand!"

Aldric twitched as if he had been stung, and the fog of pain cleared somewhat from his eyes. That was the knowledge he had been seeking, the reason why his mind had not been on the fight. Breaking ground, he enveloped yet another thrust in a sweeping circular parry, trapped cu Ruruc's blade in Widowmaker's deep, forked quillons and twisted it from the sorcerer's hand. He sent the weapon skidding out of reach with a kick from one booted foot, then as Kalarr dived after his *taiken,* Aldric ran the other way. "Here, *altrou!*" he cried. "Throw it!"

The Dragonwand flashed across the hall as Gemmel hurled it like a javelin, but it landed in the palm of Aldric's hand more like a falcon settling on a trusted perch. If he had expected his several wounds to heal at once, the *eijo* was mistaken—but if he had expected Kalarr to be dismayed, his wish was more than granted. As the Alban swivelled on one heel and lashed out with the talisman, cu Ruruc flung himself out of its path so hastily that he almost fell.

"Now, warlock . . . shall we try again?" gasped Aldric, levelling Ykraith's carved dragon-head at Kalarr's face. "With the odds not quite so stacked against me this time, eh?" He assumed a *dyutayn* position, handling the Dragonwand as he would a second *taiken.* "Well, come on, you scarlet bastard," the *eijo* hissed, teeth bared in a tight-lipped feline snarl. "Or must I go after you? Come on!"

Kalarr whirled his sword down in a blow to shatter armour and go cleaving on through flesh and bone, but the great cut never landed. Aldric sidestepped, warding off the blow with Isileth as he began a gliding turn. Both blades met amid a shower of sparks and a steely screech before Kalarr came charging past, carried by the momentum of his fully-harnessed body.

Ignoring what it did to his torn hip, Aldric slewed his

upper body round and stabbed out with Ykraith. Its crystal flame drove between cu Ruruc's shoulders, punching through lamellar scales as if they were thick parchment, and the Echainon stone flared so blue and vivid that for just an instant it cast shadows. Then its light went out.

Cu Ruruc chuckled thickly as he reached behind him to pluck the Dragonwand out of his flesh as if it was the sting of some small, irritating insect. There was no blood either on its point or on his back.

Aldric said something under his breath as the sorcerer turned once more to face him, this time with both sword and talisman outstretched. When he saw the young man's startled, disappointed face, cu Ruruc laughed aloud.

He was still laughing when Widowmaker scythed down onto his helmet, splitting its vermeil metal and the coif beneath, silencing his laughter, dazing him. Echoes of the impact rang down the pillared hall. Kalarr reeled, and the weapons slithered from his nerveless fingers to clash against the floor. A thin, bright crimson trickle wandered down his face, as if the battered helmet bled.

Aldric looked at the blood, the pallid skin, the dark, unfocused eyes, and drew a long breath deep into his lungs. His armoured fingers clenched the braided leather of Isileth's long hilt, double-handed, tighter, tighter, the blade beginning to tremble as his energy came boiling up as it had done against Duergar. Except that this way was the *kailin*'s way, *taiken-ulleth*, and clean.

"No . . . my son . . . !" The *eijo* winced as a daggerlike feeling of memory and loss bored into him, and stared again at Kalarr's face. It was . . . changing. Shifting even as he watched to a blue-eyed, white-bearded, lovingly remembered outline. A face that had been dust and ashes these four long years, and yet . . . Something hot and painful swelled up in the Alban's chest; his throat grew dry and choked so that the name he spoke was just a muted whisper.

"Haranil-*arluth* . . . ?" Aldric whispered, wanting to believe. "Oh, father . . ." The wise, dignified face smiled benignly from inside its vermeil war-mask, then the figure leaned forward slightly to lift something from the floor. There was a faint sound of steel.

And the charm broke. Haranil's face crumpled, became again cu Ruruc's visage grinning past an upraised longsword— and collapsed again into a smear of oozing ruptured tissue. Kalarr's spell had not been illusion but true Shaping, an enchantment of High Magic that his weakened body was unable to maintain. And for which he paid the price.

Widowmaker blurred out in a single thrust that had four years of grief and hatred riding on her blade. "*Hai!*" Aldric shouted as the *taiken* hammered home, an unstructured, formless cry that unleashed power from deep inside him to drive the longsword half her length in armoured bone and muscle.

Isileth burst between the *tsalaer*'s lacquered scales, snapped two ribs below and sliced the vessels leading from the wizard's heart, then slowly, slowly twisted one half-turn before she wrenched free. This time blood spewed from the wound as if from any ordinary man and spattered on the floor with a sound like rain, laying ruby droplets over Baiart's shrouded face and on the once-more softly glowing stone of Echainon. Aldric backed away, his features immobile, wondering why he had not taken off the suppurating head. To leave it on was to invite a dying curse . . . although cu Ruruc should have been beyond the power of speech.

Yet he was not. Slumping to his knees, Kalarr stared upwards at his slayer's face, lips fumbling to shape the words that refused to come. "It seems that . . . all along . . . I have underestimated you, Talvalin," he croaked at last. His mouth twisted briefly as a spasm of pain ripped through him; then it relaxed and even tried to form a smile. "Sh-should have known . . . a better k-killer than myself." He coughed and pink froth dribbled down his chin. "Foolish, I . . . I'll not make . . . that m-mistake . . . ah—! again . . ."

The smile remained fixed as all life left his face, and he slumped forward into a final First Obeisance at Aldric's feet. The *venjens-eijo* stared down at the corpse for several seconds, oblivious to the gore that puddled boot-sole deep. His oath was fulfilled, his vengeance now complete. Was it sweet? Aldric did not know; all he could taste was blood and fear and sourness in his gullet. With a single double-handed sweep he lopped off Kalarr's once handsome head, but did not bend to pick it up. The thing repelled him.

Uttering a small sound lost between a snarl and a half-stifled sob, he kicked the grisly trophy out of sight.

*

"He is dead, Lord King. By his own choice and his own hand in the rite of *tsepanak'ulleth*. I . . . did not witness it."

"I see." Rynert looked beyond Aldric's respectfully bowed head and caught Dewan watching them both with an odd expression on his face. Almost like a smile. "You knew," the king continued, "that such a suicide would forestall my seizing Clan Talvalin's lands? *If* I intended such a step."

Aldric looked up, and all the stiff-lipped pride of sixty generations was frozen on his face. The grey-green eyes remained unreadable. "Of course I knew it, *mathern-an*. If I said otherwise I would be a liar or a fool. But my concern was first and foremost with my brother's honour. Believe me or not, as you will."

"I believe you, Aldric-*arluth*." Rynert used that title quite deliberately, watching for a reaction. It was not what he had expected.

"I would . . . would plead exception from the title for a while yet, Lord King," the young man ventured softly. "I was never trained for it and . . . *Mathern-an arluth*, this citadel holds memories for me; too many for my peace of mind. In a year, maybe. Or two. Appoint a castellan to hold this place for me—until I come back."

"Come back from where, my lord? Valhol, perhaps?"

"I think not, Lord King. The memories are there as well, you see."

"Then if you should venture to the Empire—"

"*Mathern-an*, why should I do that?" Something in his tone of voice suggested Aldric's question was not as naïve as he made it sound, and Rynert let a faint smile cross his face.

"As a favour to your . . . to a valuable, high-ranking friend, shall we say?"

"Why not? I may well visit the Drusalan Empire after all. Sometime or other."

"When. . . *If* you do, then convey, ah, certain messages of some delicacy to my allies there. Prokrator Bruda and—''

"Lord General Goth?"

"Quite so. You know what the situation of the Empire is; those two want no more wars of conquest and especially no invasion of this realm. They need my personal assurances that I believe them. You, Lord Aldric, are of sufficient rank to carry such assurances. Certain codes and phrases will be implanted *here*,''—Rynert almost, but not quite, touched his fingertips to Aldric's head—''where they will be forgotten by yourself until Goth and Bruda speak words which will release them. Only then will you remember. Do you understand me?''

Aldric understood—and did not like it very much. "Is that all?" he asked, a little sharply. Rynert smiled again, without amusement now, and shook his head.

"Not quite. If there is any favour you—and Isileth—can do to further prove my friendship, then I expect it to be done. Purely as a token of good will, you understand?''

"I probably do . . .'' Aldric fitted a sardonic, careless grin on to a face which did not want to carry it; then he rose, bowed as a clan-lord and walked swiftly from the room. He was uncertain which would have been more hazardous, his acceptance or a blunt refusal. Somehow he fancied the refusal would have made him feel more comfortable . . . Then he shrugged. The thing was done, one way or another.

*

It was chilly in the courtyard; the sun had not yet risen and there were threads of mist hanging in the air. Aldric swung into his saddle and with a packhorse in tow, rode out of Dunrath and cantered east to join the Radmur road. From the ramparts of the donjon, three people watched him go.

"Hold this place till I come back," King Rynert muttered, somewhat dubiously. "Now that we've let him go, will he come back at all?''

The rider and the sun crested the eastern slope together, so that he was lost in a glare of white light and golden vapour. Gemmel leaned against the battlements and watched, even though there was nothing he could see. The enchanter made no reply to Rynert's question. He might not even have heard it. Within the fortress walls, a bell signalled the coming of dawn.

"He will," said ar Korentin firmly. "Duergar and cu Ruruc learnt that much, to their cost. Aldric Talvalin always comes back. When it suits him, and in his own good time."

Warmed by the sun, the mist thinned from the empty ridge, then faded and was gone.

DAW

TANITH LEE

"Princess Royal of Heroic Fantasy"—*The Village Voice*

THE BIRTHGRAVE TRILOGY
- [ ] THE BIRTHGRAVE   (UE2127—$3.95)
- [ ] VAZKOR, SON OF VAZKOR   (UE1972—$2.95)
- [ ] QUEST FOR THE WHITE WITCH   (UE2167—$3.50)

THE FLAT EARTH SERIES
- [ ] NIGHT'S MASTER   (UE2131—$3.50)
- [ ] DEATH'S MASTER   (UE2132—$3.50)
- [ ] DELUSION'S MASTER   (UE1932—$2.50)
- [ ] DELIRIUM'S MISTRESS   (UE2135—$3.95)

OTHER TITLES
- [ ] THE STORM LORD   (UE1867—$2.95)
- [ ] DAYS OF GRASS   (UE2094—$3.50)
- [ ] DARK CASTLE, WHITE HORSE   (UE2113—$3.50)

ANTHOLOGIES
- [ ] RED AS BLOOD   (UE1790—$2.50)
- [ ] THE GORGON   (UE2003—$2.95)

NEW AMERICAN LIBRARY
P.O. Box 999, Bergenfield, New Jersey 07621

Please send me the DAW BOOKS I have checked above. I am enclosing
$_____ (check or money order—no currency or C.O.D.'s).
Please include the list price plus $1.00 per order to cover handling costs.

Name _____

Address _____

City _____ State _____ Zip Code _____
Allow 4-6 weeks for delivery.

DAW

DAW PRESENTS THESE BESTSELLERS BY
MARION ZIMMER BRADLEY

DARKOVER NOVELS
- [ ] DARKOVER LANDFALL   UE1906—$2.50
- [ ] THE SPELL SWORD   UE2091—$2.50
- [ ] THE HERITAGE OF HASTUR   UE2079—$3.95
- [ ] THE SHATTERED CHAIN   UE1961—$3.50
- [ ] THE FORBIDDEN TOWER   UE2029—$3.95
- [ ] STORMQUEEN!   UE2092—$3.95
- [ ] TWO TO CONQUER   UE2174—$3.50
- [ ] SHARRA'S EXILE   UE1988—$3.95
- [ ] HAWKMISTRESS!   UE2064—$3.95
- [ ] THENDARA HOUSE   UE2119—$3.95
- [ ] CITY OF SORCERY   UE2122—$3.95

DARKOVER ANTHOLOGIES
- [ ] THE KEEPER'S PRICE   UE1931—$2.50
- [ ] SWORD OF CHAOS   UE1722—$2.95
- [ ] FREE AMAZONS OF DARKOVER   UE2096—$3.50

NEW AMERICAN LIBRARY
P.O. Box 999, Bergenfield, New Jersey 07621

Please send me the DAW BOOKS I have checked above. I am enclosing
$_____ (check or money order—no currency or C.O.D.'s).
Please include the list price plus $1.00 per order to cover handling costs.

Name _____

Address _____

City _____ State _____ Zip Code _____

Please allow at least 4 weeks for delivery.

DAW

DON'T MISS DAW'S RUNAWAY BESTSELLER

TAILCHASER'S SONG
By Tad Williams

"For anyone who loves and understands cats... a fantasy of epic proportions in the vein of *Watership Down* ..."—*San Diego Union*

Meet Fritti Tailchaser, a ginger tomcat of rare courage and curiosity, a born survivor in a world of heroes and villains, of powerful gods and whiskery legends about those strange, furless, erect creatures called M'an. Join Tailchaser on his magical quest to rescue his catfriend Hushpad—a quest that takes him all the way to cat hell and beyond. ...

"A felicitous felinic fantasy without the coyness that sometimes characterizes such yarns. The reader can totally believe the cat personalities and be quite worried over their fates. My compliments to Mr. Williams... a fantastic talent."—Anne McCaffrey, best-selling author of *Moreta, Dragon Lady of Pern* and *The White Dragon*

IN HARDCOVER   (0-8099-0002-5 $15.50)
NOW IN PAPERBACK   (UE2162—$3.95)

DAW

Savor the mystery, the special wonder
of the worlds of

Jennifer Roberson

☐ **SWORD-DANCER**

Here's the fast-paced, action-filled tale of the incredible
adventures of master Northern swordswoman Del, and her
quest to save her young brother who had been kidnapped and
enslaved in the South. But the treacherous Southron desert
was a deadly obstacle that even she could not traverse alone.
Then she met Tiger, a mercenary and master swordsman.
Together, they challenged cannibalistic tribes, sandstorms, sand
tigers, and sand sickness to rescue Del's long-lost brother in a
riveting story of fantasy and daring. (UE2152—$3.50)

CHRONICLES OF THE CHEYSULI

This superb new fantasy series about a race of warriors gifted
with the ability to assume animal shapes at will presents the
Cheysuli, once treasured allies to the King of Homana, now
exiles, fated to answer the call of magic in their blood, fulfilling
an ancient prophecy which could spell salvation or doom for
Cheysuli and Homanan alike.

☐ SHAPECHANGERS: BOOK ONE (UE2140—$2.95)

☐ THE SONG OF HOMANA: BOOK TWO (UE2057—$3.50)

☐ LEGACY OF THE SWORD: BOOK THREE (UE2124—$3.50)